PRAISE FOR THE NOVELS OF MARY BALOGH

SIMPLY MAGIC

"Balogh continues her superb Simply romance series ... with another exquisitely crafted Regency historical that brilliantly blends deliciously clever writing, subtly nuanced characters, and simmering sensuality into a simply sublime romance." —*Booklist*

SIMPLY LOVE

"This superbly written, emotionally wrenching story of two wary people resigned to loneliness but surprised by love is classic Balogh and one of her best to date." —*Library Journal*

SIMPLY UNFORGETTABLE

"When an author has created a series as beloved to readers as Balogh's Bedwyn saga, it is hard to believe that she can surpass the delights with the first installment in a new quartet. But Balogh has done just that." —*Booklist*

"A memorable cast ... refresh[es] a classic Regency plot with humor, wit, and the sizzling romantic chemistry that one expects from Balogh. Well-written and emotionally complex." —*Library Journal*

SLIGHTLY DANGEROUS

"*Slightly Dangerous* is the culmination of Balogh's wonderfully entertaining Bedwyn series.... Balogh, famous for her believable characters and finely crafted Regency-era settings, forges a relationship that leaps off the page and into the hearts of her readers." —*Booklist*

"With this series, Balogh has created a wonderfully romantic world of Regency culture and society. Readers will miss the honorable Bedwyns and their mates; ending the series with Wulfric's story is icing on the cake. Highly recommended." —*Library Journal*

SLIGHTLY SINFUL

"Smart, playful, and deliciously satisfying...Balogh once again delivers a clean, sprightly tale rich in both plot and character.... With its irrepressible characters and deft plotting, this polished romance is an ideal summer read." —*Publishers Weekly* (starred review)

SLIGHTLY TEMPTED

"Once again, Balogh has penned an entrancing, unconventional yarn that should expand her following." —*Publishers Weekly*

"Balogh is a gifted writer.... *Slightly Tempted* invites reflection, a fine quality in romance, and Morgan and Gervase are memorable characters." —*Contra Costa Times*

A SUMMER TO REMEMBER

ALSO BY MARY BALOGH

The Devil's Web

MARY BALOGH

A DELL BOOK

THE DEVIL'S WEB
A Dell Book

PUBLISHING HISTORY
Signet mass market edition published August 1990
Dell mass market edition/January 2008

Published by Bantam Dell
A Division of Random House, Inc.
New York, New York

This is a work of fiction. Names, characters, places, and incidents either
are the product of the author's imagination or are used fictitiously. Any
resemblance to actual persons, living or dead, events, or locales is
entirely coincidental.

Dell is a registered trademark of Random House, Inc., and the colophon
is a trademark of Random House, Inc.

ISBN: 978-0-440-24307-6

Printed in the United States of America
Published simultaneously in Canada

www.bantamdell.com

OPM 10 9 8 7 6 5 4 3 2 1

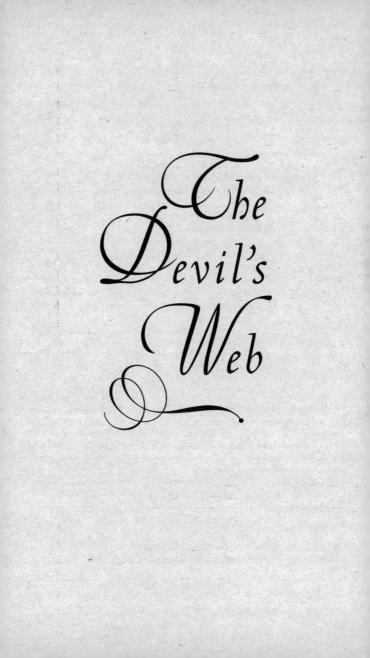

The Devil's Web

1

THE CLIFFS OF THE SOUTH COAST OF ENGLAND were visible to larboard, the morning mists having lifted, though the clouds still hung low and heavy and the sea was slate gray and heaving. The *Adeona*, one of the ships belonging to the North West Company of Canada, was bringing furs to the auction markets of London.

The cliffs of England. Of home.

A clerk of the company, one of those whose task it was to accompany the furs across the Atlantic and to transact the company's business in London, stood at the rail of the ship, one arm propping him against it, the other hand clinging to a taut rope attached to the rigging, his feet planted firmly apart for better balance, and tested the thought in his mind.

Home.

Soon he would set his feet again on his native soil, the very soil he had shaken from them four years before without a moment's hesitation. As he had once said to someone in England, though he did not care to remember whom, he had liked the sight of the sea because it represented his escape from England. And he had escaped.

But she had said that perhaps it was from himself he wished to escape and that it could not be done. For wherever he went, however far he ran, he must inevitably take himself along too.

She had been right. He had taken himself to Canada—to Lower Canada to be precise, to Montreal. And since that had not by any means been far enough, then he had become a clerk with the North West Company, a group of merchants and traders in furs, and had taken himself off with a canoe brigade beyond Lower Canada, even beyond the limits of Upper Canada, beyond the limits of civilization.

Three thousand miles beyond Montreal he had journeyed. He had spent three years there, in the Athabasca country, with only a handful of other fur-trading men and the native inhabitants of the country for company.

He could have gone no farther without falling entirely off the end of the world, it had seemed, though some men had crossed the barrier of the mountains and reached the Pacific Ocean. And of course, it was true that he had taken himself every inch of the way. The only difference was that he had come to like himself a little better while that far away from home. While that far away from his memories.

But of course he could not escape memories as effectively as he had escaped from an island. They kept intruding. They were only as far away as his mind. And so he was coming back home for a few months. He might have stayed in the interior for years—most clerks of the company did, earning partnership by slow degrees and hard work. But he had requested, and been granted, a position in Montreal for a year. And because even there he could not be free of his past, he had requested, and been granted, the task of bringing the furs to auction.

And now he was almost back where he had started.

Sometimes the mist and the water met so that he could no longer see the cliffs of southern England, but he knew they were there. And the *Adeona* was taking him very surely to London.

He did not want to be there. Or in any other part of England. Least of all in Yorkshire, where he had lived most of his life. But he would not go there. He would be working in London. There would be no time to make the ultimate journey home. And there was no point. There was nothing to be gained by going back there.

That particular episode in his life was long in the past. Long ago in his youth, when one could be expected to make mistakes. He had made one—more than one, perhaps—and he had tried to put it right. Tried until he had thought he was going mad. And failed. There was nothing he could do about it now.

It would be better to stay away from there. He was coming back to England. Surely that was enough. There was no need to worry the wound until it was quite raw again.

And yet it was that very episode from his youth that he sometimes thought would always prevent him from being entirely free.

He would not think of it. The sea was choppy. He looked down into its gray depths as the ship beneath his feet dipped and heaved. And he took off his beaver hat, which had been pulled low over his brow, in order to let the damp wind blow through his dark, overlong hair.

He probably would not have to go home to Yorkshire in order to see his parents. They would doubtless be in London to see him, and probably staying with Alex. Alex! Yes, for years before he left for Canada his sister had been the most important person in his world. She had married the Earl of Amberley after his departure and now had a son and a daughter. He longed to see them—and her, of course. It was surely worth coming home just to see Alex and discover if she had found the happiness she had never known as a girl.

She had never been allowed to be happy then. Neither had he. They had had the misfortune to have a father whose firmly held religious beliefs led him to eliminate all enjoyment from life, both for himself and for his family. And of course, there had been the dreadful quarrel between himself and his father, unresolved before he left and surely unresolvable now.

James Purnell sighed and looked up to the dimly visible cliffs of England again. Why was it that it was possible to hate and to love both at the same time? How was it that he could hate his father and reject all that he stood for and resent what his father had done to his life and to Alex's and yet at the same time love him and crave his understanding and his approval? He was a man of thirty years, and yet he seemed to have a child's need for a parent's affection.

"James?"

A light and welcome voice broke in on his thoughts, and he turned to watch the careful and somewhat unsteady approach of a small, slim girl whose brown hair was neatly confined beneath her bonnet and whose shapely form was concealed behind the folds of a heavy cloak. Her lips smiled, and her cheeks were already rosy from the freshness of the wind. Her eyes were sparkling.

"Duncan knocked on my door to tell Miss Hendricks and me that the coast of England was visible," she said, as he took her elbow in a firm clasp and guided her to the rail, where she would have something firm and safe to cling to. "And I saw immediately through the porthole that it was true. I simply had to come up on deck for a better look. England, James! I can scarce believe it."

"Your first sight of it, Jean," he said, smiling indulgently. "I can remember my first sight of Canada four years ago. I know just the excitement you are feeling."

She smiled up at him before returning her wide-eyed gaze to the distant cliffs. "It has been worth it after all," she said. "The dreadful food and the incessant motion and Miss Hendricks sick almost from the moment of our embarking." She giggled. "She has not been much of a chaperone after all, has she, the poor dear?"

"But you have had your brother to watch after you," he said.

She breathed in a deep lungful of salty air and closed her eyes. "I am so happy that Father said I could come with Duncan to join him in London," she said. "I have always wanted to see London. Is it really the most exciting city in the world?"

James Purnell smiled again. "I have not seen many of the rest of them to make comparisons," he said. "But I suppose it is exciting, if you like that type of excitement."

"You have a sister here, don't you?" she said. "And parents. You must be very happy about seeing them again."

"Yes." He gazed at the cliffs with dark, inscrutable eyes. "I was always extremely fond of Alex. She is five years younger than I. And my mother will be pleased to see me, I think."

The girl wrinkled her nose. "Well, of course she will," she said. "Will they be in London? I would dearly like to meet your family."

He looked down at her. "I have no idea," he said. "I may have to travel down into Hampshire to see my sister. She is married to the Earl of Amberley. He has a large estate close to the sea. We will doubtless sail almost within sight of their home."

"She is a countess?" she asked, her eyes widening. "You did not mention that before. And your father is a baron, is he not?"

"Lord Beckworth," he said.

"It must be wonderful to be someone of some importance in London," she said. "To have entry to all the most fashionable gatherings. And this is the time of the Season, is it not?"

"June?" he said. "So it is. But your father is not precisely a nobody, Jean. Douglas Cameron, partner in the company, respected merchant. You will have an opportunity to enjoy yourself, never fear."

"Perhaps," she said with a sigh. "But he is not exactly high *ton*, is he? Far from it. I suppose you are. Or were. And will be again as soon as you set foot on English ground. You are very fortunate."

"Yes," he said.

He had spent his first year in the Athabasca country with Duncan Cameron, the girl's brother. Naturally enough, when he had discovered his old friend in Montreal two years later, they had renewed their friendship. And he had become acquainted with Jean Cameron. He had not seen a great deal of her, as she had only recently finished her schooling at a convent, though her family was not Catholic.

Her presence on board ship had been like a breath of fresh air. Her spirits had not been dampened either by the tedium of the long days or by the indisposition of her chaperone, Miss Hendricks, a schoolmistress who was returning to England to keep house for a recently widowed brother. Jean Cameron had spent a great deal of her time with her brother and with him. She treated him almost as if he were another brother, but he was not sure he could see her as a sister. On several occasions he had resisted with some effort the urge to kiss her.

He must resist. A kiss to so young and strictly brought up a young lady would seem very little different from a proposal of marriage. And he was not in the marriage market. Not for her or anyone else.

They lapsed into silence. Jean seemed content to gaze her fill at the coast of England and to dream of the enjoyment the summer in London would bring. And James Purnell appeared to forget her presence beside him. His lean, weather-bronzed face grew hard and he gazed sightlessly at the cliffs that were so enthralling his companion.

He was thinking of another woman, yet another burden he had carried around with him for four long years. Madeline. Lady Madeline Raine. She had told him that he would take himself wherever he went. She had not also said that he would carry her around inside his head just as surely. Madeline with her bright, fair curls and eager, vital face. Madeline with her tall, slender, lithe form. Madeline, talkative and frivolous and empty-headed.

Or so he had always told himself, as if he needed somehow to convince himself that what he had felt for her had been nothing but a physical passion. Nothing serious. Nothing lasting. Only enough to haunt his every waking moment and his every dream for four years.

Though that must, of course, be an exaggeration. Pure sentimentality.

He needed to see her again. Perhaps it was to see her more than for any other reason that he was making this unnecessary journey. He must convince himself that there really was no substance to his dreams. He must rid himself of the obsession.

For he was no more free to love than he had been four years before. Free to marry, perhaps, if he so wished. But not free to love.

He would free himself of her, at least. It was necessary to see her. To see that she was six and twenty years old now, past her prime, her beauty and vitality doubtless faded.

And he doubtless would see her. She was Alex's sister-in-law, Amberley's sister. And still unmarried, according to Alex's last letter, though she had been betrothed the summer before to an officer of the Guards, wounded at the Battle of Waterloo. The engagement had been broken, however—typical of Madeline and her shallow nature. Except that perhaps she was not really shallow. Perhaps he had just made her so in his mind so that he would not love her.

Her twin brother, Dominic, Lord Eden, had married, Alex had announced in that last letter. But not Madeline. He wished she had married her officer. He could have forgotten about her then.

Perhaps.

"Will you be going to any balls, do you suppose?" Jean Cameron asked.

He looked down at her wistful face and smiled. "Not if I can avoid them," he said. But he felt again the tenderness for her youth and eagerness that he was finding hard to resist. "But if I do have an invitation that cannot be refused, I shall take you along with me—if you wish it and your father permits it, of course."

Her face lit up so that once more he had to hold himself aloof, prevent himself from bending forward and brushing her lips affectionately with his own. "Oh, would you?" she said. "Would you really, James?" Her eyes focused on a point over his shoulder. "Duncan," she called. "Come and hear what James has just promised. Oh, do come."

James Purnell looked back over his shoulder and raised his eyebrows in a rather rueful expression at his stocky, sandy-haired friend.

LADY MADELINE RAINE was sitting in a window recess in the drawing room of the Earl of Amberley's house on Grosvenor Square. She was holding her two-month-old niece on her lap and gazing down into the child's open eyes. Her twin brother, Lord Eden, the father of the child she held and of its twin, who was sleeping in his own arms, sat with her. They were a little apart from the other occupants of the room and participated both in the general conversation and in their own private one.

"What a fascination babies are," Madeline said. "Have you noticed, Dom, how a baby will always be the center of attraction in any room?"

"I have noticed that you have no eyes for anyone but Olivia," he said with a grin, "and occasionally Charles. You have scarcely glanced my way, Mad, even though we have not seen each other for almost two months until today."

"How foolish," she said, smiling back at him. "You know I am always glad to see you, Dom. There is always something missing when you are not close by. I am so glad you and Ellen came to London after all. I feared you would not come this year with the children so young and with this newfound delight of yours in the country."

"Well, you know," he said, "the chance of bringing the

children to town for the admiration of Mama and Edmund and Alexandra and you was quite irresistible. Not to mention Ellen's father, who has made no fewer than three whirlwind visits into Wiltshire already to assure himself that his grandchildren are growing and Ellen recovering her health. And of course Ellen wanted to bring Jennifer back to town to her grandfather. You must not forget that Ellen is the stepmother of a marriageable young lady, at the grand age of six and twenty. When Charlie died at Waterloo last year, he left Ellen a widow with responsibilities— Jennifer is only eight years younger than she. She is here for what remains of the Season."

"Whatever your excuse," Madeline said, "I am glad. She has green eyes, Dom, like you and me. Olivia, I mean."

"You have been enjoying the Season?" Lord Eden asked. "You are in good looks, Mad, as usual."

"It is quite shameful, is it not?" she said. "This is my ninth Season, though last year did not really count, as I was in Brussels for most of the summer. One of these days, I swear, I am going to take to wearing caps and carrying my embroidery around with me."

Lord Eden grinned and glanced down at his son, who stirred before settling back to sleep again. "Anyone special?" he asked.

Madeline's eyes sparkled back into his. "Well, of course there is someone special," she said. "Isn't there always? Actually, Dom, he is no one new. Jason Huxtable is in town and I am quite in love with him."

"*Colonel* Huxtable?" he said, eyebrows raised. "Your old beau from Brussels? I thought you had rejected him."

"Well, I have changed my mind," she said. "He is quite the most handsome man in London. He has made me an offer already."

"Has he indeed?" he said. "And?"

She laughed softly. "And nothing," she said. "I turned the question. I am not at all ready to give my answer yet. Though I think I might accept him before the Season ends, Dom. The single state sometimes becomes tedious. Geoffrey is being a little troublesome, too."

"North?" he said. "He is smitten with your charms, too?"

"Silly, is it not?" she said. "We have been friends forever and now suddenly he has begun to see roses in my cheeks and stars in my eyes and other nonsense like that. Poor Geoffrey. I really do not know how to cope with a friend turned lover."

"Madeline," Ellen, Lady Eden, called from across the room, "are you tired of holding Olivia? You must not feel obliged, you know. Shall I take her?"

"Oh, please let me have her for a little longer," Madeline said.

But her attention had been effectively diverted. Her other brother, with his daughter on his lap busily trying to undo the buttons on his waistcoat, was laughing at his wife.

"Do you realize how often you have asked that question during the past year, Alex?" he said fondly. "How am I to know beyond the shadow of a doubt if James will come or not? I can only say, as I always do, that he wrote to say he was coming and that there is no reason to suppose he will not."

"But it was last autumn when we heard from him," the Countess of Amberley said with a sigh. "So long ago. Anything could have happened since then. But your letter also said that he was coming, Mama?" She turned to her mother, who was seated beside her.

"It is too bad of him to be coming here as a common tradesman," Lady Beckworth said fretfully. "He could have come home as a decent gentleman instead of shaming us all this way."

"Oh, Mama," Alexandra said, laying a hand over her mother's, "let us be thankful that he is coming at all. If he comes. Four years seems to have been an interminable time, and for a while it seemed that he might never come home again. Will he have changed, I wonder?"

"I will not set my hopes on it," Lord Beckworth said. "It is doubtful, Alexandra, that James will have changed at his age. The manner in which he is returning—as a tradesman, to break his mother's heart—proves my point."

The countess glanced unhappily at her husband, who smiled back at her with his eyes. "I am longing to see him," she said. "Oh, Edmund, do you think he will come? And don't smile at me in that odious way. Caroline, sweetheart, don't put Papa's buttons in your mouth. I am afraid you will swallow one of them."

"So am I," the earl said, laughing and disengaging his button from his daughter's mouth. "They are made of silver."

"I am looking forward to meeting your brother, too, Alexandra," Ellen said. "You have told me so much about him. And I am sure he will come if he told you he would. He would have written otherwise, would he not?" She stooped to examine the toy brought for her inspection by Christopher, Lord Cleeves, the earl's son.

Lord Eden, smoothing a hand over the soft down on his child's head, was examining his twin closely. "Well, Mad," he said, "and what are your thoughts on the subject?"

"What subject?" she said, and flushed deeply when he

merely raised his eyebrows. "I have no thoughts, Dom. It is nothing to me."

"Madeline," he said, "this is your twin, remember?"

"Well, then," she said, suddenly finding it necessary to examine her niece's fingers with minute care, "I will be glad if he comes. I will be glad to see him. And then finally it will all be over, and I can concentrate all my attention on Jason. I am quite in love with him, you know."

"You were quite in love with Purnell," he said, "but quite against your will, I remember. You did not choose to love him, as you seem to have chosen to love Huxtable. And you did not forget him easily, did you? Or forget him ever, for that matter."

"I never loved him," she said quietly, looking up into her brother's eyes. "I hated him. I disliked him. I feared him. I didn't love him, Dom. Not at all. It was an obsession. And nothing will have changed in four years. I want to see him again, that's all. I need to see him again so that I can prove to myself that it was a foolish obsession of the past. And I want happiness, Dom. I am tired of being alone. I want children, like you and Edmund."

"All right," he said. "Don't upset yourself, Mad. I was not teasing you. I want you to be happy too, it may surprise you to know. And I remember Huxtable as a thoroughly worthy character."

"Anyway," she said quietly, "perhaps he will not come. Olivia is getting restless, Dom. What shall I do?"

He laughed. "I think only Ellen can do the doing," he said, turning to smile at his wife, who was approaching them. "Perhaps Olivia can have a meal in peace for once, if Charles continues to sleep. He is quite ferocious when he is hungry. It is going to be difficult to persuade this one that a prime gentlemanly virtue is allowing a lady to go first."

Madeline reluctantly gave up the baby to her sister-in-law and watched the two of them leave the room. She sighed inwardly and glanced at her twin, whose attention was focused on the baby in his arms. She had still not quite adjusted her mind to the fact that Dominic was married and the father of two. And seemingly perfectly happy and domesticated.

They had been restless together for several years and like each other in their enthusiasms and tendency to fall in love routinely and out of love before any marriage could be contracted. And then he had met Ellen when she was still married to his best friend, and married her himself only months after her husband was killed at the Battle of Waterloo. Ellen was perfect for him. And he was happy, and therefore she was happy.

But sometimes there was a dreadful feeling of loneliness. A loneliness she hid, as she had always done, in increased activity and gaiety. This was perhaps her busiest and brightest Season yet.

But she loved Jason Huxtable. And she would be happy with him. He was a man and not a boy. The year before she had betrothed herself to Allan Penworth and broken off the engagement in the autumn. But that was excusable. He had been wounded in battle and she had nursed him back to health. They had both mistaken their dependence on each other for love.

This was different. There was no dependence on either side. They were both strong and independent individuals. It was real love. She had drawn back from accepting Jason's offer only because she had made so many mistakes in the past. But she would accept him before the summer was out. She was six and twenty. If she did not marry soon, she never would. And she would hate to go through life without the experience of marriage and motherhood.

She wished James Purnell were not coming. It was not fair. It had taken her months, perhaps years, to recover from his leaving. It was not fair that he should come back now to throw her feelings into turmoil again.

And why should there be any turmoil? There really had been nothing between them except a mutual dislike and a strange, inexplicable attraction.

If only she had not hated him as well as disliking him, perhaps she could have forgotten him more easily. But the manner of his leaving had caused intense hatred, an emotion she had been unfamiliar with and unable to cope with.

They had met, by accident, out of doors during a summer ball at Amberley Court in Hampshire, and he had kissed her. They had danced together to the distant sounds of the music from the ballroom, and he had kissed her. If it could be called a kiss. It had been far more than that. He had made love to her in all but the ultimate way, and she had given herself to him, even for the ultimate consummation.

She had loved him during that moment of total madness. All dislike and distrust had faded, and she had offered herself to him. She had even told him that she loved him. She had humiliated herself that much.

And he had put her from him, sneered at her, told her that it was lust only he felt for her, and told her to leave him if she knew what was good for her. She had gone and never seen him since. He had left Amberley that same night and sailed for Canada a few days later.

She had been totally destroyed. It had taken her months to put herself back together again, to regain her spirits and something of her old self-esteem. And she had come to hate intensely the man she had loved as intensely for a few insane minutes.

She wished he were not coming back.

"When is the very soonest he could possibly be here?" Alexandra was asking of no one in particular, having found it impossible to concentrate on any other topic of conversation for longer than a few minutes.

"About now," the earl said, smiling gently at her. "Or if not him in person, then a letter from him. You should have some definite news soon, Alex."

She smiled apologetically at him. "I'm sorry," she said. "I am becoming a bore, am I not?" She turned to her mother-in-law, the Dowager Countess of Amberley. "Do tell me about the opera last evening, Mother. You must be very happy to have Sir Cedric Harvey back in England again. You missed him last year when he was away in Vienna, did you not?"

Perhaps he would not come, Madeline thought. Perhaps she was living through all this agony for nothing. Perhaps he would not come. Perhaps he would never come.

Would she be able to bear never seeing him again? Never in this life?

She caught her twin's eyes steady on her and flushed. Sometimes it was an uncomfortable feeling to know that she had a brother who knew her and understood her almost as well as she knew and understood herself.

2

JAMES PURNELL WAS SITTING INSIDE THE EARL of Amberley's town carriage with his sister. She held his hand firmly clasped between both of hers. He was looking at her with mingled amusement and wonder.

Amusement because she was like a child with a new treat, her cheeks flushed, her eyes sparkling, her words tripping all over themselves. Wonder because she was so changed. Gone was the quiet, serious, demure Alex who had accepted life for whatever it offered. And in the place of the old Alex was the woman he had always known she could be, the woman he had always hoped she would become and had always feared she never would.

"I did not send word, just as I said last night I would not," she was explaining to him. "I want it to be a surprise."

He laughed outright. "But you cannot expect your mother-in-law to greet the surprise with quite the wild excitement you showed last evening when I was ushered into your drawing room," he said. "Indeed, Alex, she may show no enthusiasm at all about my arrival."

"Oh, there you are wrong," she said. "She is the dearest person, James, though I know that mothers-in-law are reputed not to be, and she knows just how much I have looked forward to your coming. I have had to exercise the utmost restraint all morning not to dash off a note to her with the news but to wait until this afternoon. And you must not laugh at me. Edmund has been doing quite enough of that, odious man."

He squeezed the hand that was below his own. "You are happy with him, Alex, are you not?" he said.

"Happy?" she said in some surprise. "With Edmund? Well, of course I am happy, James. Why would I not be?"

He laughed again. "I'm sorry I asked," he said. "It was a foolish question. I just happen to remember that you were destined to marry the Duke of Peterleigh before circumstances forced you to marry Amberley."

"I was not forced to marry Edmund," she said quickly. "I married him freely, because I wanted to. Because I loved him and he me. And I don't need to be reminded of the duke, James. He is in London, you know, though I have been fortunate enough not to have seen him at all. Oh, yes, I am happy, James, and very well aware of how fortunately my life has turned out."

"Well, I am glad," he said. "You know how much I hated the thought of your marrying Peterleigh. I like the children, by the way. It is quite a novelty to be Uncle James, you know."

"Christopher has been telling anyone who would listen for the last several months that his uncle was coming in a big ship," she said. "Edmund says that the two of us have sounded like a Greek chorus. James, you have changed."

"Have I?" he said, looking into her searching eyes. "In what way?"

She put her head to one side. "You are thinner," she said. "Though you look very strong. And healthy, too. Your face is thinner. And so very bronzed. Mama was not at all pleased about that, was she?" She laughed a little guiltily.

"Well," he said, "gentlemen are not supposed to expose their faces to the sunshine, you know. Poor Mama. If she would only sometimes relax and stop worrying about what people think. She quite spoiled the effect of all her scolding when she cried all over my cravat, though, did she not?"

But Alexandra was still concentrating her looks on him and appeared not to hear his words. "It is not just your appearance, though," she said. "You have changed in other ways, haven't you, James? You look less haunted. Have you learned to live again in Canada? Have you put the past behind you? I can quite forgive you for going if that is the case."

"Four years have passed, Alex," he said quietly. "And a great deal has happened in those years. Yes, I have a new life there. I am content."

"Ah," she said, sighing, "then I must resign myself to losing you again at the end of the summer. You will go back again. Do you have anyone there, James? I mean, is there any special lady?"

"I lived in the interior," he said, "where there are no white women at all. Only the native women. Very beautiful many of them are, too, and it is quite customary for the men to take them as wives. But they are of a different culture, Alex. When the men come out, they must leave the women behind, and the children too. It would be a cruelty to bring them out into a world they do not know. I would not wish such heartbreak on myself."

"Ah," she said.

"There is a little Scottish girl, though," he said, "from Montreal. Jean Cameron. Her father is a partner in the company and is in London at the moment. She came across in the *Adeona* with her brother. I have promised to take her to some of the entertainments of the Season."

She smiled brightly at him. "And she is special?" she asked. "I will like her?"

"Yes to both questions, I would imagine," he said. "But that does not mean you may start planning my wedding, Alex. She is just a child. A very sweet child."

"A very *special* sweet child," she said, lifting his hand to lay briefly against her cheek. "I can hardly wait to see Mother's face when she sees you, James. And Madeline's."

He smiled at her. He had discovered the night before, of course, that Madeline was not staying at her brother's house on Grosvenor Square. He had not known if she was at her mother's. She had not been mentioned before this moment. He had not even known if she was in London.

"She still is not married, James," Alexandra said. "Can you imagine? She was betrothed last summer, of course, and we all were very fond of Lieutenant Penworth. But they were not really meant for each other. Dominic was telling us two days ago that Mr. Penworth and Ellen's step-daughter, Jennifer Simpson, are promised, though her grandfather has not given his approval yet. I think Madeline is going to marry Colonel Huxtable."

"Huxtable?" he said.

"A Guardsman," she said, "and wonderfully handsome, though the uniform helps, of course. They met in Brussels last year. She told Edmund and me that he has made her an offer already and that she will probably accept before the end of the Season. Will that not be splendid? Ah, here we are."

So he was to meet her again. In her mother's drawing room, doubtless in the presence of other guests. And she was in love again. Almost betrothed again. Soon to be married.

Well, it was as well to meet her this way. Now, before he had time to think about it. Casually. He would look at her, greet her, converse politely with her for a few minutes, and put behind him once and for all the obsession of four years.

He stood outside the doors of the drawing room, his sister's arm in his, her animated face smiling up into his, while the butler announced them. He smiled back.

The room was crowded with people, though only a remote part of his mind knew it. He saw only her as he entered the room. She was not with either of the two groups into which the occupants had divided themselves, but was partway across the room, obviously on her way to greet them. Except that it was clearly not him she had expected to greet. She stopped, frozen, in her tracks.

Time rolled back as if it had never been. Madeline. She was exactly as he remembered her, only more slender and lithe, more fair-haired, more lovely, more vivid in every way. Every part of his insides seemed jolted out of place.

He saw her in a moment that was quite outside time. A moment that would always be etched on his consciousness. And yet in actual fact he did not look at her at all. His eyes touched on her and slid away and no force on earth could have forced them back to her again.

He obeyed the pressure of Alex's arm and reacted to her voice and was soon bowing over the dowager countess's hand and answering her polite queries. And he was being presented to a crowd of people he had never met before and would probably not remember again. And he was shaking the hand of Sir Cedric Harvey and settling into a conversation about his employment.

He found himself sitting with the dowager's group while Alex had joined the other group, the one that included Madeline. And all the time he talked and listened and laughed and drank tea and ate scones he was aware of her with every nerve ending in his body, aware of every move she made, every expression on her face, every sound of her voice, though he never once looked her way.

He had not greeted her, or she him. They had shown no sign that they had even so much as set eyes on each other before.

And yet he had held her in his arms. He had unclothed her to the waist and kissed and fondled her. He had wanted her with every instinct of his body and every atom of his mind. And he had been raw with the pain of leaving her for months and even years afterward.

And now they were strangers in a room together. Strangers, except that his pulses pounded with the knowledge of her. Except that he could not look at her or speak to her. Except that he felt an irrational urge to kill the handsome officer who sat beside her, and even Lord North, with whom she was making arrangements to drive later in the afternoon.

Fool! He would have given anything in the world, he felt after half an hour, if he could only go back and make that entrance all over again.

MADELINE HAD BEEN holding court in her mother's drawing room, if entertaining two gentlemen who were currently showing a marked interest in her could be called holding court. She had been laughing gaily and assuring Lord North that she would indeed have gone driving with him in the park if only the day were not so beastly cold and the rain not drizzling down intermittently.

And while Lord North had looked somewhat crest-fallen, she had turned toward Colonel Huxtable and said that yes, she was to attend the concert at Mrs. Denton's that evening with her mama and would be pleased with his escort. After all, Sir Cedric would undoubtedly be accompanying her mother, as he had accompanied her almost everywhere since his return from Vienna, and she herself should have an escort of her own.

When the butler had opened the doors of the drawing room, Madeline had looked up brightly to see who the latecomers might be. She was taken completely off her guard. She had known he was coming, of course. Alexandra had talked of little else for months. But she had not known he had come.

She did not listen to the butler's words. She saw her sister-in-law.

"Here come Edmund and Alexandra," she said gladly, rising to her feet and stepping past her two admirers to greet the new arrivals. And only then, when she was stranded in the middle of the room, did the butler's words register on her hearing and did she see that the man with Alexandra was not her elder brother.

He was different. Very much darker of complexion and more agile-looking. And his eyes were less brooding and less hostile. Very different. He had changed.

And yet he was no different at all. She was paralyzed with the sameness of him. James as he had lived deep in her memories for four years, dark and intense, seemingly coiled like a spring, an almost frightening power in him. James, more handsome than any man she had ever known, though not in a drawing room kind of way. He belonged in the wilderness and not in the ballrooms and salons of society.

And that truant lock of dark hair fallen across his forehead as it had always used to do, the one feature she had forgotten about, though it was so very familiar now that her arm ached to lift and put it back to join the rest of his thick hair.

James, as he had always been. Throwing only one brief, contemptuous glance her way before turning away to greet her mother. Though how she knew about that glance when she had not once looked fully at him, she did not know. She behaved with all the gaucherie of a girl only one day out of the schoolroom. She neither looked at him nor greeted him, but smiled at Alexandra and continued on her way to the tea tray, where she poured her sister-in-law a cup of tea, but not their other guest.

And then she rejoined her group and behaved with all the mindlessness of the most flighty of social butterflies.

"But where is Lady Beckworth?" she asked Alexandra, far too brightly and far too loudly.

"She would not come with us," Alexandra said. "She thought the weather too inclement for an outing. And Edmund would not come." She laughed. "He said that since he is of no more importance to me now that my brother has arrived, he might as well retire to the nursery and sulk. He is being very silly. He is teasing me, of course," she added, for the information of Colonel Huxtable and Lord North, who might have taken her words seriously.

"Are you going to Mrs. Denton's tonight?" Madeline asked, smiling at Jason Huxtable with a flirtatiousness that she had not intended.

"We are all going," Alexandra said. "Even Papa, if you

can imagine. Of course, he does not consider concerts quite as frivolous as other forms of entertainment. James will be coming too, naturally."

Madeline felt rather as if a giant fist had punched her just below the waist. She felt as if she had just run hard for a mile. She had glanced across the room and almost met his eyes. She drew her head back as if to ward off a touch, though he was clear across the room from her and really had not looked at her at all.

"I have just had a thought," she said, and heard in some dismay the high pitch and volume of her voice. But she seemed unable to do anything about it. She turned to Lord North and laid a hand lightly on his sleeve. "When a gentleman offers to take me driving, I immediately visualize a curricle or a phaeton. You were not by any chance offering a closed carriage, were you, Geoffrey?"

"It could certainly be arranged," he said, brightening.

"I should not even dream of accompanying you in a closed carriage without the presence of my maid, of course," she said gaily. "But one advantage of having been on the town forever is that one does not have to pay heed to all that faradiddle."

"On the town forever, Lady Madeline?" Lord North said gallantly. "Why, you look not a day older than the newest young lady in town."

"Gracious!" she said, tapping his arm and laughing merrily and altogether too loudly across at the colonel. "I am not at all sure I take that as a compliment, sir."

She was aware of Sir Cedric and Mr. Brunning in the other group smiling across at her. And she could not stop herself from smiling. She could not force herself to be quiet and let the conversation continue around her.

She was behaving as she had always behaved in the

presence of James Purnell. He had always despised her as silly and empty-headed. She had always been aware of his contempt. And yet she had always lived up to his expectations when he was in the same room. She had never been able to act naturally with him. Except perhaps on that last occasion, when she had offered herself to him and told him she loved him.

Her cheeks burned with shame at the memory.

She wished she could relive the last half hour, have another chance to do it right, to greet him civilly, to behave with the coolness and poise of a mature woman. Oh, she wished she could have the time back again.

When Lord North rose in order to return home for his town carriage, all the guests took his doing so as a cue to take their own departure.

"I shall look forward to seeing you again this evening," Alexandra said, kissing her mother-in-law's cheek.

"Of course, dear," the dowager said. "We will see you there as well, Mr. Purnell?"

He answered her question, bowed, and extended a hand to her. Madeline turned away and took an effusive farewell of Colonel Huxtable.

"I AM QUITE SURE this cannot be real. Any minute now I am going to wake up and find it is all a dream." Jean Cameron clung to James's arm and looked behind her at the grand carriages that were disgorging their elegant passengers and ahead to the shallow marble steps leading to the open front doors of Mrs. Denton's house and numerous impeccably clad footmen.

"But it is real," he said very quietly so that Alexandra and Edmund, walking behind them, and his parents walking ahead, would not hear. "And I can pinch you to prove it if you wish, though I assure you the pain is not necessary. And moreover, you look quite as pretty as any other young lady within my line of vision."

She had wanted to come. He had seen that in her face as soon as he had called on her at her father's house. At the same time she had been filled with misgivings. Her clothes, which had been perfectly fashionable in Montreal, would be laughed at in London, she had said. And her manners, which had been quite acceptable in Montreal society, would appear awkward here. Besides, he was being kind. He could not really want her with him when he would have his mother and father and his sister and brother-in-law, the earl, for company.

But he had wanted her with him. He had not had to use any hypocrisy in assuring her of that. Her anxiety and her eagerness had appeared very endearing to him after the artificiality of Madeline's behavior earlier that afternoon. But he would not think of that, or of her, again. He had been right in his original impression of her. She was shallow and silly. Certainly not worthy of the kind of obsession that had haunted him for four years. He would put her from his mind. He was free of her now at last.

Jean blushed and looked at him with large, questioning eyes when Alexandra turned to her inside the crowded hallway and suggested that they go together in search of the cloakroom. She seemed quite overawed by the fact that she was being addressed by a live countess. His parents proceeded on their way upstairs.

He found himself smiling gently down at the girl as he released her arm and feeling a definite surge of tenderness for her. And of nostalgia for Canada, where he had met her and where he had learned to live in relative peace with himself. He wished he were there now. He wished he had not come back.

There was no sign in the hallway of the dowager Lady Amberley's party. They might be upstairs already in the concert room. Or theirs might be among the crush of carriages still outside. He hoped Alex and Jean would not be long. He felt alone and exposed, standing with his brother-in-law, his hands clasped behind his back.

And he wished again that he could relive that afternoon, or rather that he had lived it differently at the time. It could have been all over now, just as it was in his emotions. He had seen her and realized that she was every bit as lovely and as attractive as she had ever been. And he had heard her and known that she was as foolish as he had ever thought her. He had understood and accepted that he could never have loved her, that he had invented the woman who had lived unwillingly in his dreams throughout his exile from England.

But he had ignored her. And having done so once, he had set up an awkward situation that could only get worse with every meeting. Or with every nonmeeting. Why had he put himself in this ridiculous situation when she was nothing to him?

He listened to his brother-in-law's amiable chatter and watched the doorway with unease and the hallway leading to the ladies' withdrawing room with impatience. Just like a schoolboy who did not know how to conduct himself in company.

"Ah," the Earl of Amberley said from beside him, "we have not been abandoned after all, James. The ladies are returning, having assured themselves, doubtless, that the unthinkable has not happened and a curl worked loose during the carriage ride here." He smiled at his wife.

"Are you satisfied that you are as beautiful as I told you you were when I helped you down from the carriage, Alex?"

"Yes," she said. "Having looked in the mirror, I can safely say that you were quite right, Edmund. I apologize for having doubted your word."

The earl chuckled and Jean looked up into James's face in some surprise. It seemed to amaze her that an earl and his countess could joke with each other. James offered her his arm and smiled reassuringly at her.

"I am so afraid to walk into that room," she said breathlessly as they climbed the stairs. "You will let me hold to your arm the whole time, James?"

"Of course," he said. "And then all the gentlemen will look at you and from you to me with envy."

"Oh, how silly," she said, and giggled.

What she did not know was that he was as nervous about walking into the concert room as she was. They were among the last to arrive, and the room was crowded already. He was very glad of the excuse of having Jean on his arm to save him from having to look all about him. And he was not sorry for the crowded room and the necessity of sitting on some of the few vacant chairs close to the doors.

But for all that he did not need Alex's words.

"Your mother is sitting clear across the room," she said to her husband. "And Madeline and Aunt Viola. What a shame there are no empty seats near them, Edmund."

"But you can all content yourselves with smiling and nodding at one another," he said, "something you would all feel foolish doing if you were sitting next to one another. There are compensations for every annoyance, you see, Alex."

"I see you are in one of your nonsensical moods," she said, tapping him on the arm with her fan. "I shall confine my conversation to James and Miss Cameron. Perhaps I will have some sense from them."

"If I were you," the earl said, "I would satisfy myself with no conversation at all. The music is about to begin, and you may annoy your neighbors if you chatter."

But crowded as the room was, and as much as he had not looked about him, James had known exactly where Madeline was the moment he walked through the doors. She was wearing a jonquil-colored gown and she was seated between her mother and the Guardsman who had been paying court to her that afternoon. The one she was about to marry, according to Alex.

And he was welcome to her, too.

The pianist was seated at the grand pianoforte in the middle of the room. Looking at him, James found it very difficult to keep his eyes focused there and not to let them stray beyond to fair curls and flushed cheeks and shining eyes, which he knew to be green, and an enticing mouth curved upward into a smile. He was surprised to see that she concentrated on the music, her eyes not moving from the pianist.

Just as his own did not.

"Which is the earl's mother?" Jean whispered. Her voice became anxious. "I will not have to meet her, will I, James?"

He assured her at the time that she would probably not, since the room was so crowded. And indeed, he was proved correct. During the interval, when Sir Cedric Harvey went for refreshments, the dowager countess stayed where she was, talking with her sister-in-law, Mrs. Carrington.

But Madeline did not stay where she was, although for a while she spoke with the colonel and with the couple who sat in front of them. After a few minutes, she got to her feet with the young lady with whom she had been talking, and the two of them began to make their way across the crowded room.

James became engrossed in his conversation with Jean and Alexandra. And felt again like the schoolboy he had not been for more than twelve years.

MADELINE APPLAUDED with enthusiasm at the end of the pianoforte recital. She was enjoying herself immensely. The music was good, she had Jason Huxtable sitting beside her, easily outshining any other gentleman in the room with his scarlet regimentals, and she had her mother and Sir Cedric on one side of her, and Aunt Viola and Uncle William on the other side of Jason, and her cousins Anna and Walter Carrington in front of them, Anna with Mr. Chambers and Walter with Miss Mitchell.

Edmund and his party were clear across the crowded room. She had scarcely noticed their entrance and had paid them no attention beyond a smile and a nod in their direction. Except that he put even Jason in the shade with his dark evening clothes and his vividly dark hair and complexion. James Purnell, that was. And except that there was a young lady clinging to his arm, even after they had seated themselves. A very young lady, a stranger. A pretty young lady, on whom he looked with a fondness he had never directed her way.

Not that it mattered one little bit, of course. She was having a marvelously enjoyable evening with the company she had.

"Mama and I called on Dominic and Ellen at Lord Harrowby's this afternoon," Anna said, turning around in her seat. The gentlemen had gone to fetch some lemonade. "We went to see the babies really, of course, though we pretended to be calling on Dominic and Ellen." She giggled.

"I know," Madeline said. "I find myself doing the same thing."

"They were awake," Anna said, "and I was allowed to hold Olivia. She is quite adorable, isn't she? Charles would not be picked up. He was exercising his lungs. Ellen says that he has still not reconciled his mind to the fact that he is a twin and must share everyone's attention. He deserves to be ignored, she said, when he is being so cross. But for all that she picked him up and kissed him and soothed him, and Dominic laughed at her and told her that he could see already that all the disciplining of their children was going to fall on his shoulders."

"From what I have seen," Madeline said, "they are one as bad as the other."

"It seems strange to see Dominic in a nursery, doting on two babies," Anna said with something of a sigh. "Just a year ago I was still swearing to anyone who cared to listen that I was going to marry him." She giggled again.

"You don't seem to be pining away with grief," her father said, entering the conversation unexpectedly. "Sawyer three weeks ago, Dartford two weeks ago, Bailey last week, Chambers this week." He was counting off on his fingers. "And Ashley fits in there somewhere too. One of these days, Madeline, I am going to embarrass puss here by calling one of her young men by another one's name. Sometimes I wish we were Catholic. I could pack her off to a convent and have some peace."

"William!" his wife said, horrified. "What a thing to say. Take no notice of him, Madeline. He does like to tease, you know. Everyone knows that Anna is the apple of his eye."

Madeline laughed and took her glass of lemonade from Colonel Huxtable.

"Mr. Purnell is looking very handsome," Anna said. "He always did. I wonder if he remembers me. I was just fifteen when he was at Amberley four years ago, and everyone else ignored me. But he was very kind, I remember, just as if he understood perfectly well how horrid it is to be fifteen and neither a child nor a woman. He has probably forgotten me."

"Ah," Madeline said, smiling at the colonel, "it is cool and tastes very good, Jason. I wish Mrs. Denton would direct that some windows be opened."

"Let's see if he does remember me," Anna said, laying a hand on Madeline's arm. "Do you think we can cross this crowded room without being trampled on?" She laughed lightly after ascertaining that Mr. Chambers was talking with someone else. "We can pretend that we have gone to pay our respects to Edmund and Alexandra. He really is excessively handsome, is he not, Madeline? Who is the lady with him? I am jealous already. She is very pretty."

"I don't know," Madeline said. "I have never seen her before." They were on their way across the room already, their arms linked. She had really had no choice in the matter without making a pointed refusal. A refusal to greet her own brother and sister-in-law? It had been out of the question. Her heart felt as if it were attached to the soles of her slippers.

And she found to her own annoyance that as usual when James Purnell was anywhere in the vicinity she could not behave with any naturalness. She did not know whether to smile or not. And when she decided to smile, she did not know how brightly. And she could fix her eyes only on her brother and felt she would surely drown or die if she let them slip anywhere else. Just as she had felt when watching the pianist earlier, without hearing one note he had played.

She despised herself heartily. She had not felt so gauche since she had stepped out of the schoolroom a decade before.

3

HE EARL OF AMBERLEY SMILED AT HIS SISTER and his cousin and kissed the latter on the cheek. "You are growing lovelier by the day, young Anna," he said. "And what are you up to? A great deal of mischief, by the look of it."

"Coming to say good evening to my favorite cousin," she said almost in a whisper, looking up at him with large and dancing eyes, "and hoping that Mr. Purnell remembers me."

"Ah," he said, looking at Madeline and giving her the suggestion of a wink, "I thought it strange that you would risk being crushed and jostled coming across here just in order to get a closer look at your, er, favorite cousin, my dear." He looked back over his shoulder and raised his voice. "James, you are to step over here immediately or sooner, if you please, to see if you recognize this young lady."

Anna blushed hotly and looked reproachfully at the earl. She kept her hold of Madeline's arm. And so Madeline, who had been forming the hasty plan of paying her compliments to Lord and Lady Beckworth, was held in place as James Purnell turned toward them, his dark eyes boring into her for an uncomfortable fraction of a second.

And the pretty young girl who had been clinging to his arm all evening was still there, looking flushed and anxious. And small and dainty and helpless and altogether as if she belonged to him.

"Miss Carrington," he said after his eyes had rested on Anna for a few moments. "I scarcely knew you because you have grown up since I saw you last and are considerably more lovely. But yes, I remember you perfectly well."

Anna's discomfort vanished instantly. And finally, when it was too late, she released Madeline's arm. She smiled dazzlingly up at James. "You were at Amberley the year Edmund and Alexandra were betrothed," she said. "I was sorry when you left so abruptly. You were the only gentleman there who did not treat me as if I were a fifteen-year-old nuisance."

"Poor little Anna!" Edmund said, and grinned. "You would have met Madeline this afternoon, of course, James."

And finally there was nowhere else to look except right at him. Their eyes met at last, and held.

"Yes," they both said abruptly and simultaneously.

He was the first to break eye contact and to move his head rather jerkily to one side.

"I would like to present Lady Madeline Raine and Miss Anna Carrington, Jean," he said. "Edmund's sister and cousin. This is Miss Jean Cameron from Montreal in Canada."

From Canada. He must have brought her with him. Were they betrothed? Married? But no, something would have been said. The girl was curtsying to her and flushing. Madeline nodded to her.

"From Canada?" Anna was saying, enthralled. "How

splendid. You simply must tell me all about it at some time. Are there many bears there? And wolves?"

The girl laughed and immediately looked even prettier than she had a minute before. "People here have funny ideas about Canada," she said. "But then, I had funny ideas about England, too. I don't think I would have been wholly surprised to find the streets of London paved with gold."

The two girls began to chatter. And Alexandra drew her husband's attention to something her mother had said. Madeline was aware suddenly that she was standing silently beside an equally silent James Purnell. She looked up at him rather nervously to find his eyes on her.

And she was dismayed a moment later to find that she had immediately lowered her eyes to the fan she held in one hand.

"The pianist is marvelously accomplished, is he not?" she said. "I was held spellbound throughout his recital."

If anyone had said those very words to her, she would have been hard put to it to keep a straight face. All she needed to add was a titter. And then she heard it, a moment after the words were spoken.

"The pianoforte is not my favorite instrument," he said.

His voice always surprised her. One did not expect a man of such vivid and almost harsh looks to be so soft-spoken or to have such a cultured voice. But it angered her, too. He never had known how to conduct polite conversation.

"Well, then," she said, opening her fan and fluttering it before her face, "perhaps you will enjoy the soprano better in the second half. Or do you not enjoy sopranos, either?"

He raised his eyebrows and looked down at her. "Not particularly," he said. "I would prefer a contralto voice."

And she was left staring at him, while conversation flowed around them. He made no attempt to continue their own conversation. Memory stabbed at her. He had always been this way, looking at her with unconcealed contempt and showing his scorn for her conversation by not participating in it beyond monosyllables.

How could she ever have persuaded herself that she loved him? How could she have convinced herself that for a short while at Edmund's ball he had returned that love? How could she have so humiliated herself as to pine for him after he had gone?

She turned sharply away. "I think the concert is about to resume," she said to Anna. "We should find our way back to our seats." She smiled at Jean Cameron and raised a hand in farewell to her brother and sister-in-law. She ignored James Purnell.

And James bowed and smiled at a bright-eyed Anna and watched her turn to make her way through the crush of people toward the other side of the room again. Or rather, to be quite honest with himself, he watched her companion.

She was more beautiful than she had been. Indeed, she had never been an unusually lovely woman. It had always been the glow and vitality in her face that had drawn all eyes her way. But she was that rare kind of woman who grows more beautiful with age and the development of character. He had felt his breath catch in his throat when he had finally looked full into her face from close quarters.

And he was as awkward with her as he had ever been. Unable to think of anything witty or profound to say to her, and taking refuge in surliness and silence. He had always been thus with her, and when she had flared up at him on a few occasions when they had been together at Amberley that summer, then he had lashed out at her, accusing her of an empty-headedness that could find entertainment only in meaningless chatter.

He had even convinced himself that it was true. And could still do so, he supposed. Her behavior that afternoon in her mother's drawing room had been loud and silly. Her remarks of a few minutes before had been mundane. But he need not have answered as he had. He might have agreed with her for the sake of civility.

He found it possible to be civil with all the world, it seemed, except with Madeline. And except with his father, perhaps. He glanced uneasily Lord Beckworth's way. They had scarcely spoken since his return. And he still had not decided whether it was not better that way.

"They were very civil, were they not, James?" Jean was saying from beside him. Two spots of color high on her cheekbones gave her a glow of prettiness.

"And why would they not be?" he asked, his eyes twinkling down at her, "unless they were jealous of your loveliness, of course."

Her face lit up with merriment. "You say the silliest things," she said. "Miss Carrington is very amiable, James. And Lady Madeline is quite lovely. I am amazed that she would condescend to take notice of me at all. She is with that splendidly handsome officer, is she not?"

"It would seem so," he said. "And now it would seem we are to be entertained by a famous soprano. Are you enjoying the music, Jean?"

She turned bright eyes on him and lowered her voice to a whisper. "I am enjoying every single moment," she said.

"I am storing up the memories to tell Papa and Duncan and Miss Hendricks. And to last me a whole lifetime. This is me, sitting shoulder to shoulder with members of the *ton*."

He laughed at her and squeezed her hand as it rested on his arm. And across the pianoforte he caught the eye of Madeline, who was also laughing and tapping the colonel's arm with her fan. They both looked quickly away again.

THE COUNTESS OF AMBERLEY had persuaded her husband to host a dinner and ball in honor of her brother's return to England. It had not been difficult to do since she had discovered long before that the earl found it impossible to refuse her anything that was within his power to give. And yet it had been difficult to ask for since she knew that he was a hermit at heart and did not enjoy grand social occasions.

"But just this once," she had said, twining her arms about his neck and looking apologetically up at him. "Because James is here, Edmund, and is not like to be here again for many years or perhaps ever."

"If you wish us to give a ball," he had said, "then we will do so, Alex. You do not have to win me over with arguments."

"I think perhaps he will go back to Canada and marry Miss Cameron," she had said. "She is a very sweet girl, though very young. Do you think they will suit?"

"I have no idea," he had said, "not being of a match-making turn of mind. All I know and care about is that you suit me."

"And will Madeline marry Colonel Huxtable?" she had

asked him. "He is quite splendid, Edmund, and is one of the few gentlemen I have seen with Madeline who has the strength of mind she needs in a husband. Will they suit?"

He had smiled and kissed her. "Go and make up your invitation list," he had said. "With any luck ours will be named the ball of the year, with two betrothal announcements during the course of it. How about Anna and Chambers? And Walter and Miss Mitchell? Have I forgotten anyone?"

"Horrid man," she had said, laughing. "You are quite odious."

But plans for the dinner and ball were put into action from that moment on. Whether he liked it or not, James thought rather ruefully as he ruffled his nephew's hair and kissed his niece the following morning as he left the nursery with Alexandra.

"You will bring Miss Cameron?" Alexandra asked. "She is a very sweet girl, James, and has quite unaffected manners."

James hesitated. He could see how easy it would be to fall into a trap. There was a certain security in clinging to Jean. And yet he was not sure that he wished the two of them to be considered a couple. He was not sure at all.

"She is enjoying London vastly," he said. "I am sure the chance to attend a ball would be the pinnacle of bliss to her. Perhaps you would send invitations to both her and her brother, Alex. Will you?"

She looked at him and smiled. "Yes, that will be the way to do it," she said. "Am I being overeager, James? Edmund always laughs at me and tells me that I have become a committed matchmaker since my marriage. But can I help it if I wish everyone to be as happy as I am? I thought perhaps Miss Cameron was the one. Am I wrong?"

"I don't know," he said. "I am fond of her, Alex. At the moment that is all. Maybe there will never be anything else. And maybe there will."

"Oh, well," she said, placing her hands on his shoulders and offering her cheek for his farewell kiss, "I will not complain. I am only too happy to see that you are alive again, James, and not looking at the world with cynical eyes, as you were still doing four years ago. I am so glad you closed the book on the past."

He kissed her and left. And wondered for surely the dozenth time whether he had done the right thing in coming home. For Alex was wrong. He had not put the past behind him. He had shut it beyond his consciousness for several years so that he had been able to live again. But with every day he now spent in England he felt himself more and more hemmed in by it all.

Douglas had said that he might take time off if he wished, since there was really very little to keep two clerks busy in London. And a part of him felt pulled back to Yorkshire. There was nothing to take him there. The home there was his father's. Even in the years following his attainment of his majority, when he had still been at home, he had not been allowed any hand in the running of the estate.

And there was nothing else to go back for. She had not lived there for nine years. For five of those years he had been unable to discover where she had gone or whether she was contented or desperately unhappy. It was improbable that he would be able to find her now. And what would he be able to do even if he did discover her whereabouts? It was nine years after the event.

There was nothing he could do, no point in going back. And yet he was being haunted again by the old sense of helplessness and guilt, by the old chains that robbed him of all freedom and that made it impossible for him to grasp at any happiness for himself.

He had destroyed so much: the honor and the happiness and the freedom of another person, one whom he had loved. More than one person, in fact. All through his own carelessness and thoughtlessness. And because he had never been given the chance to atone, he must carry around the guilt for the rest of his life. He must be his own unending punishment.

He had not talked with his father. Every time he went to visit Alex, he persuaded himself that he would arrange for time alone with his father and have some plain speaking with him. It was something they had not done in years, if ever. Nine years before, they had talked. But there had been raw passion then to stand between them and communication. And after that, five years of near silence. And now four years of total silence.

He must speak with his father. Perhaps there could be some releasing of the burden.

Or perhaps he would live out the summer and go back to Canada to forget again, or to put the whole thing so far back in his consciousness that it would be as good as forgotten. Perhaps he would go back into the interior and take himself a native woman as wife. Perhaps he would stay there, as a few men did, for the rest of his life, and never return either to Canada or to England.

Or perhaps he would marry Jean and settle with her in Montreal. He could do worse. A great deal worse.

And he wondered again, as he had wondered before, why he could contemplate marriage with Jean but not with Madeline. Why was it that he was in reality as free to marry either woman, but felt that there was some insurmountable barrier that kept him from Madeline?

Was it that she lived in England and he would be forever tied to his memories if he married her? If she would have him, of course. Hell would probably freeze over before she would. Though, of course, there had been an occasion when she had told him she loved him, when she had been his for the taking. A long time ago.

He shook off the thought. He could not even begin to understand his conflicting feelings for Madeline. Attraction, revulsion; love, hate; admiration, contempt; longing, dread; how could he possibly contemplate a courtship and marriage with her?

Whereas his relationship with Jean was pleasant and tranquil. There was no deep love, perhaps, on either side. But then affection was a far more soothing emotion than love.

And now, on the very day when he had decided to keep himself away from places where Madeline was likely to be, he found himself committed to attending a ball at his sister's house. The best thing he could do, perhaps, was something he had grown quite expert at doing. He must just block his mind until the evening came and he could not avoid the meeting. He would think of Duncan Cameron, whom he was about to take along to White's Club, and imagine what his friend's reaction would be to the news that he was about to be invited to a grand ball at the home of the Earl of Amberley.

MADELINE HAD MADE a decision. She was going to marry Jason Huxtable. It was true that he was an officer of the Guards and she had never felt particularly drawn to the life of a soldier's wife. A strange thought, perhaps, when she had almost eloped with a half-pay officer at the age of eighteen and had been actually betrothed to a lieutenant just the year before after the Battle of Waterloo. But there it was. Ideally, she would not choose to marry an officer.

But it would be foolish to reject Jason's suit just on that score. She could hardly do better. He was a kindly and a dependable man, and she was old enough to realize that those were important qualities in a husband. And she enjoyed his company. She found him attractive.

More than anything, it was time she married. Very much past time, in fact. She should have married long ago, when she would have found it far easier to adapt to a husband's ways. Now she would not find it easy to do so. But it must be done. The thought of living her life out as a spinster, forever dependent upon Edmund or Dominic, was rather frightening.

She must marry. And soon. And if she must, then she could not do better than marry Jason. She was going to marry him. And moreover, she was going to accept him at Edmund's ball. If he asked her, that was. But he had asked her once already that Season, and her woman's intuition told her that he would ask again and soon.

What more appropriate occasion than a ball given by her brother?

She was going to accept him. Perhaps she would even have Edmund announce the betrothal before the evening was over.

And so she dressed with care in a sea-green gown that she had been saving for a special occasion. And she sparkled with the knowledge that her future was about to be settled at long last. With Jason Huxtable, whom she liked as well as she had ever liked any man, and far better than she had liked most.

She was quite determined to enjoy the evening. And since she was seated at a part of the dinner table where she was surrounded by relatives and friends with whom she felt thoroughly comfortable, the evening started very well indeed. It helped that James Purnell and Miss Cameron were seated farther down the table on the same side as she with the result that she did not have to look at either of them, and did not have to listen to them either provided she kept talking herself.

If the ball had been a play she was attending, she thought with some happiness as the evening progressed, then she might have written the script. For the colonel claimed her hand for the opening set and then wasted part of his half hour on the dance floor with her by maneuvering her to the door and into a small reception room next to the ballroom and empty at such an early hour.

"I thought army officers were supposed to be the fittest of mortals," she said gaily. "Are you footsore already, Jason? For shame!"

"Not footsore," he said. "Impatient. I know perfectly well that I should wait for a later and more romantic hour. I know all about tactics in battle, it seems, but not about tactics in love. I want you to marry me, Madeline. Will you? You know that I adore you. And you did not answer me when I asked you last."

Madeline opened her fan and waved it slowly before her face. She could have written the script thus far. And she knew the ending of the play. But she had not written the middle of it, and did not know how it should proceed. "Oh, dear," she heard herself say, "I wish you would not."

"Adore you?" he said. "But I do, you see."

"No," she said. "Propose to me so early in the evening. I did not expect it quite so soon. I like you very much, Jason, and greatly enjoy your company. Oh, dear, I had hoped to enjoy the dancing for the rest of the evening."

"I hate it," he said, "when women tell me that they like me."

"You would prefer me to say that I hate you?" she asked.

"Infinitely so," he said. "There is some passion in hatred. I would be quite confident of turning it into love. Do you not feel a little more than liking for me, Madeline?"

She looked at him dumbly and waved her fan foolishly before her face. She was not at all overheated. And all the eloquence that had sustained her through dinner fled. "I don't know," she said at last. "I think I have been on the town for so long that I am no longer capable of knowing what I want or how I feel. I do not know what to answer."

"Do I understand that you are not saying an outright no?" he asked.

"But I am not saying an outright yes, either," she said, fanning her face more vigorously.

"When I broached this topic with you last year in Brussels," he said, "you told me there was someone else. I thought soon after that you must have meant Penworth since you proceeded to betroth yourself to him. But you broke off the betrothal. Is there still someone else?"

She frowned and snapped the fan shut. "There never was," she said. "I lied to you. At least, I think I lied. Jason, you really do not want to be loving and marrying me, you know. I know my mind less and less as the years go on. I mean it."

He took her right hand and raised it to his lips. "I thought you would say yes," he said. "You have sparkled this evening, and I was conceited enough to think that I was the cause."

She looked at him uneasily. "I thought I would say yes, too," she said. "Forgive me, please. I seem unable to say the words I intended to say. I like you, Jason. I think perhaps I even love you, or soon will. I think perhaps I will want to marry you. But I find that at the moment I cannot promise to do so, though I wish I could. I do wish I could. I think you should put me from your mind. I do not want you to think that I am dangling you on a string."

He squeezed her hand, which he still held. "I will take my chances," he said. "At least you are honest with me. I may ask you again sometime, then?"

She frowned up at him and considered her answer with some care. "Yes," she said, "as long as you fully understand that the answer may be no."

He grinned and leaned forward to kiss her lightly and tentatively on the lips. "If I ask to do that a little more thoroughly," he said, "will the answer be no?"

"No," she said. "I mean, the answer will be yes."

She gave herself up to his embrace far more deliberately than she was used to doing with the men who ever got close enough to her to be granted a kiss. She set her hands on his shoulders and her body against his. She parted her lips slightly.

She allowed the embrace to be as long as he chose to make it. He chose to prolong it for all of a minute, and perhaps longer. Madeline examined the experience. It was far from unpleasant. It was even mildly exciting. He felt very large and strong and masculine.

Perhaps, she thought, feeling his tongue pushing between her lips, she would find the courage when he lifted his head, to look into his eyes and tell him that she would be his wife. She wanted to be his wife. She wanted the security of marriage with him. And it would not be unpleasant. Not by any means.

James was dancing the opening set with Miss Cameron. The girl was looking very dainty in a fashionable and new gown of blue silk. James had been smiling at her as he led her out onto the floor. And she had noticed in one glance at the two of them that that lock of dark hair that had always used to fall down over his brow was there again. Far away as she had been from him, her fingers had itched to push the hair back.

Jason was looking down into her eyes. He still held her close.

"I think you are probably very good and very experienced at this," she said, smiling at him. "And I think you had better not give me any further proof of that right now, Jason, or someone might come in and collapse in a fit of the vapors."

"I am hoping to be discovered by your mama or one of your brothers," he said, "so that you will be forced to marry me."

"Gracious!" she said, laughing. "If I were forced to marry every man who has ever kissed me, I would have a veritable harem, you know. Can a woman have a harem?"

"I've no idea," he said. "Madeline, I have not spoiled your evening, have I?"

She shook her head. "Not if I have not spoiled yours," she said. "It is very flattering, you see, to be offered for by a gentleman whom all the ladies sigh over. But I would not want to hurt you, Jason, and I might, you know, if you are serious about this and if you are confident of eventual success."

"I am closer to forty than thirty in age," he said. "I think

I have learned in all those years that no one really does die of a broken heart. I will doubtless survive if you do finally reject me. And you see how jaded one becomes with advancing age? I should be declaring, hand to heart, that I will expire on the spot if you cannot declare yourself to be mine for all eternity."

She tapped him on the wrist with her fan. "The music has stopped," she said. "Lord North will be expecting me for the next set. He will doubtless have all sorts of nonsense to say to me. I have known the man forever, but he has never been silly until this year."

"I really would expire," he said, "if I thought you would ever call me silly, Madeline."

She chuckled and took his arm. And felt lost and a little frightened as they returned to the ballroom. She seemed to have lost all control over her own life. She had been so sure of herself only an hour before. Less, even. And now emptiness yawned. If she rejected Jason, what was there in her future? If she could not love him, then perhaps she could love no one.

Miss Cameron was being led onto the floor by Walter. Dominic was laughing with Ellen over some joke. Edmund was sitting beside Lady Beckworth and making conversation with her. James was not in the room.

There was a painful emptiness where the excitement had been until just a short while before. And she knew what had caused the emptiness. She was not free of him. She had not been for four years. And perhaps she never would be.

It was a thoroughly frightening prospect.

4

DUNCAN CAMERON WAS ENJOYING HIMSELF.
James watched him dance with an unknown young
lady and remembered the amusement his friend had
shown when he received the invitation.

"Heady stuff this, man," he had said, "for a simple
homme du nord, this mixing with the aristocracy. Of course,
I have been doing it for some time. I must never forget that
you are heir to a baron's title." He had clapped his friend
on the shoulder.

"You never did forget," James had said. "Do you think I
don't know why you befriended me?"

Duncan had punched him none too gently on the arm.

It amused James to know just how out of place his
friend was in such a setting, though he was undoubtedly
enjoying himself. Duncan was a man who craved the free
and often lonely life of a northman, who longed to go
back into the interior and rejoin the Cree wife and son he
had left at a trading post on the Saskatchewan River more
than a year before. He was determined to be on his way
back to them the following spring.

Jean had been so excited by her invitation that she had
been able to talk of nothing else for a whole week. Douglas
had sent her with Miss Hendricks to a fashionable and

expensive modiste on Bond Street so that she would have a gown suitable for the occasion.

And very suitable it was, too. Not that the gown accounted for all of her loveliness. She fairly sparkled. James danced the opening set with her and wished that he was not hemmed in by the etiquette of London society. He would have liked to dance with her all night, feasting his eyes on her freshness and youth, focusing his mind on the sweetness and simplicity life with her would offer.

"Is this really me, James?" she asked when the pattern of the dance brought them together. "Even in my fondest dreams, I could not have quite imagined this."

"It is real," he said. "And so are you. And so is the almost full card at your wrist. Enjoy yourself, Jean. That is what you are meant to do at your age."

"Oh," she said, looking at him wide-eyed. "I do not need to be told to do that. You are wonderful, James. This is all your doing, I know that. I do love you."

It was those last words that jolted him back to reality. For they were not the words of a young lady who was in love, but the words a girl might say to her brother or to a very dear friend. He must be careful. He must remember that a decision to marry involved two people, and not just one. It was not enough for him to decide that he wished to marry Jean. She must wish to marry him, too.

"I may remind you of that one day," he said, smiling back at her.

But of course he had not been entirely absorbed in her even though he had wished to be so. He knew that Madeline was not in the ballroom and had not been after the first few minutes of the dancing. She had left with Colonel Huxtable. And all evening she had looked even more vibrantly beautiful than usual, and had glowed with an inner happiness that could be attributed only to her partner.

It seemed wholly likely that an announcement would be made during the evening. He must brace himself for it.

Brace himself? Would the announcement affect him in any way, then? Did he care?

He felt slightly sick.

His father was not present, either. That was not at all surprising, of course, since his father never attended any entertainment that he considered frivolous. And he considered most entertainments frivolous, even sinful. He was doubtless sitting somewhere in the house, wishing he had chosen to live somewhere else during his stay in London and blocking from his hearing all sounds of merriment and focusing his mind on the God he had created for himself. A God of wrath and gloom.

James relinquished Jean to her next partner and decided not to dance himself. He felt restless and depressed. Time was slipping by and he had as yet accomplished nothing by his return home except a gradual loss of his own hard-won tranquillity.

He must speak with his father. The middle of a ball was hardly a suitable time, but then he had had nothing but suitable times since his return yet had made nothing of them. He went in search of his father.

He found him in the earl's library, alone and seated at the desk, a large, ornately bound Bible before him.

"You are not joining in the festivities, sir?" he asked rather unnecessarily. But for years he had not found conversation easy with his father.

"There are more important ways to spend one's time," Lord Beckworth said, looking steadily at his son. "We never know when we may be called upon to meet our

Maker. It is our responsibility to make sure that we are ready."

"You have not been well," James said, coming right into the room and taking up a position with his back to the empty fireplace. "Alex wrote to tell me so. The physician said you must be careful of your heart?"

"I am as well as can be expected," his father said. "I am ready, James, when I am called. Are you?"

James did not immediately reply. "After I had read that particular letter of Alex's," he said, "I applied to come to London with the furs instead of going back inland this spring as I was scheduled to do. I wanted to see you again."

His father smoothed his hands over the pages of the Bible. "Perhaps you are showing concern for the wrong father, James," he said. "Perhaps it is your heavenly Father whom you should be wishing to meet again."

James licked dry lips. "I had hoped we could be civil with each other, sir," he said. "I will be returning to Canada before the summer is ended. I will probably stay there for years. Perhaps for the rest of my life. It is possible we will never meet each other again."

His father was regarding him with a face that looked as if it were carved out of marble. "I don't believe we have treated each other with incivility since your return, James," he said. "I am trying to read the Good Book and drown out the sounds of frivolity. Do you care to join me?"

"The ball is in my honor," James said. "Alex and Edmund have thought to give me pleasure. They are showing their love for me. I hoped somehow to share the evening with you."

Lord Beckworth turned a page of the Bible.

James sighed. "It is the wrong time," he said almost to himself. "I should not have sought you out tonight." He stared broodingly at his silent father. "Nothing has changed, has it? Dora and the past will always be there between us."

His father did not look up, though his lips thinned.

James nodded after a few silent moments and left the room without another word.

The dancing was between sets. He approached a large group of young people, which included Jean and Duncan, Anna and Walter Carrington, Madeline, and a few other people he did not know.

"Mr. Purnell," Anna said, smiling brightly at him and standing to one side so that he was included in the group, "I thought you must have run off to Canada again. Jean has been telling us about the sleigh rides in Montreal during the winter months, and we have all been thinking of removing there."

He smiled at her. "Months and months of nothing but snow and ice," he said. "But it is a marvelous excuse for innumerable parties and dances, of course."

The dancing was about to resume. Walter led Jean onto the floor, and Duncan was holding out a hand to another young lady.

"Would you care to dance?" James asked Anna.

Anna looked at him regretfully. "It is already promised," she said. "But you simply must ask me again later. Will you?"

"Of course," he said, and watched her being led away by her new partner.

And suddenly the group was not there any longer, but only himself and one other young lady, who inexplicably had not yet been claimed by any partner. He drew in a deep breath and closed his eyes briefly.

"Lady Madeline?" he said, and extended a hand to her.

Her green eyes lifted to his chin and then looked up unwillingly into his. "Yes," she said. "Thank you."

MADELINE HAD FLED from the ballroom after dancing with Lord North, who had behaved in quite as silly a manner as had become habitual with him of late. Indeed, with very little encouragement he would have been making her her second offer of the night. But she gave no encouragement. She did not want to hear it.

She still felt bewildered and panic-stricken when she remembered that she had refused Jason, or as good as refused him. She had fully planned to accept, had even planned that their betrothal would be announced during the course of the evening.

But she had refused, or deferred her decision. But if she had said no now, when she had been expecting the offer and had planned her answer, how would she ever find the courage or the good sense to say yes?

Dominic was looking at her across the ballroom in that way he had of boring right through her skull with his eyes. If he came close, there would be no keeping any secrets from him, and her whole frightening foolishness would be exposed. One part of her wanted more than anything to cry out her woes on the safe and familiar shoulder of her twin. But the days for such dependence were past. He did not need the extra burden of a sister who did not know her own mind at the age of six and twenty.

She fled to the card room, where she stood looking

over the shoulder of a young man wearing a dark patch over one eye, until the hand was finished. Then he turned to smile up at her.

"Hello, Madeline," he said. "You were not at home when I called on you either yesterday or four days ago."

"No," she said. "I am almost always from home. You should have let me know you were coming, Allan. It is so good to see you again. You look wonderfully well."

She clasped her hands behind her as he lifted himself from his chair with the help of crutches. She resisted the urge to offer her help.

"Let me get you some lemonade," he said.

"That would be wonderful," she said, "but I will get it, Allan."

He laughed at her. "Yes, nurse," he said. "I will try not to argue."

She flushed. "I am rather domineering, am I not?" she said. "I can see why you did not want to marry me, Allan."

"I protest," he said. "You were the one who did not want to marry me, Madeline. I was the one who was jilted, if you recall."

She went for the lemonade.

"I really am happy to see you again, Allan," she said when she returned with their drinks. They settled side by side on a love seat in an anteroom. "But we would not have suited as husband and wife, would we?"

"No, we would not," he said. "You are far too lovely and vibrant, Madeline. You need someone very special. Someone like Huxtable, maybe?"

"Oh," she said, shrugging, "I don't know, Allan. I don't know. I have never been as happy as I was last year when you were hurt and needed me so badly. Not that I wish you back in that state, of course. But life had meaning then."

"And has not now?" he asked, taking her hand. "Poor Madeline. You have so much to give, and there are so many gentlemen falling all over themselves just in the hope of receiving one of your smiles. Yet you cannot find happiness."

"But I will," she said, smiling brightly. "And what is this I have been hearing in the past few weeks from Ellen and Dominic? Is it true that you have an understanding with Ellen's stepdaughter, Allan? You never mentioned it last summer when we were betrothed or in any of your letters since then."

He smiled rather shame-facedly. "There was nothing to tell while you and I were betrothed," he said. "Really there was not. And I have been too embarrassed to mention it to you since, as it happened rather suddenly in the days after our engagement was broken while Jennifer and I were both still at Amberley. Do you mind, Madeline? Are you offended?"

"Absolutely not," she said, squeezing his hand. "Allan, I do love you dearly. You know that. I think of you almost as I think of my brothers. And Jennifer Simpson is a pleasant young lady. I am happy for you. Is it all settled?"

He smiled. "She is not having a very good bargain," he said, "as I have told her repeatedly. A man with only one leg and only one eye is not quite a whole man. And her grandfather has told her as much. They have had some fierce arguments over me, I gather. I have told her, just this evening, in fact, that she must enjoy this Season and look at all the gentlemen she will meet with an open mind. And I have vowed to myself that I will not make her a formal offer until I can be done with these infernal crutches.

I will learn to walk again on two legs, even if one of them is not my own, or turn all over black and blue in the attempt."

"You will do it too," she said, smiling at him a little ruefully. "And to think that I once wanted to marry you because you would always be totally dependent upon my loving care. Oh, Allan, dear, I am happy for you. But where is she?"

"Jennifer?" he said, grinning. "Gone into the ballroom in high dudgeon to show me that she can enjoy herself quite well without me, thank you very much. I forbade her to sit with me all evening, you see. You would not wish to know some of the things she said in reply. They were quite unladylike."

Madeline laughed. "And talking about going back into the ballroom to enjoy oneself," she said, "I must be doing the same, Allan, or Edmund will be thinking I am sick and summoning a physician. There is nothing so enjoyable as a ball, you know."

She smiled dazzlingly at him, and he lifted her hand to his lips.

"You will find him one day soon, I promise you," he said quietly before releasing her.

Madeline, on the brink of tears, smiled determinedly and joined a group in the ballroom only a few moments before she was aware of James Purnell doing the same thing. Oh, yes, she would find him soon, all right.

She had been out of the room during the previous set, and had returned after most of the gentlemen had chosen their next partners. She became aware of the situation in some dismay only one moment before she found herself in the unspeakably embarrassing position of being almost alone with James at the edge of the dance floor while other couples were taking their places for the coming set. It was too late to make an inconspicuous exit.

"Lady Madeline?" he said, extending a hand to her.

Lifting her eyes beyond his chin to meet his was the hardest thing she remembered doing in a long while. "Yes," she said, placing her hand in his. "Thank you."

IT WAS A WALTZ. Of all the dances it might possibly have been, it was a waltz.

Madeline rested a hand on James's shoulder, set her other hand in his, and wondered if he was remembering quite as vividly as she the last time they had waltzed together. The music had been so faint that the rhythm had been felt rather than heard. The gravel of the formal gardens at Amberley had crunched underfoot. The water from the fountain had tinkled into the stone basin.

He had been staying there with his family following the betrothal of Edmund and Alexandra. And she was there, as she always was during the summer. As they all were. Even Dominic in those days had chosen to spend most of his time at his childhood home rather than at his own estate in Wiltshire. It was before he had bought his commission and long before he had met Ellen.

It had been at the annual summer ball at Amberley. She had been feeling restless, as she so often did even in those days. And for the same reason—she had been bewildered by her own powerful and conflicting feelings for Alexandra's brother. Always James. Always the blight of her life. She had wandered out into the formal gardens, not knowing that he was there before her.

He had held her correctly for a while and then drawn her against him. And after a while they had stopped moving. The music and the waltz had been forgotten. That was the time when during an embrace that had grown hotter and more intimate over the course of several minutes she had offered herself to him in all but words. The time when she had told him she loved him. And the time when he had told her that he felt nothing for her but lust. She had not believed him at the time, although she had left him there and although he had left Amberley that same night without another word to her or any message left for her.

She glanced up, hoping that he would be looking about him at the other dancers, hoping that he would be smiling sociably. Hoping that he would not be the old James, whom she had disliked and feared. And loved. She met dark, unfathomable eyes. That lock of hair had fallen across his forehead again. Sometimes things were so frighteningly the same that she wondered if she had imagined the four intervening years.

She licked her lips nervously and watched his eyes follow the movement of her tongue.

"It is a pleasant evening, is it not?" she said, smiling. "I am glad. Edmund and Alexandra do not like to entertain, you know—or to be entertained, for that matter. They are never happier than when they are at home alone with the children. But the evening is turning out well. I think everyone who was invited must have come."

"It would seem so," he said. He did not return her smile. "The room is quite crowded."

"Of course," she said, "it is all in your honor. Alexandra has been very excited since your letter came last summer to say you were coming home. I don't think they would have left Amberley for any other reason even if it is the Season. They like the greater freedom of the country for the children's sake."

"I have expressed my gratitude to Alex," he said.

"Have you met Ellen?" she asked. "She is so lovely tonight dressed in blue."

"Alex took me to call on them," he said. "Lady Eden is quite charming."

Madeline listened to herself in some dismay. And she felt the bright social smile frozen to her face. She always knew she was going to behave just so with him, yet she seemed quite powerless to stop herself. Because he was so silent and because he looked at her always with those unsmiling eyes, she was always totally unnerved. She felt like a butterfly caught and spread by pins for his inspection.

She deliberately relaxed the muscles of her face and shifted her gaze to the hand that rested on his shoulder. They danced in silence for a while. And would dance in silence forever and a day before she would break it.

"You have not changed," he said at last.

She looked back up into his eyes. "Is that meant to be a compliment?" she asked.

"Most women, I suppose, would be glad to be told that they had not changed in four years," he said.

"But you did not approve of me four years ago," she said, and flushed. "You did not like me."

"But I never disputed the fact that you are beautiful," he said.

Madeline's stomach felt as if it had turned a complete somersault inside her. "It was my character of which you disapproved, then?" she said.

"That was a long time ago," he said.

It seemed he had nothing left to say. And she had done with nervous prattling. Or with any honest effort to initiate a conversation to which she could expect only monosyllables in reply. She tried to concentrate on the music and the couples dancing around them.

But he was so very unmistakably James. He was leaner, stronger. But James, nevertheless. She would have known him at a touch, blindfolded. Her heartbeat would have known it and the muscles of her legs and the blood beating through her temples.

She was touching him again, one hand on his shoulder, the other resting in his. And she could feel his other hand warm at her waist. She had spent so many weeks, even months, reliving his touch, at first with a desperate misery, and later with a dull unwillingness. So long. And now she was touching him again. And he was a stranger again. Yet so familiar that her throat ached with the tears she must withhold.

He still disliked her. He still despised her and withheld from her even the common courtesies he would accord any other woman. She wondered why he had asked her to dance.

"Why did you ask me to dance?" she asked.

He raised his eyebrows. "It seemed the civil thing to do," he said. "This occasion is for dancing, is it not?"

"Was it because Anna said no and I was the closest lady to you apart from her?" she asked.

"Yes, I suppose that is the reason," he said. "Are you offended?"

"No," she said. But she was offended. Or hurt, perhaps. Or outraged at honesty that did not try to mask itself in tact and good manners. "Why should I be offended?"

There was nothing else to say. Madeline waited tensely for the music to end and guessed that her partner was no less eager to be rid of her. What neither of them had realized, she discovered with dismay when the music actually did draw to an end, was that it was the supper dance they had been engaged in. The members of the orchestra laid down their instruments.

"There is no need for you to lead me in to supper," she said hastily.

"But there is every need," he said. "Good manners dictate that I now offer you my arm and take you in. Do you think I have forgotten such niceties of polite behavior in the North American wilderness, Madeline?"

This time it was her heart that somersaulted. And all at the sound of her given name on his lips without the formality of her title before it. Was she a green girl fresh from the schoolroom to be so affected by one word spoken by an attractive gentleman?

She placed a hand on his arm without replying.

THE EARL OF AMBERLEY seated his wife at a table in the supper room. "I don't care if it is not quite the thing to lead my own countess in to supper," he said. "I have been apart from you quite long enough for one evening, Alex."

"I am not arguing," she said. "You do not need to defend yourself to me, Edmund. I was hoping that James would dance the supper dance with Miss Cameron. She truly is a delightful girl, is she not? And I do not care at all that some people might say that she is not quite *haut ton*. But I suppose it was unrealistic of me to expect some sort of announcement tonight."

"Probably," he said, smiling at her with amused affection. "Here come Ellen and Dominic. They are together, you see. I feel reassured."

Lord Eden held a chair so that his wife could seat herself beside Alexandra. "We have been upstairs feeding the babies," he said, "and giving them strict orders to sleep through until a decent hour of the morning. Or rather, it would be more accurate to say, I suppose, that Ellen has been feeding the babies. Have we missed anything startling? Madeline has not contracted or broken any engagements, has she?"

"Not to my knowledge," the earl said. "But North has a tendency to gaze on her like a lost puppy, poor devil."

"I do believe she is at last serious over Colonel Huxtable," Alexandra said. "Indeed, when I saw him draw her aside during the very first set of the evening, I thought perhaps matters would come to their conclusion tonight. But no matter."

"Here she is with Mr. Purnell," Ellen said, looking toward the doorway. "I cannot help thinking that they make a rather splendid couple. It is a pity you cannot persuade him to stay in England, Alexandra."

Her sister-in-law looked at the approaching couple, arrested. "James and Madeline," she said. "Gracious, I had never thought of it before. How very splendid that would be. But of course there is no chance. He is to return to Canada before the summer is over, and Madeline has eyes for no one but the colonel these days. Oh, Ellen, do you think there is the faintest chance?"

Lord Amberley pursed his lips and looked with marked amusement across the table at his younger brother. But Lord Eden, his face quite serious, was gazing across the room at his twin sister.

Jennifer Simpson and Lord North, Duncan Cameron and Miss Marshall were also approaching their table.

5

JAMES STOOD UNDECIDED IN THE DOORWAY, looking about him. Should he choose an empty table? One occupied by strangers? Or one with family members? His companion's hand burned through his sleeve and through his arm.

"Shall we join your brothers?" he suggested.

"Yes," she said.

He had been determined this evening to treat her no differently from the way he would treat any other lady. He would ignore her if he could, he had decided. And if he could not, then he would behave toward her with a cool courtesy.

And what had happened? He had been rude to her again. He had agreed with her suggestion that he had asked her to dance only because her cousin had been engaged to dance the set with someone else. And he had made almost no effort to match her attempts at conversation. He had felt quite unable to prevent himself from putting on the usual defenses against her. He had become surly.

Sometimes he did not understand himself at all. And sometimes he angered himself. He seated her at the table and found himself quite unable for the moment to smile at any of its occupants.

"James," Alexandra said, her cheeks flushed, "I had no idea there would be such a crush here tonight. Everyone must have come out of curiosity, knowing that it is all in your honor."

James managed a grin at her. "More likely it was out of curiosity to see the Amberley ballroom," he said. "I gather it is not used a great deal."

"For which I make no apology," the earl said. "One ball a year is usually quite sufficient for my peace of mind, and the neighbors at Amberley Court would be severely disappointed if we were to discontinue the annual ball there."

"You must realize what a great honor is being done you, Purnell," Lord Eden said with a chuckle. "Edmund has a reputation in town as something of a hermit. Yet here he is, playing amiable host to the *crème de la crème*."

"You will all be making Mr. Purnell decidedly uncomfortable to know that he is the cause of all this," Ellen said, giving him a quiet smile. "I for one think it all very splendid, and I am glad you came home and made it all possible, sir."

Madeline was sitting straight and silent in her chair beside him, not at all her customary sociable self.

"I danced with Mr. Cameron earlier," Jennifer Simpson said, smiling at that gentleman across the table. "He told me that he has traveled thousands of miles inland by canoe, climbing in and out of the boat constantly to pass rapids and waterfalls. It sounds like the most exciting job in the world."

"But do you prefer this part of the job?" Ellen asked Duncan. "Coming to England, I mean?"

"It is a novelty to be invited to English parties, I must confess, ma'am," Duncan Cameron said. "And to waltz.

But I do believe the lure of the wilderness is in my blood. I am hoping that next spring I can be on my way back there."

"Do you feel the same way, James?" Ellen asked.

Madeline's hands were twisting in her lap, he could see out of the corner of one eye. He turned cold for a moment when he realized that he had been about to reach out to take one of them in his.

"In my blood?" he said. "I am not sure I would put it quite like that. But it is a great experience. One comes face-to-face with oneself when surrounded with such vast emptiness and such harsh living conditions. I can well imagine that it could become essential to one's being."

"You make it sound very romantic," Jennifer said.

"Of course," Duncan said with a grin, "there are the mosquitoes and black flies to eat one alive in the summer and the snow and the ice to bury one alive in the winter."

They all laughed. James was watching Madeline's hands. White, long-fingered hands. She was twisting a ring on her right hand. Those hands had once touched him with desire. They had been warm on his face and in his hair.

Her hands clenched suddenly in her lap, and when he glanced quickly into her face, it was to find that her jaw was set and she was staring down at her hands. He looked away from her.

Duncan was describing how the *voyageurs,* or canoe-men, portaged all the contents of the canoes and the canoes themselves around rapids. He added some details of his own. It was inevitable, James supposed, that people here would be curious about their lives as fur traders. He did not resent the questions.

His father, he noticed, had come for supper, but he had

not approached their table. He was seated with the dowager countess and Sir Cedric Harvey.

Madeline's hands were alternately still and fidgeting. She had scarcely spoken. And for his part, he could not recall a time when he had felt quite so suffocatingly uncomfortable. He turned to her impulsively. Only a few people had risen and left the room. Most were still eating.

"May I escort you back to the ballroom?" he asked.

She rose to her feet as the other occupants of the table looked at them in some surprise.

"To some private room," he said to Madeline as they left the dining room. "We need to talk for a few minutes."

If she felt surprise, she did not show it. Or reluctance. He had half expected her to refuse to be alone with him. She led him to a small room at the front of the house. A morning room, he guessed.

She crossed the room to the fireplace as he closed the door behind him, and she set both hands on the mantel, above the level of her head. A single candle burned there.

He stood just inside the doorway, his hands clasped behind him, his feet set slightly apart.

"Is there anything we can do about this awkwardness between us?" he asked.

He thought she would not answer. She gripped the mantelpiece and stared downward. "I suppose," she said at last, "we could contrive to stay away from each other. I would leave London if I could. But it is not easy being an unmarried lady in our society. My mother is in town, as are my two brothers. It seems that I have no option but to remain here too."

"I thought Lady Madeline Raine lived for London and the Season," he said. "You must dislike me indeed if you would leave rather than have to meet me."

"Of course," she said, and she lowered her hands and turned to face him, "the frivolity of London society is the only thing I am capable of enjoying. I had forgotten that you discovered my darkest secret years ago, the secret that I have a brain full of feathers. And as for my disliking you, you have never given me reason to do otherwise."

"Ah," he said, advancing one step farther into the room, "plain speaking. I found it difficult meeting you again this summer. And no easier after the first time. I have noticed that you share my embarrassment. I suppose the nature of our last encounter before this year has something to do with it."

"Where was that?" she asked. "I have forgotten." She raised her eyebrows coolly, but she flushed.

"You are a liar," he said. "There is no reason why we should both remember that occasion quite so vividly. Even at the time we were both undoubtedly adult, and embraces happen between adults. But the fact is that we do remember it, and it has created this awkwardness. Is it because I left so abruptly and did not face you the following morning?"

"It was, as I remember, a rather hot embrace," she said, lifting her chin. "It was doubtless due to the moonlight and the music and perhaps the wine. There was nothing particularly unusual about it, sir. I am sure you have done the like with many women, as I have done with many men."

"I suppose I owed you marriage after what happened," he said. "But instead I left."

She laughed. "Then it was doubtless as well you did," she said. "You might have found my reception of a marriage offer somewhat humiliating. You are the very last man on this earth I would ever consider marrying, Mr. Purnell."

"And yet," he said coldly, "you told me on that night that you loved me."

Her eyes flashed at him, and he knew that was the one detail he should never have confronted her with. He had done so only because her words had inexplicably hurt.

"Well," she said, "you have called me liar this evening. It seems I was a liar then, too. You at least were honest, I seem to recall. You told me that it was nothing but lust you felt. I was a lady. I would not admit to a purely physical craving. I dressed it up in respectable terms. How could I have loved you? You treated me with as much contempt then as you have shown me since your return."

"Your problem," he said, "is that for years you have had nothing but adulation from the gentlemen around you. You have come to expect it as your due. If a man does not fawn on you and sigh over you, you feel insulted."

"What a ridiculous notion," she said. "Your problem, sir, is that you have never felt it necessary to afford other people the common courtesies. You smile when you wish, and you speak when you wish. And it is not very often that you wish to do either. It is your moroseness and your silence that create awkwardness."

"Ah, the old story," he said. "I remember your saying as much four years ago. And on one of those occasions I remember undertaking to entertain you for the whole of a walk of two miles or more. And what was the point, pray? I will wager that you cannot now recall a single word I said to you on that occasion."

"Well, there you are wrong," she said, her nostrils flared and her eyes still flashing at him. "You told me about your years at school and at university, and I mistakenly thought that after all perhaps you were human."

"Both our voices are rising," he said. "I suppose it was inevitable that we quarrel. We always seem to have done so. I should not have brought you here. I merely thought that perhaps we could behave like civilized beings at last. It seems I was mistaken."

"And if you are," she said, making no attempt to lower her own voice or accept his veiled suggestion that they hold on to their tempers, "it is entirely your own fault. You need not talk of 'we' and 'us.' I am perfectly willing to behave in a civilized manner at any time. It is you who have decided that boorishness is an acceptable form of behavior."

"I might have known," he said, "that you would not have changed at all, that you would be just as childish now as you ever were."

"Oh!" she said, and her lips clamped together while her bosom heaved. "I don't believe there can be a more despicable man alive than you, James Purnell. I was prepared to be civil to you, for Alexandra's sake and Edmund's. But I find that my dislike of four years ago has turned into a full-blown hatred. I hate you, sir, and I believe it would be in both our interests if we make every effort to avoid each other during what remains of your stay in England. The time cannot go fast enough for me."

"Or for me, either," he said, making her a half bow, and standing aside as she swept by him and out through the door. She did not stop to close it behind her.

James stood where he was and shut his eyes tightly.

God! Oh, God.

What had he said to her? What unspeakable atrocities had he said to her to make her so furiously angry? The dreadful thing was that at the moment he could not for the life of him remember.

He could only recall that in the supper room he had had the impulsive idea to take her aside, to talk to her, to try somehow to clear the air between them, to have done with the ridiculous and paralyzing awkwardness between them.

It had seemed like a good idea.

Who had started hurling insults at whom?

Had he started it? He could not remember. All he did know was that within minutes they had been glaring and yelling at each other and that he had felt a blind instinct to hurt her, to set her down, to humiliate her.

But why?

God!

He set a hand up over his eyes and closed them again. Why did he want to hurt her? And why did it hurt him so badly when he succeeded? Was that it? Was that what he was trying to do? Hurt himself?

But why would he wish to hurt himself? Why punish himself? Punish himself for what?

For loving her? *Did* he love her?

Did he have the right to love her? To love any woman? Did he have the right to seek happiness with any woman?

With any woman who was not Dora? He had loved Dora. He had told her so. And he had shown her so. And then he had left her to the unthinkable nightmare of the consequences of that love. He had not done so knowingly, of course. He had not known what she had had to endure until it was too late to help her. By the time word reached him at university, Dora had been married off to John Drummond and sent off with him to an unknown destination.

He had been unable to save her. Incapable of saving her. He could not be blamed. He had told himself that over and over down the years. He could not be blamed.

But her life had been ruined forever. And was he to seek happiness for himself? He, who had not had to take any of the consequences of his irresponsible love for Dora?

He threw back his head and gazed sightlessly up at the ceiling. Madeline. He had just hurt her again, as he knew he had hurt her four years before. Was she to be punished because he had been weak enough to fall in love with her when he was not free to love?

And did he love her? Did he not dislike and despise her? Did he love her?

JENNIFER AND LORD NORTH, Duncan and Miss Marshall had also returned to the ballroom.

"Oh, dear," Alexandra said, turning to her husband, "it was a thoroughly good idea of Ellen's, but I don't think there can be any truth in it. James and Madeline did not look as if they were enjoying each other's company, did they? I have never seen her so quiet. And James could not wait to return her to the ballroom. What a great shame!"

The earl smiled at her in some amusement and covered her hand on the table with his own. "Why all the world cannot be persuaded to be as happy as you and I, my love," he said, "I could not say. But that is the way of the world. It is full of foolish people."

"I have never seen Madeline so out of spirits," Ellen said, looking up at her husband. "It is true then, what you told me, Dominic?"

"It would seem so," he said, touching her cheek briefly

with one knuckle. "Poor Madeline has fallen hard, and only she can pick herself up. A mere twin is quite helpless. How many times have I danced with you, love? Can we risk one more without becoming social pariahs?"

"Fallen?" Alexandra said, frowning. "Madeline? Have I been missing something, Dominic? Do you mean for James? But they used to dislike each other quite intensely, if you will forgive me for saying so of your sister. I can remember that."

"Yes, they did," Lord Eden said, taking his wife's hand in his and getting to his feet. "And still do, apparently, Alexandra. Altogether too much for casual acquaintances, would you not agree?"

Alexandra was left to frown down at her plate. "Did he mean that there is hope after all?" she asked the earl when they were alone. "James and Madeline. I cannot imagine how I had never thought of it. It would be so wonderful that I can scarce think of it without bursting with excitement, Edmund. But he used to dislike her so. Was it because he really liked her, then?"

"Alex," the Earl of Amberley said, getting to his feet and drawing back her chair, "I had better return you to the ballroom and search out my next partner without further ado. It would not be at all the thing to obey instinct and kiss you in the middle of the supper room. You are quite adorable, and quite disastrous as a matchmaker, my love. You might be better advised to locate the nose on your face."

"Oh," she said flushing, "what an odious man you are, Edmund. It is true, then? James and Madeline. How perfectly splendid."

• • • •

JAMES WAS DISCOVERING that there really was not a great deal of work to be done. There were trading goods to be received and sorted and listed ready for taking back to Montreal late in the summer—those goods that would be traded to the people of the native tribes in exchange for the furs they hunted. But Douglas Cameron was doing all the negotiations related to that task, and only one clerk seemed to be necessary for the more monotonous parts of the task. He and Duncan shared the work.

The situation was somewhat similar to that faced by the wintering partners and clerks—those who worked inland where the furs were gathered. There were busy days, yes, but there were also long, slack weeks between. One's presence was necessary but not constantly required. One had a great deal of spare time.

The difference was that in the vast North American wilderness one was thrown very much on one's own resources. There was hunting to be enjoyed when one was not working, and playing cards and reading and conversing, if one was fortunate enough to share the post with another partner or clerk. There was some dancing. And, if one had been wise enough to take one of the daughters of the country to wife, there was making love.

Here there were all the amusements of London to enjoy. And perhaps more. Three days after the ball he received two separate invitations. The first he would perhaps have refused if he had not met Jean even before going home to find it there. But she had received hers already, and she was ecstatic.

"James," she said, coming into her father's house all rosy-cheeked from an outing, "has Duncan told you? I can scarce believe my good fortune. I keep thinking that it surely must now have come to an end, and then yet another wonderful thing happens."

"No, I have not told," her brother said with a grin, "it having escaped my mind, Jean, until this precise moment. You may have all the joy of impressing James with the news."

"We have been invited to the picnic," she said, her hands clasped to her bosom, her eyes shining at him.

"The picnic?" he said, amused, raising his eyebrows.

"At Richmond," she said. "The one Sir Cedric Harvey is organizing. I was never more surprised in my life as to find that Duncan and I have been included in his guest list. And all on account of you, James. You will be going, of course?"

"This is the first I have heard of it," he said. "But no, Jean, I don't think I will go. There is too much to do."

Douglas Cameron chuckled. "Then it must be that you are chasing the ladies around, lad," he said. "I am not exactly wearing your fingers to the bone, now, am I? Go and enjoy yourself. I have told Duncan the same. I shall manage without the two of you for one afternoon, I do not doubt."

"This consorting with the rich is head-swelling business, man," Duncan said. "Sir Cedric Harvey is the Dowager Countess of Amberley's particular friend, is he not?"

"But you must come, James," Jean said, her eyes pleading. "It would appear most strange if Duncan and I put in an appearance and you did not. Please?"

"Of course he will go, lass," her father said. "I will go one further, James, my lad. If you wish to take yourself off to Yorkshire for a few weeks or down to your sister's place, well, I daresay Duncan and I will hold the fort while you are gone. Eh, Duncan?"

James smiled. "It seems I am set about with people determined that I will enjoy myself," he said. "How am I to resist? I will give in gracefully."

Jean clapped her hands in delight, and Duncan slapped his friend on the shoulder.

"You'll owe me one," he said with a grin, "for doing all your hard labor for a few weeks."

So he was doomed to attend the picnic, James found even before he had seen his own invitation. And there was worse to come.

He was sitting in the nursery of the house on Grosvenor Square that same afternoon, his niece sitting solemnly on his knee playing with his watch on its chain, Alexandra sitting on her heels on the floor in front of them. Christopher was painting quietly at the other side of the room.

"You probably don't know how honored you are," Alexandra said. "Caroline does not take to many people. Apart from Edmund and me and Nanny Rey, Ellen is about the only other person who is allowed to pick her up. And now you. I am very glad. She must know how much her mother worshiped you as a child."

"Past tense?" he said, touching the child's soft dark curls. "You no longer worship me, Alex?"

She smiled. "You know I do," she said. "You cannot imagine how I have waited and waited for your coming, James. And how now I am willing time to a standstill. Must you go back?"

He looked at her with the smile that would have been imperceptible to anyone but her. "I must," he said quietly.

"I thought just perhaps you would decide to stay," she said. "You seem different. I thought perhaps you would have put the past behind you. You have not?"

"I have learned to live again," he said. "But it is easier in another country, Alex. You are the only person here I really regret having to leave."

"Not Mama and Papa?" she asked wistfully. "Have you not been able to mend the quarrel with Papa, James? I hoped you would."

"No," he said. "It is unmendable."

She sighed. "And all over Dora," she said. "Oh, James, she really was not worth all the agony you have lived through and the rift with Papa. I did not know her well, but she seemed very shallow. I am sorry. Forgive me."

"I have had to forget Dora," he said, lifting his quizzing glass for his niece, who was looking for a new toy.

"It is as well," she said. "Is there anyone else, James? Miss Cameron, perhaps? You hinted a while ago that she may be someone special. Or Madeline, perhaps?" Her tone was casual.

"Madeline?" he said. "Spare me, Alex. I have never met anyone with whom I was less compatible. You are joking of course. And Jean?" His expression softened. "I am very fond of Jean. But I am not quite sure yet how fond."

"I wish you could come to Amberley," she said. "How lovely it would be to get away from town and have you all to myself for a few weeks. I don't suppose it would be possible, would it?"

"It would," he said, smiling at her just to see her expression suddenly light up. "Douglas told me for the second time just this morning that I may take a holiday if I wish."

She scrambled to her feet. "You will come to

Amberley?" she said. "Oh, James, you will see the house again and the portrait Edmund has had done of me and placed in the gallery, and we will go riding on the beach and up on the cliffs, and..."

"Mama!" Christopher's voice was impatient, it being the third time he had called for his mother's attention. "Come and see."

"You are finished?" she asked, turning a glowing face to her son. "Let me see, then, sweetheart."

Caroline wriggled off James's lap so that she too might see the completed painting.

The fates must be against him, James thought. After the disaster of the ball, he had resolved to have nothing more to do with Lady Madeline Raine. He would not even see her again unless pure chance caused their paths to cross. He would put her out of his mind and out of his life, even before he sailed with the *Adeona* again.

And now? It was too much to hope that she would not attend the picnic that was to be hosted by her mother's particular friend. And she always went to Amberley for the summer, did she not?

Good God, he would be living in the same house as she for a few weeks. And in the secluded atmosphere of a country home.

Perhaps she would go elsewhere. When she knew he was going to Amberley, perhaps she would stay in London. Or perhaps she would go into Wiltshire with Lord and Lady Eden. Lord Eden was her twin, after all, and there had always been a close bond between them.

Perhaps she would stay away from Amberley.

And perhaps hell would freeze over, too.

. . .

SIR CEDRIC HARVEY rode out to Richmond Park in a closed carriage with the Dowager Countess of Amberley and Lord and Lady Beckworth.

"You must be warned," the dowager had said to him a few days earlier when he had been making plans for the carriages, "in case you have forgotten, that Lady Beckworth must not be exposed to moving air no matter what the weather, Cedric. And now that her husband is no longer in the best of health, she will be doubly cautious."

And so he rode with his friend and his guests in a carriage with the windows tightly closed on a sweltering hot day in late June when everyone else traveled in open carriages or on horseback.

"But it does not matter, Louisa," he had said, "provided only they come. Strange people, the Beckworths. I could never understand people not simply enjoying life when it is so short and the future so full of uncertainties. They do not seem overjoyed to have their son at home, do they?"

"The foolish people are ashamed that he works for a living," she had said. "They cannot simply rejoice that he is alive and well. My anxieties when Dominic was in the army for three years taught me to treasure every moment with my children."

"But then you always did, Louisa," he had said, touching her hand.

"I am so very pleased," the dowager said now to the Beckworths as they were riding to Richmond Park, "that you will be coming to Amberley for a month. It is so much more relaxing to be in the country, is it not? And you will enjoy being close to the children for a while longer, ma'am."

"If only Alexandra would not allow them to be taken outside so frequently," Lady Beckworth said fretfully.

"The sea air is most injurious to their health, you know. I have warned her that Caroline is like to grow up in delicate health."

Lady Amberley smiled. "And you must be looking forward to spending more time with your son, sir," she said, "before he returns to Montreal."

Lord Beckworth inclined his head. "I have learned to live without him, ma'am," he said. "All is as God wills."

Altogether, Lady Amberley found, it was a great relief to descend from the carriage when they reached their destination and to find everyone there before them and in noisy high spirits.

Jennifer, Anna, and Miss Cameron were with Dominic's twins and young Caroline, although two nurses had been brought along to care for them. Christopher was perched on his father's shoulders, holding tight by a fistful of hair. Madeline was laughing over something with Colonel Huxtable, Walter and Mr. Chambers. Dominic and Ellen were talking with Allan Penworth. Alexandra, her arm linked through James's, was blushing over some doubtless teasing remark that William was making. Viola Carrington was looking flustered and indignant, as she so often did at her husband's quips. The Earl of Harrowby appeared to be deep in conversation with Duncan Cameron.

It was, the senior Lady Amberley thought, a very pleasant scene for a picnic. And she was particularly glad to see Madeline looking happy. Though one could never be sure with Madeline. Often the happier she looked, the more restless and unsure she was. The dowager saw a great deal more than she ever disclosed. She was worried about her daughter.

But this afternoon was no time for worry. She turned to smile at Sir Cedric.

"It is far too early for tea," he announced. "There are acres and acres of delightful greenery to be explored and enjoyed before we even think of eating."

He took the dowager's arm and held it firmly to his side as Lady Beckworth indicated that she would sit down on one of the blankets.

"We will walk," he said.

6

$\mathcal{J}$EAN CAMERON HAD STROLLED AWAY FROM the babies to join James. She smiled brightly up at him and took his arm. She looked entirely happy. "Is it not beautiful here, James?" she said. "I had heard that the English countryside is quite lovely, but I have not had an opportunity to see much of it until today."

He covered her hand with his and smiled affectionately down at her. "Let's walk," he said. "And you may feel English grass beneath your feet and see English trees above your head and breathe in English country air."

"And next week we will be at Amberley," she said, her eyes sparkling up into his. "Anna says it is quite the loveliest spot in England. Oh, James, I can scarcely wait."

It had clearly been the right thing to do, James reflected, looking into her happy face, to ask Alex if she would invite Jean into the country too. Because the girl would thereby be made entirely happy, he had explained to his sister and convinced himself. There could be no other reason why he would want her there with him.

"Let's enjoy today first," he said. He looked about him and raised his voice. "Would anyone care to join us in a walk?"

Anna and Mrs. Chambers, Walter and Jennifer, Dominic

and Ellen were all agreeable to the walk. Madeline, who was standing quite close by, James noticed, her back to him, made no move, though the colonel looked down at her inquiringly.

It was the first time he had seen her in more than a week. She was dressed all in yellow, sunshine yellow, and she looked more vivid and more lovely than ever. But she had scarcely looked at him, and she had not acknowledged him.

It was as well under the circumstances. He had made up his mind to stay completely away from her. He did not want her walking with him and Jean. He wanted to be able to concentrate his attention on his companion.

He brought his mind back to her. They were strolling among trees. Jean had thrown her head back so that the shade of the branches and the sunlight played over her face. She was smiling.

"I could stay here all my life," she said. "I love this country, James."

"You would miss the winters and the snow and the sleigh rides," he said.

"Perhaps the sleigh rides," she conceded, "but not the long, long winters. Oh, definitely not those. I wish I could stay."

He laughed. "By Christmastime you would probably be crying for home," he said. "As it is, you will have wonderful memories. I'm glad for you, Jean. I was hoping you would not find your stay here dull."

"Thanks to you," she said, "it has all been wildly exciting, James. And there is more to come. Oh, how all the girls at school would envy me if they knew."

They were a little behind the rest of the group. It would be the easiest thing in the world to slow his footsteps, to become lost among the trees, to take her into his arms and kiss her. She was very young and fresh and pretty. Very kissable.

And he needed to hold a woman and kiss her. With warmth and affection, and just a manageable dose of desire. A woman who would not constantly make him feel guilty. One he could feel free to love, free even to marry if he so chose. A woman who was not Madeline.

But if he kissed Jean, he would be making a very clear declaration of intent. She was too young to dally with. He would be telling her by his actions that he wanted her as a wife. He did not know at all what her feelings on the matter were. Sometimes he thought that she clearly favored him. At other times he thought that she saw him only as a type of elder and rather indulgent brother.

But Duncan would expect him to marry his sister if he kissed her. And so would Douglas. Even if he were to go back inland with the fur brigades and could be expected to remain there for years and probably take a native woman for a wife, they would still expect him to marry Jean once he had kissed her. For those country marriages, of course, were unsanctioned by either church or state.

It would be an expensive kiss. And he was not at all sure that he was prepared to pay the price.

He smiled down at Jean and quickened their pace.

During the next few minutes Anna overheard Ellen remark to Dominic that when they got back it would be time for her to take the babies into one of the carriages in order to nurse them. If those babies were to be played with, Anna declared, there was no time to be wasted. And it seemed that Jennifer and Jean agreed with her. The men and Ellen were left laughing as the three of them marched off, arm in arm, in the direction of the carriages.

"Abandoned for a pair of bald babies!" Walter complained. "The cut direct."

"Those ladies recognize a handsome lad when they see one," Dominic said. "Charles has a pair of fine gray eyes. He inherited them from his mother."

Ellen smiled at James. "Anna and Jennifer have been the best of friends since they met last summer," she said. "I am glad they have adopted Miss Cameron too. She is a charming young lady. She seems to be enjoying herself."

"She is," he said. "She has just been telling me that she wishes she could stay in England."

"Oh, dear," she said, "what will her father have to say to that?"

He began to stroll back slowly beside her and her husband. It was quite understandable, he thought, that Jean had been so captivated by the English countryside. He was feeling a quite strong nostalgia himself, walking among the trunks of large and ancient oak trees. Although he had renounced his home and now thought of Canada as the place where he belonged, there was indeed no place like England.

He looked about him and breathed in the heavy scents of summer.

And his eye was caught by a flutter of yellow, lighter and flimsier than any leaf or petal. He looked again. She was almost out of sight, leaning up against the trunk of a tree, only a part of her muslin skirt and one bare elbow visible from where he stood. And she seemed to be alone.

"I'll catch up to you," he said to the others, and looked about him as they strolled on. He stood there awhile, uncertain what to do. Instinct had stopped him. Common sense told him to move on. But common sense had never figured largely in his dealings with Madeline Raine.

He walked among the trees until he could come around the one against which she stood and see her fully.

She must have heard his approach. She did not seem unduly startled. She did not move either, but merely looked at him. Her head was back against the trunk of the tree.

"Madeline?" he said. "What is it?"

"YOU DO NOT WISH to go walking?" Colonel Huxtable asked Madeline.

"In a moment," she said. "I must talk to Allan first."

But it was merely an excuse. Allan Penworth was sitting on a blanket and seemed quite content to be doing so and talking with her Uncle William and Lord Harrowby.

"Are you feeling abandoned, Allan?" she asked, smiling at him. "Would you like Jason and me to stay here too? We would not mind at all."

"Absolutely not," he said, breaking off his conversation with the other two men. He grinned. "I have already quarreled with Jennifer and sent her on her way. Not you too, please. But you will never give up being my nurse, will you, Madeline? Wait until you see me with my new leg. I will have a race with you and win, I will wager."

"Well," she said, "you had better not wager your whole fortune, Allan. I always was rather good at footraces. It is what came of always pursuing boys when I was a child in the hope that they would let me play with them. Dominic would never simply say yes."

But she really must turn back and begin the walk, she thought, since Jason clearly expected her to do so and there was really no reason whatsoever why she should not. Except that there was one member of the group who she wished fervently was at the other side of the ocean again already. But she would see him at the bottom of the ocean before she would admit to him or to anyone else that she was afraid of his presence.

The others had had time to get far enough ahead, anyway. And why should she care if they caught up to the group and were compelled to walk with them? She had Jason to walk with and talk with.

She smiled at him and took his arm.

Jean Cameron had been looking quite radiantly happy. Surely far happier than the summer's day and the picnic and the company could account for. She had looked up at James as a new bride looks up at her groom. And he had looked back at her—she had seen it before she had turned away—with gentleness and affection and tenderness. He had been smiling. He had looked at Jean in a way he had never once looked at her. Not even on that one occasion when he had kissed her with something she had thought was tenderness.

And it did not matter. It did not matter how he looked at Jean or she at him. It did not matter if they loved each other, if they would marry after their return to Canada. It simply did not matter.

Except that it mattered a great deal.

"How clever of me to make that excuse of talking to Allan for a moment," she said gaily, looking archly up at Colonel Huxtable. "Now I have you all to myself."

"You may regret your cleverness," he said, looking back at her in some amusement. "I may take you among the trees, Madeline, and kiss you breathless and keep you captive there until you have promised to marry me."

"Ooh," she said, batting her eyelids at him and lowering

her voice to a seductive murmur, "is that a threat or a promise, sir?"

He lowered his head and whispered in her ear. "Both."

They both laughed.

He was quite remarkably handsome, Madeline thought, with his very military bearing and blond wavy hair. It should be possible to fall in love with him without any effort of will. Years ago she would have tumbled headlong and been dreaming of marital bliss with him long before this. He was a younger son, but he was heir to an inheritance from an elderly aunt. He would probably sell out of the army when he inherited, he had once told her, though he was in no hurry for that day to come. He was fond of the old girl, and the life of an officer suited him.

Perhaps if she tried very hard . . .

James and Jean had fallen somewhat behind the others. Jean was walking with her head thrown back, as if her surroundings and her companion had put her into an ecstasy of enjoyment.

"Jason," Madeline said, clinging more tightly to his arm, "let's not follow the others. Let's be alone together for a little while."

"Gladly," he said. "I just wish I had a deep dark den to take you into. Your family would hear no more of you today. Or perhaps for several days."

"I'm serious," she said. And she looked up into his face, noting his good looks as if she had never seen him before, knowing his good nature and his steadfastness, knowing that he was surely the most eligible suitor she had ever had. Far better than she deserved.

He turned her to their left, away from the path that the others were following, and they strolled for a while in silence among the ancient oaks. Until he stopped and turned to her, and she set her hands on his shoulders and looked at him expectantly.

It was a light kiss. His mouth was closed over hers. His hands, holding her firmly by the waist, kept her a little away from him.

But it was not enough. Not nearly enough. She joined her hands behind his neck and looked down at his lips when he raised his head.

"Jason," she whispered, "hold me. Kiss me properly."

He tried to kiss her properly. But propriety was the last thing on her mind. She put herself full against him and twined her fingers in his hair. She moved her mouth over his, willing it to open, licking at his lips with her tongue.

"Kiss me. Kiss me," she whispered desperately when his mouth moved to her cheek and her ear. "Jason." And she pressed even closer when his embrace grew more ardent, wanting to lose herself entirely in him, wanting to be taken into him. And moving desperately against him when her mind would not let go and allow sensation to take its place.

When he put her from him finally, so that she was leaning against a tree trunk, his questioning face still very close to her own, she touched his cheek with her fingers and spoke breathlessly. "Let's get married, Jason. Marry me soon."

But he continued to look deep into her eyes. "What's the matter?" he asked.

She laughed softly. "The matter is that I have come to my senses," she said, "and realize how much I want to accept your offer. Is my capitulation so strange that you must look at me so? Frowning instead of smiling?

Have you changed your mind? Do you no longer want to marry me?"

"I want to marry you now as I have done for the past year," he said. "The question is, do you want to marry me?"

"Have I not just proved it?" She laughed again. "And I am not at all sure that you are not honor-bound to marry me now, Jason, having just kissed me so. Or rather, to be quite honest about the matter, having allowed me to kiss you so. Can we announce our betrothal when we get back to the others? Can we marry this summer?"

But instead of laughing and hugging her and twirling her about as she expected him to do, he continued to search her eyes with his own. Madeline felt a coldness settle deep inside her.

"You are a very unhappy person," he said, "aren't you? I felt it in you last year in Brussels on that day when I first broached the subject of marriage between us. And I have felt it all this spring. Despite all the exuberance and bright smiles and dazzling beauty. It is fairly bursting from you today. I can't take advantage of your unhappiness, Madeline."

The coldness was replaced by a hot flush that she could feel creeping up her neck and into her cheeks. "You are rejecting me," she said, pressing her head back against the tree, trying to laugh.

He shook his head. "No," he said. "I am trying to look after you, to protect you from yourself. I have known it, of course. I have known that I do not really have a chance with you. But I have hoped. Now I know that there is no hope."

"You are the best thing that has ever happened to

me," she said. "Jason, I care for you deeply. I do want to marry you."

"No," he said, flicking her cheek with one finger. "Temptress!"

She felt turned to stone. She closed her eyes.

"Can I help, Madeline?" he asked. "I am not very expert with women, perhaps, but I have had men under my command for many years and have had vast experience with hearing their woes and helping solve them. Can I help? Sometimes it is a great relief just to unburden oneself of one's thoughts. And I have a broad shoulder if you wish to avail yourself of it."

"Jason," she said. She did not open her eyes. "I am sorry, I am so very sorry. I have been desperately wanting to love you, to marry you, and to will my life into a happy-ever-after ending. But I have been utterly selfish. I have been using you and not thinking of your happiness at all. How could I make you happy? I have been thinking only of myself. I am so dreadfully sorry."

There was a thread of humor in his voice when he spoke. "You must not add guilt to your other burdens," he said. "Not at all, Madeline. I am not a victim, you know. I am a man of six-and-thirty years who has risen to the rank of colonel of the Guards. A man of some firmness of character, I suppose. I have known and understood you better than you think. And I have pursued you regardless. But I would never have allowed you to deceive either yourself or me. If you had married me, it would have been because you truly wished to do so. I have never been in danger of being your victim."

"I'm sorry," she said again. "I would love you if I could, Jason. I so very much want to love you."

"I have wanted it too," he said. "But you are not to think

you have broken my heart or destroyed my life, Madeline. I think I am too old for such romantic and poetic sentiment. You must not burden yourself with that idea. Do you understand?"

She looked at him hopelessly and knew her loss. And knew that she had hurt him despite his words. And she had used him cruelly.

"I'm sorry," she said.

"Come." He stood away from her and offered his arm. "I'll take you back to the others. I daresay it is almost time for tea."

"I can't," she said. "I need to be alone for a few minutes. Will you go back without me, Jason? It is not far, I am not like to be devoured by either bears or bandits, you know."

He looked about them. "Very well," he said. "But Madeline, you are not to torture your conscience over me. Please? Smile at me. We will still have to meet back at the picnic site without drawing everyone's attention and having everyone guessing what might have happened out here."

She smiled bleakly at him. "I shall smile and be gay," she said. "I promise, I will not have anyone suspecting that you tried to steal a kiss from me."

"Then they will all think me a thorough slowtop," he said before grinning at her and turning to stride away.

Madeline did not think she had ever felt more dreadful in her life. She could not think of a way in which she might have acted more selfishly. She had used Jason without any regard at all to his feelings. Had he accepted her suggestion, she would have rushed into a marriage with him without pausing to allow herself any further thought. And she would have made him unhappy for a lifetime.

Her own terrible misery held her motionless against

the tree, her hands behind her and resting against the bark, her head, too, thrown back against it. But it was not the self-pity that mattered. What mattered was that she had been willing to use another human being for her own ends. Despite Jason's insistence, she would find it very hard to forgive herself for that.

She heard them several minutes later—the members of the other group. First the chatter and giggles of the girls, and then Dominic's voice and Walter's. But they were a safe distance away. And they would not see her, hidden as she was by the broad trunk of the oak. She did not want to be seen. She was not capable yet of putting on her social self.

But she heard the footsteps coming. And she knew without any doubt at all whose they were. She could have run. She could have shown herself and smiled brightly and called out to the others or merely spoken to him.

She stood where she was and did not move even when he stepped around the tree and stood in front of her. She merely looked at him.

"Madeline?" he asked. "What is it?"

"I REALLY SHOULD KEEP Lady Beckworth company," the dowager Lady Amberley said to Sir Cedric Harvey as they strolled across a wide lawn. "But I find it quite unbearable to sit constantly."

"And so you should," he said. "You are a mere girl, Louisa."

She laughed. "With three grown children and four grandchildren?" she said. "Hardly a girl, Cedric."

"You don't look any older than when I first knew you as Edward's bride," he said.

"It is strange, is it not?" she said. "One grows older. One counts the years passing and feels that one is growing older in wisdom. But I don't feel old. And fifty-two is not such a dreadfully advanced age, is it?"

"That is what I keep telling myself," he said. "Though I have white hair to suggest that perhaps it is."

"Oh, not white, Cedric," she said, looking up at him, her head to one side. "Silver, my dear. And very distinguished."

"I thought my life was at an end when Anne died," he said. "I thought the rest of my life would be merely a case of waiting patiently for the end. That was twenty-two years ago. She seems very far in the past, poor Anne. I can remember her only by her portrait." He sighed.

"And Edward has been gone for fourteen years," she said. "The pain is almost beyond endurance for a long, long time, is it not? And then there comes the guilt when one hears oneself laugh with real amusement or realizes that a day has passed in which one has not thought consciously of that person even once. But he was all the world to me while he lived."

"No one having seen you together could ever dispute that," he said.

They strolled on in companionable silence.

"I missed you during all that time in Vienna," he said at last. "All of you. I did not realize how much. I have come to think of you all as family."

"But you are family," she said. "You were when Edward was still alive. And you were like a rock on which we all leaned when he died so suddenly. Edmund was so young. Depending on you became a habit with all of us."

"In fact," he said, "it is amazing that Dominic was able

to make such a wise marriage without having access to my expert advice."

She laughed. "Ellen is a dear girl, is she not?" she said. "Definitely my favorite daughter-in-law. Equal with Alexandra, of course."

"And who are we to find for Madeline," he asked, "now that I am here to lend my expert counsel? Huxtable?"

"She is fond of him," she said with a sigh. "But there is a spark missing somehow. Madeline is like all the rest of us, you see—Edmund, Dominic, and me. There has to be a spark. I do not believe she will accept him, though I may, of course, be wrong."

"Purnell, then?" he said after a small hesitation.

"James?" she said. "Ah, you have noticed it too, have you, Cedric? Yes, there is definitely a spark there, is there not? More than a spark. A raging fire, I would say. Though it drives them apart instead of bringing them together. He is a strange young man. Far more approachable than he was when Edmund first met Alexandra, it is true, but strange still. There is an inner tension. An anger, perhaps. He does not get along well with his father, but then who could? And I am being uncharitable again. I shudder for Madeline if she should end up with James. And I despair for her if she does not. And never let me tell you that age has brought me tranquillity, Cedric."

He patted her hand and laughed down at her.

MADELINE DID NOT MOVE, or answer for a while. Her face was quite without color, James noticed.

"Nothing really," she said at last. "I have just rejected a good man, that is all."

"Huxtable?" he said. "Why?"

She shrugged. "I am too caught up in the frivolity of a London Season, I suppose," she said, her voice bitter. "If I were to marry one man, I would have to forfeit the admiration of all the others."

He stood looking down at her, his hands clasped behind him. Her gaze was fixed beyond him. "I thought you were fond of him," he said.

"I was." She closed her eyes briefly. "I am. I think I have waited too long. I should have married in my first Season. I would have adjusted to a husband at the age of eighteen. Now I have waited so long that I want the moon and the stars and the whole universe too. I cannot be satisfied with simple goodness and kindness and devotion."

He merely stood there looking at her. But then she had long passed the stage of expecting James Purnell to speak when there was a silence. Not that she would admit to herself that it was James to whom she talked. She had not looked at him.

"Sometimes," she said, "one yearns for something. For the ultimate in happiness. I yearn for it, and I don't know where to look for it any longer. And I don't know if I would recognize it if I found it. And the longer I look, the more selfish I grow. For I think only of my own happiness. I think I have lost the ability to make someone else happy. If I ever had it. And I suppose we can never be happy unless we can also give happiness." She shifted her gaze to him at last, and her eyes were troubled and intensely green. "Why am I talking to you like this?"

"Because I am here, I suppose," he said. His hands behind his back were so tightly clenched into fists that his fingernails were cutting into his palms.

She laughed and looked away among the trees. "You

are the perfect person to talk to, anyway," she said. "One is unlikely to be interrupted."

"You are very upset," he said. "Did he hurt you in any way?"

"No!" She looked sharply back to him. "No, not in any way at all. I am the one who did the hurting. I have just taken a good look at myself, that is all. And I do not like what I have seen. I don't think I am a very pleasant person." She laughed rather shakily as the silence lengthened. "And you are not the one to contradict me on that or to reassure me, are you?"

"I hated myself for years," he said. "They were dark, lost years. Useless years. Don't do that to yourself. Life is too short as it is." There was a desperate need in him to take away her pain. His hands clenched even more tightly.

"Kind words from James Purnell?" she said, looking up at him with a smile. "This must be a first."

And then she could feel nothing but total astonishment and humiliation as his face blurred before her eyes and a raw ache swept upward from her chest into her throat and nose. She dared not move.

And he felt rather as if a knife were twisting in him. He felt so powerless to help her. She was Madeline. "I am not quite a monster," he said. "Not quite the devil, though you may think I am." And his hands unclenched at last.

Her humiliation was complete when she felt both his thumbs brush at the tears that had spilled over onto her cheeks. His fingertips were light against the sides of her face.

"I am not good company," she said, appalled at the thinness and high pitch of her voice. "You had best go away."

"But then I never expect you to be good company, do

I?" he said, his own voice more bitter than he had intended. And he lifted his thumbs and brushed away two more tears.

She stayed back against the tree, her hands flat against it behind her back, the back of her bonnet resting against it. And she closed her eyes and tried to keep her mind working rationally.

Was his kiss so vastly different from Jason's? He held her face cupped in his hands, whereas Jason's had been at her waist. But his lips were closed as Jason's had been. Like Jason, he did not touch her with any other part of his body.

There was no difference. None at all, except that her knees felt as if they were made of jelly, and her insides somersaulted, and she could feel her mouth trembling quite out of control against his. And she wanted to cry and cry.

Her lips were cool and wet and salty from her tears, and they trembled against his own. Lips he had kissed once—no, twice—a long, long time ago, and lips he had been kissing ever since in those unwary waking moments when dreams were remembered. Not the lips of any other woman, though he had kissed many in his time.

Madeline's. She was Madeline. He had been able to think of no other way to comfort her. Or himself.

Her eyes had cleared when he lifted his head. He was looking into her—not into her eyes, but into her—with those dark eyes of his. There was no trace of a smile on his face. But then there was none on hers either. She looked back, no more able to look away or to say anything than she would have been able to stop breathing.

Her eyes looked back into his with no defenses. There

was none of the customary gaiety and sparkle in her look. She was pale and vulnerable. As was he.

When he kissed her again, she moved her hands finally from behind her and set them at his waist. And she let his mouth open over hers and paid no more heed to the trembling of her lips. She stopped thinking and comparing. She clung to his waistcoat beneath his coat and allowed herself finally and at long last—after four endless years—the luxury of feeling.

James! James!

All she had ever wanted, or would ever want.

But he did not bring her against him. He did not deepen the kiss.

"You see?" he said eventually, not at all in the voice she had expected to hear, the voice that would have matched her own feelings. "You needed company after all."

She had been too vulnerable. He could not take advantage of her vulnerability. But he was James Purnell and she Madeline Raine. His only alternative was to hurt her. And he did so quite unavoidably, without ever wanting to.

She spun away from him, brushing twigs and creases from her muslin skirt, undoing the strings of her bonnet so that she might tie them afresh. "It will be teatime," she said. "Everyone will wonder where we are."

But he caught at her shoulder from behind as she would have rushed away. It was a firm grip, which she would not have been able to shrug off even if she had felt like trying.

"Madeline," he said quietly, "it would not work. There is nothing at all except this. We cannot be five minutes together without quarreling. We are two very separate beings who by some strange quirk of fate happen to feel a powerful physical attraction for each other. There is really nothing else. And we are from different worlds. Literally. In little more than a month's time I will be gone. It would not work."

"No, it would not," she said. "But you were right just now. I did need the company. And the comfort. I feel better already. Thank you."

She took his arm since she could scarcely walk beside him all the way back through the trees and across the wide lawn without touching him. And they walked back in total silence.

And if this was feeling better, she thought with grim humor as the carriages and the blankets and the company came into sight, then feeling merely good must be death itself.

And James walked beside her and cursed himself. For if it was true that they could never agree, then perhaps his cruelty and his moroseness with her were to blame. And if it was true that there was a powerful physical attraction between them, then it was also true that he felt the pull of a far deeper emotion. And if it was true that a relationship between the two of them would never work, then he had only his past to blame. His thoughtless and irresponsible past.

He really would not need his father's hell as punishment for his sins. He lived there very effectively already. A hell of his own making.

Madeline smiled brightly at her mother when the latter raised a hand in greeting as they approached.

"Are we late?" she called gaily. "I hope Dom has not devoured all the lobster patties. He used to have a dreadful habit of doing that."

Her twin pulled a face. "I have been sitting in the carriage with Ellen and Charles, playing fond husband and father," he said. "I have not even peeped into the hampers yet, Mad, to see if there are lobster patties or not."

Madeline relinquished James's arm and took her brother's. "Let's look together, then," she said. "I'm starved."

7

$\mathcal{J}$N SOME WAYS IT FELT GOOD TO BE SIX AND twenty years of age and free, Madeline often thought. One was not burdened with a tyrannical or peevish or inattentive husband or with a brood of noisy and bad-tempered children. Neither was one hemmed in by all the restrictions on one's behavior that being a very young lady imposed.

Life had been good to her. She had taken well with the *ton* during her very first Season, and she had remained popular ever since. Younger ladies liked to be seen with her. They liked to copy her fashions. Younger men also seemed to feel that they gained in consequence if they were part of Lady Madeline's court. And older men treated her with more deference than they showed the younger girls.

There were definite advantages to being past the first blush of youth and still unattached. There were also, of course, disadvantages. One was not entirely free. When one's family decided to disperse from London even before the Season was out, one had little choice but to attach oneself to some of them.

She would have liked to stay in town. There she could lose herself in the whirl of social activities, and surround herself with admirers. There she could to a certain extent choose her companions. And there she could keep her mind off herself.

It would have been possible to stay. The Carringtons were not quite ready yet to return home. Perhaps they would stay another week, Aunt Viola said. Perhaps two, Uncle William added, merely to watch his wife become cross and flustered. But one week or two would not help Madeline a great deal. Sooner or later she would have to remove herself elsewhere.

Probably to Amberley Court. She did not want to go to Amberley.

She thought perhaps she would go into Wiltshire with her twin. Until she talked to him about it, that was.

He and Ellen were in a salon with Ellen's father when she called one afternoon. Dominic was holding Olivia and entertaining her by waving a quizzing glass from its ribbon before her eyes, pendulum fashion. Lord Harrowby had Charles and was making him smile. Ellen was sitting beside her father.

It was a disturbingly domesticated scene, Madeline thought. Sometimes it was becoming hard to realize that Dominic was her twin. He and Ellen seemed as reluctant as Edmund and Alexandra to leave their children in the nursery all day under the care of their nurse.

"Come into the library," Dominic said to Madeline, relinquishing his daughter to Ellen's care. "There's less chance there that you will have some baby dribbling all over your dress."

"But you know the babies are my only real reason for coming," she protested, smiling.

"On this occasion I think not," he said as he closed the library door behind them. "I am conceited enough to think that I am the reason. What's bothering you, Mad? I could see as soon as you were shown in that something is."

"Really, nothing," she said, "except that you are leaving for Wiltshire the day after tomorrow, and Edmund is leaving for Amberley. And I won't see you until goodness knows when, and we have always been close, haven't we, Dom? And yet if I ask to come with you, I will be imposing my presence on a family group and Ellen may resent it, though she will be far too polite to say so. And if I go with Edmund I will be interfering in a family party. For Alexandra does not see her parents often, and of course she does not see her brother for years at a time. So I am caught between the devil and the deep blue sea."

"Am I the devil or the sea?" he asked, reclining back against a large oak desk and crossing his arms over his chest. "Since when have you dreamed up this nonsense of not being welcome either with Edmund or with me?"

"Dom," she said, "you cannot conceive of what it is like to be a woman and unmarried at my age. It did not strike me fully until recently, perhaps because you were not married either. But it is a terrible feeling to be a spinster and to not quite belong anywhere."

Dominic grinned.

"Oh, you horrid man!" she cried, temper flaring. "I might have known you would have no sympathy at all. Now that you have Ellen and two babies all at once, you are wallowing in domestic bliss, and I may go hang for all you care."

"Mad!" he said, putting his head to one side and opening his arms. "Do you want to punch and pummel me? Come on, I won't even defend myself."

"Stupid!" she said. "We are not children still to fight

each other, Dom. Though sometimes I wish I could have those days back. They were so uncomplicated. May I come with you to Wiltshire?"

"No," he said.

She looked at him as if he had just slapped her face. She flushed painfully.

"You should not have come to me, you know," he said. "You should have gone to Ellen. I know you altogether too well. I think you are thoroughly convinced by this unwanted-spinster-relative image of yourself you have dreamed up. I am not at all convinced. It's Purnell, isn't it?"

She frowned. "What can James possibly have to do with all this?" she asked.

"Only everything," he said. "He is going to Amberley, so of course you must avoid it at all costs. Is it really very painful?"

She stared at him for a few moments and then turned to walk away from him. She stood staring out through one of the windows. "I have to end it once and for all," she said. "I don't want to see him again, Dom. I can't spend a month at Amberley with him. Please don't say no. Let me come with you."

His voice came from just beyond her shoulder when he spoke next. "Last year when I returned from Brussels," he said, "Ellen wanted nothing more to do with me. She did not want to see me. And the pain was so dreadful that I wanted to go away and forget. The fight for her seemed too impossible to win and too painful. I probably would have gone, too, if I had not discovered just in time that she was with child. We fought it through, Madeline. I dread to think what my life would be now if I had given up so easily."

"But that was different altogether from my case," she said crossly.

"Of course it was," he said. "In details it was very different. In essentials I think it was much the same. You love Purnell. You want to cut off the pain now, when you can still feel somewhat in control of it. You are afraid that after another month the pain will be unbearable and will destroy you."

She rested her forehead against the window, "Can you promise me that it will not?" she said. "It is easy for you, Dom, to look back and see that following Ellen to Amberley last year was the best thing you could have done. But there is no hope for me. For even if by some strange chance he did make me an offer and I accepted, we would not be happy together. I am incapable of making him happy, because he does not like me. And I could not be happy with his morose nature. Let me come with you."

He took her by the shoulders and turned her to him. "Will you trust me?" he asked. "We have always known each other almost better than we have known ourselves, haven't we, Mad? I can't look into the future. I can't make promises for you. It may well be that if you go to Amberley, you will have a broken heart at the end of a month. Perhaps it will throw a blight on the rest of your life. But if you don't go, you will never be free of what has pursued you and haunted you for four years."

"Geoffrey will marry me," she said.

"North?" he said scornfully. "That is not even a good try, Mad. What has happened to Huxtable? Rejected already, at a guess. Now, having given my little sermon, I will say this. If you will do us the honor of spending the summer with us in Wiltshire, both Ellen and I will be delighted. I know I speak for her too. She thinks of you as a sister and is very fond of you. You may come with us the day after tomorrow. But for your sake, I hope you don't."

"Oh, horrid!" she said, leaning forward to rest her forehead against his neckcloth. "You have turned into a horrid, very grown-up and wise man, Dom. You are quite as bad as Edmund. I far preferred it when we bit and scratched."

"I never did either," he said. "I slapped and punched and swore. And what a beautiful compliment about my being like Edmund. I could do a great deal worse. Come and have tea now, and you shall let us know tomorrow what you have decided to do. There will be no reproaches, by the way, and no more sermons."

She lifted her head with a sigh. "I don't really need until tomorrow," she said. "Miss Cameron is traveling down to Amberley with Mama and me. It would be unmannerly to absent myself, would it not?"

"No comment," he said.

"And our trunks are packed," she said. "And some of my things are hopelessly mixed up with Mama's. I suppose it would be easier for me to go with her."

"Yes," he said.

"I don't suppose Edmund and Alexandra will mind too much, will they?" she said. "I have been spending my summers at Amberley for so long that I must be hardly distinguishable from the furniture."

His lips twitched. "Quite," he said.

"And there are so many friends and neighbors to be visited," she said, "that I can be away from home for most of every day."

"A good point," he said.

"And then, of course, Miss Cameron will be there, and she will be with him all the time. It is likely that I will scarce see him and never have to converse with him."

"You are being very sensible about the whole thing," he said.

She punched him suddenly with a hard jab to the stomach. "And you are being horrid," she said. "Don't you dare laugh at me, Dominic Raine. You know I can tolerate anything except being laughed at."

"Quite so," he said soothingly.

And so Madeline found herself less than a week later at Amberley, and wondering how she could have thought of going anywhere else. There was the gray stone mansion in the valley, which was surely one of the loveliest houses she had ever seen and which had always been home. And the valley was peaceful and green, and the cliffs wild and windblown, and the beach flat and golden when the tide was out.

And there were the Courtneys glad to see her home, even Howard, the oldest son, now one of Edmund's tenants in his own right, and for many years her faithful admirer. And the Mortons and the Cartwrights and the Lampmans and the Misses Stanhope and the rector and his wife. And Mr. Watson, who had recently married. And Uncle William and Aunt Viola would be back soon.

It was good to be home. And if there were some visitors with whom she was less than comfortable, well then, it was easy enough to avoid them. The house was large enough and the countryside much larger.

And she had to endure for only one month. The *Adeona* was to sail in August.

• • •

IF JEAN HAD BEEN EXCITED by London and delighted with Richmond Park, she was enraptured with Amberley Court. It seemed she could not have enough of walking and riding and even running out of doors. The state apartments of the house and the family portrait gallery enchanted her. She frequently spent an hour at a time in the nursery or out on one of the lawns, playing with Christopher and trying to coax smiles from Caroline. And she loved the neighbors and their friendliness. Jean had stood in awe of the English. She had not expected to be taken notice of by any of them. She had certainly not expected any to befriend her.

Before Anna's return one week after their own arrival, she spent much of her time with Madeline. And Madeline could not help but like the girl, whose sunny nature matched her own as it had used to be. They went visiting together when the dowager Lady Amberley was too busy entertaining Lady Beckworth or escaping for private walks with Sir Cedric.

Jean loved to visit the rector and his wife, whose home was anything but the tidy, quiet haven one might expect of a rectory. Seven children had been given the freedom of the house, and used the privilege to its full advantage. The eighth would doubtless join them when he once learned either to crawl or to walk. And the rector's wife sat amid the chaos, huge with the ninth addition to their family, beaming goodwill on all comers.

And she loved to visit the Lampmans and their two quiet, well-behaved children, although Rose was not quite four and Paul not quite two. Lady Lampman took her into the flower garden and the rose arbor and the orchard, and Jean thought that she had never in her life seen anything more splendidly colorful. And Sir Perry teased her about her accent, which was not quite Scottish and not quite French and not quite anything else either.

"But quite, quite charming," he added, his eyes twinkling when he was not sure that she knew he was teasing.

She liked the Courtneys, who lived in a large house and were clearly prosperous tenant farmers, but who were so friendly and so cozy that she felt quite unthreatened by their grandeur. Large, genial Mr. Courtney, creaking inside his stays, showed her his prize boars and a large number of their twenty-three cats. There would not be so many of the latter, he said with a rumble of a laugh and a creak, now that his Susan was from home. She was living in London with her brother-in-law, Lord Renfrew, and his good lady, preparing for her wedding to Viscount Agerton in St. George's in the autumn.

Her first husband, Jean understood, had been killed at Waterloo just as Lady Eden's had been.

Mrs. Courtney showed her her vegetable garden.

The Misses Stanhope showed her their treasures of lace and displayed a great deal of interest in her Scottish ancestry on her father's side and her English ancestry on her mother's. Both Mrs. Morton and Mrs. Cartwright plied her with cream cakes and tea and kindly questions. And Mrs. Colin Courtney wanted to know all about Montreal and thought it must be wonderful to have been all the way to the new world, while Colin and his older brother, Howard, talked with Madeline and smiled at Jean occasionally and talked with her when Mrs. Colin paused for breath.

Jean was very happy, and she told James so whenever they were together. They frequently were together, always in company with some other people, usually the earl and his countess or Anna and Walter Carrington after they had come home. They usually walked with their arms linked.

"If I lived in this part of the world," she said to him on one occasion when they were walking inland along the valley, the river on one side, trees on the other, "I don't think I would ever leave, not even to go to London for a Season. Would you, James?"

"I have heard Edmund say," he said, "that he likes going away merely for the pleasure of loving his home even more when he returns to it."

"Oh, yes," she said. "I am sure that is true. Have you ever known such friendly people, James? They have not made me feel a stranger at all."

"How could they?" he said with a smile. "You are so very friendly yourself, Jean. It is enough to make one smile just to look at you."

She laughed. "I think it is my accent they smile at," she said. "While to me it seems funny that everyone here talks as you do. James, I am so very, very happy." She laid the side of her head very briefly against his arm.

James was rather glad at that moment that his sister and brother-in-law were coming along behind them. He would have taken her into his arms and kissed her and asked her if she would take him into her own happiness— though he would not have used those exact words. He would have asked her to marry him. And he was not quite sure yet. Either for her sake or his own.

MRS. MORTON PAID A CALL personally at Amberley Court only two days after the earl resumed residence there, in order to invite all family and guests to a dinner and evening party. She had come as soon as she decently could, she explained quite candidly, in the hope of extending her invitation before the Courtneys had completed their own plans. It was usually the Courtneys who won such races. Though, of course, this year they were somewhat preoccupied by the coming nuptials of Susan. Mrs. Courtney would be leaving for London soon, and even Mr. Courtney would exert himself on this one occasion to go to town for a few weeks.

But the Courtneys were not to be outdone. Their own dinner and informal dance was set for two evenings after the Morton party.

"It is going to be a busy month," the earl told his wife with a sigh and a smile combined. "We had to miss giving the annual summer ball last year. I am sure no one will let us get away with such a thing this year, Alex. We might as well hold it early so that we can make it a celebration for your brother too."

"I will begin to associate the ball with his leaving," she said. "The last time he left it was in the middle of the ball. But it should not be quite as bad this time. I think he really must be fond of Miss Cameron after all, don't you, Edmund? I think perhaps they will be happy together."

"Yes," he said. "I just wish Madeline were not quite so determinedly gay. It makes me tired just to look at her."

"And I sometimes think that James is so attentive to Miss Cameron as a defense against stronger feelings for Madeline," his countess said with a sigh. "Oh, dear, Edmund, why do people have to be so foolish? I don't think the two of them have exchanged a dozen words since they have been here."

The earl had no answer or comfort to offer.

But what Alexandra had said was true, or almost so. They had probably exchanged more than a dozen words, since just a bare "good morning" and "good night" used up four in a day. But they had certainly not spoken more words than were necessary or looked more looks than they could decently avoid during the first week at Amberley.

It was a nasty surprise to both when they realized one morning that Jean had asked each of them to ride down onto the beach with her. And both had accepted without realizing that the other had been invited.

Madeline was very relieved to see Howard Courtney at the house. He had just finished some business with Edmund. Howard had been a playmate all through their childhood and had declared undying love for her when he was eighteen and she seventeen. He had remained faithful for years after that, and watched her with adoring eyes whenever she was at home. He had never asked her to marry him, realizing that the social gap between the daughter of an earl and the son of a tenant farmer was insurmountable.

She was thankful he had never asked. She was extremely fond of Howard, as who could not be? His placid temperament and good nature extended back to his early childhood. And though he had never been handsome, and already showed signs of acquiring some of his father's portliness and of losing some of his fair hair, he was pleasant enough looking. But she had never felt more than affection for him. She was thankful that in the past few years he had kept his adoration contained if, indeed, he still felt it. She hoped he did not.

She smiled dazzlingly at him now and hoped fervently that he would not misunderstand. For James Purnell had accused her four years before of breaking Howard's heart.

"Howard," she said, "you simply must save Miss

Cameron and me from the dreadful fate of having to share one gentleman between the two of us for the remainder of the morning. Will you come riding on the beach with us and Mr. Purnell?"

Jean too turned her sunny smile on him. "Oh, will you, Mr. Courtney?" she asked. "It is such a beautiful day and simply made for pleasure. I hate to think of your riding back home in order to work."

Howard smiled his usual placid and good-natured smile and agreed without further persuasion.

Madeline, riding along the valley in the direction of the beach, went to such great pains to converse with both Howard and Jean so that Howard would not think that she was flirting with him that she succeeded only too well. As their horses stepped from grass to sand and turned to walk along the beach, Howard drew his horse alongside Jean's and proceeded to tell her of his turnip crop, for which he had great hopes.

And so Madeline found herself looking sideways into the dark eyes of the man she had successfully avoided for almost two weeks. And so James found himself looking into the green eyes of the woman he had successfully avoided for an equal period of time.

"You are enjoying your stay here?" she asked, and wondered immediately why she always said such foolish and unnecessary things to him.

"Yes," he said. "It all looks very familiar." He glanced to the cliff that towered to their right. "The pathway we descended is somewhat farther along, I believe."

"Yes," she said, pointing ahead. "It begins almost across from that black rock."

"The occasion of one of our more vicious quarrels, I recall," he said.

"Yes."

"It was a long time ago," he said. "We have both done a great deal of living since then."

"Yes."

"And it seems to me," he said, "that we have switched roles. I was the one at that time who was berated for answering in monosyllables."

"Yes," she said. And when the silence lengthened, "I cannot speak with you. I am always conscious of what I must say, and therefore what I say is of no value at all. And you think I am foolish when in reality it is just the words I say to you that are foolish."

"And does my opinion matter to you?" he asked.

"I suppose not," she said. "But no one likes to be despised, for all that."

"I have never despised you, Madeline," he said. "Oh, perhaps at first. Yes, I think perhaps I did then. But I have not in the past four years. I do not now."

"Have you ever thought of me in the past four years?" she asked. And she looked ahead of her and all around her, and despised herself for asking the question. As if the answer mattered to her.

"When you are alone a great deal of the time," he said, "you think of a great many things. The people and events of your past. Your own reactions to both. Yes, I have thought of you, as I have thought of everyone else I have ever known."

Well, she had asked for it, she thought, as a pain of something knifed through her heart. But she could not let it alone. "And what have you thought of me?" she asked.

She did not think he would reply. He was silent for a long time. "That I was a fool," he said, "ever to have allowed myself to feel an attraction for someone so eminently unsuitable for me. And someone for whom I was equally unsuitable. That I was a fool not to have stayed that night and the following morning so that I could see you with lust gone and know again and let you know how impossible it all was. That I was a fool ever to think of coming back here again."

"And you still think so now," she said, her eyes directed between her horse's ears. "That you are a fool where I am concerned."

"Not exactly," he said. "We understand each other, I believe. And we both know that for a reason neither of us understands fully it is impossible. When I go away, I will finally be able to leave you behind me."

Again that knifing pain. "Will you?" she said.

"Yes."

"And you will not think of me again," she asked unwisely, "when you are off in the wilderness alone once more?"

"No more than of anyone else," he said. "Besides, I may stay in Montreal. I may have reason to ask to stay there."

He was looking ahead to Jean Cameron. And this time the pain came crashing at her from all directions and she could no longer ask the questions that might make it finally unbearable.

"And you," he said. His eyes bored into hers for a moment. "What will you do when I am gone?"

"I am going to marry Lord North," she said, smiling dazzlingly at him. Poor Geoffrey had not even asked her, she thought, but he would. It would take only one such smile. "We have known each other forever. We will be comfortable with each other."

"I see," he said. "And you will be content to be comfortable, Madeline?"

"Oh, yes." She laughed. "I am practically in my dotage, you know. I think I am past anything else."

"And if anything you have said to me in the past month is calculated to confirm me in my old opinion that you are foolish," he said, "those words are undoubtedly it."

She could not tell from his expression, though she looked directly into his eyes, whether he was serious or teasing. But how could James Purnell tease? It was surely an impossibility.

She shrugged. "Miss Cameron is undoubtedly being unwise enough to show interest in Howard's farming," she said. "He may just go on forever, you know. You must do what you did the last time we quarreled on this beach. Then you told me stories about school. Now you must tell me stories about the land where you stayed for three years. What did you call it? Ath—?"

"The Athabasca country," he said. "Very well, then, Madeline. I shall do as I did then. I shall tell you to relax and merely add a 'Really?' and a 'How splendid!' in the appropriate places. I will entertain you."

And she was entertained, too. For the very first time, she realized much later as she rode back up the valley with Jean while Howard told a new audience about his turnip crop, she had forgotten herself and him and their surroundings and had been enthralled by his stories of a northern land that sounded as if it must be on a different planet, so remote was it from anything in her experience.

She did not think she had removed her eyes from his face during the telling. But she had seen the thin, angular, darkly handsome face and the live, dark eyes of a fascinating storyteller. Not the forbidding, rather frightening face of the James she knew.

And now she was almost sorry that she had not

allowed them to ride along in their customary uncomfortable and rather hostile silence. For she had had a rare glimpse of him as a real person. And it had been a glimpse of a person she could like and be drawn to. Not just by the power of a physical attraction but by the compelling fascination of his character.

She fought, as she had fought for four years, not to put her feelings into words. For if she did so, then the pain would be unbearable indeed. Dominic had put it into words, of course, two days before they left London. But she would not remember the words or acknowledge their truth. She would not admit to herself—and never would—that she loved James Purnell.

And James, for his part, riding along the valley with Howard, listening with part of his attention to an enthusiastic account of turnip crops and boars that might one day rival his father's and drainage schemes that would increase his acreage, watched Madeline and marveled at what had just happened.

For though he was accustomed to people's curiosity about life in the far Northwest, both in Canada and in England, and though he had accustomed himself to answering that curiosity, no one else had ever opened the floodgates of his memories and observations as she had just done. Though she had only requested the stories. She had not said a word once he had begun.

It had been like talking to himself, thinking to himself, a skill he had become expert at. And when he had glanced at her in the telling, it had not been Madeline he had seen, the Madeline with whom he always felt taciturn and watchful and gauche, the Madeline he had always been convinced would not care a fig for him or his life. It had been a vibrantly beautiful woman whose green eyes and parted lips had shown her engrossment in what she heard.

He had spoken to her for how long—twenty minutes? half an hour? longer?—without any self-consciousness at all or any danger of running out of words. Just as if she were a silent but totally sympathetic part of himself.

Damnation!

8

"ARE YOU NOT READY YET TO GIVE UP THIS whim of yours, James?" Lady Beckworth was leaning heavily on her son's arm and taking a turn with him about the formal gardens in front of Amberley Court.

"Whim, Mama?" he said, shortening his stride to match hers.

"That is all it ever was," she said. "Done in order to defy your father and break his heart. Is it not time to come back home?"

"Do you mean to England as opposed to Canada?" he asked. "Or are you talking about Yorkshire and Dunstable Hall?"

"Your father is a sick man, James," she said, "for all he does not show it. You are his only son. Despite everything, despite your stubborn and wayward disposition, you are still his son. Do you think it does not hurt him to see you engaged in vulgar trade? Do you think it does not break my heart?"

"Mama," he said, covering her hand with his own, "don't say such things. I remained your son and his through all the trouble with Dora. I stayed for five years afterward, living in hell, because I was your son. And it was hell. You must admit that."

"If it was, it was of your own choosing," she said, drawing a handkerchief from her pocket and dabbing at her eyes with it. "Though how you can say such a thing, I don't know. Beckworth is a saint, James. He has never ceased praying for your soul. And besides, it was Alexandra who kept you at home, not your papa. And not me."

"Mama," he said, "I love you. I have always loved you. But it became impossible for me to live at home any longer. You must have seen that. And it would be impossible now. I cannot talk with Papa. He cannot see me as a person at all. He can see me only as a sinner."

"If you came back home," she said, "and were a dutiful son, perhaps he would see that you are repentant."

"It cannot be done," he said, taking his own large handkerchief from a pocket and stopping to dry her eyes himself. "Don't cry, Mama. You have Alex and the children. And I will continue to write to you, as I have done over the years. It will be better that way."

"And you will probably marry that dreadful girl merely to spite him," she said, sniffing and resuming their walk.

"Jean?" he asked in amazement. "Jean a dreadful girl?"

"Her father is in trade," she said, "and her brother. And she speaks with such a dreadfully vulgar accent, James, and is such a colonial. Will you shame your father with such a bride?"

His face became instantly hard and expressionless, his eyes burning and inscrutable. "When I choose a bride, Mama," he said, "I will, I hope, choose someone for my own comfort. And she will be no one to shame either me or you. I have not asked Jean yet."

"You ought to offer for Lady Madeline," she said. "She can be shockingly vulgar and flirtatious, and Amberley allows her altogether too much freedom, but she has the birth and breeding, James. You must remember that you will be Beckworth yourself one day."

"I will never marry Lady Madeline Raine," he said quickly. "Mama, I have been back in England for a month. I have a month left. Can we not just enjoy being together? I am thirty years old. Can you not accept me as I am? I so long for reconciliation with you and Papa. I long for the peace of your love."

"Well, of course we both love you, James," she said. "The very idea that we might not! The Good Book tells us we must love, and your Papa lives by its word. It is your own love that is lacking. You will persist, then, in returning to that heathen land and in marrying that vulgar girl?"

"I will be returning to Canada in August," he said. "I have made no offer for Jean."

"But you will," she said bitterly. "I can see, James, that you are bound and determined to kill your father. I wonder how you will live with yourself or ever reconcile your soul with your Maker when you hear that he is dead."

"Mama." They had reached one of the stone fountains in the gardens. He released her arm and stood with both hands on the edge of the basin, gazing into the water that was spraying into it. "Please don't lay such a burden on me. I will speak with him again before I leave. I will try to reconcile with him. Will that please you?"

She was crying again. "Will you?" she said. "And beg his pardon for all the shame you have brought him in the past? And assure him that you will come back home and be his dutiful son? And that you will offer for Lady Madeline? Will you, James? For my sake, will you? I want my son back. I lost you and Alexandra both together. I miss you."

"Oh, Mama!" He took her into his arms and let her sob on his shoulder. And he threw his head back, his eyes tightly closed, his teeth clenched hard together.

MADELINE WAS LYING flushed and laughing in the grass later that same afternoon. She was out of breath after having played an energetic game of chasing with her nephew, with a few pauses to swing Caroline around in a circle. Christopher was now lying on his stomach at the bank of the river, watching for fish. Caroline was picking off the heads of the daisies, which dotted the grass despite a gardener's care.

Alexandra was sitting on a wrought-iron bench, sewing.

"Poor Madeline," she said. "You will be exhausted. You should not encourage the children to drag you all to pieces, you know. They have learned that there are certain things that Mama will do with them and certain things that are quite beyond the limits of her energy."

"Ah, but I do not see them as often as you do," Madeline said. "It is easy to be an aunt, Dominic assures me."

"You should be a mother," Alexandra said. "You should not delay much longer, Madeline. Having children is very uncomfortable for nine months—or for much of that time, anyway—and downright painful for several hours. But it is a glorious experience, nonetheless, and one not to be missed."

Madeline grinned at her. "I would need a husband," she said. "The world would be scandalized if I tried it without."

"I wish..." Alexandra said. And then in a rush, "I wish

you would find someone with whom to settle down happily, Madeline. I had hoped . . . Oh, never mind."

"No," Madeline said, closing her eyes and plucking at the grass on either side of her, "never mind."

"You did not want to go with Anna and Miss Cameron?" Alexandra asked cheerfully.

"No." Madeline smiled without opening her eyes. "I must be getting old. They seem such children to me. Going off giggling with Walter to call on Colin and Hetty, who seem equally infantile for all that they are married already and not so very much younger than I. And planning then, the lot of them, to visit Howard. No, such an outing is not for me, Alexandra. Howard has become a dreadful bore since acquiring his own farm."

"But he is working so very hard," Alexandra said, "and is a very worthy citizen, Madeline. He will doubtless be as prosperous and as respectable as his father."

Madeline pulled a face. "He used to be in as much mischief and earn as many punishments as the rest of us as a child," she said. "Oh, dear, Alexandra, we are all grown up, aren't we? And Howard is doing what he should be doing. He is settling to a life of sober hard work. And Dom is doing what he should be doing. He is making a home of his estate and raising a family. And then there is me."

"Some people take longer to find what they want," Alexandra said, putting aside her sewing. "It will happen eventually. The summer is very dull for you, is it not?"

Madeline sat up and brushed at her hair and dress. She smiled. "Not at all," she said. "There is the Mortons' party tonight and the Courtneys' two nights hence. And Aunt Viola cannot decide between a grand picnic and another evening party. But you may be sure that there will be something. And there is the summer ball here. And the regiment is back and some of the officers invited to the Mortons' tonight. They must be handsome. It is a necessary qualification for a commission, you know. And the Lampmans were expecting visitors to arrive yesterday, including one gentleman who seems to be unattached and is almost bound to be youngish and handsome and rich and eligible." She laughed. "My choices are about to become dizzying, Alexandra."

"Well." Alexandra reached down to take the palmful of daisy heads her daughter was offering. "How very lovely, angel. We shall put them in water as soon as we go inside. I hope you are right, Madeline. I know you miss Dominic. I am sorry he did not come this year, but I fully understand, of course, and am very delighted that he and Ellen are happy enough to want to be at home alone together."

"Me, too," Madeline said, and lay back down and yawned.

"James is off on his own," Alexandra said, looking briefly down at the closed eyes of her sister-in-law. "He would not even come to luncheon, and then he went galloping off up the hill onto the cliffs. I would have gone with him if he had given me one word of encouragement."

"Sometimes people need to be alone for a while," Madeline said after a short pause. "Perhaps he finds the house crowded. He has been used to being alone. Very alone for four years."

"Yes." Alexandra frowned. "I thought when he first returned that he was changed. He seemed confident and happy. He had lost that brooding and haunted look that was his mask for several years. But it is coming back."

Madeline swallowed. "Perhaps he is like Dom," she said. "Dom hates saying good-bye. He always says that he wishes he could snap his fingers the day before he is due to go somewhere and be gone, all farewells unsaid. Perhaps he is thinking that he will have to say good-bye again in a few weeks' time to you and your mama and papa."

"Perhaps," Alexandra said with a sigh. "I had hoped... Oh, Madeline, I had hoped...But it doesn't matter. It is time I took the children back to Nanny Rey before Christopher falls in the water. Are you coming?"

"I think I'll stay here for a while," Madeline said, "and be utterly lazy. There is no more delicious combination than grass and sunshine."

She might even sleep, she thought a few minutes later, watching the bright glow of her eyelids and feeling the pleasant warmth of the sun on her face.

Lady Lampman's niece, Priscilla, was paying a visit with her new husband and the latter's older brother. And Miss Letitia Stanhope had sighed just the day before over the handsomeness of Captain Hands of the local regiment. She would meet both of the single gentlemen that evening. And perhaps more officers too. Perhaps none of them would be eligible in any way. And perhaps they would.

But however it was, that evening she was going to begin a new life. Within the next year at the longest she was going to find herself a husband. And if she chose with the head and not the heart, she ought not to find the task difficult at all. She was fortunate enough still to have her looks and still to be attractive to men. And many of the men of her acquaintance were perfectly sensible and kindly.

She had frightened herself in London with the realization that she really was a spinster relative, a hanger-on, tolerated because she was a sister, and even loved by both

Edmund and Dominic and, she thought, by their wives. But nevertheless, she did not belong with either of them, or even with her mother, who had a life of her own and was enjoying her independence. There was nowhere where she really belonged.

But she would belong. Even a dreary marriage would be preferable to spinster status. And there was no reason why any marriage she chose to make should be dreary.

She was going to put behind her an infatuation, an obsession that had lived with her for four whole years, even when she had not realized it. Every good man with whom she might have allied herself in that time had been rejected because he did not have the thin dark face or the burning, penetrating eyes, or the wayward lock of dark hair or the brooding morose nature or the compelling sexuality of James Purnell.

No longer. The sensible part of her knew that even if the obstacles to their marrying could be removed—and they could be removed quite easily, since there was no insurmountable barrier between them—it would be the unwisest move of her life to marry him. She wanted him, she ached for him, with far more than mere lust. But she would never be happy with him. There was just something there that made it impossible for them ever to be happy with each other.

And so she must let him go when he left. She must watch him go and steel herself against all the agony that that would involve—for try as she would to be nonchalant, she knew that there would be agony. And then she must let him go into her past, into the past of nostalgia and mild regrets. Into the past so that he would have no influence whatsoever on either her present or her future.

Tonight her new life would begin—a new life as yet

unknown, but neither a tragic nor a dreary life. It was not in her nature to turn inward upon herself and brood upon an unhappiness that could not be helped. So there was some goodness, some happiness, ahead. And perhaps that evening she would see a glimmering of what it might be.

It was an exciting thought. Madeline drifted off to sleep.

THE MORTONS were not able to offer their guests any dancing, much to the mortification of Mrs. Morton, who had never been able to persuade Mr. Morton that they needed a pianoforte when they already possessed a spinet on which the girls could practice their scales. A spinet was all very well for scales and finger exercises, she had always argued to deaf ears, which in more private moments she had sometimes called doltish among other lowering things. But it was no good at all for musical evenings with one's friends. And absolutely impossible for dancing.

Their son-in-law, dear Hetty's husband, Colin, was, of course, proficient on the violin, but it was humiliating to expect one's guests to dance to its scrapings when the Courtneys could always call upon the skill and experience of Miss Letitia Stanhope to play their pianoforte, which they had bought years before even though they had had but the one girl. And the Earl of Amberley, of course, always hired a whole orchestra to play for the summer ball.

Mrs. Morton made the best of a bad situation by organizing cards and charades, and sharpening her conversational skills, and having colored lanterns hung in the trees all about the terrace and lawns, and having her cook prepare such mounds of food and bowls of punch that the Courtneys would be clearly outdone. Not that one wanted to outdo one's neighbors, of course, she explained to a husband whose nose was deeply buried in a horse journal. But the Courtneys would have all the advantage of their dance.

It was gratifying to find, though, on the evening of the party, that all the guests arrived in the highest of spirits. The dowager Countess of Amberley and Sir Cedric Harvey were smiling and gracious, and Lady Beckworth amiable, though she asked to be seated as far as possible from the open French windows in the drawing room. Lord Beckworth had declined to come on account of his health, poor man.

Mr. Carrington loudly declared to Mr. Morton that they must suffer through another evening of what the ladies considered to be genteel entertainment, and Mr. Morton chuckled his appreciation, while Mr. Courtney's stays creaked from his laughter. Mrs. Carrington looked reproachfully at her husband and assured everyone within hearing that he was teasing.

All the other neighbors arrived in good time and good spirits. Sir Peregrine made Miss Letitia blush by admiring her new cap, although it was not new, that flustered and pleased lady confided to Mrs. Courtney. But dear Sir Perry was very kind. And such a mischief he had been as a child, too. Did Mrs. Courtney remember the time when...? And the two ladies were off into a comfortable coze.

Lady Lampman presented her niece to the company, though most of them remembered her from a visit she had made with her mama and papa and grandpapa a few years before. Now she had acquired a good-looking young man for a husband. They all greeted Mr. Henry Clark and his even better-looking older brother, Sir Gordon Clark. Such a head of auburn curls he had, and such a fine figure of a man for all the young ladies to fight over.

Not that he was the only one, of course. Captain Hands, with his dark hair and curled mustache, was a very distinguished gentleman indeed, and Lieutenant Cowley of pleasing countenance. And there was neither a Mrs. Hands nor a Mrs. Cowley.

Anna Carrington and Jean Cameron had their heads together and were doing a deal of whispering and giggling and looking conscious. And Lady Madeline was bright-eyed and glowing as she had always been for as far back as anyone could remember. And exciting the notice of the captain, if not that of all three new gentlemen to the neighborhood.

Lady Amberley had been gracious enough to put in an appearance with the earl. She never had put on airs since acquiring the title four years before. She sat by the windows with Lady Lampman beside her to keep her company, though the earl rarely took his eyes from her for more than five minutes at a time, any more than Sir Perry did from his lady.

Mr. Watson sat beside his new wife while she blushed and made conversation with Hetty. Mr. Watson, that quiet poet farmer, was clearly in love.

And Mr. Purnell was as quiet a gentleman as he had been several years before when he had first come to Amberley with his sister, before her marriage. And as handsome a gentleman, despite the dark bronzing of his complexion, which must have come of being out in the sun without a hat. He would lose all his hair that way before he was forty, if he were not careful. See if he wouldn't.

Altogether, Mrs. Morton thought, as her guests settled in for an evening's modest entertainment, she could feel thoroughly satisfied with all the work she had done and all the anxieties she had suffered and all the sleep she had lost worrying that something would go wrong.

Her party was going to be a success.

"THOSE CURLS!" Anna was whispering to Jean. "Don't you just long to wind them around your fingers?"

They both smothered laughter.

"He is quite well-looking," Jean said, taking another look at Sir Gordon Clark. "Are you being untrue to Mr. Chambers already, Anna?"

"Pooh!" the girl said. "He did not even make me an offer before we came home. He merely said that he would do himself the honor of calling upon me next spring when we were in town. I would not give him the satisfaction of remaining single that long."

"You are not nursing a broken heart?" Jean asked.

Anna giggled. "The only time I had a broken heart," she said, "was when Dominic told me last summer that I must stop telling everyone that I was going to marry him. I had been doing so since I was ten years old, you know. It had come to be a habit. And almost indecently soon after that he betrothed himself to Ellen. And when I was all ready to see him as a noble figure of tragedy—because she was already increasing, you see, and he was doing the decent thing—it became very obvious to me that he was also head over ears in love with her. That was very lowering to the spirits, believe me."

"You speak of Lord Eden?" Jean asked. "He is very handsome."

"Don't remind me," Anna said. "I have never met a man more so. But Sir Gordon Clark has definite possibilities.

And the added attraction of a dimpled chin, Jean. My heart is quite aflutter, as my eyelashes will be if I do not school them to propriety. I do hope Madeline does not decide to set her cap at him, for she will surely win him if she does."

Jean smiled and nodded across the room to where Madeline was in close and animated conversation with Captain Hands. "There is your answer, perhaps," she said.

Anna put her head to one side and studied the captain from head to foot. "A little too broad in the shoulders and chest," she said. "And I have never admired mustaches, have you, Jean? I imagine they would tickle."

Again the smothered giggles.

"Not the gentleman himself," Anna said, "but the lady kissing him. Have you ever been kissed, Jean? It is the most delightful experience, I do assure you. I let Mr. Chambers kiss me on two separate occasions, though I am sorry now that I did. And he did not do it near as well as Mr. Sindon did it last year. Have you allowed Mr. Purnell to kiss you yet?"

"James?" Jean said, startled out of the giggles. "Gracious, no. Why should I let James kiss me? Or why would he want to?"

Anna looked at her with some interest. "I thought he was your beau," she said. "Is that not what everyone thinks? Is that not why you are here?"

Jean flushed. "James my beau?" she said. "But of course not. He is old. I think he must be thirty or close to it. The same age as Duncan. He is like Duncan to me, only very much kinder. He is not my beau."

"Oh," Anna said. "I wish I had known sooner. For he is definitely the second most handsome man I have ever known and I liked him exceedingly when he was here last, for he was the only one of the adults who took any notice of me at all except for Dominic. And I remember how my heart fluttered when he returned this year and we met him and you at that concert in London. But I thought he was yours, and I decided to do the honorable thing and not steal him from you."

This time the giggling was so noticeable that Mrs. Carrington looked meaningfully at Anna.

"We will have to find you a beau as well, then," Anna said. "Not Sir Gordon, because I have first claim. And not Captain Hands, because he has eyes for no one but Madeline at this precise moment. And that mustache would definitely tickle. It will have to be Lieutenant Cowley, I'm afraid. The kindest thing that can be said about him is that he is pleasant looking. And he does have a rather sweet smile. There is, of course, Howard Courtney—" Anna glanced to her mother and decided not to giggle again, "if you fancy being a farmer's wife."

"It must be a very pleasant life," Jean said somewhat wistfully. "In this part of the world, anyway."

Anna looked at her and forgot her resolve not to laugh. "Oh, famous!" she said. "We will marry you to Howard and keep you in the neighborhood for the rest of your life."

"Sh!" Jean said, and flushed.

The two girls were soon separated by the necessity of playing charades with the other young people. Sir Peregrine chose Jean to be on his team, and James Purnell chose Anna to be on his.

"But Sir Perry is bound to win," Anna protested loudly, "for he and Madeline are by far the best players at charades for miles around." But she was pacified at the fact that she had been chosen first by Mr. Purnell and that Sir Gordon

Clark was also on her team. She winked at Jean when Sir Peregrine named Howard Courtney.

Anna did not get her kiss that evening, much to her chagrin, even though both Sir Gordon and the lieutenant were sitting with her at one point in the evening, and though Sir Gordon walked out into the garden with her. Unfortunately, his brother and sister-in-law chose to accompany them. And the garden looked so very romantic that Anna could have cried.

Both Jean and Madeline were kissed.

Jean strolled out on the terrace after the charades were over with James and the earl and countess. And she looked up at James and saw that indeed he was handsome and not so very old after all. But she smiled at Anna's suggestion that he was her beau. When he smiled back at her, she almost shared the joke with him, but his sister and brother-in-law were close by and might think such a topic of conversation indelicate.

"I like all these people," she said instead. "I am having such a very good time, James. Are you?"

He smiled down into her eyes just like a very dear brother and covered her hand with his. "Yes, I am, Jean," he said. "What are you going to do for enjoyment next winter, I wonder, after having such a wonderful time here?"

"I shall relive it all," she said, "and spend my time dreaming. And I will have you to reminisce with, for you will not start back into the interior until next spring, will you?"

But when they went back inside, she saw Howard Courtney sitting all alone, and though he did not look unhappy, she could not bear that anyone not share the warm glow that the evening was bringing her. She went to sit beside him.

"Do you spend many such sociable evenings?" she asked. "You must be very thankful to live in such a neighborhood if you do."

"I could not imagine living anywhere else, Miss Cameron," he said.

"You have never dreamed of traveling?" she asked.

Howard pondered a moment. "No," he said.

Jean smiled warmly at him. "I can very well understand why," she said. "When you live in surely the loveliest part of the world, there is little point in traveling elsewhere, is there?"

"I feel exactly that way," he said. "Though I have not been anywhere else, of course, to compare. I have to go to London in the autumn for my sister's wedding. It will be my first visit there."

"You will like it," she said, "and then be so happy to come home again."

"Would you care for a walk outside?" he asked. "Everyone else seems to be out there."

"I have just come in," she said. "But it is far cooler and lovelier out there." She jumped to her feet.

And when they were outside and she took his arm and closed her eyes and breathed in deeply and exclaimed on the scent of roses, he took her to see them, though the rose garden was around at the side of the house and not lit by the lanterns and could not be seen clearly at all. But it could be smelled.

"I will never forget this scent," she said. "We have roses in Montreal, but there is something special about the smell here. I will always think of it as the smell of England. I love England."

And that was when Howard kissed her. A fumbling kiss, surely his first as it was hers. He kissed first her cheek in the darkness and then her lips. And though the embrace lasted only a brief few seconds and was conducted with closed lips and bodies not touching, they were both breathless when it was finished and both thankful for the darkness that hid their blushes.

"I am sorry," he said.

"I am not," she said hurriedly.

"I had better take you back to the lawn," he said. "I wasn't thinking. I should not have brought you here."

"But I'm glad you did, Mr. Courtney," she said, taking his arm and tripping along at his side as he hurried around the path that led to the back of the house and the lawns and the lanterns.

And if he was not exactly handsome, she thought, blushing anew at the thought of her first kiss and smiling though there was no one to see her in the darkness, then it really did not matter. For he was courteous and kindly, and she felt comfortable with him despite the blushes. And he worked hard to earn an honest living just as her papa and Duncan did.

9

MADELINE DID NOT FLIRT. ALTHOUGH HER cheeks were flushed and her eyes shone and her lips were curved into a smile, and although her whole manner sparkled through much of the evening, her behavior was wholly spontaneous. She felt happy. She had made a decision, and she was going to live with it.

She liked Captain Hands as soon as she met him. He was not a great deal taller than she, but his broad and strongly muscled chest and shoulders gave the illusion of height. And being a soldier, he bore himself well. He had a handsome enough face and his dark brown hair was thick and shining.

But more important than his appearance, he was a serious young man, who looked her very directly in the eye and conversed earnestly on any topic she chose. He was very different from her usual choice of flirt. Indeed, he could not be called a flirt. Usually she liked to engage gentlemen in light bantering conversation and teasing flirtation. She had realized only the year before in Brussels that she did so in an unconscious effort to hold them at arm's length. Only a few men, like Jason Huxtable, had penetrated beyond the barrier that she had erected around herself.

But on this occasion she was building no barriers. She asked the captain in all seriousness about his family and home, about his life as an officer and his aspirations for the future. And although she conversed with other people and joined in wholeheartedly with the game of charades and laughed with Perry when their team won handily, her attention was entirely given over to cultivating this new acquaintance, this new hope for her future.

Not that she had any wish to be an officer's wife. Although she had once almost eloped with a lieutenant and actually had been betrothed to one the year before, and though she had seriously considered marrying a colonel only a few weeks before, she did not really think the life would suit her. But she was not going to make excuses to remain uninvolved with any man. She was going to give every possible relationship a chance.

She and the captain walked outside before supper, as several of the other guests did, and they breathed in the fresh air and the scent of the roses together and admired the lanterns and strolled the perimeter of the lawns. The rhododendron bushes were in full bloom and must be appreciated to the full.

"They are overpowered by the roses," Madeline said, "but they smell just as sweet." And she stepped up to one bloom and breathed in its fragrance. "How lovely the summertime is."

Captain Hands must have agreed with her. He must have thought she matched the loveliness of her surroundings. He stood beside her with hands clasped behind his back and leaned forward and kissed her.

She resisted the urge to react in any of the glib ways she normally would have done. And normally she would have been annoyed. She had been taken by surprise. A kiss for Madeline was usually something granted rather than taken. She smiled at the captain when he lifted his head.

He regarded her gravely. "Do I owe you an apology?" he asked.

She continued to smile. "Only if you are sorry," she said. "But I would be sorry if you are."

He said no more and Madeline turned to stroll onward. They resumed their conversation as if it had not been interrupted at all.

It was a thoroughly promising beginning, she thought as they returned inside and were called to supper and her attention was taken by her Aunt Viola. A comfortable friendship had begun, with a hint that it might turn into more than friendship. She liked the captain. There was nothing whatsoever about him that might be considered threatening.

There was something decidedly threatening about James Purnell. He came to sit beside her as she took supper at a table with Aunt Viola, Mr. Cartwright, and the Watsons. His arrival there was totally inexplicable and disturbing since he might have sat anywhere he pleased. There was an empty chair beside Miss Cameron.

But he came to sit beside her instead. And spoke not a word to her. He answered a string of the inevitable questions about Canada from Aunt Viola and Mr. Cartwright and then proceeded to draw the very shy Mrs. Watson into conversation. And he did so with a skill and gentleness that soon had her talking freely about the family and home she had left twenty miles away. Mr. Watson smiled with obvious gratification that someone had been able to draw his wife out of her shell.

Madeline felt only indignation. Why was it that he was

capable of so much humanity with other people? Young and shy girls could always provoke compassion in him, it seemed. They reminded him perhaps of Alexandra as she had used to be.

And that fact would explain why he had never shown either gentleness or compassion to her. She had never been shy.

"Would you care to walk outside?"

There was a subtle change in his voice, an almost imperceptible hardening, which made Madeline realize immediately that he was addressing her. When she turned from a contemplation of Anna and Jean, Howard and Lieutenant Cowley at the other side of the room, it was to find his dark eyes on her, as unfathomable as ever in their expression.

No good whatsoever could come of it. It was strange beyond belief that he would even suggest such a thing. They would be merely punishing themselves and each other by being deliberately alone together. Besides, she had made a satisfactory start to a new life and a new attitude just that evening. She was pleased with herself. She was almost happy.

"Thank you," she said, smiling at him, "that would be pleasant."

And when he rose to his feet and pulled back her chair for her, she smiled around at the other occupants of the table and turned to the doorway.

JAMES HAD BEEN WATCHING Jean all evening. And trying, as he had been doing all afternoon up on the cliffs, to make decisions. But he was no nearer settling the course of his life. He had succeeded only in making his brain race along out of all control so that he could not think clearly at all.

He played cards with the elder Miss Stanhope, Sir Cedric, and Mrs. Courtney. He led one of the teams of charades, a team that lost ignominiously and amid much laughter to the other. He conversed with anyone who happened to be at his side during the evening. And he watched Jean.

She was very young. She liked to whisper and giggle with Anna Carrington. She was also very sweet and even-tempered and sociable. She even had quiet, plodding, good-natured Howard Courtney taken with her.

She would be a perfect wife. Pretty and dainty, cheerful, easy to entertain. He could live in Montreal with her and forget his past and this disastrous attempt to come to terms with it. He thought he would possibly be able to arrange it that he stayed in Montreal. And if he could not, then he could leave the company. There were plenty of other ways to earn a living in Montreal or other parts of Upper or Lower Canada.

It was what he should do. And he should settle the matter now, as soon as possible, so that his mind could be at peace, his future assured. He should make his offer for Jean now, while they were at Amberley, though he would not be able to speak with her father until they returned to London. But they could make an unofficial announcement. And then he would be safe.

But of course nothing was ever as simple as that. His mother's words haunted him. He had not been able to shake his mind free of them all day. Years ago he had decided that he must take himself right away from his parents. It was impossible to please them, impossible to penetrate the armor of religion and morality they had put on. And he had gone—all the way across the Atlantic Ocean and thousands of miles beyond that.

But he had come back. And the decision was there to make all over again. For despite everything, despite the fact that they were impossible to please, they were his parents and he loved them. And he could not shut from his mind the possibility that somewhere deep inside they had feelings for him too. Indeed, his mother had shown them just that morning.

He had shamed them by going into business. That accusation he could shake off quite easily. He would shame them further by marrying Jean, who was not socially acceptable according to their standards. That too he could shake off. He had broken their hearts by leaving home and going so far away. But there was no living with them. They must have known more peace of mind since he had left, just as he had. He had never publicly begged their pardon or God's for the way he had behaved over the whole ugly affair of Dora. But then he had not wronged them nearly as much as they had wronged him. And his relationship with God was a private matter between the two of them, and not his parents' concern at all. Besides, he did not know their God and was not sure that he had one of his own.

And if his father died—*when* his father died—he would have the burden on his conscience of knowing that he had been responsible for precipitating his death.

He did not believe it. He would not believe it. But the thought had weighed on him and bowed him down all through a nightmare of a day.

So he watched Jean. And contemplated defiance. Though defiance was for schoolboys, not for thirty-year-old men who had set the course of their lives years before.

Returning to Canada was not defiance. Marrying Jean would not be defiance. If such actions killed his father, the responsibility, the guilt, would not be his.

He watched Jean and saw Madeline. She was in his every waking moment and in every cycle of his dreams. She was in his blood. And his mother wanted him to marry her. He would be showing filial duty and love by marrying Madeline and remaining in England.

His mind grappled with decisions; his conscience throbbed with denied guilt; his blood pulsed with Madeline. And during a short stroll outside with the Lampmans he looked off into the darkness beyond the lawns and the lanterns and saw her share a brief kiss with Captain Hands of the regiment stationed nearby.

When he entered the supper room, one of the last guests to do so because Miss Stanhope had engaged him and the Lampmans in the telling of a particularly lengthy anecdote about her brother Bertie, there were several empty seats. There was one across the table from Alexandra. There was one next to Jean. And one next to Madeline. He would sit beside Jean, he decided, and ask her to take a walk with him afterward. Perhaps the time would seem right for his offer. He would wait and see.

But his steps took him to Madeline's side, and he sat by her through supper without once looking at her or talking to her. And every pulse in his body was beating with awareness of her by the time they had finished eating. Conversation throughout the room was animated. No one showed any inclination to rise and return to the drawing room.

"Would you care to walk outside?" he asked Madeline, without any conscious decision to do so.

And she smiled at him, accepted, and rose from her chair.

"It is a beautiful evening," she said, taking his arm as they stepped beyond the French windows. "And there is something particularly enchanting about lanterns in the trees, is there not?"

"Yes," he said, strolling with her across the grass.

"Mrs. Morton has outdone herself," she said. "She always likes to feel that she has put on the most memorable entertainment of the summer."

"Yes," he said. And when he turned his head a few silent moments later to look down at her, it was to find her glaring ahead with fixed eyes, her jaw set in a hard and stubborn line.

He kept on walking when they came to the edge of the lawn, following a path through the bushes, not knowing where it led. There was an orchard beyond, lit only by the light of the moon and stars.

"Hands is to be the lucky recipient of your favors for the summer?" he asked, hating himself even as he heard the words he had spoken.

Her head turned sharply in his direction. "Oh, definitely," she said. "You cannot expect me to resist the lure of a young and unattached gentleman, can you? It would be as impossible for me to avoid flirting with him as it would to stop breathing."

He wanted to apologize to her. But all the frustrations of the day converted into irritability against her. "Yes," he said, "I know that quite well."

"Then your question was redundant," she said. "I made a careful assessment of Sir Gordon Clark, Lieutenant Cowley, and the captain, and decided that the last gentleman was the handsomest of the three. So I began my flirtation without further delay. Over the next few days, of course, I will have to make careful and discreet inquiries as to the relative wealth and prospects of the three. My victim may change identity as a result. But only under extreme circumstances. On the whole, it is a handsome face and physique that hold most sway with me."

"Understandable," he said. "I wonder you even give thought to wealth and prospects since matrimony is always the last thing on your mind anyway. Flirtation is the breath of life to you. I wonder if you write down the names of all your conquests. You must have a bookful already."

She looked up at him all amazement, eyebrows raised. "Oh, sir," she said, "if you had ever been inside my bedchamber, you would have seen that one wall beside my bed is pockmarked with small gouges in the wallpaper. So much more permanent and impressive a record than a mere list of names in a book, don't you agree?"

"You kissed him," he said. "Almost in public. Have you no shame?"

She laughed suddenly, still looking up at him. "Pardon the rudeness," she said, "but you sounded remarkably like your father at that moment, James. 'Have you no shame?'"

The small vestiges of his control snapped. He whirled on her, grabbed her by the upper arms, and shook her roughly. "You will leave my father out of this," he said through his teeth. "I will not permit you to insult him."

She spread her hands defensively on his chest. She was breathless. But she tipped her head back and continued to laugh up at him. "No," she said, "I am not ashamed. I like to be kissed. I like to be appreciated. And I don't care the snap of my fingers for your contempt or disapproval,

James Purnell. I will kiss and flirt with whom I like, and you may go to the devil with my blessing."

Some of his rage had receded. The hopelessness, the frustration, remained. He looked down into her laughing, scornful face.

"I think I am the devil where you are concerned, aren't I?" he said, and took her mouth with his.

He would have let her go when she struggled. He would have released her completely and turned from her so that she could find her way back to the house and safety. But her struggles were not to free herself but merely to release her arms from imprisonment against his chest. She wrapped them about his neck and pressed herself against him and opened her mouth so that his tongue plunged unimpeded into the soft heat beyond her teeth.

And her temperature soared with his. She moved against him, at first with taut desperation, and then with slower, more knowing movements, feeling him with her breasts and her hips and thighs, rubbing intimately against him, moving her shoulders back from him so that he could fondle her breasts, so that his hand could slide down between them.

And he wanted her with every pounding beat of the blood coursing through him. He wanted her with a physical agony that only their standing position and the barrier of their clothing held in check. But he lifted his head away from her eventually and stepped back with her to lean against the narrow trunk of a fruit tree. He held her head firmly against his chest and waited for sanity to return.

She was drawing audible and deep breaths and letting them out with shuddering difficulty.

"Madeline," he said finally, "what are we going to do?"

It took her a while to answer. Her voice was breathless

and shaking when she did so, though the words were light. "Straighten our hair and our clothing and go back to the house, naturally," she said, pushing away from him and concentrating her attention on brushing at the skirt of her gown.

He stayed back against the tree. "There is no way it could work, is there?" he said, gazing at her bent head, willing her for the first time in all his acquaintance with her to contradict him.

She did not look up. She must be finding many creases in her gown. "No," she said, "absolutely none. I hate you, James. I think I really do. But you see how incorrigible I am? I cannot resist kissing and flirting even with you."

"You were not flirting," he said.

She lifted her head and smiled dazzlingly at him. "Ah," she said, "but the essence of really expert flirting is that one's victim thinks one to be in true earnest. Did you think I was serious? Poor James. I am sorry, you know, if I raised hopes where there cannot be any. I am quite heartless, you see. A worthy adversary for the devil, wouldn't you agree?"

He stayed where he was when she began to walk in the direction of the house. But she turned back to him and smiled. "It might be the occasion of dreadful gossip," she said, "if we arrive back separately when everyone saw us leave the dining room together. Let us walk back sedately together, my arm in yours. What shall we converse about? Canada again? I fear the topic must be becoming tedious to you. The weather, perhaps?"

"The weather seems a safe enough topic," he said through his teeth. "We have been having an unusually long spell of heat, even for July. When do you think it is likely to break?"

"Oh, not until you have sailed in August," she said airily. "It would not be cruel enough to break before then, surely. Edmund's ball would be quite spoiled."

"There are more people on the lawn again," he said. "How fortunate, since that topic was in danger of playing itself out. Shall we join your aunt and uncle?"

"You may do so," she said, withdrawing her arm from his. "I am rather chilly. I am going indoors."

He watched her wave a hand at the Carringtons and walk in leisurely fashion in the direction of the house. She stopped along the way to talk with the captain and the lieutenant and Anna.

THE EARL OF AMBERLEY sat in his dressing gown on the side of the bed he shared with his wife. He had just straightened up after kissing her.

"Witch!" he said, smiling ruefully at her. "It is the wrong time, is it not? The dangerous time?"

"Yes," she said, folding the blankets neatly beneath her arms. "I just wish my need for you would move in cycles as my body does, Edmund. Though that would not help you at all, would it?"

"Is this house party working?" he asked, deliberately changing the subject. "Is James happy, do you think? And is he associating with your father at all?"

"No and no," she said with a sigh. "But there are a few weeks left, Edmund. I have great faith in the atmosphere of Amberley. It brought you and me together when we were all ready to go our separate ways. And it brought Dominic and Ellen together when things had gone dreadfully wrong between them. Maybe James will straighten himself out here too."

The earl got restlessly to his feet and paced to the window, where he stood staring sightlessly out.

Alexandra broke a lengthy silence. "If you are not going to lie down properly," she said, "you might as well put your mind at rest, Edmund, and go to her."

"She is probably sleeping by now," he said.

"I doubt it." She sat up and reached for his hand as he came toward her. "She was crying quite hard when we passed her room. Go to her, love. I would go myself, but you are her brother. And more to the point, I am James's sister."

"Madeline never did cry often," he said. "But when she does, she sobs and hiccups for all to hear."

"You were right all along," she said. "It never has been James and Jean Cameron, even though he has told me that he may marry her. It has always been James and Madeline. I was so happy when they left the dining room at the Mortons' together after supper. But their faces afterward, Edmund! Smiling and talking, both of them—with empty, empty eyes. I could shake the two of them. And cry oceans of tears over them. Go to her."

"Dominic should be here," he said. "He would know what to do. I was always something of an outsider with those two, you know."

"Oh, nonsense," she said. "Of course they are close. They are twins. But you are her elder brother. She adores you."

"I will go and see what I can do, then," he said. "If she is still awake, she will probably throw pillows at my head or worse. But what are brothers for?"

But Madeline was not in her room as he saw after he had knocked quietly and turned the knob of the door to look inside. He went downstairs to the conservatory, which had always been her private hideout and Dominic's, though neither of them knew that he knew.

She was huddled up into one corner of the window seat that ran around three sides of the room, clasping her knees, with her chin resting on them. The only light was that coming through the windows from the outside. He sat down close to her without saying a word.

"I couldn't sleep," she said. "The night is too lovely."

"I heard you crying," he said.

She was silent for a while. "I want to go to Dominic's," she said. "Will you let me go, Edmund? He said I might spend the summer with him and Ellen if I wished. May I go? Tomorrow?"

"Of course," he said. "If it is what you really wish, Madeline. Is it?"

She rested her forehead on her knees. "I feel so lost without him," she said. "That is absurd to say, isn't it, when I was without him for three years during the wars. But it was different then. He was in constant danger and I was constantly worried about him. He was still at the center of my life. Now he is married and happy and settled elsewhere. And they have their babies. Am I being very self-pitying? I know I am, so you need not answer me."

"Do you resent Ellen?" he asked gently.

"No!" She jerked her head up and looked directly at him. "No, I love her, Edmund. I really do, both in her own right and because she is just perfect for Dom. No, I'm not jealous of her. Just . . ." She sighed. "Just a little empty without him, that's all."

He reached out and touched one of her hands. "I'm not Dominic," he said. "I can't compete and wouldn't want to. But I have always loved you as much as he has, Madeline.

Will I do as a substitute tonight? I knew where to find you, you see. I have always known."

"Poor Edmund," she said. "It must be dreadful to have a twin brother and sister and no others at all. But we always worshipped you, you know, Dom and I. You could never do any wrong in our eyes. And if we were far less full of mischief after Papa died, it was because we could never bear to see the look of reproach in your eyes when you confronted us. Papa was fair game because he was a father. But you were our brother. Our idol."

He chuckled and squeezed her hand. "Nighttime is sometimes a dangerous time to talk," he said. "One says things one may regret forever after. I shall hold this idol business over your head, you know."

She leaned the side of her head against the window and smiled. "I was so proud of myself tonight," she said. "I had decided, you see, that it was time I looked sensibly to my future. I have promised myself that I will marry within the year, and I have set about finding myself a kindly and sensible husband. Someone as like to you as possible. I will not say that I chose Captain Hands as soon as I saw him, for that would be utterly absurd. But I began something, Edmund. I talked with him. I mean really talked. And I did not flirt, which is what I have a dreadful habit of doing just so that I will not have a close relationship with any man."

"He seems worthy enough," he said.

"Yes, he is." They were both silent for a while. "I have to continue what I started tonight, Edmund. Not necessarily with the captain. I am not saying I am going to maneuver him into marriage whether he likes it or not and whether he is suitable or not. But I must continue. I will not go to Dominic's. I will not run away. I am six and twenty years old and no child. And I have always prided myself on being independent. It has been a self-delusion, I think, but I am going to make it true."

"Do you want to tell me what happened with James?" he asked. "But only if you wish. I will not pry."

"I wish I could," she said. "I wish I knew myself what is happening with James. He has blighted my life for four years, you know."

"Has he?" he said. "There was something even when he was here last, then? I'm sorry, Madeline. I did not notice. I had thoughts for no one but Alex during that summer, I'm afraid. But blighted? That is a strong word, is it not?"

"We bring each other nothing but the most dreadful misery," she said, "and we can do nothing but quarrel and hurl insults at each other when we are together. Yet we cannot seem to stay apart. He kissed me tonight, Edmund. Oh, I kissed him too. We kissed each other. But it was after we had said dreadful things to each other and before we said more dreadful things."

"You love him?" he asked.

She laughed without humor. "It is hardly love," she said. "But I am terrified, Edmund. I'm terrified that I will never be able to put him from my mind. I don't love him, but I'm afraid that he will make it impossible for me ever to love anyone else. And it is no idle terror. It has already proved true for four years. I couldn't love Jason. I wanted to so very much. I think I may always regret losing him. But I couldn't love him."

There was silence for a while. "I wish I could think of a wise answer," he said. "I wish I could live up to your image of me, Madeline, and solve all your problems with a few words. Alas, it cannot be done. All I can say is that love is a strange thing. Never the same from one couple to another and never the easy, euphoric thing that one expects. It was not easy for Alex and me, though I don't think you know the full story. And it was not easy for Dominic and Ellen—and we doubtless don't know the full story there either.

"But somehow the four of us fought it through. And I can tell you from personal experience that for Alex and me it has been worthwhile. And that is the most foolish understatement I have ever made. I think Dominic would say the same, though doubtless he would phrase it better than I have done. Perhaps it will be worthwhile for you too, Madeline. Fight for what you want, dear."

She smiled. "If I just knew what I want," she said. "Oh, but I do know. I want contentment and peace, Edmund. I want an end to all the uncertainties. I want to be respectably married. I want some children before it is too late. I don't want James. For life could never be tranquil with him. We would forever fight." She swallowed and closed her eyes. "And love."

"Come here," he said, and he held her while she cried for the second time that night.

"There," she said when she was finished. "Now I have soaked your nightshirt and given myself two swollen eyes and a headache. And we have not solved any of the world's problems. Tears never were worth the effort of crying them."

"I remember once," he said, "asking a woman to marry me. She refused me and told me that she could give me only friendship and comfort. She told me that I needed passion. I really did not agree with her. Until I began to love Alex very soon afterward, that is. I think you need passion as badly as I, you know. If I were you, I would not settle for anything less."

"But that may mean settling for nothing at all," she said.

"Yes," he said with a sigh. "That is always the risk. But I don't think so, Madeline. I really don't think so. And I know that is small comfort. I am no miracle worker, you see."

She smiled at him, the side of her head against the window again. "No miracle worker, perhaps," she said. "But I'm glad you came, Edmund. I have always loved you, but I have never really thought of you as a brother like Dom. You have always been up there on a pedestal. But you are just as dear as he is. Every bit as much." She leaned forward and kissed his cheek. "Alexandra will still be awake, won't she, waiting for you? And she ought not to be awake this late. Or you. Thank you for coming."

"Come on," he said, "I'll take you back to your room. Are you going to be all right? You are not going to sob into your pillow all night?"

"Edmund!" she said brightly. "If I did that, I would have puffy eyes at breakfast. Have you ever known me to put on such a dreadfully public display?"

He thought a moment. "Yes," he said. "When I was taking Dominic and Perry and Howard and a few others fishing when you were ten, and Mama forbade you to go because you would be the only girl. And Papa refused to be wheedled. You cried all night and pouted all through breakfast. And Dom pouted all through the fishing trip and kicked Perry in the shin when he was unwise enough to swagger and comment on how grand it was to be all men together."

She giggled.

"Hush!" he said. "You will wake everyone up."

10

THE WEATHER CHANGED THE DAY AFTER THE Mortons' party so that no one could wander outside during the Courtneys' dinner and dance two evenings later, and the Carringtons' picnic had to be changed to an indoor tea. And at Amberley the music room and the library and the nursery became favorite haunts of the inhabitants seeking employment.

During the following two weeks the weather was chilly and unsettled. But somehow everyone managed to resume the visits and the shopping trips to the village and the rides.

Anna declared to Jean that it was a shame the weather was not cooperating. It was true that she had seen Sir Gordon Clark on several occasions and had conversed with him each time. "And I am sure he is as taken with me as I am with him, for he always arranges matters that he sits next to me, you know. But we are always in a room full of other people, Jean."

"But they are staying for Lord Amberley's ball," Jean said. "Perhaps you will be able to have some time alone with him there."

Anna pulled a face. "As like as not," she said, "he will kiss me there but will think it far too soon to declare himself. And then he will be returning home with Mr. and Mrs. Clark. I am doomed to be a tragic spinster."

"At the age of nineteen?" Jean said, and smiled. "You are very elderly, Anna."

"And poor Jean," Anna said. "You have scarce seen Lieutenant Cowley, have you, except at the Courtneys' dance. This is not turning into a very delightful summer after all. You have seen far more of Howard. It is a pity we cannot turn him into a romantic lover for you. He is really very sweet, you know, but dreadfully dull."

"I don't find him so," Jean said. "But then I have not moved in such exalted circles as you all my life."

Anna did not pursue that line of conversation. "I have had a letter from Jennifer," she said, her eyes growing round. "She has had two offers since we left town, both from gentlemen I have never heard of. At least, she had one offer and another was made to her grandfather. She says she may not accept either as she has a string of beaux. It does not sound like Jennifer to be so wild, but she does sound as if she is enjoying herself immensely." Her tone was wistful.

"What of Mr. Penworth?" Jean asked. "I thought they had an understanding."

"But they had some nasty quarrels," Anna said. "Jennifer's grandfather did not favor his suit, and Mr. Penworth told Jennifer she must not feel bound to him and she must go out and enjoy herself and meet other gentlemen. And Jennifer told him that if he was going to feel sorry for himself because he could not offer a whole body, he might go hang. He has gone home to Devonshire. Jennifer pretends not to care."

"I liked him," Jean said. "I think he is very fond of Jennifer, poor gentleman. And she of him."

Anna sighed. "One longs and longs to be grown up, doesn't one?" she said. "I dreamed of being eighteen and having a Season and meeting handsome gentlemen even apart from Dominic and falling in love with one of them and marrying him and living happily ever after. But life is not nearly as simple when one finally does grow up."

"It's the rain," Jean said soothingly. "When it clears away, you will not feel near as gloomy. After all, Sir Gordon is still here, and there is still the ball to look forward to before he goes away."

"Yes." Anna brightened. "And I really must feel those auburn curls before he leaves. He has already asked if I will reserve the first waltz for him."

Jean was restless. Time was slipping by. Soon she would be returning to London and thence to Montreal. It was something she looked forward to. She wanted to see her father and Duncan again, and it would be good to be home and to see all her old friends there. But even so, she willed time to a standstill. She knew that for the rest of her life she would treasure her memories of England and the people she had met there.

"James," she said one morning, finding him at last in the long gallery staring out a window along the valley toward the sea, "I have hunted all over for you. Come walking with me?"

He turned to smile at her. "It may be a little damp underfoot," he said. "Will you mind?"

"My hem will get wet," she said, "but I can change my dress when we come home again. It is no great matter."

They walked slowly along the valley he had just been looking at through the window. It was a cold, raw morning with heavy gray clouds overhead and a wind buffeting them from the direction of the sea.

"Oh," she said breathlessly, "this is glorious. Isn't it lovely, James?"

He bent his head so that he could see into her face around the brim of her bonnet. "Yes, very lovely," he said. "Two rosy cheeks and two sparkling eyes. A slightly reddened nose too, but I am too gentlemanly to mention that."

She laughed gaily. "I meant the weather, silly," she said. "Isn't it lovely?" She closed her eyes and lifted her face.

"I thought that perhaps now you have tasted how dreary English weather can be," he said, "you would be impatient to be gone back home again."

"No," she said, "not impatient. I want to enjoy what is left of my time here."

They strolled in comfortable silence for a while.

"James," she blurted at last, "may I talk to you? I would talk to Anna, but she would giggle and make something silly of it. Or I would talk to Lady Amberley or the earl's mother, for they are both very kind ladies, but I would feel young and foolish. May I talk to you?"

"But of course," he said, clasping the hand that rested on his arm. "What is it, Jean? Troubles?"

"No," she said. "Maybe nothing at all. Maybe nothing will happen and I will feel very foolish for having said anything to you. But I really don't know what to do if it does happen."

He smiled gently down at her. "And what do you think might happen?" he asked.

"I think Mr. Courtney might ask me to marry him," she said.

He missed a step and gazed down at her in some amazement. "Mr. Howard Courtney?" he said. "He is seen as something of a confirmed bachelor, I believe, even though he is younger than I. He has been courting you, Jean? I'm sorry—I must have lost my powers of observation. I had not noticed."

"He likes to sit beside me and talk," she said. "And he kissed me at Mrs. Morton's party. I have never been kissed before."

"I am all amazement," he said. "And what are your feelings, Jean? He is a thoroughly worthy gentleman, I am sure. A trifle dull, perhaps."

"That is what everyone thinks," she said, "but he is not. He likes to talk of his farm and his work, but there is nothing dull about that. I like him. I feel comfortable with him. And I liked his kiss."

He did not say anything for a while. "You are very young, Jean," he said. "You would be living in a strange country far away from your family."

"I know," she said. "And he has not even asked me and may not do so. Maybe he has never even contemplated doing so. And I shall feel very foolish and find it difficult to look at you if he does not. But I must be prepared, you see, because he may ask me and it is a huge and difficult decision that I would have to make."

"Is it perhaps that it will be your first offer and you feel you should accept in case it is your last?" he asked. "If so, think very carefully, Jean. I can see more objectively than you, perhaps, and I can assure you without any doubt at all that you will not lack for offers during the next several years."

"I have thought of that," she said, "for it is very flattering to be kissed and to have one's company sought out. But I don't think it is that, James. This will sound foolish, because as Anna says Mr. Courtney is not a romantic figure of a man, and as you say, he is a little dull by some standards—but I think I love him, James. I have a warm feeling here"—she spread her free hand over the ribs beneath her bosom—"whenever I think of him, and I know I will miss him of all people when I return home."

"Then it seems that the only thing we have to hope for," he said with a smile, "is that Howard Courtney will have the courage to make his proposal before you leave here and that your papa will agree to your marriage. I don't think there is any other decision to make, is there?"

"Oh," she said, turning to him, her eyes shining, "do you think so, James? Do you really think so? You don't think I am being foolish? I thought perhaps you would laugh, and I would realize that it is not the thing at all."

"Well," he said, looking gravely down at her, "you do not see me laughing, do you, Jean?"

She threw her arms about his neck, stood on tiptoe, and kissed him smackingly on the cheek. "Oh, I do love you," she said. "I wish you were my real brother, and not just Duncan's friend."

"Brothers can be adopted," he said, hugging her. "I would be honored."

She kept her hands clasped behind his neck as she leaned back and grinned impishly up at him. "Do you know what Anna thought?" she said, and giggled. "She thought you were my beau, James. Isn't that silly? And not at all flattering to you, for you are very handsome and very distinguished, and any of the loveliest ladies of the *ton* would fall all over themselves if you but looked on them with favor. Besides, you will be a baron someday."

"Very silly," he said, patting the sides of her waist and matching her grin. "No one in his right mind would expect someone as fresh and pretty as you to ally herself to an old man like me."

She wrinkled her nose at him. "You are not so very old," she said. "I daresay you are not above thirty at the most. James, promise me faithfully that you will not laugh at me if Mr. Courtney says nothing. I shall feel very foolish indeed."

"I have a dreadful memory," he said. "What have we been talking about this morning, anyway? We are far from the house already, I see, and must have been talking about something or there would have been an embarrassing silence between us. It must have been the weather. We have been talking about the weather, have we? Shall we begin the walk back? I see the hem of your dress is heavy with damp. Was there anything left to say about the weather? I really can't remember what we have already said. This is what happens when one is once past his thirtieth birthday, you know. A dreadful fate!"

She took his arm again and tripped along beside him. "Silly!" she said. "You are silly, James."

He was feeling stunned—all his plans blown to the winds. When she had found him in the gallery, he had been working up his will and his courage to go and find her. He was going to do it that very day, he had decided. He was going to end this indecision and betroth himself to her. He was going to announce it, even though he would not have a chance to talk with Douglas until their return to London. He was going to announce it so that he could feel safe for the remaining days of his stay at Amberley.

But she had spoken first. And he was stunned at his own total blindness. An attachment had been forming under his very eyes, and he had seen none of it. All of Jean's attention to him and affection for him were those of a very young girl to an older man, a brother figure.

He truly did not know what they talked about on the return walk to the house. He was stunned—and a little embarrassed and humiliated.

And a great deal relieved.

ON THE SAME MORNING, the dowager Lady Amberley rode up onto the cliffs with Sir Cedric Harvey. They tethered their horses when they were a safe distance from the edge, and walked along, the wind whipping against them.

"And blowing my words right back down my throat," Lady Amberley said.

"But I can hear them," he said, drawing her arm firmly through his and lowering his head against the wind.

"We are quite mad," she said. "But if I had had to sit quietly indoors another hour with that woman, Cedric, I would have started to commit murder, or worse. And how dreadful I am being."

"You are always so very courteous and gracious, Louisa," he said. "Everyone needs some chance to let out real feelings."

"I could shake her," she said. "All she does is complain of damp and drafts, even though Edmund has ordered fires blazing half up the chimney in the drawing room every day for the past two weeks."

"She is upset," he said. "Beckworth shuts himself up in the library most of the time, and she is very much aware that she will be losing her son again next week."

"I know," she said, contrition in her face as she looked up at him. "You are being my conscience, Cedric. I feel for her. I know what it was like to see Dominic go on his way more than once and not know if I would ever see him again. I am dreadfully heartless, aren't I?"

"No," he said, patting her hand. "Just very human. For however much one may sympathize with Lady Beckworth, one cannot but deplore the fact that she seems to have no inner resources with which to cheer herself up."

"I am glad Alexandra is very different from her mama," she said, "though I found her shedding a tear in the nursery yesterday when Edmund was away at the village on business and she was not expecting my arrival. She was very flustered and tried to tell me she had something in her eye before she laughed and told me she was indulging in a fit of the dismals because her brother will soon be on his way."

"They are very close," he said, "and always have been, as I remember." He looked at her consideringly for a moment. "You should get right away for a time, Louisa. Have you never dreamed of traveling? To the north and Scotland, perhaps, or to the Continent?"

She laughed. "Edward and I used to talk about it constantly before we married and for two months afterward," she said. "But Edmund began to put in an appearance, and he put an end to all our dreams. To those dreams, anyway. New ones came instantly to take their place, of course. And we were very well blessed."

"But now," he said, "two of your children are well settled and have family dreams of their own. And Madeline will not be far behind. She and Captain Hands seem very taken with each other. She appears to take him more seriously than I have seen her with anyone else. It's time for new dreams, Louisa."

She smiled and turned her head away from a particularly strong gust of wind. "One thinks there will be nothing else," she said. "One has children, and one's life is so taken up with theirs that one thinks that that will be the whole of life. For Edward it was, of course, poor dear. But then one comes out at the other end of it, and discovers that life still has something to offer. A future. Some excitement, perhaps."

"I would like to travel the Continent with you," he said.

"I would like it too." She smiled up at him. "But it would not be very proper. Perhaps we can organize a party. There must be several of our friends who have not fully comprehended the fact that the wars are over and Europe is safe for travel again."

"It would not be improper if we were married," he said.

"Cedric!" She stopped walking and looked up at him in pure amazement. "Was that a proposal? Was it? We cannot marry. We are friends."

He looked a little sheepish. "And friends cannot marry?" he asked.

"But you love Anne," she said. "And I love Edward. We can never duplicate those loves with each other, my dear."

"Anne and Edward are very far in our past," he said. "In the meantime, Louisa, we are alive. And I have grown very fond of you. I did not realize just how fond until I was away from you last year."

"But married, Cedric," she said. "I have never thought of you in terms of marriage. Of intimacy. Did you have in mind a marriage in all its meanings?"

He grinned at her suddenly. "I had hoped that I would have enough youthful energy left to make love to you, yes," he said.

Lady Amberley blushed. "Oh, gracious," she said. "I am speechless, Cedric. I am as flustered as a girl."

"Perhaps you would like to think about it," he said, "instead of slapping my face and giving an instant rejection. Will you think about it?"

"It will be very hard to think of anything else," she said. She searched his eyes and blushed again. "Gracious, Cedric, I have never once thought of such a thing. You were Edward's dear friend, and have been mine for years. I have never thought of our being lovers. Yes, I will think of it, my friend. And I think—yes, I am sure—that my head is quite, quite free of cobwebs again. Oh, goodness, how very foolish. Edmund and Dominic have two children apiece and their mama is up here on the cliffs listening to a marriage proposal and finding it quite impossible to stop blushing."

Sir Cedric took her arm through his again. "We will change the subject," he said, "and you will tell me as you usually do up here how you would love to paint the sea and how you always find it impossible to do so to your satisfaction. But before you do, you must assure me that whatever you decide, our friendship will not end. It won't, Louisa?"

"What a ridiculous notion," she said. "How could we not be friends? The greatest frustration on a day like this, you know, is that the water and sky would be so very exciting to paint and yet it would not be within the bounds of possibility to stand an easel up here in this wind or keep paper on it or paint on the brush. And I cannot paint from memory. I have to be right there, feeling and hearing and smelling the scene as well as seeing it."

THE DAY BEFORE THE BALL was the first lovely summer's day for weeks. A hastily organized party of young people rode up the hill west of Amberley and past the

Carringtons' house, where Anna and Walter joined the group, and along the top of the valley to the old ruined abbey where the picnic was to have been two weeks before.

"It was almost totally destroyed at the time of the dissolution of the monasteries," Madeline explained to Captain Hands. "It must have been large and very beautiful."

"But it made a marvelous playground when we were all children," Walter said. "We could hide for hours and not be found."

"Susan and I were sent to hide once, I remember," Madeline said, "and we stayed concealed forever, giggling and proud of ourselves until we discovered that every last one of you boys had crept down into the valley looking for fish in the river. Susan cried oceans and I was so furious that I punched out at all of you. I think that was the time I gave Dom his black eye."

"Susan was still crying when we arrived home," Howard said. "And then she cried all evening too because Papa gave me a thrashing."

They all laughed.

Madeline was feeling relaxed. James Purnell was not with them, having decided to spend an afternoon with his mother and sister. It was only when she thought of the reason for his doing so that her stomach threatened to turn the old somersaults. He would be leaving in two days' time. He and Jean Cameron would be starting their return journey to London, with a maid, the afternoon after the ball.

But she would not think of it. She would only will the two days to pass as uneventfully as the previous two weeks had done. She had not seen him alone in all that time, and had exchanged no private conversation with him. He had been as intent as she on preserving a distant civility.

And apart from that one lapse at the Mortons' party and afterward when Edmund had found her in the conservatory, she had everything to be proud of in her new life. She had not thought it would be so easy. Captain Hands was a serious young man on whom flirtation would not have worked at all. In the past few weeks they had talked their way into an easy friendship. He had not kissed her again, but there was Edmund's ball the next day.

It would be good to have a betrothal to announce at the ball. The euphoria of it would carry her safely through the ordeal of the next few days. And would carry her contentedly through the remainder of a lifetime.

The two of them rode on at a leisurely pace while the others dismounted in order to explore the ruins of the old abbey.

"I was fortunate to be stationed here," Captain Hands said. "It is a lovely part of the country."

"I think so," she said. "But of course, I am partial."

They talked easily on, without having to give conscious thought to the topic.

"You will be at my brother's ball tomorrow?" she asked as they turned their horses' heads to walk back again. "In the country even one absentee is sorely missed, you know." She smiled at him.

"Indeed, I would not miss it," he said. He looked at her and hesitated. For once he looked uncomfortable in her presence. "I have an apology to make, Lady Madeline. One I should have made a long time ago."

"Oh, goodness," she said. "What can you possibly have done to offend me?"

"I kissed you," he said.

She laughed. "And you think you owe me an apology for that?" she asked. "It was nothing, I assure you. I am no green girl."

"You are very lovely," he said, "and very attractive. I forgot myself."

"And at the time I believe I was quite glad that you did," she said. "Please think no more of it."

"But I did you wrong," he said. He glanced swiftly at her and ahead again. "And someone else."

"Oh?" She smiled brightly at him.

"I am promised to someone else," he said, "and have been almost since our infancy. Our parents are planning betrothal celebrations for Christmastime. I am fond of her and owe her better than to be dallying after someone who is lovelier than she."

"But you must not exaggerate," Madeline said. "You have not dallied with me. We shared one very brief kiss on the evening we first met and since then have developed a companionable friendship. That is hardly infidelity, sir."

"I should have told you sooner," he said. "I have been feeling guilty."

Madeline laughed. "If every man who has ever kissed me were to feel that he had somehow compromised me and himself," she said, "I am afraid there would be a large number of guilty hearts strewn around England. If I had known that you took that one so seriously, I would have disabused your mind a long time ago. I had quite forgot it, sir."

"It is kind of you to say so," he said.

"Indeed, now you have made me feel guilty," she said. "Because obviously something that was so carelessly given might have been taken seriously if circumstances had been different. You remind me to be more careful in future, for I would not wish to hurt any man by raising hopes that I am not prepared to satisfy."

"I am greatly relieved," he said, "and I have learned my lesson, I assure you. Will you dance with me tomorrow night?"

"I will be mortally offended if you do not claim me for at least one set," she said with a laugh. "We are back to the others already. What a shame! I would have liked to hear about your soon-to-be betrothed. What is her name?"

During the leisurely ride back to Amberley, Madeline did not know quite whether she more wished to laugh or cry. There was cause for laughter, certainly. She had just been given a memorable lesson in humility. She had been so very confident that any man she chose to smile at would be only too happy to marry her that she had not once considered the possibility that Captain Hands would not make her an offer. It was very amusing. And she was surprised to find that she really did find it so.

But there was also cause for tears. Her new life was threatening to come crashing down about her ears. And she would have no one and nothing with which to fortify herself over the coming two days.

She would just have to do it alone. And her sense of worth was certainly not so fragile that it would crumble at one setback. Besides, she thought, totally ignoring the conversation about her for a few moments and concentrating hard on the state of her own emotions, she was not about to suffer a broken heart over the captain. She did not love him at all. She had merely considered that he might be a sensible choice of husband. There must be any number of such sensible choices just waiting for her to make them.

On the whole, she decided, laughing at some absurdity of Walter's that she had only half heard, it would be better far to laugh. It was not easy to laugh at oneself, but it was doubtless good for the soul.

ALEXANDRA WAS STROLLING across the lawn at Amberley, leaning on her brother's arm. Lady Beckworth had not, after all, spent much time with them. She had retired to her room after half an hour in the drawing room with them, with a headache.

"You should have gone riding with the others," Alexandra said. "We have not had many days like this lately. It is a shame to be confined to the house and grounds."

"I can't think of anywhere I would rather be at the moment," he said.

She smiled at him. "Edmund would have stayed," she said. "But I knew he was pining for exercise, and Christopher has been pleading to go to the beach. They will doubtless have a good run, the two of them with Caroline, and come back with apple cheeks and raging appetites. Edmund knew I wanted to spend this afternoon with you."

"I just wish there were not this parting facing us," he said. "It is always hard to say good-bye."

She held more tightly to his arm. "Don't talk about it, James," she said. "Tell me, are you looking forward to being back in Montreal? I mean, really looking forward to it?"

"Yes," he said. "I found myself again when I was there, Alex. But I am not as strong in myself as I thought. Apart from you and the children, there is only depression here. And a sense of my own inadequacy."

She touched her temple to his shoulder. "I am a very happy person," she said. "But I will not be fully so until I hear that you are finally contented, James. I mean fully contented, with nothing missing from your life. Are you still planning to marry Miss Cameron?"

"No." He smiled. "It seems that I have been adopted as elder brother. But I think I like that relationship better than husband."

"Oh, dear," she said. "Is that how she sees you?"

"Entirely," he said. "With a smacking kiss on the cheek to prove it, and a cheerful judgment that I am silly."

"What about Madeline?" she asked quietly.

"No," he said. It sounded for a moment as if he were struggling for words, but he did not speak them. "No, Alex."

"Ah," she said, and let the matter drop. "Have you talked to Papa, James? Are you going to leave without doing so?"

"You seem to have a reasonably good relationship with him," he said. "How do you do it?"

"By refusing to do anything but love him," she said. "When he scolds and frowns and moralizes, I merely put my arms about him and tell him that I love him. And then he scolds and grumbles and mumbles until I leave the room. But I think he is not displeased. Poor Papa. He is so intent on living the virtuous life and being without sin that he cannot show his love. Love is weakness to him. Edmund taught me a long time ago that it is only love that matters."

"I must talk to Papa again," he said. "I don't suppose I shall ever forgive myself or ever live at peace with myself if I don't. And yet I know that it will be quite as pointless to do so as it was the first time. And I can't quite picture myself listening to him and then kissing him and telling him that I love him."

"You are his son," she said. "His heir. And so he loves you most and finds you most impossible to love, James."

He stopped walking suddenly. "I am procrastinating," he said. "I have done so all month here. But I can't leave it until the day of the ball, can I? And certainly not until the day after. Are you ready to go in, Alex? I'm going to find him out right now."

"Leave me, then," she said. "I need a little more air and exercise."

He turned to leave, his face hard and serious.

"James?" she said.

He turned back to her and she walked quickly toward him. She put her arms about his neck and kissed him warmly on the cheek. "I love you," she said.

He smiled somewhat grimly. "Am I now supposed to scold and grumble and mumble but not be entirely displeased?" he asked. He kissed her on the cheek. "I love you too, Alex."

11

ORD BECKWORTH, HAVING TAKEN A SOLITARY stroll up along the valley earlier in the afternoon, was settled in the library with a book, as he so often was. He looked over the top of it and set it down when his son came into the room.

"It is a lovely day again," James said lamely. "I have been walking in the garden with Alex."

"Hm," Lord Beckworth said. "She ought to be in the nursery with her children."

James let the remark pass. He took the chair across from his father's. "I will be leaving here the day after tomorrow," he said. "We will probably set sail for Canada within the week."

"It will be as well when you are gone," the other said. "Your mother does nothing but cry when you are here. I hope you are proud of yourself."

"Neither proud nor ashamed," James said carefully. "It is my chosen life, and I have worked hard and honestly to establish a place for myself. I am sorry if it does not meet with your approval and Mama's. I really am sorry. I hoped to return with your blessing and your love."

His father looked at him with the steady, cold eyes that

had always been able to cause other eyes to drop before them. James's eyes wavered and held.

"You forfeited both a long time ago, James," Lord Beckworth said.

James closed his eyes and leaned his head back against the chair. "You do not love me," he said. "You can offer me no peace. And yet you resent the fact that I went away and that I am going away again. What do you want of me?"

"I want nothing," Lord Beckworth said sternly. "I am merely your earthly father, James. I believe another Father demands a change of heart in you, a repentant heart, and a dutiful and a filial heart. I see no signs of repentance in you despite your protestations of need."

James sighed but did not open his eyes. "I was so very young," he said. "Can you not make allowances for youthful wildness and rebellion?"

"You had been brought up to the straight and narrow path to salvation," his father said. "I cannot forgive the sins of fornication and riotousness. I do not have the power to offer such forgiveness. The shame and the suffering to your mother and Alexandra and to me I could forgive. And I have forgiven them even as I am to expect forgiveness. But I cannot forget them for as long as your heart is hardened."

"I loved her," James said, "with all the ardor of a young and first love. Whether I would have continued to do so I do not know. That does not matter now. I was twenty and she seventeen. It was wrong, yes, to lie together as we did. The consequences showed that. We could have learned to take the consequences together. Perhaps we would have been happy; perhaps not. But we should have been allowed to put right what we had put wrong."

"I would not have seen my son married to a slut," Lord Beckworth said fiercely.

James opened his eyes and gripped the arms of his chair. But he held on to his temper. "Dora was not a slut," he said. "She gave me a husband's privilege, which she should not have given and I should not have taken. But she was not a slut. She was young and in love."

"Youth does not excuse such sin," his father said. "And even at the time you would not show the proper shame. There were all the eruptions of violence. And years of sullen anger afterward. Your mother and I had a great deal to put up with, James. And you expect me now to forget?"

James surged to his feet and began to pace the room. "Why did you do it?" he asked. "I could never make proper sense of it. She was very young, it is true, and I can understand that you were ambitious for me since I was your only son. I can see that you might have thought my future would be blighted by a marriage when I had not even finished at university. But she would not have been an ineligible match, by any means. She was the Duke of Peterleigh's ward. She was not a nobody."

"She was a slut," Lord Beckworth said.

James paused in his pacing and pushed back with some impatience the lock of hair that had fallen across his brow. "If she was," he said, "then I was the male equivalent. You knew I loved her. You must have known something of the heartbreak you would cause. Why did you marry her off in such haste to Drummond? You and Peterleigh between you? I don't blame Peterleigh so much. He was in London and doubtless did not know the true state of affairs. I am sure you would have covered the truth in your communications with him. And her brother would not have acted alone—he would not have stood against you and

Peterleigh. You are the one who did it all. Paid off Drummond. Intimidated Dora. Prevented her from communicating with me and not doing so yourself until it was too late. Why did you do it? Just tell me."

"I did it to save us all from scandal," his father said, his voice rising. "I did it to save my son from the embraces of a whore. I hoped that you would be capable of acknowledging your sins and freeing yourself of them before your immortal soul was put in eternal danger."

James stopped pacing and stood looking down at his father. "Did you not know how you would destroy me?" he asked. "Or her? Did you have no compassion whatsoever for the feelings of a young girl who had no one but a young brother and an absent guardian to defend her? Did you not see that you gave me no path to redemption? And did you expect me to find my way back to God when you withdrew from me even the restrained signs of love that you had shown me through my childhood and boyhood? Did you not see how very wrong you were?"

Lord Beckworth slammed a fist on the arm of his chair. "Enough!" he said. "You are unchanged, unregenerate. Your sin must be turned from yourself and thrown onto me. It was always so. I am loaded down with enough guilt, James, without taking yours on my shoulders too. I am burdened with the sin of having been a too indulgent father. If I had not spared the rod when you were a boy, perhaps I would not now be responsible for the peril your soul is in."

"Spared the rod," James said quietly. "Did you? I dread to think what Alex and I might have suffered if you had been a harsh parent, then. It seems to me that the rod figured very prominently in our upbringing. Perhaps if there had been less rod and more love, I would have been a little more responsible in the expression of my love for Dora. Perhaps I might have saved her from great suffering."

Lord Beckworth's breathing was loud and harsh. "You dare to preach to me about love?" he said. "You dare to stand there and say these things to me?" His hand went to his chest.

James was down on one knee before his father immediately. "Is something wrong?" he asked. "Your heart?"

"The only thing wrong with me," Lord Beckworth said, sinking back in his chair and letting go of his rage, "is having to listen to an undutiful son."

James sighed. "I did not come here to accuse you," he said. "Time has cleared my vision. I can see that what you did, you did with what you thought were my best interests at heart. I no longer hate you or even blame you. Occasionally we all do wrong things from right motives. Only time can prove us right or wrong. The past is the past. Nothing can change it now, and who is to say that it was all wrong, anyway? Let's forgive each other and forget, shall we?"

His father laughed. His hand was still over his heart. He was still breathing quickly. "You forgive me," he said. "You impudent puppy."

James pushed himself to his feet again. "Very well, then," he said wearily. "It's unimportant. Let us not part bitter enemies. Forgive me, then, will you? For all I have done to offend you, forgive me."

"You can best show your sorrow to me," his father said, "by going from this room to your own and falling on your knees and begging forgiveness from above."

"Give me your blessing." James held out his right hand. "Don't let me go without your blessing."

His father ignored the hand. "If you are truly contrite,"

he said, "you will give up this vulgar pursuit of yours, James, and come home where you belong. I cannot give you my blessing to go and break your mother's heart."

James's hand closed upon itself. "Well, then," he said, "so be it." He turned to leave the room. But he paused with his hand on the doorknob and turned back to look at his father. "I love you," he said. "Despite everything, you gave me life and you sheltered me and brought me up according to what you believed true principles. I would like to leave with your blessing. It will always hurt me that you would not give it. But you must remain true to yourself to the end, I see. I will console myself with the belief that your very anger with me shows that you also love me." He opened the door and shut it quietly behind him.

Lord Beckworth closed his eyes and clenched his teeth hard. His hands gripped the arms of his chair with such force that his knuckles turned white.

THE STATE APARTMENTS, the pride and joy of the Earl of Amberley, were always opened for the annual summer ball and for a few very special occasions, like weddings. Dinner was served in the state dining room, and the ball-room was so decked out with flowers that it was indistinguishable from the garden beyond the French doors, Sir Cedric said. The flowers and the splendid clothes of the guests were multiplied in grandeur by the long mirrors that stretched along one wall.

"I can remember what an agony the ball always was after I was past about my twelfth birthday," Anna told Jean as they stood fanning themselves against the mirrors, waiting for the dancing to begin. "I was brought over here, as we always were, to sleep in the nursery, and we were allowed to creep into the minstrels' gallery to hear the orchestra and to see all the fashions and watch the opening quadrille. I say 'we,' though for the last few years it was just me. I thought the time would never come when I would be allowed to come downstairs and dance too."

"I think Nanny Rey has Christopher up there now," Jean said, peering up at the minstrels' gallery, which had never been used as anything but a not-so-secret hideout for the children of the family. "I heard the countess say that he was too excited to go to sleep."

"Mr. Purnell is to dance the opening set with you?" Anna asked. "How fortunate you are. He has not signed my card yet, though he surely will, will he not? I am still chagrined that I did not know he was not your beau. I might have had him on his knees before me by now. But how heart-wrenching a parting there would be tomorrow. Perhaps it is as well I did not know." She giggled. "I was truly annoyed when Lieutenant Cowley asked for the first set before Sir Gordon had a chance to do so. But all is well. He has asked for a waltz, and that comes second."

The earl began the ball by leading his countess onto the floor.

"I think all our guests are enjoying themselves," she said beneath the sounds of the music.

"But of course," he said. "It is strictly forbidden not to enjoy oneself at the Amberley ball, you know."

"Did we enjoy our first?" she asked.

He grimaced and took one of her hands in his. "I was to break our engagement the next morning," he said, "because you wished to be free and I wanted to do the noble thing. And then you announced its end at suppertime, to Mama and your parents. And I had to continue to host the ball and smile and smile. No, it was not my happiest evening, I suppose."

"It was not mine, either," she said.

"Of course—" he brought his mouth close to her ear, "the hours following the ball more than made up for any unhappiness during it."

"Yes," she said.

"A memorable night," he said. "Our first lovemaking." He smiled at her. "Up in our hut in the hills. Where Christopher was conceived."

"Edmund," she said, flushing, "this is not at all proper conversation for such a time and place. Will any romances flourish here tonight, do you think? Anna and Sir Gordon Clark, perhaps? And Madeline and Captain Hands? They really seem to deal splendidly together."

"We will hope for at least one," he said.

Anna achieved one of her goals, as she confided to Jean during supper. Sir Gordon Clark had kissed her and expressed a hope of seeing her and renewing his acquaintance with her in London the following spring.

"I shall die if Papa will not take us," she whispered, round-eyed. "He has been saying that we will definitely not go there for a third Season in a row, but Papa is such a dreadful tease that one never knows when he is serious and when he is not. Mama says that I can wrap him around my little finger. I do hope that is true. I am going to set to work on him tomorrow."

"Do you think Sir Gordon really meant it?" Jean asked.

"Of course he meant it," Anna said. "He kissed my lips and my temples—and my throat, Jean. He kisses quite divinely. And the feel of those curls around my fingers! I am deep in love, I promise you. And he is to be here for almost a week more. Who knows what will happen during that time?"

There was no more chance for whispered confidences. Their supper partners had brought them plates of food.

But Jean would have had nothing to confide anyway. She had danced every set, and everyone had been obligingly kind to her, but Howard Courtney had not asked for her hand even once. Perhaps he would not have done so at all had she not caught his eye quite by accident across the supper room and smiled at him. As it was, he came to her directly after supper and asked for the set of country dances to follow.

Jean could have wept at the intricacy of the steps, which separated them for most of the set and did not permit conversation even when they were together. She smiled her way through a half hour of energetic frustration.

"I should say good-bye," she said in desperation, smiling gaily as he led her across the floor when the music finally ended. "I shall be leaving tomorrow and probably will not see you again after tonight."

"You will be missed," Howard said. "You are well liked in this neighborhood."

"I have liked it here," she said, holding on to her smile by sheer willpower. "I will always remember everyone."

Captain Hands was bowing and asking if she was free for the next set. She turned her smile on him.

"Miss Cameron has promised it to me," Howard said hastily.

"That's right," she said. "But thank you, sir. Perhaps later?"

Captain Hands bowed and withdrew.

"I-I'm sorry," Howard stammered. "I don't know what came over me. Did you want to dance with him?"

"No," she said, looking up at him. "I want to dance with you, Mr. Courtney."

"It is a waltz," he said. "I never could learn the steps. I'll probably tread all over your feet."

"Perhaps we could stroll on the terrace," she suggested, and blushed at her own boldness.

"Will you?" he asked.

She nodded and took his arm.

"You will be looking forward to seeing your father and brother again," he said.

"Yes, sir."

"And to returning home."

"Yes."

"Do you like sailing?" he asked. "Does it make you sick? Or frighten you?"

"Neither," she said. "It is just a little tedious, that is all, and the food monotonous."

"You will be glad to see the end of the crossing, then."

"Yes, sir."

There were other couples on the terrace, enjoying the coolness of the evening air. There seemed to be nothing else to say. But instead of turning back when they had strolled the length of the terrace, Howard continued on down the steps that led to a wide lawn below.

"I will miss you," he said.

"Will you?"

"I don't mingle very well with others," he said. "Words do not come easily to me. I have only my own life to talk about and there is nothing very exciting about that."

"Conversation does not have to be exciting," she said.

"Interesting is enough. Another person's life is always interesting."

"You are kind," he said. "Your life in Canada must be exciting. Life on an English farm is quiet and a constant round of routine activities. Social life is not very active, especially in the winter and spring."

"Winters are long in Montreal," she said, "and life is frequently tedious. I don't think routine would be dull when it involves the changing of the seasons and the living things of nature."

"I have had my own farm for only a year," he said. "The house seems large and very quiet after my father's house."

"I daresay he thought the same about his when he started out," she said.

"You would miss your family if you were separated from them by an ocean," he said.

"Yes, sir," she said, "though Papa has been back and forth to England for years."

He stopped walking suddenly and pulled her awkwardly into his arms. He kissed her just as awkwardly and so hard that she could feel her teeth cutting her lip. He released her as abruptly as he had seized her.

"I do beg your pardon," he said. "You will find my advances offensive. I am seen as a dull and plodding fellow, I know. And the description is accurate. That is what I am."

"I see you rather as sturdy and amiable, sir," she said. "And I am not offended."

He had her hands in his and was holding them so tightly that Jean had to concentrate on not wincing.

"Then Mr. Purnell will doubtless challenge me if he sees us," he said. "You are to marry him? It is fitting. He is a gentleman."

"I am not going to marry Mr. Purnell, or anyone else that I know of," she said.

"If I just had more to offer you," he said. "If I were a gentleman of wealth and position. Or if I were more of a dashing fellow. I had better take you inside. I ought not to have brought you down off the terrace."

"I don't want a gentleman of wealth and position," she said. "I would be uncomfortable with such a husband, Mr. Courtney. My father has worked hard all his life to make a respectable living. I grew up in an atmosphere of industry. And I don't want a dashing fellow. I would not be comfortable with him. I want a cozy home of my own and a husband whose company and devotion I can depend upon."

"You don't want me," he said firmly, squeezing her hands a little harder, so that she bit her lower lip.

"I can't answer that unless I know I am being offered you," she said.

"Would you?" he asked hesitantly. "If I asked you?"

"Marry you?" she asked.

"Would you?"

"Yes, I would, sir," she said.

"Will you marry me?"

"Yes, I will, Mr. Courtney," she said, wasting a dazzling smile on the darkness.

"But perhaps your father will not allow it," he said.

"And perhaps he will," she said.

"But you are to return to him tomorrow," he said, "and sail for Canada next week."

"Yes."

Somehow his arms were about her waist and hers about his neck.

"I'll travel to London tomorrow," he said with sudden

reckless decision, "before you. You must tell me where to find him. I have never been there before."

"Oh, will you, Mr. Courtney?" she asked. "You will ask Papa?"

"I'll leave in the morning," he said. " Shall we go inside and tell my parents, Miss Cameron? They will be very happy, I assure you."

"Had you not better kiss me again first?" Jean asked shyly. "You have not kissed me since we were betrothed."

"I am afraid I don't do it well," Howard said. "I have never..."

"Neither have I," Jean said. "We will learn together, shall we? Will you call me Jean?"

He kissed her fiercely again until he felt her fingertips against his cheeks. And then they explored each other's lips awkwardly and tentatively and gently.

"I may be a dull fellow, Jean," Howard said at last, "but you will always have my devotion. I can safely promise you that because my father has always been devoted to my mother, and it has always been my goal to emulate him."

"I love you, Howard," Jean said.

He looked at her, arrested, in the darkness. "Do you?" he asked in some surprise. "Do you really?"

IT WAS AN EVENING to be proud of. She had moved through it with the dignity of her years—not with determined and forced gaiety, and with no flirtatiousness. She had been cheerful and gracious. She had talked with all their neighbors and friends and danced every set with a different gentleman.

But there were limits to one's endurance. Madeline was

proud of herself, and she knew that she would not break but that she would go on to live her new life, and be happy with it too, for it was not in her nature to be unhappy for any length of time. But there were times for unhappiness, and there was one such time looming very close ahead.

The next few days would be ones of excruciating pain. She knew it and accepted the fact. If she tried to deny it, then she would not be able to endure. She would be her former bright and flighty self and she would be out of control of her own life.

She must live through the next few days and weeks with as much fortitude as she could muster. But she must expect to be submerged in misery on occasion.

One such occasion came toward the end of the ball, when she realized that it was well past midnight and that this already was the day of his departure. Soon the ball would be at an end and they would all go to bed and sleep until late in the morning. And then there would be a great hustle and bustle, and Lady Beckworth and Alexandra would be crying. And he would be gone.

She could not stay to dance anymore. She could not. Perhaps if she slipped away and went to bed and slept, she would sleep too long. And when she got up, he would be gone already. Perhaps she would be that fortunate.

But she could not go to bed either. It would be worse there in the silence of her own room, counting off the hours.

She went to the only place she could go, the place where she supposed she had known all evening she would go eventually. She left the ballroom by the French doors and walked around to the front of the house and the formal gardens. And she walked along the gravel paths until she reached one of the stone fountains. It was where she had danced with him and kissed him the last time. The place where they had not said good-bye because she had not known that he was going.

She stood looking down into the water of the basin, its ripples sparkling in the moonlight. And she trailed her hand through the water, noting its coolness. She did not turn when she heard the crunching of the gravel behind her. She knew who it was. There was no doubt in her mind at all. She did not need to turn.

"It's hard to believe that four years have passed," she said when the footsteps finally stopped.

"Yes," he said.

"But this time you are to do things properly," she said, turning to face him and smiling. The moon was behind him. His face was in darkness. "The proper farewells tomorrow instead of the riding off into the darkness."

"Yes," he said. "The good-byes tomorrow. Most of them. But not you. I would rather not see you tomorrow."

She wrapped her arms around herself, hugging her pain to herself. But there was no offense to be taken. She did not want to see him the next day either.

His right hand was extended. "Good-bye, Madeline," he said.

She looked at it for a long time before placing her own in it and feeling its strong clasp. "Good-bye, James."

But he did not turn to leave when their hands parted company. He stood looking at her, and she fixed her eyes on the whiteness that must be his neckcloth and concentrated on committing him to memory. For she knew she would feed on this moment for weeks to come. Perhaps for months or years.

When his fingertips traced lightly the line of her jaw

and came to rest beneath her chin, she closed her eyes and felt them there with every nerve ending in her body.

"I wonder if we might have been friends had we tried," he said softly. "Or does the antagonism go to the very roots of our characters? As does the attraction."

She could not answer. She could not have forced a single word past the rawness of her throat if it had been necessary to save her life. She kept her eyes closed and shook her head slightly.

"Well," he said, "I suppose the question is academic now."

She could no more open her eyes than she could speak. His fingertips remained beneath her chin. His mouth when it touched hers did so softly and lingeringly.

And then hand and mouth were gone, and she could hear the quiet crunching of gravel again. But she did not open her eyes. She had all the food for her memories that she would ever gather.

THE EARL OF AMBERLEY was bidding farewell to his guests, his wife beside him.

A lovely ball, Edmund," Sir Peregrine Lampman said, shaking hands with his friend. "Though I am mortally offended that your wife had no dance free for me."

"An undiscriminating lady, Alex," the earl said with a grin. "She accepts the hand of any partner who asks. Try again next year, Perry. Grace, my dear, we must thank you for bringing your niece with you tonight and her husband and brother. The young ladies have been particularly pleased with Sir Gordon, as you will have seen for yourself."

"Splendid ball, splendid ball," William Carrington said

with a beaming smile and a smacking kiss on the cheek for his niece by marriage. "But I plan to post up to town within the week, Edmund, and spread the latest gossip. You danced only once with your wife. Shocking, my boy."

"Oh, William!" his wife said, flushing and clutching at his arm. "Take no notice of him, Edmund. He does like to tease. Anyone knows that it would not be at all the thing for you to dance with Alexandra all night."

"A wonderful evening, as usual, my lord," Mr. Courtney said, taking the earl's hand in a bruising clasp and nodding genially to the countess. "Wonderful evening. I can speak for my whole family, and only wish that my Susan were here too. She will be sorry to have missed it. But her mama will be able to tell her all about it." He beamed at his host and hostess and leaned toward them conspiratorially, though his lowered voice was still several times louder than the normal voice of any of his neighbors. "Sooner than expected."

"You are leaving for London very soon?" the earl asked, smiling at Mrs. Courtney. "You must give our regards to Susan, if you please."

"It's very good of you to say so, I am sure, my lord," Mr. Courtney said, still in his lowered voice. "Mrs. Courtney will be leaving tomorrow. Mr. Purnell has graciously consented to her riding in the carriage with Miss Cameron instead of a maid. And Howard is to ride along with Mr. Purnell. I can whisper to present company, my lord and lady, though there can be nothing official, of course, until the young lady's papa has given his consent."

The earl looked with polite interest at his neighbor and at a flushing Howard behind him.

"Miss Cameron has this very night accepted the offer of

our Howard," Mr. Courtney announced in triumph. "And Mrs. Courtney and I are brimful of pride and pleasure."

"Why, Howard!" The earl stretched out a hand to his tenant and shook his heartily. "My congratulations. I am sure you have made a wise choice. Where is Miss Cameron?"

She was standing a short distance away, her arm drawn through James's, looking anxious and embarrassed. She seemed considerably more relieved after the earl had kissed her cheek and the countess had hugged her.

"I hope you will not think I have taken advantage of your hospitality," she said.

"I have been scheming for all of a year to get Howard suitably married off," Edmund said. "My tenants need wives, you know, if they are to have prosperous farms and comfortable homes and contented hearts. I could not have chosen better myself."

Jean looked up at James, who was smiling reassuringly down at her, and shyly across at her betrothed. He hovered in the background while his mother and father felt constrained to hug her once more before taking their leave. She felt rather as if every bone in her body had been squeezed almost to breaking point when she emerged from Mr. Courtney's fond and fatherly embrace.

"Another daughter to love soon enough," he said, chucking her under the chin. "And for you another papa as soon as ever you leave the altar, my dear. I am well blessed indeed. Well blessed."

Alexandra was looking at her brother with a pale face, which showed clearly that she had lost all interest in any conversation going on around her. And he looked back, his smile fading.

12

JAMES PURNELL AND DUNCAN CAMERON WERE standing side by side on the deck of the *Adeona*. They were both leaning on the rail, looking out across the river to the city of London. The ship would sail with the tide.

"I am glad I have had a look at it, even if only once," Duncan said. "But I can't say I am sorry to be leaving. Give me a quieter life any day."

"Yes," James said. "I have never been overfond of London."

"Yet my father has chosen to stay here for yet another winter," Duncan said, shaking his head. "I don't think I could stay even for one."

"You must admit he has good reason to change his mind," James said. "It would be a very lonely feeling for Jean to wave the both of you good-bye when she is not even married yet."

"You think she will be happy with Courtney?" his friend asked. "I must confess I think she could have done better for herself. She certainly has all the looks in our family, anyway."

"The Courtneys are quite prosperous," James said, "and very industrious. They are well respected. And there seems to be a great deal of family affection among them. I think she stands as good a chance for happiness as she would in any other marriage."

"Well," Duncan said, "it's her choice, I suppose. For myself, I have a hankering to get back to my woman and our son. I confess to having found English beauties insipid. Next spring I'll be on my way back with the brigades. You too, James?"

His friend shrugged. "I daresay," he said. "One can do much worse with one's life."

They lapsed into silence, the one allowing his thoughts to slip ahead of him to the country he was going to and ahead in time to the following spring when he could join a canoe brigade again and leave civilization behind him until he found the small trading post he would call home and the black-haired woman and the chubby black-eyed child he had left behind him well over a year before.

James could not think ahead. His thoughts were still firmly anchored in the island he was leaving. He watched idly the little boats on the river, each busy about its own business. And he saw his mother with a handkerchief pressed to her eyes and Alex pale and smiling and hugging him close. And his father, who had surprised him by coming outside to the carriage when he left and shaking hands with him, though his face was as if carved out of marble and his eyes cold.

He had not asked himself too closely what it had meant. He preferred to assume that there was after all love for him in his father, a love that could not or would not express itself in words. There was a small measure of peace—very small—in the assumption.

Madeline had been noticeably absent, though she had been standing at the front window of the long gallery. He had seen her there when he looked up, desperate for one more sight of her. She had not ducked back out of sight. And she had not smiled or made any acknowledgment of his half-raised hand.

One of the small boats appeared to be making its way toward the *Adeona*. James watched it without interest or curiosity.

He should have tried, perhaps, to make a friend of her. He had known as soon as he first set eyes on her again that he had not worked her from his system. He had known that his attraction to her was many times stronger than it had been before, because it had had four years in which to grow. He should have tried to make something of it.

Instead, he had allowed resentment and attraction to war inside him every time he had been in her presence. Resentment and fear.

Fear that he would love her too dearly and bring her to love him, and then find that he could not offer her a whole heart, a guiltless heart. Fear perhaps that if he acknowledged his love, it would be taken away from him as the first had been. Fear that she would be destroyed by his love as Dora had been.

He would not think of it. He was going away for good this time. He would never see her again.

"He looks familiar," he said to Duncan, frowning and pointing to a man wrapped in a cloak and sitting in the middle of the little boat that was approaching. "Who is he?"

But the answer came to him before his friend could look and shake his head and declare that he had never seen the fellow in his life. He was one of the servants at Amberley Court.

His father! Something had happened to him. He could

feel his heart pounding and the blood beating against his temples.

He was at the head of the ladder when the servant finally climbed on board. He looked questioningly at the man, who merely handed him a letter in silence.

"Is anything the matter, James?" Duncan Cameron asked a minute later.

"It's my father," James said, staring down at the brief and hastily written note in his hand. "He has had a heart seizure."

"Oh, man," Duncan said, clapping his friend on the shoulder. "Bad, is it?"

"Amberley seems to think so," James said. He gazed down at his letter for another minute before crumpling it in his hand and looking at Duncan with sudden decision. "Do you think you can see to having my trunks brought up here while I talk with the captain?"

Duncan clapped him on the shoulder again before disappearing below.

Less than half an hour later, James Purnell was sitting in the little boat beside the servant from Amberley, raising a hand in a final farewell to his friend, who stood at the rail of the *Adeona* again.

"ALEX." The earl took her by the shoulders and spoke quietly into her ear. "You must come and rest, my love."

She was sitting beside her father's bed, listening to his loud and labored breathing, watching his half-closed eyelids and his white, cold hands on the covers. Her mother was sitting behind her at the window, weeping, the dowager Lady Amberley at her side.

"What?" she said.

"You must come and rest," the earl said again. "You have been sitting here for five hours."

She rose obediently and allowed him to lead her from the room, one arm about her shoulders. "I think he is better," she said. "His breathing is steadier."

"You must rest," he said, leading her to their bedchamber. "You have not slept, Alex."

"Did you notice?" she asked, obeying the pressure of his hands and sitting on the edge of the bed while he stooped down to remove her slippers. "Do you think he is getting better, Edmund?"

He got to his feet, his task completed, and framed her face with his hands. "We will hope so, my love," he said. "But we must keep in mind what Doctor Hanson has said."

"He is wrong," she said, bending her head forward as his hands began to remove the pins from her hair. "I know he is wrong, Edmund. Papa is a strong man. And he has recovered from a seizure before."

He bent and kissed her lips before disappearing briefly into her dressing room to fetch a brush. He began to pull it through her hair. "Fifty strokes only," he said, "and then you are going to lie down. And you are going to sleep. I will stay here until you do, and there will be stern words, I promise, if you are not asleep within ten minutes."

"You will call me, Edmund, if anything...?" She looked up at him frantically.

"I will call you," he said.

"And if James comes?" She watched him take her brush back to the dressing room and waited like a child for him to fold back the bedcovers before lying back against the pillows. "He will come, Edmund, won't he? Your letter will have reached him in time? And he will come?"

He covered her up, kissed her again, and lay down beside her, on top of the covers, his hands clasped behind his head. "The letter may have been too late," he said. "The ship may have sailed. We both know that, Alex. We should know for sure tomorrow. Peters should be back then. Go to sleep, love. You have only nine minutes left in which to avoid a severe scolding."

She turned her head to look at him. "You have always said I need not be obedient to you," she said.

"If women are allowed to change their minds," he said, "then men are allowed to be horrible liars. Stay awake for eight and a half minutes longer, and you will see just how ferociously I can enforce wifely obedience."

She closed her eyes and smiled fleetingly. "I would love to see it," she said. "But I don't think I can stay awake long enough. Remind me to defy you some other time, Edmund."

He had a reply ready, but he looked at her closely and did not make it. He lay where he was for ten more minutes before removing himself from the bed and the room.

MADELINE WAS STANDING on the arched stone bridge across the river, leaning on the balustrade and staring down into the waters that flowed beneath. She had wandered a little way from the house, and drew in slow breaths of fresh air.

She had just seen Sir Perry on his way. An hour before it had been the rector, though Edmund had taken charge of his visit. And a little while before that Anna and Walter had ridden over when she and Sir Cedric were already entertaining Mr. Courtney and Mr. Morton.

The task of dealing with the almost constant flow of

callers fell largely on their shoulders. Lady Beckworth and Alexandra, of course, were spending every waking moment in the sickroom, and Mama was there much of the time. Edmund had the estate business to see to, and he was trying to be both mother and father to the children.

She did not mind doing her small part. Besides, Sir Cedric was a pillar of strength and comfort, as he always had been during times of crisis. She could remember as far back as the time when her father died, curling up on his lap and crying her heart out because Mama had completely collapsed and Edmund had been walking about in a white-faced daze and Dominic had been swaggering around, refusing to show any emotion because he was twelve years old and a man.

Madeline smiled down unseeingly at the water below her. Just a week before she had been wondering what she would do with herself during these days between James's departure from Amberley and his setting sail, how she would keep thought and emotion at bay. None of her carefully laid plans had worked for the first five days.

The pain had been searing and fraught with panic and desperation. If she left now, she had thought a dozen times a day, without any delay whatsoever, taking time only to saddle a horse, perhaps she would be able to reach him in time, in time to …

But there her thoughts had always balked. In time to what? Beg him to stay? Beg to be taken with him? Beg that they try what he had murmured almost to himself at the fountain during the ball—try to become friends? How could they be friends with an ocean between them?

And then on the fifth day Lord Beckworth had collapsed in the drawing room after dinner, and since then the house and all their lives had been in turmoil.

And what now if he should come back? What if Edmund's letter had reached him in time and he had decided to come back rather than sail for Canada?

Madeline glanced up the eastern hillside, up the road that formed the main approach to the house. She realized that she had been doing so every few minutes since she had left the house. Yet even if he came, the earliest they could expect him was the next day.

And what if he came? She was unprepared for his coming. She did not know how she would cope with it.

And what if he did not come? She was unprepared for his not coming. She did not know how she would cope with that either.

There was a lone rider coming down the hillside. But it was not he. He could not be expected until the next day. It would be Mr. Watson or Miles Courtney or someone else. But she straightened up and watched the horseman, and intuition and an accelerated heartbeat told her who it was even before he was close enough for her to see him clearly.

She stayed where she was, turning as he rode closer so that her back was against the balustrade and her hands gripping its top behind her back. His face was pale and unshaven. His tired dark eyes bored into hers as he drew his horse to a halt on the bridge.

"He is still alive," she said.

"Still?" His voice was harsh. "He was not expected to be, then?"

He was waiting for an answer, his eyes holding hers. She shook her head briefly. She thought he was about to say something else, but he did not. He loosened the reins and gave his horse the signal to proceed.

Edmund was waiting on the steps, she saw when she turned her head to look toward the house.

• • •

IT WAS SOME LATE HOUR of the night. James had no idea
what time it was. Indeed, the last few days and nights had
so run together in his mind that he was no longer able to
say what day of the week it was. He had slept for five
hours—at least Edmund had told him it was that long—
after his arrival, after he had hugged his mother and Alex
and had spent an hour standing by his father's bedside,
gazing down at him.

He stood there again now—he had not sat down at all
in this room. His mother was sitting at the window, her
head nodded forward on her chest. Alex had gone to bed,
on the combined insistence of himself and Edmund and
her mother-in-law.

His father's breathing was so labored it was almost a
snore. His eyes were half-open. His hands lay on the covers exactly as they had earlier in the day, when James had
arrived. He had not moved.

The doctor had said there was no realistic hope of recovery. His father was going to die.

James touched the back of one of his father's hands. It
was cold. "Papa," he said, "can you hear me?"

He had no memories of playing with his father. None
of the sorts of memories that Alex's children would have.
Only memories of standing at his father's knee, reciting
Bible verses and other lessons, feeling those keen eyes on
him. And memories of a rare look of pride in those eyes
when he got it all right, without faltering.

He had always wondered, but had never discovered the
truth, if his father had sometimes followed him with his
eyes when he knew himself unobserved, as he had done
occasionally with Alex. Eyes that were softened from
their usual coldness and sternness. Eyes that hinted at an

affection that was never allowed to show itself more openly.

"Don't die," James said. "Open your eyes and know me."

He could remember his mother hugging and kissing them as very young children, and occasionally covering up some mischief, like the time when she had had his muddy clothes smuggled down the back stairs to the kitchen after he had been on a forbidden jaunt out onto the moors. But she had been taught in time that such displays of affection were weakness and would merely encourage waywardness in her children.

"Just one look," he said. "One look of kindness, Papa."

He had feared and worshipped his father. He had spent his childhood and a large part of his boyhood striving to live up to his father's expectations of him. He had not often rebelled, and when he had, he had been consumed with guilt and remorse afterward and a terror of the wrath of both his father and God. He had spent years yearning and striving for his father's love, feeding himself on those few looks of pride.

"Give me your blessing before you die," he said to the comatose man on the bed. "Even if only in a look."

And then there had been school and university and the realization that life was not as harsh in all homes. In some homes there were open expressions of love. In some homes weakness and waywardness and disobedience were treated leniently, smoothed over by the power of love.

And so he had rebelled against his father in the name of love. He had taken Dora, who had grown up on the neighboring estate to theirs with her brother, as wards of the Duke of Peterleigh, and he had loved her and deliberately shown her a free expression of his love. She had not been reluctant. And he had dreamed of a life of love with her.

He had dreamed of freedom. But even without his father's terrible interference, he would not have been free. He knew that now. For he carried his chains inside himself. They were part of his upbringing, part of his character. He was incapable of love, incapable of making love the guiding force of his life.

He could only look at love from the outside and know that he would never be on the inside. Madeline had been right when she had told him years before that he would never be able to run far enough because he would always have to take himself with him.

"I love you," he said to his father. "Tell me that you love me, Papa. Set me free."

He had destroyed Dora. It was not his father who had done that. He had done it. For if he had not lain with her in a fine gesture of defiance against what he had been taught was right, his father would have had nothing to interfere with. Dora would have been free to grow up and choose her own husband or else have someone far more suitable chosen for her.

He could not blame his father for what had happened to her. He was to blame. His one real attempt to love had ended in disaster. He had destroyed another human being.

"Forgive me," he whispered to his father. "I forced you into that difficult situation. It was all my fault, not yours. Forgive me, Papa."

He did not know how much later it was when his father's breathing changed. He listened to it tensely for a few minutes and then crossed the room and opened the door quietly to send the servant who was sitting outside for his sister and brother-in-law. He walked over to his mother and touched her gently on the shoulder.

It was a whole hour after that before his father died.

LADY BECKWORTH DECIDED that it would be madness to try to take her husband's remains back to Yorkshire for burial. The funeral would take place at Amberley, in the village of Abbotsford. He would at least be close to his daughter.

She was not capable of much decision making. She went into a state of collapse after her husband's death and no one was capable of bringing her any comfort, although both her son and her daughter spent much of their time with her, and the earl and his mother attended to her every need.

The funeral was set as far into the future as possible, five days after the death, and Lord Beckworth's sister was sent for. A letter was sent too by servant to Lord and Lady Eden.

And so Madeline had the enormous comfort on the fourth day of seeing her twin's carriage cross the bridge, skirt the formal gardens, and draw up outside the main doors. Ellen was with him.

"Dom," she said an hour later when they had walked outside to take some fresh air. Ellen was sitting inside, holding Alexandra's hand. The babies had been taken upstairs to the nursery. "You can't know how glad I am to see you."

"A house of death is not a happy place to be," he said. "And he lingered for several days? That must have put an extra strain on everyone."

"James arrived here in time at least," she said. "For that

I will always be thankful. Imagine how dreadful it would have been for him, Dom, to have got here the next day to find his father dead already."

Dominic shrugged his arm free of hers and put it about her shoulders. "He looks as if he is turned to stone," he said. "Quite as he used to look when we first knew him. He looks as if he does not feel a thing."

"But he does," she said. "I can look at him now and know that there is a great deal going on behind the granite exterior."

"You are privy to Purnell's feelings, then, Mad?" he asked. "He speaks to you? Things are better between you?"

"He has not spoken to me since the afternoon when he arrived back here," she said. "And as far as I know, he has not once looked at me or shown any awareness of my existence. No, things ended when he left here after Edmund's ball, Dom—if they had ever begun, that is. I thought it would be difficult having him back here again. But it is not so. We are like strangers who are not even aware of each other any longer."

"Except that you know he is suffering," he said.

"Except that I know he is suffering," she agreed.

"Well," he said, squeezing her shoulder, "I daresay he and his mother will leave here soon after the funeral. And even if they don't, Ellen and I have come for only a week. You will come back with us and stay for as long as you wish. We are finding that Amberley is not the only place that has friendly neighbors. We will be able to offer you an almost active social life. And a few eligible bachelors too."

She rested her head briefly against his shoulder. "The poor gentlemen," she said. "Do you know that you have designs on their freedom, I wonder? I will come. And I warn you that I have vowed to marry within the year. I don't at all relish my present situation as everyone's spinster aunt. Four times already. You don't have another set of twins on the way yet, by any chance?"

"After only four months?" he said. "Poor Ellen. No, I thought perhaps you would want to take a turn next."

"Then for sure," she said, "I must find a husband. I cannot keep you and Ellen waiting indefinitely. Are any of those neighbors of yours tall and blond, Dom? And below five and thirty years of age? And charming? With at least ten thousand a year?"

"I can think of three without even trying," he said. "Wiltshire breeds them handsome, Mad."

"Ah," she said, "now you tell me. Oh, Dom, I am so happy, happy, happy to have you home again."

Mrs. Deirdre Harding-Smythe arrived later the same evening with her son, Albert. She hugged and cried over Alexandra and her sister-in-law while Albert shook hands with his cousin and congratulated him on his newly acquired title.

James looked at him coldly and blankly.

"You are Beckworth now," Albert said. "Your life's dream has been fulfilled, James, and you no longer have need to go back to the new world to seek adventure."

"So I am," his cousin said with a stiff inclination of the head, "and so it has and so I don't."

Albert looked a little confused and turned away to take Alexandra's hand and raise it to his lips. "My dear cousin," he said. "How very well you look in black. It complements your dark coloring."

Alexandra frowned and said nothing.

Albert looked up into James's stern and immobile

face, flashed him a foolish smile, and turned to Lady Beckworth.

"Aunty!" he said, his voice vibrant with soft sympathy. "It is really for the best, you know. This world was not good enough for Uncle. I always did say so, as I am sure you will recall, and I have been consoling Mama with the same sentiment all the way from London."

Lord Eden spoke into his sister's ear. "Are you quite sure he has to be blond and tall with ten thousand a year?" he murmured. "Perhaps I can find you someone closer to home."

She gave him a speaking glance. "I always did say he was a toad," she whispered to him, "as I am sure you will recall. And I will regale your ears with the same sentiment all the way to Wiltshire."

"Ah, Lord Eden, Lady Madeline," Albert said graciously. "So pleased to renew our acquaintance and so sad that it has to be in such very sad circumstances. My uncle was a saint, you know. But then, of course, you had the pleasure of his company here for a month before his tragic demise."

He sat down beside them and favored them with his superior conversation for half an hour. Both Madeline and Dominic found themselves envying Ellen. She was upstairs in the nursery consoling her son, who had not taken kindly to the journey.

JAMES SAT CLOSE to one of the windows in the drawing room, occasionally looking out at the darkness. The curtains had not been drawn even though it was quite late in the evening already. And he looked down at his black clothes and across the room at his mother's and his aunt's.

He was dead, then, and buried. It was all over. Alex's neighbors, who had filled the church and come back to the house, many of them, at Amberley's bidding, had all returned home. They had been unstinting with their sympathy. They were kind people. He wished he had been able to respond better to them.

Lord and Lady Eden were sitting on either side of his mother. Lady Eden had an arm linked through hers and was talking earnestly to her. She was a gracious lady. But then, of course, she knew all about the loss of a husband. She had lost her own only the previous year.

Amberley had taken Alex upstairs just a short while before. She was close to exhaustion after all the tensions of the past several days.

He had hardly spoken with her since his return from London. What was there to say? That she was taking it hard was clear to him, and she doubtless knew that he was not unmoved either by the death of their father. But what could he say to her when even the thoughts inside him were leaden?

The dowager countess had stepped outside with Sir Cedric Harvey a few minutes before, leaving Madeline talking with his aunt and his cousin.

He looked at her—for the first time since his return. She was wearing a gown of subdued lavender. She was sitting very straight on her chair, her hands clasped loosely in her lap. The customary sparkle was missing from her face. She was pale and looked as if she had not slept for several nights. She looked very beautiful.

That worm Albert was ogling her and trying to charm her.

But then Albert could probably do her a great deal less harm than he could. The chains were still locked about his heart and always would be now. He was a force only of destruction for other people. If his father died, his mother had said to him a few weeks before, he would be responsible for that death.

He would not believe it. With his head he did not believe it. But with his heart? He had not been the son his father wanted, the son he had striven for so many years to be. And whose fault was that? His father's or his own?

He would never now know for sure if his father had loved him. He would never be free.

Madeline was flushing. Her lips had tightened. Albert was smirking and saying something to her that James could not quite hear.

He felt a flash of anger. But she was capable of taking care of herself. He must leave her alone. He must make no move toward her.

He got to his feet and walked across the room. "Would you care for some fresh air, Madeline?" he asked.

She looked up at him, startled.

"Fresh air would be good for you, I am sure, James, my dear," his Aunt Deirdre said. "If you think it would be showing the proper respect for your father, of course. But I cannot see any great impropriety when you will be on Lord Amberley's land."

James kept his eyes on Madeline.

"Lady Madeline will need a chaperone, cousin," Albert said. "It would not do to start any gossip at such a time, as I am sure you are well aware. You must remember now that you are no longer simply Mr. James Purnell. You are Beckworth."

"Thank you," Madeline said, getting to her feet. "I shall fetch a cloak."

13

THE DOWAGER COUNTESS OF AMBERLEY AND Sir Cedric Harvey crossed the stone bridge and turned to walk slowly up the valley.

"It is always something of a relief to have a funeral over," she said. "But then, of course, the real pain begins for close family members. The emptiness, the full realization of their loss. Oh, Cedric, I do feel for Lady Beckworth. She doted on her husband, did she not?"

"One wonders if she has the inner resources to combat such a loss," he said. "Of course, she has Alexandra and the children. And her son was brought back in time and will surely not now return to Canada—not this year, anyway."

Lady Amberley sighed. "The cool air feels so good," she said. "And I do feel like a truant from school, Cedric. Should I have stayed, do you think?"

"Ellen was doing very well with Lady Beckworth when we left," he said. "You have a gem of a daughter-in-law there, Louisa. And Mrs. Harding-Smythe was all ready to offer consolation when needed, you may be sure. Relax and enjoy your walk."

"Oh, I will," she said. "I am so thankful that it is not this year you are away. I don't know what I would have done without you in the past month or so. You are so very sane."

"That is the strangest compliment I have ever been paid," he said. "Is it a compliment?"

"Of course," she said. "Cedric, I cannot help thinking constantly of what you said a while ago. Did you mean it?"

"About wanting to marry you?" he said. "It is hardly the sort of thing I would say in jest, Louisa."

"I cannot get beyond the barrier of our friendship," she said. "It embarrasses me to think of you in any other way, you know. And that is foolish, for you are a handsome man. I have looked at you with new eyes in the past week or so, and I have seen that. But I have never seen it before. You have been just Cedric, my friend."

"We have the trees and the river and the moonlight," he said. "The perfect setting for romance. Why do we not put the matter to the test? Let me kiss you."

"Here? Now?" she said. "It seems very foolish."

He stopped walking and turned her to him. "If it turns out to be foolish," he said, "it will remain our secret. There are absolutely no witnesses, you see."

He lowered his head and kissed her on the lips, a light kiss, with his hands on her shoulders.

"I am very thankful for the darkness," she said when he lifted his head again and looked down at her. "I am quite sure I am blushing like a girl. You will think me gauche, Cedric. It has been a long time, you know."

"Well, then," he said, "we must try kissing like a man and woman rather than like a boy and girl."

He drew her into his arms and kissed her again, open-mouthed. His hands moved over her back, holding her full against him. Her own hands came to rest on his shoulders.

"Not so gauche after all," he murmured against her mouth several minutes later. "Beautiful, Louisa."

She rested her forehead against his shoulder. "It has been fourteen years," she said, "and only ever with Edward before that. You have not been celibate since Anne, have you? I am afraid you are far beyond me in experience, Cedric. You showed me that just a moment ago. I will not be able to satisfy your needs. I think it would be best for us to remain just friends."

"But I am not offering you the position of mistress," he said. "I am not hiring you to cater just to my physical needs. I want you as my wife—companion, friend, and lover. I know there has been only Edward, Louisa. I do not expect an experienced courtesan. But if you think that you do not stir my blood, you have not been paying close attention in the past five minutes."

"This is so foolish," she said. "I have three grown children and four grandchildren."

"Are you afraid, Louisa?" he asked.

"Yes." She lifted her head and looked up at him. "I had thought that part of my life was long over, you see. I have learned to take pleasure from my children's lives. And I have built a life of my own, with a circle of good friends. A quiet life of dignity and refinement. And now I find that after all there are sensual pleasures still within my reach. With my closest friend. Yes, I am afraid, Cedric. I am afraid that all will be ruined. It is like stepping out into the darkness when one has a world of light and warmth behind one."

"I always thought you were an expert on love," he said. "You and Edward had a perfect marriage. And your children are capable of deep love, an apparent testament to your teaching and example."

"I have always believed that it is love that has given my life meaning," she said.

"But you are now afraid of love?"

She frowned. "Of physical passion," she said, "not of love."

"Are the two quite separate things, then?" he asked. "Will you destroy the love between us, which has shown itself so far in friendship, if you marry me and share my bed? And—heaven forbid—enjoy doing so?"

"Ah," she said, turning and gazing down at the dark waters of the river, "now I see you are using our friendship against me. You have always been so sensible—so sane, as I was mad enough to put it only a few minutes ago—and I have been in the habit of listening to you and thinking that anything you said must be wisdom."

"And what I have just said is not?" he asked. "Is it because of Edward, Louisa? Is it because you loved him totally and lost him and almost lost yourself in the process? If you could go back, would you reject him or else keep yourself aloof from him so that you would not suffer as much from his passing?"

"No, of course not," she said. "I would not have had one moment of my marriage with him different, even knowing what the end was to be."

"Is it that you cannot free yourself of your love for him to love again?" he asked. "Or is it that you are afraid to love me because I must die one day and may do so before you?"

She turned to him and smiled. "I agreed to be kissed," she said, "not to have my soul searched. I also agreed to walk, not to stand on the riverbank being interrogated. Well, sir?"

"Well, madam," he said, "I perceive you are a coward. For shame, Louisa. Now, has a definite answer been given here? Have I been rejected out of hand? Or have I been given a maybe?"

"A definite maybe, Cedric," she said. "Will you give me time? I must confess that you have me mortally terrified. I had hoped that when you kissed me, we would both discover how foolish it would be to change the nature of our relationship. But instead I have found that the idea has its attractions. I am just very much afraid."

He took her arm, drew it through his again, and patted her hand. "We will walk on and change the subject, then," he said. "I shall stay until the end of August, Louisa, if I may, but I must put in an appearance at my own estate then. Will you be going to London soon?"

"Yes," she said, "once the household is back to normal again after this dreadful upset. With a wife and two children, Edmund has every right to be left alone. Besides, my interests are in my own home in town."

"I shall be sure to be there by the end of September," he said.

"The Bassets should be back from their tour of Europe by then," she said. "We must invite them for dinner one evening, Cedric. They are sure to have no end of interesting stories."

They resumed their stroll along the valley.

JAMES TURNED TO THE RIGHT when they were outside the door. But he did not walk along the valley toward the sea, but up into the hills. He did not keep to the path that would have taken them up onto the cliffs, but moved across the hill, following no path at all. Madeline doubted that he even knew where he walked or had any planned destination.

His arm was taut beneath her own. His face was hard and set, his eyes fixed ahead of them. She wondered if he even remembered that she was with him.

She did not speak. She could feel need in him with every nerve ending in her body. And whether he remembered it or not, whether he regretted it or not, he had chosen her as his companion. He had shown a need for her.

She was content to walk at his side, to give him, perhaps, some measure of comfort. Perhaps she would never walk with him again, never have another chance to give him anything, even her silent support.

But he had need of more. She knew as soon as he stopped walking and swung her around against him and held her to him and lowered his mouth to hers. She knew, and she yielded to the pressure of his arms, and lifted her face to his.

She knew that he needed a great deal more, that this was no romantic night of love, that his kiss was no embrace in itself. She felt his need as a tangible thing, and whether he knew her clearly or knew clearly what he did, it did not matter. For he had chosen her and now he was turning to her in his need.

And there could be no thought of denying him, for love can only give. As soon as it began to demand something in return, even if only a promise, then it was no longer love. And finally, without the medium of thought or reason, she knew that she loved him, that it was him, the world was him and life was him and ultimately nothing else mattered. Or ever would.

There was nothing gentle about either his mouth on hers or his tongue, which ravished. And nothing gentle about his hands, which first strained her to him and then explored with unsubtle desperation. She held her mouth open for him and relaxed to the roving and searching of his hands. And her fingers smoothed gently through his hair.

The ground was hard beneath her back, despite the grass, when he tumbled her down. But she reached for him and took his mouth to hers again while his hands pulled roughly at her clothes and dragged away undergarments. And when he came down on top of her, she ignored the discomfort of a hard ground that did not give beneath their combined weights, and allowed herself to be positioned for the ultimate giving. She stroked her fingers through his hair.

The shock of pain as he stabbed into her had her closing her eyes very tightly and biting down hard on her lower lip, but she did not cry out and she kept her trembling fingers gentle against his head.

It was all discomfort and pain: the uneven hardness of the ground, his weight on her, his ungentle entry, the deep urgent movements that followed, each stroke pushing her more firmly against the ground, the growing soreness. She was biting both lips before he finished, and concentrating every effort of will on not sobbing aloud.

But the need to sob was occasioned only in part by the physical discomfort. It had far more to do with a full realization of what was happening, of what she was doing, and of what the probable consequences would be.

He was using her for his need. Not really Madeline, but a woman's body with which to soothe his grief. When it was over, he would take her back to the house. He would leave within a few days, and she would never see him again. And all her carefully made plans for the future would be useless. There could never now be anyone else, not even for a comfortable marriage of convenience. There could never now be anyone but James.

And perhaps he would leave her with child.

But she would have cried, if she had allowed herself to do so, not with misery or remorse, but with a realization that it was all inevitable. This was the way it had to be, the way it had always been and always would have been however much she had tried to delude herself in the future. For James was as much as a part of her as her heart was or her brain, and quite as essential to her being as either.

And so after he had finished in her, his face pressed to her hair, she did not push against him as she might have done, to release herself from some of the pain. She kept one hand in his hair and rested the other about his shoulders, and let him relax his full weight against her. And she would have endured the pain all night. She closed her eyes and concentrated on memorizing every touch of his body against hers and in hers.

But he moved away far too soon and lay on his back at her side, not touching her, one arm beneath his head, staring up at the stars.

"Albert was right, you see," he said tonelessly. "You should have brought a chaperone."

She did not reply.

"So, Madeline," he said after another minute of silence, "you have been caught in my web." He turned his head to look at her, his face taut and hard, his eyes mocking. "The devil's web."

She looked back at him but said nothing.

He looked at her with a twisted smile. "It seems that you have no choice but to marry the devil," he said. "You will doubtless be delighted. I am sure that becoming Lady

Beckworth will be a dream come true for you. You were a fool not to bring that chaperone."

Madeline sat up sharply and hugged her knees. "I don't regret what has happened," she said. "And I have been caught in no web. This was not ravishment. And you have no need to offer me marriage."

"Brave words," he said. "You would risk bearing my bastard?"

She lifted her face to the sky. "You do not need to offer me marriage," she said.

"I am afraid you have no choice," he said quietly from the ground behind her. "I have just had your virginity, Madeline. We must now play out the part expected of us by society. We are not free agents after all. You are Lady Madeline Raine, sister of the Earl of Amberley. I am James Purnell, Lord Beckworth. People like you and me do not take a roll in the hay and shake hands and go our separate ways. They marry."

"We cannot marry," she said. "We would be miserable together."

"It seems to me," he said, "that we are rather miserable apart. If we must settle for one of the two miseries, it might as well be marriage. We have no choice anyway. We made it an hour ago. We both knew when we left the house what was going to happen and what must happen after that. There is nothing more to be said."

He got abruptly to his feet and strode away from her. She dressed herself quickly, with shaking fingers, and went after him. But he had not gone far. He stood looking down into the valley, his face hard again, his eyes bleak. She stood silently beside him.

His teeth were clamped so firmly together that they felt as if they might crack. But he could not relax his jaw. He stared down into the valley as if it were daylight and he had set himself to counting every blade of grass there. But he could not withdraw his gaze. His hands were clenched into fists at his sides, his fingernails digging painfully into his palms. But he could not stretch his fingers.

For if he moved a single muscle, he would break down entirely. He would grab Madeline, who was standing silently beside him, and sob out all his pain and despair.

He could not so demean himself. He had been brought up to a stoical self-discipline. It was almost impossible for him to show his deepest feelings to another human being.

Especially such feelings. An aching grief for a father he had loved and had been unable to draw close to. A gnawing guilt over the knowledge that he had disappointed his father and spoiled the last ten years of his life. An emptiness of despair over not knowing for sure if he had been loved or if he had been forgiven. And now he would never know.

Madeline. Every ounce of feeling in him wanted to turn to her so that he could sob out his grief in her arms. So that he could seek love again, risk love again. So that he could tell her that what had just happened had been love, the instinctive reaching out for the one person who meant more to him than the whole world.

But he could not turn to her. He dared not move. He would come all to pieces if he moved.

Love! How could he ever persuade her that what had just happened was love? He had taken her quite cruelly. He had hurt her. He had said and done nothing that would even suggest tenderness. He had not made love to her. He had taken her, used her for his need.

But he loved her. God, he loved her. He would give his life if only he could make her happy.

Was there anything he could say? Anything he could do? What had he said a few minutes before? Something doubtless to hide his feelings, to hide the pain of rejection that must come when she had recovered from shock and pain.

He had ravished her. God, he had ravished the one woman in this world he would die for.

He stood as if turned to stone.

"He did not love me, you know," he said after several minutes. "Or Alex. Or my mother. He was cold and unfeeling to the core. I asked for his love before I left here. I asked for his blessing. He gave me only a handshake and no words at all."

"He had very high standards of behavior," Madeline said. "But who knows what his inner feelings were?"

"He was incapable of love," he said. He turned to look down at her, and knew that the tension inside him had not uncoiled at all. His eyes were cold and unfathomable. "Like father, like son, I suppose. You cannot expect love to flow from the members of such a family."

"Your mother loved him," Madeline said, "and she loves you. Alexandra is capable of great love."

"Then perhaps it is a malady just of the men in the family," he said. "You must hope that you will bear me female children only. We had better go back to the house. We have a betrothal to announce. Is it distasteful to have a funeral and a betrothal both within the same day, do you think?"

"We should wait," she said. "And perhaps there should be no marriage at all. James, we must think about it, talk about it more."

But he could not think, and he could not talk. Not

about the feelings closest to his heart, anyway. And he could not lose her now. He would die rather than lose her.

"I shall leave for London in the morning," he said, "and return with a special license. We will marry within a week, Madeline—in the chapel at Amberley before I take you into Yorkshire. There is no point in delay. I am eager to begin this new life of mine, to return to a home I swore I would never see again."

"James," she said, "this is madness. You ..."

He spread one hand behind her head and kissed her again, his mouth as hard and ungentle as it had been before.

"Hush," he said. "You are mine now. You have given yourself to me. I will make the decisions from now on."

Madeline shivered, but she bit her lip and did not tell him, as she had been about to do, that he sounded just exactly like his father. And she did not tell him, as she might have done and as her self-respect told her to do, that she would not marry him, that he could not force her to do so.

She took his arm silently and walked back to the house with him. They did not exchange one word on the way.

MADELINE LIVED in something of a daze during the following week. A deliberate daze. She could not think clearly, and she did not want to do so. She would leave her thinking to do during the following week, after she was married.

James was not able to make his announcement immediately on their arrival home. His mother fell sobbing into his arms, and it took the combined efforts of James, Ellen, and Mrs. Harding-Smythe to calm her down and persuade her to sit down and sip some tea.

But the announcement was made. And Madeline was surprised when Lady Beckworth threw her arms about James's neck and kissed him and called him her dear, dear son. And she hugged and kissed her future daughter-in-law too. Only later did she resume her crying, and lament the fact that her dear Beckworth would never know.

There did not seem to be any objection to the haste of the marriage, either. It seemed that Lady Beckworth interpreted James's decisions as a sign that he was taking on himself the responsibility of his new position.

And so he left the following morning for London. They had not had a private word together since they were out on the hillside.

"Are you quite sure, Madeline?" Edmund asked her the night of the betrothal, taking both her hands in his when they were left alone in the drawing room and looking directly into her eyes. Alexandra had retired to bed some hours before. "There is a heightened emotion surrounding such events as funerals. And I know you have a regard for James and must sympathize with him in his loss. Are you sure you want to marry him?"

"Yes," she said, "it is what I want, Edmund."

He frowned. "Something is wrong," he said. "You are not smiling. James did not look overjoyed, though of course one would not expect him to forget what day this is. You did not sit together or speak together all evening. Reassure me. I want you to be happy."

"I will be happy," she said, releasing her hands from his and putting them about his neck. "He is what I want, Edmund. And is it not quite typical of you to be showing concern for me when you must be worried about Alexandra and eager to check on her. Don't let me keep you."

She hugged him before smiling at him and preceding him from the room.

Dominic was in her dressing room waiting for her when she went upstairs. He was lounging against her dressing table, playing absently with a brush.

"Well," he said, tossing down the brush and getting to his feet. "Hugs?"

She let him hug her tight, and rested her head briefly on the safety and comfort of his shoulder.

"Why aren't you happier?" he asked her, holding her at arm's length.

"Lord Beckworth was buried today," she said. "It cannot be a time of great rejoicing."

"This is your twin, love," he said. "What's the matter?"

She looked at him before letting her eyes fall before his. "I am marrying the man I love most in all the world," she said. "The man I would be miserable without for the rest of a lifetime. And yet I know I will not be happy with him either, Dom."

"Does he not love you?" he asked.

She shook her head.

"Why is he marrying you, then?" he asked.

She shrugged and reached out without thought to do up a button that had come undone on his waistcoat.

"Are you increasing?" he asked.

She looked, startled, up into his face and flushed. "No!" she said.

"But there is the chance that you might be, isn't there, Mad?" he said. "You have been with him."

"Just tonight," she said. "He needed me. And I love him. Nothing mattered but that I loved him."

He nodded. "But it should have been a mutual need and a mutual love," he said. "And perhaps it is, too. I don't pretend to understand Purnell, Mad. He is so withdrawn and his face is always so impassive that it's impossible to know the man. But something obviously draws him to you. Perhaps you will be able to penetrate behind the mask. And perhaps you will find there is love there after all. I hope so."

"I have to marry him," she said. "I could not say no, and he would not allow me to, anyway."

"No," he said, "I know you have no choice. And so I know this is the real thing for you, Mad. With all the others the choice was always yours. I know you have to marry him, so I won't give any brotherly lectures. I could do so, you know, because from the outside this seems all wrong. I'll only hug you again and wish and wish that you will be as happy in your marriage as I am in mine. You know I'll always be here for you, don't you? Anytime you need me."

"Yes, Dom," she said. "I know."

Her mother was pleased for her.

"He is a hardworking young man," she told Madeline next morning after James had already left, "and takes his responsibilities seriously. He is rather reticent, it is true, and somewhat severe in manner, but then Alexandra was much like that too when she first met Edmund. Love and marriage and children have brought out all the charm and love that were hidden within. They had a harsh upbringing, you know. You will do for James what Edmund has done for Alexandra. How could you fail, dear, with your sunny nature? Do you love him?"

"Yes, Mama," Madeline said. "He is the whole of life to me."

Her mother smiled and kissed her on the cheek. "Then what more is there to say?" she said. "Your mother and fa-

ther and your two brothers married for just exactly that
reason. I would say you are in very good company. James
is a good young man. I shall be proud to have him for a
son-in-law."

Alexandra sought her out the same morning even before breakfast. "I feel guilty," she said, taking both her
sister-in-law's hands in hers, "to be feeling any happiness
today. But I am happy, Madeline. James is home to stay.
And what is far more precious even than that, he is going
to marry you next week." She hugged Madeline hard.

"If something good could come of Papa's passing," she
continued, "it is that James will stay in this country and go
back home to Yorkshire again. And that he will be taking
you with him as his wife. He will be happy with you. And
I have always wanted his happiness more than almost
anything else in life."

Word spread long before the week was out, and callers
arrived daily to pay their respects to Lady Beckworth and
to wish Madeline all the joy of her coming nuptials.

Fortunately, it was a time in which it was easy to keep
the mind in a daze. Easy and very desirable. For though
she knew that she had to marry James—for a variety of
reasons—she knew too that there was no happily-ever-
after ending waiting for her the other side of the altar.

There was the memory of James sneering at her and
telling her she had been caught in the devil's web. There
was James telling her that he was incapable of loving, as
his father had been. James kissing her and loving her without any trace of tenderness. And James telling her to hush
because she was his possession now and he would make
all the decisions affecting their lives.

And there was herself not making any protest against
anything he had said or done. She who had fought her

14

THE DOWAGER LADY BECKWORTH WAS SOB-
bing in James's arms. She was very happy for him.
Her life was over, she said. There could be no more happiness for her with his papa gone. But James had shown
himself their son again. He was not going back to that
heathen land but was on his way to Yorkshire and
Dunstable Hall. And he had made a very eligible marriage. She was more proud of him than she could say. He
was looking so very handsome on his wedding day.

She cupped his face in her hands and kissed him
soundly.

Then Alex was hugging him and laughing and saying
how wonderful it was to be sending him off only as far as
Yorkshire.

"Have a safe journey," she said into his ear. "And be
happy, James. For years you wanted only my happiness—
and your wish was granted. Now I want yours. And you
will be happy, I know. You and Madeline are meant for
each other."

Edmund was holding out a hand to him and smiling.
"Well, James," he said, "it seems that we liked each other
so well as brothers-in-law that we had to do it again."

James shook hands with him.

"Have a safe journey," Edmund said. "And look after my sister."

"As you look after mine, I would hope," James said in all seriousness.

His Aunt Deirdre was awaiting her turn to hug him and wish him a good journey.

Madeline was in her mother's arms, he saw at a glance. Eden and his wife were standing close to them, their arms about each other's waists. Madeline turned and lifted an arm about the neck of each.

"You had better get on your way as fast as you can," William Carrington said, gripping his hand firmly, "before the ladies drown themselves and each other. There is something about weddings that always has them turn on the waterworks."

"Well, William," his wife said, "weddings are serious business. You look very handsome, James, my dear—I may call you that now you are our nephew by marriage, may I? But I can see that you want only to snatch up your bride and be on your way." She gave him a hearty kiss on the cheek.

Albert was hovering in the background.

Madeline was hugging Anna and Walter. She was not dressed in black. He had forbidden her to do so when she had mentioned the subject on his return from London the day before. There would be no mourning clothes for her. She had not been related to his father in any way when he died.

She was in tears, but smiling. His new mother-in-law was hugging him.

"James," she said, "I am so proud to have you as a son-in-law. Welcome to my family, my dear. Now, my experience is that these farewells can go on forever and ever. I would suggest that you disengage Madeline from William's embrace and make off with her." She smiled at him. "I can see that all this sentimentality is making you thoroughly uncomfortable."

By the time he crossed the distance between himself and his wife, she was holding one of Ellen's hands in both of hers and talking very fast and very eagerly to Dominic. He took her by the elbow.

"It's time to leave, Madeline," he said. He should smile at her. A bridegroom should smile at his bride, especially when all her family and all his were looking at them and were themselves smiling. But he could not force the muscles of his face to obey his will.

"Oh, yes," she said breathlessly, "of course."

She came with him immediately and allowed him to hand her into his father's carriage, now his—the carriage they would share by day for a week or more until they arrived at his home.

There was a great deal of noise and laughter. More tears. Edmund closed the door of the carriage and smiled and lifted a hand in farewell. And they were on their way.

Married two hours before, husband and wife, and on their way into a future together.

"You would have liked a large wedding, doubtless," he said. "In St. George's or elsewhere in London." He had meant his tone to be sympathetic. It sounded stiff, even cold.

"I always dreamed of getting married in the chapel," she said, "with just family present. That is where Dom and Ellen were married last year because she was in mourning at the time, too."

She leaned forward as the carriage began to climb the hill opposite the house and looked out the window until they were at the top of the rise and beyond sight of the valley. But even when she leaned back again, she kept her head averted. He could hear her swallow several times.

He wanted to reach a hand across to her. He wanted to move across the seat to her to dry her tears with his own handkerchief, to let her do her crying against his shoulder. He wanted to assure her that she was not losing a home but gaining one, that as much love as she was leaving behind her, there was so much more traveling with her and waiting ahead of her.

He too swallowed and turned his head to look out the window beside him.

"I expected that your mama would come with us," she said after several silent minutes.

"It will be better for her to remain with Alex for a month or so," he said. "She is fond of the children. She will go to Aunt Deirdre's after that—for an indefinite stay, I believe. She would not enjoy being at Dunstable Hall with my father not there."

Her hands were fidgeting in her lap. He would not even have to move in order to reach across and take one of them in his own. It would be a small enough gesture of support. She was his wife. He would not have to find words. Just hold her hand in his.

"James," she said, her voice shaking and breathless, "I cannot stand this. Is this what I am to be subjected to for a week of travel? Perhaps for a lifetime?"

"What?" he asked, holding his expression blank as he looked into her flushed and angry face. Though, of course, he knew very well what she meant.

"This silent treatment," she said. "This coldness. I look into your eyes and I am frightened, for I can see nothing beyond them."

"Perhaps there is nothing to see," he said.

"We were married this morning," she said. "I am your wife. Am I to be treated now like a stranger?"

"If you were a stranger," he said, "doubtless I would feel obliged to make polite conversation with you. Is that what you want? Shall we converse? Is it like to rain later today, do you think? Are those clouds gathering on the horizon, or is it merely a heat haze?"

"I hate it when you sneer," she said. "I think I would prefer your morose silence."

"Would you?" he said. "Then we will be silent. I am intent on obliging you, you see."

Her jaw set hard and her nostrils flared. "You may go to the devil," she said. "And I'll be damned along with you before I feel a moment's further embarrassment at your silence."

"You forget that I *am* the devil," he said. "You would do well to get used to me, Madeline. It seems that you are stuck with me for the rest of your life."

"Yes," she said, almost hissing the word. "But you will not find me a docile and teary-eyed victim, James Purnell. You will not drag me down with you into gloom, I can safely promise you. I shall fight you every inch of the way."

He did not answer her. He turned his attention to the window again.

And so they journeyed for the rest of the day in near silence, turned away from each other, looking through the windows as if it were a new and fascinating country through which they traveled. She took his hand to descend when they stopped to change horses and to take tea, but her chin was raised at a stubborn angle. She did not once look at him.

And he began to feel that there must be something

wrong with him, that he was treading a sure road to his own permanent unhappiness and sealing the doom of the woman he had taken to wife just that morning. He was doing so quite unwillingly but was totally powerless to do otherwise. It was as if he really did have the devil inside of him.

He had told himself during his ride to London and back to procure a special license that there was hope. It was true that he was his father's son, unloved and unforgiven by the man who had given him life. And it was true that he lived in terror of being like his father indeed, incapable of loving or bringing any joy into the lives of those closest to him.

But it was not so, he had told himself. He loved his mother. Despite the weakness of her character, her lethargy, her constant low spirits, he loved her. And he loved Alex with a deep concern for her happiness. He loved her children.

He was capable of love. He loved Madeline. He had told himself that repeatedly on his journey to London. And it was true. His need for her on the day of his father's funeral had been a monumental thing. And it had been a need not just for her body, though that was how it had shown itself. He had needed *her*. He had needed her arms about him, her voice soothing him, herself part of him.

He knew he had not been gentle. It had been her first time, and he had done nothing to ease her pain or to soothe her shock. And he had felt her pain in the tension of her body—it had not been the tension of passion.

He had taken her with the need and the desire to take her into himself, to make her forever a part of him. And of course he had known even as he took her that he must have her with him for the rest of his life. She was as necessary to him as the air he breathed. He could not possibly let her go.

He loved her, he had told himself during the interminable days away from her. So far he had shown his love only in the fight he had made against the inevitable, and in the selfish grasping to satisfy his own needs.

When he got back to her it would be different. He would smile at her and tell her that he loved her. His wedding day would be the beginning of a new and wonderful life for both of them. He would make her a gift of himself at the altar of the chapel at Amberley, not just of his name.

Madeline and his love for her would free him. He would no longer be his father's son, no longer a product of his background and upbringing. He would be Madeline's husband and friend and lover. He would learn to laugh with her and joke with her and share the whole of himself with her.

It had been a heady dream. It had sustained him through the tedium and fatigue of a lonely journey. He had not thought at all about the old nagging guilt, the old need to punish himself for his destruction of another's happiness. He had given himself up to his dream.

But a dream was all it had been. One cannot after all change one's nature in a matter of days, he had discovered the day before on his return to Amberley. The will to change was not enough.

And yet it was not his nature to be surly to the point of rudeness. It was only with Madeline he was so. He could not seem to treat her even with common courtesy. After sustaining himself for days with the need to be back with her, he had avoided being alone with her all the day before. And when she had contrived to be alone with him during the evening, he had been abrupt and domineering and downright cruel to her.

"James," she had said, "I do not know what I should wear tomorrow."

He had looked at her with cold eyes. "I thought women arranged such matters as a bride's clothes," he had said.

"But I don't know if I should be in mourning," she had said. "I have black dresses. Should I wear one for our wedding? Will you expect it?"

And instead of taking her hands in his and smiling at her and telling her that he wanted his bride to be like the sunshine, as she usually was, he had looked at her without any expression at all.

"You will not wear mourning on account of my father," he had said. "Try wearing a black dress, Madeline, tomorrow or any other day in the next year, and I shall tear it off you and rip it to shreds before your eyes."

Because he loved her and wanted her to brighten his life, not add to its gloom, he might have added. Because he did not want her tainted by the gloom that had always hung like a pall over his own family. He did not want to look at her and see mourning. He wanted to see the hope, the light of his life, in her.

But he had said none of those things. He had stood, his hands clasped behind his back, watching her flush, waiting for her to turn away and seek out other company.

He had hated himself and realized that his dream was as insubstantial as those that trailed through his sleep at night.

And so he sat beside her on their wedding day, knowing with each passing mile that he had bullied his wife into a marriage that would bring her nothing but an enforced hell.

• • •

MADELINE WAS WALKING back and forth in the rather magnificent bedchamber of the inn where they had stopped for the night. She was wearing a white silk and lace nightgown. Her hair had been freshly brushed by her maid and lay in soft curls about her face and along her neck. She was waiting for her husband to come to her.

Waiting in anger. She would not deny him, of course. They were at a public inn, and he could scarcely take himself off to another room. Besides, she had a feeling that he would insist on taking his conjugal rights and he would doubtless be able to force himself upon her. Not that that would daunt her if she really wished to deny him. She would be quite unabashed by the necessity to yell and scream and punch, kick, and claw. She would enjoy doing so even knowing that he would be able to subdue her with ease.

If they were not at the inn, she might try it. Though she would certainly not enjoy being taken against her will. Better to give herself with at least a semblance of willingness.

But she was angry. At herself. She had come out of her daze—with a crash. And what in the name of all that was wonderful had she done? She had married a man without humor or feelings, a tyrant who had married her for some mysterious reason of his own. Perhaps to degrade her. He seemed to quite hate her.

And she had married him. No one had held a pistol to her back or her temple and forced her forward to the altar. No one had bullied her except him. Mama, Edmund, Dominic: all three of them would have supported her and defended her if she had said but one word. All three would have continued to love her even if it did turn out that she was increasing.

Besides, she did not need to hide behind the strength of her family. She could have said no herself. There was no way on earth he could have forced her to marry him if she had just said no.

But she had married him. Because she loved him, she had persuaded herself and told everyone else during the week he was away. Love? Could she call her feelings for him love? They were more a strange and frightening need to be dominated and degraded and hated. She had walked the length of the chapel that morning on Edmund's arm, knowing quite well what she did and what sort of man he was she was marrying.

She deserved her fate. She deserved it if he turned out to be far worse than the morose tyrant she already knew him to be. It would serve her right if he turned out to be a wife-beater.

She almost wished he would. He would present her with the perfect excuse to deal him a few punches of her own.

The door opened behind her and she turned to face her husband, her chin raised in defiance, her eyes steady on his.

"Well," he said, closing the door behind his back. He was wearing a blue dressing gown. He had come from his dressing room and through their private sitting room. "You do not look like the typical blushing, timid bride."

"I do not need to," she said.

"Ah, no." He undid the silk sash of his dressing gown, removed the garment, and tossed it onto a chair. "You were ravished on a hillside a week ago."

"I was not ravished," she said.

"You will have a softer rest for your back tonight, anyway," he said, and he reached out for her and brought her against him.

She would not deny him. She would not impede him in any way. But she would not respond. He might take what he wanted; she would not give. She looked steadily into his eyes.

He brought his mouth to hers, open, hard, and demanding as it had been at their last encounter. She opened her own obediently. His hands explored her boldly. She did not cringe or pull away.

He was smiling down at her then—except that it was not quite a smile. "Ah, I see how it is," he said. "I was accused of giving you the silent treatment earlier. Now you retaliate with the cold treatment."

She smiled back with a smile that was not a smile. "Yes, James," she said.

"We will see." He stooped down and picked her up and strode to the bed with her. He tossed rather than laid her down on it. And he stooped down, grasped her nightgown by the hem, and stripped it up her body and over her head. He dropped it to the floor beside the bed, peeled off his own nightshirt, and joined her there after snuffing the candles.

It was no fair contest, of course. He was so very much more experienced than she. The rough lovemaking of the last occasion she could have withstood—she could have held herself aloof from it. But she had no chance whatsover against what he now began to do to her.

His mouth took hers, teased it, opened it. His tongue reached inside and touched lightly and circled and stroked. And his hands roamed over her, feathered over her, pausing unerringly in places that had her gasping and squirming, rubbing lightly with his palm, arousing with his fingers, smoothing with his thumbs. In her nakedness and inexperience she stood not a chance. She lost the battle—if she had ever begun to fight it—the moment his mouth began to follow the path his hands had blazed.

Her hands twined into his hair, explored the muscles of his shoulders and back. Her mouth searched for his when he was kissing her eyelids and her ears. And her body arched to his, was on fire for his.

By the time he covered her on the bed and penetrated her, she was aware only of the fact that he did not hurt her and that he was moving in her with an intensity that fast created its own need.

She moaned.

And his hands gripped her by the shoulders hard enough to bruise, and he slowed until she could catch his rhythm. He moved with her, thrusting against her need.

She was lost beyond even knowing. Or caring. She was being taken to a world she had dreamed of for years but had never expected to enter. The ache, the unbearable ache, was growing in her until she thought she could not bear it any longer. But she knew there was a world beyond. And she knew that it was James who was taking her there.

She knew it was James. She was lost to all reason and thought. She was bodily need and sensation only. But she knew he was James. He could not be anyone else. There could be no one else. She moved against him and held him to her, giving and taking, giving and taking. Loving and being loved.

Nothing else mattered now. She did not want to have to think ever again. Better far to feel. To love him with her instincts, with her instincts to know herself loved. To abandon herself. She wrapped her arms about his waist and stopped her own movements. She pushed down against him in final surrender. And allowed herself to be taken, to be fully taken wherever it was he would take her. Where only he could take her. Where she wanted to go only with him.

His hand moved from her arm and clamped over her mouth at the final moment so that her cry was muffled.

"Hush," he said. "Hush."

But the hand relaxed as he pushed into her once more and sighed his own release against her hair.

She let herself slip into sleep. He moved away from her, and the lightness and the coolness and the relaxed feeling of well-being were delicious. She did not want to open her eyes, or speak, or think. She slept.

But only for a short while. He was pulling a sheet up over her, his movements slow and designed, it seemed, not to disturb her. But she woke, and opened her eyes to find him still leaning over her, his dark eyes looking down into hers.

The room was lit only by the lights of the innyard below. But in the moment of waking there was an illusion of depth to his eyes, and her hand lifted of its own volition, it seemed, to push back the lock of dark hair that was, as usual, down over his brow.

But it was a trick of the half-light. By the time he lay back down beside her, his eyes were mocking again.

"Well, Madeline," he said, "it seems that as always we have something to hold us together. And whether we do or not, we have a marriage to get on with. A church ceremony this morning, the consummation tonight. We are husband and wife. A marriage made in heaven, would you say?"

She did not want to let reality in. She did not want to see his eyes mock her or hear his voice do likewise. She closed her eyes and said nothing.

"Well," he said after a brief silence, his voice no longer mocking, but flat and expressionless, "you will not try coldness with me again, Madeline. Anything else but that. I did not marry you for coldness."

"Why did you marry me?" she asked, neither moving nor opening her eyes.

He shifted position. She thought he would not answer. She turned her head away from him.

"For light," he murmured finally. But he said no more and she was not sure she had heard him correctly. And even if she had, she did not know what he meant.

But he did not need to give such a command. She would try other things, as many things as she could think of to show him that she was no poor-spirited creature to be worn into submission by a moody and tyrannical husband. She would fight a good fight. But coldness would not be one of her weapons. What was the point in using a weapon one knew to be totally useless?

She could be anything with him but cold.

He proved it to her twice more during their wedding night, and many more times during the remaining nights of their journey into Yorkshire.

MADELINE'S SPIRITS DIPPED with almost every mile they traveled north. The landscape became bleaker and the weather gray and chilly. Despite the length and tedium of the journey, Dunstable Hall came upon them altogether too soon. Surely they would pass into more picturesque surroundings eventually, she had thought for all of two days.

But her new home was not in a beautiful part of England. And the grounds of the house, seen when their carriage had finally turned past heavy stone gateposts and iron gates, were not designed for maximum beauty. A thick covering of trees on the slopes to either side of them, creating artificial darkness for a quarter of a mile, and bare lawns closer to the house. No formal gardens. Apparently no flower gardens at all.

The house was magnificent from the outside, far larger and more imposing than she had expected. But it was austere, fitting its surroundings well—a rectangular house with six rectangular towers, flat-roofed, the only feature to lighten its look the many long windows.

Her husband stared from the carriage window with her, his expression quite inscrutable.

"I had thought never to come back here," he said, more to himself than to her. "I must have imagined my father was immortal."

"So this is where you grew up," she said. "And Alexandra." It explained a great deal, she thought, and did not know quite what she meant by the thought. And here was where she would live with this man. And where her own children would grow up.

"I might have expected as much," James muttered from beside her.

His jaw had tightened, she saw at a glance, though she was soon looking back through the window at two long, straight lines of erect and motionless servants, standing facing each other across the cobbled courtyard where their carriage would stop.

Word had preceded them, and the staff of Dunstable

Hall had turned out to greet their new master and his bride.

James presented Mrs. Cockings, the housekeeper, and Mr. Cockings, the butler, to Madeline, and then walked beside her the length of one row of servants, across the cobbles, and back down the length of the row opposite.

Madeline was reminded of something. Some familiarity lingered at the back of her mind, just beyond conscious thought. And then she remembered with a shock and a quite inappropriate urge to giggle. When she had been in Brussels the year before, she had watched many military reviews. The troops had stood no more perfectly at attention, their eyes had been directed no more unrelentingly and unmovingly forward, nor had their expressions been more woodenly unsmiling when being reviewed by the Duke of Wellington himself than the servants of Dunstable were for James's inspection and her own.

The Cockingses had not smiled either, she thought in some fascination as Mrs. Cockings made polite inquiries about her journey and led her into the house and up a wide oak stairway to her rooms.

And if the woman's gray hair were scraped back from her face with any more severity, it surely would be dragged altogether from its roots.

That was another thing, Madeline thought with a frown, noting with unexpected relief that the two long windows in her bedchamber made it a light and seemingly airy apartment. All the maidservants had looked just the same, all with hair severely drawn back from their faces and confined in a neat knot at their necks. Apart from the inevitable differences in hair coloring and in height and build, they had all looked identical.

Mrs. Cockings stood in the middle of the bedchamber, her back ramrod straight, her hands clasped at her waist. "Your maid will be in the dressing room, my lady," she said. "You will wish to freshen yourself. Tea will be served in the drawing room immediately. After that, you will perhaps care for a bath?"

Madeline smiled. "I can think of nothing I would like more," she said. She crossed the room to one of the windows and looked down on green lawns and trees. "How lovely it will be not to have to get up tomorrow to yet another day of carriage travel."

"I shall await your instructions in the morning, my lady," the housekeeper said, making no response to the invitation of the smile. "In the meanwhile I have taken the liberty of arranging the dinner menu with the cook."

"I am sure whatever you have ordered will be quite acceptable," Madeline said with another smile.

"And I have given instructions to the servants that evening and morning prayers will be held in the main hall instead of in the kitchen, beginning this evening," Mrs. Cockings said. "Tired as you both must be, I am sure Lord Beckworth will not wish to miss that routine."

Madeline tried not to gape. She inclined her head in what she hoped was a dismissive gesture. "Thank you, Mrs. Cockings," she said.

The housekeeper crossed the bedchamber and held open the door into the dressing room. "I shall also take it upon myself, my lady," she said, as Madeline passed her, relieved to see that her maid was already in the room and busy unpacking brushes and combs, "to see to it that your maid is clothed in the proper uniform of the house and given instructions on the correct grooming as expected by his lordship."

"Thank you," Madeline said, turning in the doorway and looking quite dismissively at her housekeeper. "We will speak in the morning, Mrs. Cockings. But please make no move on the last matter. My maid is permitted to dress and to groom herself in any manner that I consider fitting."

"With all due respect, my lady," the housekeeper said, "I believe his lordship will be adamant on the matter. Perhaps..."

"Thank you, Mrs. Cockings," Madeline said firmly, and walked into her dressing room.

If her spirits had been sinking during the past few days, she thought, plunging her face into the cold water her maid had poured into a bowl, they had now arrived right down inside her slippers.

One consolation, she thought with wry humor, was that they had no further to sink.

15

JAMES FELT RATHER AS IF HE WERE LIVING WITH bated breath. He had been at Dunstable Hall for almost two weeks and there had been no major unpleasant incident either at the house, or in the neighborhood, or with his wife. Could he dare hope that life would settle into a comfortable peace?

But it was an uneasy peace.

The Cockingses were not pleased. Not that it was easy to divine their mood, it was true, since never in all the years of his acquaintance with them had he seen either one of them smile or frown or show any outward sign of emotion.

Cockings had hovered at his elbow the day of his arrival, after the housekeeper had taken Madeline to her apartments. Among other things, he had informed his master that he had taken the liberty of arranging that prayers be conducted in the grand hall that evening instead of in the kitchen where they were always conducted when the master was from home.

Half an hour of Bible reading and prayer during the evening and fifteen minutes during the morning had always been the strict and immutable rule at Dunstable Hall.

He had said nothing but had let the servants assemble after dinner. And he had taken Madeline with him to face their silent rows and informed them that from that day on there would be no formal prayers.

"There will, however," he said, "be the half hour in the evening and fifteen minutes in the morning when you may all be free to occupy yourselves as you please. Those of you who wish to conduct devotions may do so privately or in groups organized among yourselves as you will."

There was murmuring, soon quelled by a look from Cockings and his wife.

"I believe you have twenty minutes left this evening," James continued. "You may go and use the time as you wish."

"With all due respect," Cockings said after the bewildered servants had dispersed, "Lord Beckworth was very strict on the question of prayers."

James said nothing but merely turned his stare on the man.

Cockings bowed stiffly. "It will be as you wish, my lord," he said.

"There is always more work to be done than there is time to do it," Mrs. Cockings said. "I shall see to it, my lord, that everyone is decently occupied."

"Perhaps I did not express myself clearly," James said. "What I meant to say was that every servant in this house, yourself included, Mrs. Cockings, will have a little free time both morning and evening."

"Yes, my lord," she said, inclining her head.

But he knew that neither of them was pleased.

Madeline burst into giggles when they had returned to the drawing room. "Oh, James," she said, "it was priceless.

Did you see their faces? And you pokered up so splendidly. I think the Duke of Wellington himself would have quailed before you."

He was standing facing the fireplace, a grin on his face. He was only just containing his own laughter. But there were memories too. Memories of aching limbs and of boredom. Memories of numerous punishments for both himself and Alex if they had moved a muscle during the half hour or yawned—hours spent on their knees in the schoolroom, reading the Bible, missing meals.

He had rejected his father's God years before. It was only during his stay in the vast empty wilderness beyond Canada that he had begun to wonder if perhaps there were not a God after all. But one quite different from his father's. He would not want that God even if He existed. He would fight such a God to the death.

By the time he turned away from the fireplace, it was too late to share his laughter with Madeline. He surprised both himself and her by what he said.

"I shall spend the time, morning and evening, in private meditation," he said. He meant it. He had a curiosity to read the Bible for himself. Was the God of the Bible entirely a God of wrath? Memory suggested to him that perhaps He was not, though that was the overwhelming impression he had grown up with. "You may use it as you wish, Madeline."

The laughter died from her face. She appeared uncertain how to respond to his words. And he was embarrassed by his pronouncement. He stood and looked sternly at her, his hands clasped behind his back until she flushed and crossed the room to the pianoforte, where she spent the following hour.

He seemed to have no way of talking to her. And the

more he told himself to relax and say whatever he wished to say to her, the more impossible it became to behave with her in any sort of natural manner.

Even before the incident with the prayers he had had the opportunity to establish a more affectionate relationship with her. When they had gone in to dinner, he had placed her at one end of the long table and taken his seat at the other.

"Is it necessary," she asked with the hint of a smile, "to sit such a distance apart, James?"

He had not thought to question the arrangement. They were merely occupying the places his mother and father had always occupied.

"Cockings," he said, "move her ladyship's placing to my right-hand side, if you please. And that will be a permanent arrangement."

When she sat there, smiling at him with dancing eyes, he looked back. "Are you more comfortable now?" he asked.

He was not quite sure why her smile faded instantly and her eyes turned hostile.

"Perfectly, I thank you," she said in tones that he realized matched his own. But he had not intended to speak coldly or to look at her with hostility. He was pleased to have her beside him.

"James," she said, her tone still chilly, her back quite straight and not touching her chair, "I have been informed that you will require my maid to wear the ghastly uniform of the house and to wear her hair scraped back into a bun as all the other servants do. I will not have it, I would have you know. I will not stand for such petty tyranny."

"Good Lord, Madeline," he said, annoyed that she

should think the order had come from him, "do you think I care what your maid wears? Don't be ridiculous."

They began their soup in silence.

"I consider that the house servants, with the exception of the butler and my valet, are your domain," he said, realizing how revolutionary his words were for this house. His mother had never had charge of anything. "You may make any changes you wish, Madeline."

And he listened in some dismay to his tone, imperious, offhand, as if he did not care about anything that had to do with her world.

"Good," she said. "There will be changes, I assure you."

They ate the main course in silence.

"I like my bedchamber," she said brightly at last. "It is light and airy."

"I hope you will like mine as well, then," he said, "since that is where you will be sleeping."

"Will I?" she said. There was color in her cheeks and a light in her eyes that caused him a surge of desire.

But he was aware of what he had said aloud in front of the butler and two footmen, standing like wooden statues at the sideboard, and of what was in her face. And instead of merely smiling at her or else dropping the subject entirely, he had to make matters worse.

He looked very directly into her eyes. "Try sleeping anywhere else," he said, "and I shall come to fetch you."

She recoiled rather as if he had slapped her. And he knew that the words had been neither provocative nor teasing. They had sounded like a threat.

In the week and a half following their arrival at Dunstable Hall he learned to stay away from her as much as possible during the day and to confine his conversation to purely mundane household matters. And there was a sort of peace between them. Madeline was busy learning the workings of the house and imposing her will on Mrs. Cockings. The maid who brought their breakfast on the fourth morning had curls peeping from beneath her cap—and smiled and blushed at Madeline's compliment.

Madeline seemed not actively unhappy.

And if he was quite incapable of showing her his love in words or by facial expressions, then he tried to make up for the lack at night. She was like a drug to him. He had been totally addicted to his need for her long before they arrived at Dunstable Hall.

But it was a need not only for personal gratification. The need was just as strong in him to love her, to make of their beddings a beautiful and fulfilling experience for her too. And his main comfort, his main hope, during the early days of their marriage was that he was having considerable success. She enjoyed their lovemaking quite as much as he did and she was learning how to increase both her own pleasure and his.

If only he could murmur something to her in words! But he could not, so he would not brood on the matter. On the whole his marriage was developing a great deal better than he had feared on their wedding day.

Though there was no cause for great rejoicing, of course. After they had been home a week, she informed him with a look almost of defiance on her face that she was not after all with child.

"Well," he said, hiding his disappointment, "then it seems you need not have married me after all, Madeline. You might have slipped through that web to freedom."

"That is not why I married you," she said.

"Why did you?"

"I don't know," she said after a pause. "Perhaps an unconscious desire to be punished."

No, there was no great harmony in their marriage. Only a cautious peace.

He was devoting much of his days to traveling his estate with his bailiff, learning about the workings of his holdings. Even though he had lived at home until he was six and twenty, his father had never allowed him any hand in the running of the estate. His ignorance was almost total.

The living conditions of his laborers and their wages were deplorable, he began to discover. His tenants had grievances that had long been ignored. There was a great deal of work to be done. But he spent those first weeks looking and listening, making no hasty judgments, making no inexperienced decisions that time might prove disastrous.

He almost forgot that there was a world beyond the boundaries of his land. In his father's time there almost had been no other world. There had been almost no socializing with neighbors, since almost all of them had been judged at one time or another ungodly. There had been no playmates for him and Alex, except each other. Any child with whom they might have played would only lead them astray.

And so it was something of a surprise to be invited to a dinner and evening party at the home of Mr. Hooper, a prosperous landowner whose land adjoined his own on the west side. The Hoopers had been cut from the late Lord Beckworth's list of acquaintances after a boundary dispute twenty years or more before.

"We have had an invitation to dinner at the home of our neighbors next week," he told Madeline, going to her immediately in the morning room, where she was writing letters.

"Have we?" she said. "I was beginning to wonder if we had any neighbors, though there seemed to be plenty of people at church last Sunday."

"My father did not associate with many people," he said. "Perhaps they think I will be like him. And perhaps I am."

"No, you are not," she said. She smiled impishly at him in an expression he had not seen very often directed his way. "Tessa, the upstairs maid who limps a little, was caught outside the stables last night kissing one of the grooms. Mrs. Cockings informed me that both servants were instantly dismissed."

"Hm," he said, embarrassed. "Doubtless I will regret having intervened."

"You told Mr. Cockings this morning that they were to stay, and be allowed to marry too. I understood from the way Mrs. Cockings told the story that such scandalous goings-on would not have been tolerated in your father's time, James."

"Well," he said gruffly, "the man is a good groom."

"Ah," she said, "that explains your generosity. I have had letters from Anna and Allan Penworth this morning."

"Penworth?" he said with a frown. "He is writing to you? Does he not know you are married?"

"Of course he knows," she said, "or why would he be sending the letter here? We have corresponded frequently during the last year. He has been using his artificial leg until he is all over black bruises, he says." She laughed. "Just imagine. I betrothed myself to him thinking that he would need me for the rest of his life. He is a wonder. He says he may go back to London for the Season next year."

"Well," he said, "you will not be going."

"I did not expect to," she said. She frowned. "Why that look?"

"If you think I will tolerate your writing to old beaux and planning to meet them," he said, "you do not know me, Madeline. You may regret your choice of husband, but you made the choice."

She flung down her quill pen, splashing ink over the half-written sheet on the escritoire before her, and jumped to her feet. "What are you suggesting?" she said. "That Allan and I are exchanging love letters? That I am exchanging them with half a dozen other men too? Or a dozen? That I am planning clandestine meetings with them all? How dare you speak to me so."

"You always were an incurable flirt," he said. "I don't know why I should expect you to change now."

"And you always were a humorless tyrant," she said. "I don't know why one incident with your servants deceived me into thinking that perhaps you had changed. In future, James, I will not even try to share my correspondence or any other part of my life with you. I shall keep it all to myself and you may think or imagine what you will."

"I am devastated," he said. "We have had such a close relationship until now."

"Perhaps in time I *will* take a lover," she said. "I imagine that the day may come when I will want a little brightness and excitement in my life. And I certainly will get neither from you."

He was across the room in a few strides and gripped her arms in a grasp that had her visibly wincing. "If I cannot put excitement into your life," he said, "perhaps it is because your palette is jaded from too much empty frivolity. And you will try taking a lover at your peril,

Madeline." His eyes narrowed on her; his breath quickened.

She looked up at him and laughed. "Go on," she said. "I believe your next move is to turn me beneath your arm and beat me until I have to lie facedown on my bed for the rest of the day. Or else to kiss me so fiercely that my lips will be swollen and bruised for a week. Don't disappoint me, James. Play the part of the heavy-handed lord and master. You do it so well."

He dropped his hands and stood staring at her, his shoulders drooped. And the fight went out of her eyes. She dropped them to his chin.

"I think perhaps your father talked to your mother and to you in that way," she said. "But you will not talk to me like that and get away with it. And if you ever strike me, I shall hit back. If you ever use me in anger or out of a wish to punish, I shall leave you." She looked back up into his eyes.

"I will never strike you," he said, "no matter how much you provoke me. As for the rest, if you ever leave me, I shall come and bring you back again. Even if you take yourself to the far corner of the world. You are my wife, and you will remain so for as long as we both live."

Because I need you. Because I love you. Because I want and want and want to make you happy. Because the thought of your turning to another man drives me insane. He looked deeply into her eyes, his expression a mask, and turned and left the room without another word.

He sent an acceptance of the Hoopers' invitation.

IT WAS A GREAT RELIEF to Madeline to discover that they were after all to attend at least one entertainment. For the first week after their arrival at Dunstable Hall, she had not really noticed the lack of visitors. She had been too engrossed in adjusting her life to a totally new environment—a large and gloomy house, which had no need to be gloomy at all, a severe and humorless house-keeper, who for years had run the household as if it were an army post, and a moody, surly husband.

It was not an easy adjustment to make. There was a great dragging at her spirits, and the temptation to just give up the struggle was enormous. The house had always been run very well, it seemed. Why not allow it to continue to do so rather than have a daily battle of wills with Mrs. Cockings? And there was no pleasing her husband. She had tried. Several times she had tried to pretend that he was just like any other man of her acquaintance. She had tried to smile and talk to him as if she expected answering smiles and words.

But he had that way of looking through her with those dark eyes, which were themselves inscrutable. And a way of speaking that was abrupt and to the point. And no way at all of smiling.

The temptation was to ignore him, to withdraw into her own world. But it was not in her nature to be aloof, and she had to live with this man for the rest of her life. Besides, she wanted to share her life with him. For a reason that totally escaped her comprehension, she loved him.

But how could one share with a man who was so totally unresponsive?

Except in bed. She could please him there as he pleased her. She could have basked in the glory of their nights together. She could have lived on the love she received and gave there.

But she could not. If anything, the very satisfactory nature of their sexual life made her more dissatisfied. He had always admitted to an attraction to her. And it was becoming increasingly obvious that the attraction was only physical and that that was the reason he had married her. He wanted her for his bed. He would put up with the irritation of her presence in his home during the days so that he might use her at night.

It was not a flattering realization. She felt very much less of a person than she had done before her marriage. And so she had to fight on. If she did not, she would have to sink her mind in the degradation of knowing herself her husband's plaything and nothing else.

Sometimes she hated him.

And at the end of the first week she became aware of the loneliness of their existence and wondered with some unease if they would ever visit or be visited. How could she invite visitors if she had never been presented to any of their neighbors?

The dissatisfaction began at about the same time as she discovered that she was not with child. She was severely disappointed and depressed for a few days, though she told herself how ridiculous she was being. There had been only the two weeks of their marriage and the one encounter the week before that. Perhaps by the end of the next month she would be more fortunate. Or at the end of the next. Perhaps she would have to be patient for several months.

But she was six and twenty, the same age as Ellen, who had two children already, and a year older than Alex. Perhaps she would never have children of her own. Perhaps in addition to everything else, their marriage would be childless.

It was a ridiculous fear after two weeks of marriage.

She was very relieved at the invitation from Mr. and Mrs. Hooper, and James's acceptance of it.

"How old are they, James?" she asked when they were in the carriage on their way to Moorton Grange. "Do they have a family? Will we be the only guests, do you suppose, or will there be others?" She felt as excited as if she were a girl again on her way to her first party. And in a way there was something quite new in all this. She was going to her first entertainment as Madeline Purnell, Lady Beckworth. She would be meeting her neighbors for the first time.

He was sitting against one corner of the carriage, looking at her with eyes that might possibly hold some amusement. It was so hard to tell with James. "In their fifties, probably," he said. "They have five children. The three oldest are married and away from home. I am not sure about the other two. I have no idea if there will be other guests or not."

"But the invitation said evening party as well as dinner, did it not?" she said, looking at him in some triumph. "That must mean there will be other guests."

"I suppose so," he said.

He seemed more approachable than usual. Madeline glanced down at her pale green dress beneath her pelisse. "Will any of them mind that I am not in mourning?" she asked. "I look very noticeably not so next to your black, James."

"Why the devil should I care if they mind or not?" he said.

"Your father was their neighbor," she said.

He laughed and turned to look out the window. "Well," he said, "I should care if you were in mourning, Madeline.

I have already told you what I would do with anything black you chose to wear in defiance of me."

She sat back in her seat, her mood deflated for the moment. "There was no need for that," she said. "You know there has been no question of defiance. You have no cause to speak as if you are cross with me."

"Then why do you worry about what our neighbors will think?" he said. "Your business is to please me, is it not? Do you care what your neighbors think of you?"

"Yes, of course I do," she said. "I am to live here for the rest of my days as your wife. I must live close to them for the rest of my life also. I hope to make friends and friendly acquaintances. Of course I care about pleasing them. And as for pleasing you, if I were to make that the sole aim of my life, I would be doomed to terrible failure, wouldn't I? You are impossible to please."

"It pleases me when you are not constantly crossing my will," he said.

"If you want a docile little mouse," she said, "you married the wrong woman."

And she felt thoroughly cross, her mood of a few minutes before in ruins. Her evening was spoiled. Except that she was not going to allow him to do any such thing to her. She was not going to allow him to dash her spirits whenever they had the misfortune to be in company together. She had set out to enjoy the visit, and enjoy it she would.

She turned a sunny face to her husband again a couple of minutes after their last words.

"Will we be able to entertain, James?" she asked. "Dunstable Hall is such a splendid place for guests."

"You are the mistress of the place," he said. "If it pleases you to entertain, then we will entertain."

She laughed lightly and looked at him with twinkling eyes. "If it pleases me?" she said. "Can it be that you think it part of your business to please me, James? As it is mine to please you? And will I please you if I turn out to be an accomplished hostess? Will you be proud of me?"

"You are in a strange mood," he said. "Like a child being given a treat."

"But I am being given a treat," she said. "I am being taken to the Hoopers' party and my husband has just said that we may entertain if it pleases me. James—" she stretched a hand across the distance between them and laid it lightly on his, "you are in grave danger of becoming human." She laughed gaily.

But of course, she thought a few moments later, having retrieved her hand and turned to look out the window and try to revive her spirits yet again, he took it all wrongly. His jaw set even as she laughed at him, and his eyes blazed at her.

"It pleases you to mock me," he said. "That is all I get for trying to treat you with some kindness, Madeline?"

"But I was not mocking you," she said, her eyes widening in dismay. "I was teasing."

"Pardon me," he said, "but people who are scarcely human do not always recognize teasing."

"Oh, you are being ridiculous!" she said.

"Of course," he said, turning his head away from her.

MOORTON GRANGE was a sizable gray stone house, though it was not nearly on the scale of Dunstable Hall. There were several guests. James realized by the effusive, yet rather anxious greetings of Mr. and Mrs. Hooper that he and Madeline were the guests of honor. They and their neighbors were doubtless curious to discover if he would be like his father, or if they might look to him as more of a social leader in the community. Although he had grown up at Dunstable Hall and lived there until four years before, he was in all essential ways a stranger to them.

He presented his wife to Mr. and Mrs. Hooper and Miss Christine Hooper—Timothy Hooper, it seemed, had moved away from home just the year before; to Reverend and Mrs. Hurd; to Mr. and Mrs. Trenton, Mark Trenton, and Miss Henrietta Trenton; to Mr. Palmer and his sister; and to Carl Beasley, whom he was surprised to see if indeed the party was in his honor. And there were more guests still to come.

Madeline fairly sparkled, of course, as she always did in company. He could see that within ten minutes of their arrival she had enslaved most, if not all, of the company. And during dinner there was a great deal of animated conversation and laughter from the other end of the table, where she sat at Mr. Hooper's right.

"We have arranged for music and cards, my lord," Mrs. Hooper explained to him. "My Christine wanted dancing, and I am sure the young people would have enjoyed it, but we said no for this occasion on account of the recent passing of your father."

Miss Palmer played the pianoforte after dinner, and Mark Trenton sang. Miss Hooper played the harp, and Madeline was prevailed upon to play the pianoforte too, though she protested laughingly that her neighbors might never again press her to do so.

"Well, Beckworth," Carl Beasley said at James's elbow, "so you have come home."

"As you see," James said. "And you are still Peterleigh's steward?"

Beasley inclined his head. "I believe we were all somewhat surprised to learn that you were bringing home a bride," he said. "Did you discover that after all the great love of one's life can fade? Or did you consider it expedient to add a wife to your new title?"

"Perhaps you would prefer to discover the answer for yourself over the next few years," James said.

They had been friends of sorts at one time—as far as he had been able to form any friendship during his growing years. They had ridden together, fished together, dreamed of their future together. Carl had been the ward of the Duke of Peterleigh, the son of a cousin of the duke's. He had come to live on Peterleigh's estate at quite a young age. As had his sister, Dora.

"Ben and Adam Drummond would not come tonight," Carl said with a half-smile. "I am afraid I am a more curious fellow."

"I am obliged to you," James said.

The Drummond brothers were prosperous tenants of Peterleigh's. They were a little older than he and Carl, and never close friends of his. They were never anything to him, in fact, until their younger brother, John, married Dora.

"Had you heard that John Drummond is back?" Carl asked, looking casually about him, and watching his former friend at the same time.

"No," James said just as casually. "I have not had a chance to hear much local news."

"Some people have wondered if that fact precipitated your decision to return so soon after the death of your father," Carl said.

Yes, Benjamin and Adam would doubtless wonder. And perhaps John. And Carl himself.

"No," James said, "I had not heard."

"My sister has four children now," Carl said.

"Has she?" James was watching Madeline receive the praise of their neighbors on her performance and laughing and taking the offered hand of Mr. Palmer to rise from the bench.

He could feel the blood pounding at his temples. Dora was back. As simply as that. Years before, he had felt that he had moved heaven and earth and not found her. Yet now he had been back for two whole weeks and not known that she was there too.

She had four children. Dora with four children. Three of them John Drummond's.

He would see her again. He would see what had become of her, what he had done to her.

And he would see his child at last. His son. He had throttled that much information out of Carl, though never the boy's name. He would be almost nine years old now.

"I must go and make the acquaintance of Lady Beckworth," Carl said with a smile.

James watched him cross the room to her. He soon had her smiling and talking with animation. Carl was a tall, athletic-looking gentleman, whose blond wavy hair always looked slightly tousled. James had not realized until that moment how attractive his former friend had grown.

16

MADELINE HAD ENJOYED THE EVENING vastly. She had remembered Alexandra's saying how wonderful and friendly a part of the country Amberley was and how different from the place where she had grown up. And she herself had been at Dunstable Hall for more than two weeks without any communication with their neighbors beyond a few tentative nods at church. But all was to be well after all.

"Miss Palmer is to call for tea tomorrow, James," she said in the carriage on the way home. "She seems a very sensible lady. She taught at a girls' academy for four years, but came back to keep house for her brother."

"I am glad you like her," he said.

"Miss Trenton and her brother are to call one day so that I may go walking with them," she said. "And Mr. Beasley has offered to take me riding about the Duke of Peterleigh's estate. His grace does not come home very often, he says."

"He used to come for a few weeks in the summer," James said.

"Well, I am glad he is not here," she said. "I have never liked the man since the time when he was supposed to be promised to Alexandra and gave her that famous snub the evening she became betrothed to Edmund instead. You were there too. I remember feeling amazed that you could look so fierce without actually doing violence." She laughed.

"She was intended for him from childhood on," he said, "but I can only feel thankful that he did see fit to snub her. She might still have married him else."

"Mr. Beasley is his relative?" Madeline said. "And he has chosen to remain as the duke's steward. He is very amiable."

"He was Peterleigh's ward," James said.

"He has a sister too, doesn't he?" she said, turning her face to him in the darkness of the carriage and smiling. "It is a pity she and her husband were unable to attend tonight. Her husband is one of the duke's tenants. He has been unwell. Mr. Beasley said we will ride by their farm and call upon her."

"If you wish to go walking or riding anywhere, Madeline," James said, "You have only to tell me so and I shall take you. You have no need to impose on neighbors."

"Impose?" she said. "But they all offered. I did not beg. Besides, doing things together is part of friendship, is it not? And I am determined to make friends among our neighbors here."

"I won't have you on Peterleigh's land," he said.

"Why?" she asked, looking at him, amazed. "Because he snubbed your sister, James? But that was such a long time ago. Besides, he is not in residence and is not expected. Mr. Beasley says there is a splendid orchard and organgery beside the house."

"I said you will stay away from there," he said.

She was silent for a moment. "I take it that is an absolute command?" she said.

"Yes." He was not looking at her. His profile was set and hard. "Stay away from there, Madeline. And from Beasley."

"Oh, now I understand," she said. "Mr. Beasley is a young and single gentleman. A handsome one too. You are suspicious and jealous. That is what this is all about, is it not?"

He looked across at her, his eyes very dark in the shadows. "It is not at all the thing for a married lady to be riding about with a single gentleman," he said.

"Oh, nonsense, James!" She clucked her tongue and turned her head away to the window in annoyance. "You just do not wish me to make friends, that is all. You want me all to yourself, though why you want that is a mystery to me, because you clearly dislike me and disapprove of everything I say or do."

"I do not dislike you," he said.

"Then you must be a very good actor," she said.

"Madeline," he said, "I don't . . ."

"I wonder you do not lock all the doors in Dunstable Hall and bar all the windows," she said. "You could carry the keys in a large bunch at your waist. And allow me outside only when I am chained to your wrist or with one of the Cockingses on either side of me, perhaps."

"You are being foolish," he said.

"But of course," she said. "In your eyes I am capable of nothing else, am I? And if you think I am going to obey you in this matter, James, then you will be sorely disappointed. I will choose my own friends and occupy my time with them as I please. And if you don't like it, then you really must lock me up or beat me."

"Beasley means mischief," he said. "Stay away from him, Madeline."

"Are you going to make me?" she asked, her eyes narrowing.

"If I possibly can." he said.

And so she was annoyed again, furiously annoyed, her evening finally in ruins. She had thought to be friendly with him on the way home. She had thought he would be pleased that she liked their neighbors and was already making friends among them. And he had looked so very handsome all evening in his own austere way, dressed in his black mourning clothes. She had felt near to bursting with love for him.

But there was definitely no pleasing him at all. It was tempting, for very pride's sake, to give up the attempt. But giving up would mean a lifetime of very real misery. Perhaps the misery was to be there anyway, but she was not going to hold the door open and invite it in.

"Would you care to organize a dinner for a few weeks in the future?" he asked. "It would make you happy to do that, would it not, Madeline?"

It was surely an olive branch. She turned to smile dazzlingly at him. "Yes," she said, "that would be lovely. Perhaps by then I will have met even more people, and we can invite them all."

"I will leave the planning to you, then," he said.

"James," she said later when they were in their bedchamber, "I have seen very little more of this place than the house and the immediate grounds. Talking this evening about walking and riding with other people has whetted my appetite. I think I will go riding tomorrow."

"But not alone," he said. "Or if you do, you must keep

to the roads and pastures. Not out onto the moors. You will get lost."

"Oh, nonsense," she said, "I am not a child."

He came across the room to where she was standing beside the bed. "And I am not a man to be defied at every turn," he said quietly to her. "I know this area well. The moors are dangerous, Madeline. It is very easy to get lost out on them. I will have your promise not to ride out there alone. Not for years to come, at least. Now, if you please."

"James," she said, smiling and touching his chest with one light hand, "I will promise on condition that you promise to take me riding out there within the week."

"You want me with you?" he asked.

"Yes, I want you with me," she said, letting her other hand join the first. "You are my husband, aren't you? My bridegroom of one month? Promise to take me riding."

"So that we can quarrel every step of the way?" he said.

"I will not promise unless you do," she said. "I shall go out onto the moors every day of my life just to defy you and then we will quarrel even more. Take me?"

"Yes," he said, "I'll take you, of course. You don't need a promise for that. But don't think I have forgotten yours, Madeline. Your promise, if you please."

"Oh, very well, then," she said, "though I am sure you are being ridiculous. I promise not to ride out onto the moors unless you or someone of whom you approve is with me for—how long?"

"Five years."

"For five years," she said. "There, are you pleased now? You have a nice docile, obedient wife."

She tried to coax a smile from him with her own, but he gazed darkly back at her.

"Promise me not to get involved with Beasley," he said.

She put up a hand and spread her fingers over his mouth. "Let's leave it at that," she said. "Let's not quarrel any more tonight. I get so mortally tired of quarreling." She grinned. "Especially when you are always in the wrong."

He took her by the wrist and gazed into her eyes. She could see deeply into his, to what might have been pain. But his face was expressionless.

She shook her head slightly. "Don't say any more," she said. "Please, James, don't say any more."

By day she could despise herself for the way she always abandoned herself to his lovemaking, for the way she had learned to participate in it and take full pleasure from it. She could despise herself for catering so willingly to his only need for her.

But by night there was only James and his unhurried, expert lovemaking. And her need to touch and be touched, to love and be loved. She had learned to be naked and unembarrassed with him on the bed, even with the candles burning. And she had learned how and where to touch him, how to arouse him, how to heighten his pleasure when he was in her. She had learned how to move for her own pleasure, how to let tension build, when to let tension go and trust him to bring her to a climax.

And so instead of quarreling further, they made slow love and found in each other's body all the harmony, all the rightness, that was absent from the other aspects of their lives.

And Madeline, lying beneath her husband and moving with his rhythm during the minutes when their desire built to a crest, was as usual beyond all thought except that this man who was loving her was James and that she loved him with all her heart and soul as well as with her body. And as usual she wanted to say his name as she buried her hands in his hair—to say it over and over again against his mouth, into his ear.

James, James.

But there was always just enough reason left, just enough pride, that she knew that to do so would be to degrade herself. For as things were, he would know only that she had a physical craving for him as he had for her. She could not hide that so made no attempt to do so. But if she once said his name while he loved her, then he would know. And then he would know too that he had it in his power to make her his slave.

She would rather die with her love undeclared than become his slave.

And so they finished their lovemaking with incoherent cries, but with no words at all. And after he had lifted himself away from her, he lay staring up at the canopy above their heads in the flickering light of the single candle that still burned, while she lay turned away from him, staring off into the shadows.

Both were physically satisfied and very close to sleep. And both were very much alone again. And both were very unhappy.

JAMES WAS RIDING ALONE along the banks of a stream that divided part of his property from that of the Duke of Peterleigh. He was returning from a visit to one of his tenants, who had complained more and more loudly since he had realized that he was being listened to that his rents were too high. James agreed, though he had not told the man so yet. He wished to consult a little more closely with his bailiff.

It seemed that every tenant's rent was too high and every laborer's wages too low. His instinct was to recognize the injustice and put it right immediately. But of course, when one was the owner of large tracts of land and responsible for every soul who lived upon them, justice was not always an easy thing to detect. For if he should bankrupt himself in order to benefit those dependent upon him, then eventually they would see no benefit at all from his generosity or sense of right.

It was a tricky business, as he was becoming well aware.

There were some people ahead of him, on the bank of the stream. Children, probably, fishing. He had come to that particular spot himself as a lad, when he could get away from the house, to fish with Carl Beasley.

The grass was wet beneath his horse's hooves. It had rained steadily for four days after their visit to the Hoopers. There had been no chance to keep his promise to take Madeline riding out onto the moors. But she seemed not to have been actively unhappy. She was busy planning the dinner they were to host the following week. Palmer and his sister had called on them one afternoon, the young Trentons on another.

And she had been busy writing letters. She made a point now of telling him from whom she received every letter, her chin lifted defiantly, but of telling him nothing about the contents of those letters. There had been no more from Penworth, and indeed he felt foolish for the objection he had made to that particular correspondence. Her betrothal to Penworth had been ended the year before, and there had seemed to be no particular attachment on either side during the spring in London. She had had letters from her mother and both brothers, from Ellen, from Anna, and from Jennifer Simpson. There had been letters addressed to both of them from Alex and Jean, whose wedding had been delayed until Christmastime on account of her future sister-in-law's wedding planned for that month.

Madeline spent much of each morning writing long letters in reply. She never offered to let him read them. He sometimes wondered what she wrote about. What did she say about her new home? About him? Did she tell the truth? Or did she pretend that all was well? He somehow could not imagine Madeline divulging the true state of their marriage to anyone, except perhaps to her twin.

There were three children on the bank, the youngest one in tears, the oldest scornfully ignoring him. The middle one, a girl, was patting the infant on the back reassuringly. They had one fishing rod among the three of them. The oldest boy was holding it.

"What is the matter?" James called across the stream. "Is the little lad not being given his turn?"

The child wailed more loudly when he realized that he had an adult audience.

"It is just that he rolled his ball into the water and Jonathan will not get it for him," the girl said, continuing to pat ineffectively.

"The water would not reach even to his waist where the ball is," the boy called Jonathan said, not even looking up from his rod. "Let him get it himself. He was told not to play so near the edge."

"Can't you see that he is frightened?" the girl asked. "And I can't go in. I'm wearing a dress."

James swung down from his horse with a smile, though he was not particularly feeling a smile. "Perhaps I can risk it," he said. He looked down into the water, which was swollen from the rain. "Hm, I don't think my boots would survive it, would they?" He sat down on the bank to pull them off one by one.

The little boy had forgotten to cry. The older boy's attention had been fully diverted from his fishing. The little girl was giving advice.

"I would not go in if I were you, sir," she said. "You will get your breeches and your stockings wet."

James winked at her. "But I don't have a mama at home to scold me," he said.

The two little boys laughed.

The ball was quite visible and easily retrieved. He was soaked to the knees after he had finally handed it back to the smallest child and climbed out on his side of the stream again, and was facing the ticklish problem of whether to pull his boots back on again or go riding home in his stockinged feet with his boots beneath his arm. He shrugged and pulled on the boots much to the amusement of the boys and against the advice of the girl.

"Where do you come from?" he asked, though he knew the answer very well. He had to hear it in words.

"Mama is visiting Uncle Carl," the girl said.

"And who is your mama?" he asked, grimacing with some distaste as he pulled on the second boot.

"She is Mrs. John Drummond," the girl said. "But she is a cousin to the Duke of Peterleigh and we have come to live close to here all the time, where Mama and Papa used to live before they moved to Somerset, where we were all born. I am Sylvia Drummond, and this is Patrick. Jonathan is the oldest. And there is Lester too—he is the baby."

"Indeed," James said, vaulting into his saddle again. "I am pleased to make your acquaintance. I am Beckworth."

"Oh," the girl said. "You are the one with the new bride. Uncle Carl was telling Mama about her. You had better gallop home, sir, before you catch your death."

James smiled again, touched his hat with his riding whip, and turned his horse's head for home.

The two younger children were fair and somewhat stocky, like John Drummond. And with the coloring of Dora too, of course. The eldest boy was tall and thin. His thick dark hair fell over his eyes. And the eyes in his thin face were dark.

His son looked like him.

Jonathan. He had not known his name.

He had felt nothing for the boy beyond a certain curiosity and wonder. Wonder that he had fathered a child whom he had not seen until that day. He had wondered if he would feel a rush of paternal love. He had felt nothing.

But his son! His own flesh and blood.

He urged his horse into a canter. Not so much because his feet and legs were uncomfortably wet and cold, but because Madeline was at home. He wanted to be with her.

MADELINE WAS RIDING ALONG the banks of the same stream the following afternoon with Henrietta and Mark Trenton. She rather enjoyed their company, since they were both cheerful and full of conversation. And it was a beautiful late September day after four days of rain and the gloomy clouds of the day before.

Indeed, she would have been perfectly happy if only James were with them. But he had an appointment at the house with his man of business and had been unable to come.

And why would she want him with her anyway? she

asked herself as she laughed at something Mark said and launched into an anecdote of her own. He would surely have ruined the afternoon with his taciturnity and lack of humor. And she surely would have ended up quarreling with him over something—after they were alone, of course.

It was better to be away from him.

But she felt a twinge of guilt, and was immediately annoyed with herself, when a voice hailed them from among the trees on the other side of the stream and the handsome figure of Carl Beasley, also on horseback, appeared.

"Well met," he called, sweeping off his hat. "Are you out riding? And you have two lovely ladies to yourself, Trenton? This will never do."

He had a very attractive smile, Madeline noticed, responding to it. He had white, even teeth.

"But a sister does not count," she called back. "And I am a married lady. Poor Mr. Trenton is not to be envied after all."

"Why do you not bring your horses to this side of the stream?" he asked. "We could take a ride up to the house and orchard."

Madeline was quite glad afterward that Henrietta was the first to reply. She realized that she had been about to make an excuse. She did not like to consider why she would have done so.

"May we see the dogs?" Henrietta asked eagerly. "Have the puppies grown much? They were such darling little creatures the last time I saw them."

"I believe they can still be classified as puppies," Carl said with a smile, holding his horse still while Mark led the way across the stream.

They had to ride in single file through the trees, but when they came within sight of the manor, Carl Beasley drew his horse alongside Madeline's.

"This was a fortunate encounter," he said.

"Yes." She smiled. "I promised to go riding with the Trentons when we were at Mr. Hooper's party, but the weather has not been suitable until today. Unfortunately, my husband is otherwise engaged this afternoon."

"Ah, yes," he said. "Beckworth was never one to indulge in such frivolities as an afternoon ride for the sake of riding. Are you feeling very dull at Dunstable Hall?"

"Not at all," she said hastily. "I have been finding a great deal to do with myself."

"Have you?" he said. "But of course, the place and your marriage are all new to you. You must take a firm hand with Beckworth, though, ma'am, and not allow him to keep you closeted at home." He smiled to take any sting from his words.

"But he encouraged me to organize next week's dinner," she said. "You have had your invitation?"

He inclined his head. "And have penned an acceptance already," he said. He turned back to the Trentons. "The dogs are in the stables. Perhaps you would like to look at them while I show Lady Beckworth the orchard."

Madeline would have preferred to go to the stables too. Not that she had minded for the past several years being alone with a gentleman. She had scoffed at the idea of chaperones after passing her twentieth birthday. And she was not, absolutely not, going to allow James's ridiculous notions of what was proper determine her behavior. It was true that Mr. Beasley was a very attractive man, but that made no difference to anything. She smiled determinedly.

"The house looks quite magnificent," she said. "Do you live there all alone?"

"Except on his grace's rare visits, yes," he said, dismounting from his horse and lifting her from hers before turning both horses over to a waiting groom. "It has been my home for many years. I had my sister with me, of course, until her marriage."

"I still have not met her," Madeline said.

"Her husband has been sick for more than a month," Carl said, taking her arm on his and strolling with her in the direction of the orchard. "They have not been at church or at any entertainment in that time. She was here yesterday with her children. She is curious to meet you."

"Is she?" Madeline said. "I shall look forward to the meeting, then. Oh, what splendid apple trees you have."

"We are rather proud of them," he said. He looked at her and laughed. "I wonder if Beckworth will try to prevent your meeting with Dora."

"With your sister?" she said in surprise. "Why should he?"

His eyes twinkled at her. "There was a time when he was somewhat smitten with her charms," he said. "But I should not be telling tales. They were both very young. Doubtless, he forgot about her long ago."

"I daresay," Madeline said. "When I think of gentlemen I was smitten with years ago, I can scarce put a face to their names."

"We sometimes do foolish things when we are young, don't we?" he said, opening the door of the orangery and allowing her to precede him inside. "Beckworth went quite berserk when Dora married John Drummond and moved away with him. He seemed to think there was some conspiracy against him. He succeeded in blacking one of my eyes and breaking my nose. He might have done the same with John's older brothers had he not been unwise enough to tackle them both together. The foolishness of youth!" He laughed lightly.

"Gracious!" Madeline said. "Are you serious, sir? Whyever would he do such a thing?"

"You have not discovered Beckworth's violent side?" he asked. But his voice was teasing. "This was many years ago. I am sure he learned long ago to control his impulses. And I suppose he thought himself sufficiently provoked. He seemed to think...But never mind that. It is ancient history, and I must look to my sister's reputation. Besides, you are Beckworth's new bride. I would not want to tell tales. I am sure his new attachment far outstrips the old. I have told you all this only because it was a long time ago and you look like a lady with a sense of humor. Now, to change the subject. We have a gardener who has a passion for the orangery. I think he does rather well, don't you?"

"Yes, indeed," Madeline said.

The door of the orangery opened at that moment to admit the Trentons.

"The puppies have grown," Henrietta said. "What a shame. I do think they should stay tiny for much longer than they do. A footman stepped out of the house as we passed to tell us that tea will be served at your convenience."

Carl smiled. "The housekeeper must have seen that we have visitors, then. Ma'am?" He extended an arm for Madeline's. "May I lead you to the house?"

"I really had not expected to stay for tea," she said. "My husband will be expecting me home."

"Ah," he said, "you show the eagerness of a bride. The chances are that he is so engrossed in business that he has not even missed you. Though he would be a fool if that is true. Half an hour, ma'am?"

She hesitated. "Half an hour, then," she said, and felt rather like a child involved in some forbidden activity.

"It seems that my nephews and niece met your husband yesterday," Carl said to Madeline during tea when there was a momentary lull in the conversation.

"Oh," she said, "is that who they were? He came home very wet after retrieving a child's ball from the stream."

"Patrick has a new hero," he said, "as well as his ball. Sylvie was only concerned that Beckworth might have caught his death of cold. May I reassure her that he has not?"

"Oh, no," Madeline said with a laugh. "The only casualty is one ruined pair of boots."

"Mrs. Drummond called upon Mama a few days ago," Henrietta said. "What a darling the baby is. He has soft blond curls exactly like his older brother and sister. Only the oldest boy looks quite different. Indeed, it is difficult to believe that he has the same parents as the others."

"Henrietta!" her brother said beneath his breath.

"What?" she asked, wide-eyed.

Carl smiled. "Jonathan is rather different from the other three," he said. "Tall and thin and dark. He does not look like his mama or papa. It is a good thing that both my father and Drummond's were dark-haired men, or there might be some embarrassment for my sister."

"Oh." Henrietta flushed painfully. "I did not mean to suggest..."

"Of course you did not," Carl said with an easy laugh. "Have another scone, Miss Trenton."

Mark jumped into the conversational gap. "Papa thinks the waters at Harrogate may help his gout," he said. "I believe we will be spending a month there before Christmas."

"Harrogate is somewhere I have always wanted to visit," Madeline said.

Less than half an hour later she was riding across the stream with the Trentons, waving good-bye to Mr. Beasley, who had accompanied them as far as the boundary, and riding in the direction of home.

James was thirty years old. He had, of course, done a great deal of living in that time. And this was his home, the place where he had lived most of the first twenty-six years of his life. Of course there would be people and events from his past that she could not be expected to know about. Perhaps one day she would persuade him to tell her more of his past.

Though it really did not matter. It would take her a week of nonstop talking to tell him all about her own past. And that did not matter at all. She was his wife now. His. All those others meant nothing whatsoever to her in comparison with what he meant.

"Mark," Henrietta said, turning to him accusingly when they were a safe distance from the stream, "whatever did you mean by hissing at me during tea? What had I said?"

"Nothing," he said, frowning at her crossly. "Nothing at all, Henrietta."

"But Mr. Beasley seemed to think that I had been suggesting that Jonathan Drummond does not really belong to his mama and papa," she said. "And you must have thought so too or you would not have said 'Henrietta!' in such an agonized voice. I could have died, Mark. If I had ever thought such a thing, I certainly would not have said it aloud. Did you have to draw attention to me?"

"Drop it," he said, glancing uneasily at Madeline and away again. "I didn't mean anything, and neither did you."

"But is there any such possibility?" she asked him.

"Henrietta!" he said sternly. "Mind your manners. We are in company."

She flushed. "I do beg your pardon, Lady Beckworth," she said. "But I was so mortified I could have died."

"That is quite all right," Madeline said. "Sometimes we all say embarrassing things without at all meaning to do so."

"But you will see what I mean when you see those children," Henrietta said. "You would never guess that Jonathan is brother to the other three."

"Have you ridden out onto the moors yet?" Mark asked Madeline.

"No," she said. "But my husband has promised to take me riding there within the next day or two. It seems that I am not permitted to ride on the moors alone." She smiled.

"It is easy to get lost," he said, "especially in winter. People have died out on the moors in the snow, sometimes within easy reach of some habitation."

They chattered easily on, Henrietta riding silently at their side for a few minutes.

17

JAMES HAD PROMISED TO TAKE MADELINE
riding on the moors within the week. And finally, after the rain, the weather seemed to have settled into an
early autumn beauty and warmth. It was perfect for riding, better than the heat of summer.

He looked forward to the afternoon ride. They had
both been busy about other business during the morning.
After a lengthy session with his man of business the day
before, he had met with his bailiff that morning to give orders that his laborers' wages be raised and repairs be made
to their homes before winter set in.

Madeline was dressed in a royal blue velvet riding habit
and jaunty hat to match. He had seen neither before. She
looked very vividly beautiful, he thought, waving aside a
groom and tossing her into her sidesaddle himself. She
settled herself and smiled down at him.

"I finally believe you about the moors," she said as he
mounted his own stallion. "Mr. Trenton said the same
thing yesterday, though he did say they are more dangerous during the winter when the snow falls."

"So you will believe a neighbor and not me," he said,
leading the way from the cobbled stable yard. But he did
not speak with annoyance. He knew she was teasing, and

he knew that having given her promise, she could be relied upon not to worry him by riding out alone.

"Sometimes I think you are overprotective," she said, but she smiled and looked as if she really did not mind if he was.

They had settled in the past week into an almost comfortable sort of amity. They had both found plenty to do during the days that did not include the other, and spent little time together. And when they were together, they did not converse a great deal. But it seemed that they were learning to adjust to each other. They were learning to avoid confrontations that could only leave both angry and frustrated.

He was beginning to dare to hope that they could be contented together. And he was trying hard to bring about that desirable state. He was not the sort of man who could make Madeline sparkle, but he was learning to live on her smiles. And she smiled at him frequently. He was pleased even though he knew that she did so in a conscious effort to keep the peace between them. He knew that she was working as hard on their marriage as he was.

"The world seems to be a vaster place here than at Amberley," she said, as they rode out north of the house. "Do you know what I mean?"

"Of course," he said. "Amberley is in a valley enclosed by hills. The slopes are covered with trees. The beach is bordered by high cliffs. It is a small, though lovely world. This is far less picturesque, far more elemental."

"I am not sure it is less beautiful, though," she said, "though I was prepared to find it so."

They did not pursue the conversation. They were far more often silent together. But she looked relaxed. She did not seem any longer to squirm with embarrassment and anger with him for not talking.

She had taken tea with Beasley the day before. She had come to him immediately on her return home and told him so, that familiar defiant lift to her chin as she did so.

"He asked us onto the duke's land," she had said, "and Miss Trenton accepted because she wanted to see the puppies, and it would have been churlish of me to refuse. And then the housekeeper saw us outside the house and sent a message that tea was to be served. I could hardly refuse. And I enjoyed my hour there, James, and found Mr. Beasley to be very amiable. I am telling you only so that you will not find out later and think that I did something forbidden behind your back."

He had looked closely into her eyes and nodded his head. There had appeared to be only defiance in her eyes, nothing else.

It had all been a long time ago. Perhaps he was being absurd to imagine that a grown man would hold a grudge for so many years. Beasley had not been entirely unfriendly at the Hoopers'. His vow of revenge had been made nine years before. It was true that the enmity had been kept very much alive during the following five years, while they had both still lived in the same neighborhood. But four years had passed since then. Dora had been married a long time and had four children now. He himself had a new bride.

James had blamed Beasley for writing to Peterleigh as soon as Dora's condition became known. He had thought Beasley his friend, and the man had known about his love for Dora and hers for him. The three of them had spent time together during that summer when he had been home from university. Yet after he had gone back and her brother learned that Dora was with child, he had not written to him at all, or allowed Dora to do so.

He had conspired with Peterleigh and James's father to avert scandal and marry off Dora as fast as could be to John Drummond, who had doubtless been paid handsomely for his compliance.

James had never blamed Peterleigh. He had been far away in London at the time and doubtless did not know the full truth of the matter. Dora was his ward. His chief concern must have been for her reputation. And so he had married her to a willing man and packed her off with her new husband to one of his estates in the south of England so that the scandal could blow itself out. If he knew that the father was James Purnell, then he would also have been anxious to avert scandal in that direction. There had always been an understanding that he would marry Alex when she grew up.

No, he had never blamed Peterleigh. He had always blamed his father and Beasley. Neither had written to him until Dora was married and gone away already, although both had known the state of his heart and hers. His father, of course, had seen her as a whore under the circumstances, and had been willing to do anything to avoid having her associated with his family. Besides, although she was a cousin of sorts to the duke, she was not quite the bride he would have chosen for his only son.

And so, with a terrible interference, he had helped arrange the marriage, had doubtless contributed financially to it, and informed his son only afterward. Informed him in such a way that only his displeasure with his son's loose morals was conveyed in the letter.

And when he had come home, in a rage of panic and despair, it was to find Dora indeed gone and no one willing to tell him where she was or exactly how she had been persuaded into doing what she had done.

Not that he had ever blamed her. She had always been sweet and placid and somewhat timid. He had cried many tears of despair, imagining her alone and with child and frightened. It would not have taken a great deal to bully her into an unwanted marriage. Had she been told that he did not want her? That question had always haunted him. He still did not know the answer. He had not seen or heard from Dora since the day he had loved her and kissed her good-bye before returning to university.

Now he had avoided seeing her, even though he had known for a week that she was back. He had spent so long trying to find her, yet now he was as diligently avoiding her.

"Alexandra told me that you used to come out here riding with her," Madeline said, "and that you used to gallop. It was strictly forbidden, she said."

"It was Alex's one defiance of authority," he said. "She used to ride neck or nothing and laugh and shriek with excitement. My father would have had an apoplexy if he had ever found out. Fortunately, he never did.

"Shall we gallop now?" she asked, her eyes shining across at him.

"No!" he said firmly. "You are not used to the terrain, Madeline. You have to learn to walk before you can run. Literally."

She made a face at him. "Killjoy!" she said without any particular venom.

"I would not particularly enjoy writing to your mother and your brothers to inform them that you had broken your neck," he said. "They might think I had throttled you, and they would probably scarcely blame me."

She looked at him and laughed, her eyes dancing with merriment. He felt his breath catch in his throat.

"I am not quite as bad as that, am I?" she said.

"Worse sometimes," he said merely for the pleasure of watching her laugh again.

"We will not gallop, then," she said. "I shall allow my horse to trot sedately at your side, my lord. You see how docile a wife I have become? Soon I shall be quite unrecognizable to my mother and brothers."

"Amberley will doubtless have my likeness cast in marble and set in the middle of the formal gardens for achieving the impossible," he said.

This time she actually giggled. He looked at her sternly, though he thought she knew that he did not feel stern.

Carl Beasley was the one he had blamed the most. For one thing, he was the person closest to Dora, the one she relied most heavily upon. And yet knowing that she loved him, knowing that it was his child she had conceived, knowing that he loved her and would have been only too happy to do the honorable thing by her, Carl had concealed the truth from him and allowed his sister to be forced into an unwanted marriage with the dull and unattractive John Drummond.

Carl had betrayed his own sister. It was for that as much as for his own agony that he had fought with his former friend until his hands had been slippery on the other's face. He had broken Carl's nose.

Carl had merely laughed at him—before his nose was broken, that was—and told him it was time he grew up and learned not to live in a fool's paradise. Did he think Dora would have been allowed to marry a Purnell when Miss Purnell was to be the duke's bride?

No amount of pleading or bullying or punching had

been able to prize from Carl the whereabouts of Dora—Mrs. John Drummond.

"Everything has been settled satisfactorily for my sister," Carl had said. "But I will not forgive you for all this, Purnell. If you had only kept yourself for the barmaids of Oxford and left Dora alone, perhaps things would have worked out differently for her. Stranger things have happened. I won't ever forgive you. And one day I will get my revenge on you. I will destroy your life as you have destroyed my sister's."

The only time they had spoken after that, until they met again at the Hoopers' dinner, was when James had gone to him almost a year later, almost mad with frustration, to choke from him the information that the child was a boy and healthy, and that Dora had come safely through her confinement. Nothing of her whereabouts.

It was ancient history. He had not seen Dora, but he did not believe there would be any traces left of his old attachment to her. Indeed, he had thought treacherously in the past few years, if he had not impregnated her, if there had not been all the drama of what had followed, perhaps the great love of his life would have died a natural death even before his next holiday from university.

Perhaps.

And certainly she was not the great love of his life. Only perhaps the great burden of his life. But that was unfair to her.

He turned to Madeline. "Would you like to get down and rest for a while?" he asked.

"In the middle of nowhere?" She looked about her and laughed. "Yes, it would be the perfect thing to do. I love the moors, James. For how many years did I promise?"

"Five!" he said firmly.

She sighed as he lifted her from the saddle and set her feet on the ground. "Four years and fifty-one weeks left," she said. "How slowly times goes."

"Would you prefer to be here without me, then?" he asked, and wished he had not done so. He was feeling so warm about the heart today that her answer might be more than usually painful.

"No," she said with a laugh. "I am afraid I would be horribly lost, James. There is not a human habitation or a recognizable landmark in sight. And you have my permission to say, 'I told you so,' sir. Not that you need my permission, of course."

"I told you so," he said.

They were beside a slight and grassy hollow, which he knew from experience would be warm and sheltered from the breeze.

"The horses will not wander far," he said, setting them free and taking Madeline by the elbow to lead her down into the hollow.

"These are what make the land so treacherous during the winter," he said. "They fill with snow, and the unwary traveler can fall into them and flounder around and panic."

"But today it is beautiful," she said, sitting down on the grass and hugging her knees. "So quiet, James. Listen."

A faint sound of the breeze. A lone bird. A horse snorting. Not silence. There was never silence in nature. But peace. Perfect peace.

James stretched out on the grass, one arm beneath his head, and watched a few white clouds scudding across the sky. He lay there in silence for a long time.

• • •

MADELINE FOUND THE SILENCE quite unembarrassing. Indeed, she was almost unaware of her companion after a few minutes, except that there was the comfortable, unconscious knowledge that she was not alone. All her senses had awakened to her surroundings.

Strange that they should do so here where the landscape was stark, where there was so little that might be called obviously beautiful. Amberley was steeped in beauty, and she had known it, but she could never remember all her senses being stretched to appreciate it all as they were here.

She had tossed her hat aside and could feel the warmth of the sun on the top of her head and the back of her neck. She could hear insects and smell heather and grass. She could feel the grass beneath her. And although the hollow had seemed so slight from horseback that it was scarcely noticeable, they were surrounded by it now, grass meeting sky, all the world contained in one small circle of vastness.

She rested her chin on her knees.

She was feeling cautiously happy. Yes. She sat very still and tested her feelings. She was feeling happy. Perhaps after all her hasty and inexplicable decision to marry James was turning out to be not such a disastrous one. Perhaps they could learn to adjust to each other's ways enough that they could live together in relative peace.

They were already doing so. They had learned not to spend too much time together and not to converse too much when they were together. Those facts did not sound promising when stated in just those words, but they were promising nevertheless. They had had no real quarrel in the past week, only a few bickering words. And more important, there had not been those spells of silent anger and hostility.

She had learned to accept his silences, not to be offended by them, but to recognize them as part of his nature. And James on his part had seemed to accept her need to talk sometimes with light banter. He was even capable on occasion of joining in as he had done just this afternoon during their ride.

It was a cautious beginning to a marriage that must last for many years if their lives took their natural course. Who knew whether their natural antipathy for each other or their mutual desire for peace in their relationship would finally prevail? Or perhaps they must always tread the fine line between the two. Perhaps they would never know total peace.

But then perhaps married couples never did.

"This reminds me somewhat of the Athabasca country," James said from behind her.

She said nothing but gave him the whole of her attention. It was so rare for James to initiate any conversation.

"Perhaps that was why I was able to settle to the life there," he said. "Some men were restless and bored almost from the moment of their arrival."

Madeline hugged her knees more tightly.

"Do you ever get the feeling," he asked, "that everything that happens in life happens for a purpose? When I sailed for Canada, I was going away, leaving something, running away. I had no notion of going *to* anything. But those four years in the wilderness were the most important years of my life."

"Do you wish you were back there?" she asked rather bleakly.

He was quiet for a moment. "No," he said. "Those

years served their purpose, but I don't believe I could settle there for the rest of my working lifetime as many men do."

She laid one cheek against her knee. She thought he had finished and was sorry. She liked to hear him talk. It happened so very rarely.

"I suppose I did not spend enough time out here when I lived here," he said. "I had to go halfway around the world to find myself. I think I found God there, Madeline." He was silent for a while. "That is a nonsensical thing to say when I do not know God or even for sure that there is a God. I was brought up to think of Him as very much involved in human affairs, very stern and judgmental, unyielding, humorless. Far more inclined to condemn than to praise. But when you are in a place like this—just earth and sky and yourself—you wonder about God."

He lapsed into silence.

"God has been mainly a Sunday occurrence for me," she said. "Though I always thought God was love, and I have always seen love all about me."

"I think perhaps," he said, "that when you are alone in such surroundings, you come face-to-face with yourself or else go mad. You learn that being is more important than doing, that perhaps God is not to be found in the noisy affairs of men but in the silence of the heart. Perhaps I am talking nonsense."

"Tell me about your life there," she said when he fell silent again. She felt a little like crying. She felt closer to him than she had ever felt before, and she did not want to lose the moment, though she realized that he had been talking to himself more than to her.

"You like to hear about it?" he asked. "It was a dull

life, Madeline. Days and days, weeks and weeks, of tedium."

"Tell me about the canoe travel," she said. And when he propped himself up on one elbow and she knew that he would do so, she stretched out on the grass beside him, her face turned to the warmth of the sun.

Perhaps there was a reason for her fascination with hearing about those years of his life, she thought. And perhaps she had just glimpsed that reason. Perhaps the key to knowing and understanding her husband lay in his experiences during that time, experiences that he seemed to be only just beginning to assess himself.

"Months of hard toil and hell," he said, "though it can get into one's blood. And I was one of the fortunate ones, being a clerk of the company. The Frenchmen who man the canoes, the *voyageurs*, live lives of unbelievable hardship. They paddle their canoes or portage them past rapids for eighteen hours of every day. And yet a more cheerful breed of men or a louder and more quarrelsome one it would be hard to find."

He launched into a lengthy account of his travels, as she had hoped he would. She listened in fascination for a long time until drowsiness overtook her. She realized a few times, with a little start of guilt, that she had drifted and not heard him at all. And finally she lost the battle and drifted right off.

"AND WHEN WE GOT BACK to the water finally," James said, "there were six mermaids sitting there in a row, all singing off-key." He grinned when Madeline made no objection to the absurd ending to his story.

He reclined on his elbow for a long time, staring at her,

her curls tousled about her face, her lips slightly parted in sleep. His eyes traveled down her slim body and came to rest at her waist. Would he be able to cause a swelling there soon? He hoped so. He passionately wanted a child. With Madeline. And he believed that she had been disappointed when it had not happened the month before.

He wanted a child that could be truly called his own. A child of his wife's.

Her riding habit had pulled up well above her right ankle. A slim and shapely ankle. He smiled.

And he leaned across her and kissed her softly on the lips.

"Mm," she said, and stirred slightly.

He kissed her very lightly again, his opened mouth over hers, his tongue tracing the outline of her parted lips and probing gently between.

"Mm," she said, and stirred again. And there was response there. She opened her mouth wider.

He had meant it just as a mark of affection. He had not fully intended to waken her. But he took almost instant fire. Inside, her mouth was moist and very warm. He smoothed the curls back from her face.

"Mm," she said once more, and her eyes opened suddenly and looked first into his and then beyond him to the blue sky.

He watched her swallow as he began to open first the buttons of her jacket and then those of the blouse beneath. Then he kissed her again while his hand completed the task and found its way beneath her shift to her warm breasts. Her nipples tautened beneath his touch.

It took him just a minute longer to remove both jacket and blouse and pull down her shift so that his mouth could continue the task of arousal that his hands had begun. An unnecessary task, though she moaned and pushed herself against him. She was ready for him. He lifted himself over her, kissed her throat, her chin, her mouth, again.

Was he mad? Had he completely taken leave of his senses? But no one ever came this way. He had been out on the moors a thousand times and never once met anyone by chance. If he was mad, it was a glorious insanity.

He moved half off her and drew her velvet skirt up to her waist. He pulled at the undergarments beneath; adjusted his own clothing; and remembered the hillside at Amberley, where he had taken her for the first time, crushing her beneath him into the hard ground, doubtless hurting her dreadfully, though she had uttered not one sound of complaint. The ground was a hard and unyielding bed for a woman in the act of love.

He had never taken her any other way.

He slipped an arm beneath her waist and rolled over onto his back. He swung her over on top of him, holding up her skirt. She looked down at him with wide eyes, her breath coming in short gasps.

"Hug my sides with your knees," he told her, helping her to position herself and then moving his hands to her hips and bringing her down onto himself.

They both gasped.

When he moved in her, she did not, as she usually did, move with him. She held tightly to him with her knees and tightened her inner muscles, and closed her eyes. He spread one hand against the back of her head and brought it down to within a few inches of his own. And she opened her eyes and looked into his.

And they continued to look into each other's eyes as

she gradually relaxed and trembled against him. And he watched her teeth bite into her lower lip.

Her skirt was in heavy folds over the both of them. And she was warm and wet and trembling beneath it all. He could not have imagined a more erotic lovemaking. He touched one naked breast with his free hand and brought her mouth down to his own.

And he slowed and deepened his movements as he felt her coming to him and came to her at the exact moment. He had never, he thought with what rationality was left to him, been more aware of Madeline as his love partner.

Her head dropped to his shoulder when the tension of climax had shuddered out of her. He nudged at her legs, helping her straighten them out to either side of his. And he wrapped his arms about her so that he might hold her in the aftermath of passion.

Even several minutes later he knew that she was not sleeping. She was perfectly relaxed but awake. As was he.

So close. They were so close to each other. They could not be closer physically. They were still joined in body. The seeds of his lovemaking were in her. And so close in other ways too. Relaxed and contented in each other's arms. Husband and wife.

It should have been so easy. So easy to say something. Anything. Her name at the very least.

Madeline.

Or even to say those most difficult words of all to say out loud—I love you.

But if he spoke, he might spoil everything. He might at best jolt her back to reality and put an end to these minutes when he held her as closely as a man can hold his woman. At worst, he might see her look at him in shock, incomprehension, derision. She had surrendered her body to him from the start. She had never made any sign that he also had a claim on her heart.

He was afraid of spoiling what little closeness with her he had. His fingers played gently and absently with her curls.

And Madeline for her part lay warm and comfortable against his lean strength, her head pillowed on his shoulder, and willed the moment to last forever. She could hear his heart beating steadily beneath her ear. She wondered if he knew that his fingers were playing with her hair and massaging her scalp.

And if the moment could not last forever, as moments never could, then she willed him to speak. To say it. To say what she sensed. It could not be just physical. There had to be more: some affection, some tenderness, some love perhaps. It had been in his kiss. She had felt it in his touch.

And she had seen it—oh, she had gazed into it—in his eyes. She had looked into his eyes for seemingly endless minutes when he had been thrusting into her. And there had been something there, some nakedness. Something almost frightening in its intensity. Frightening because she was terrified that she was mistaken.

He loved her. His eyes had told her that he loved her. She willed him to say it. Or just to say her name. Or even just to kiss her again and smile at her and let her know beyond the level of words.

She had been mistaken. She must have been mistaken. In the intensity of her own passion she had seen in his eyes what she had wanted to see there. Instead of which she had been watching rising physical desire.

She had been mistaken. He was not going to say anything.

"I told you the moors were dangerous," he said.

"Yes," she said, "so you did."

"You should not allow such goings-on outside of our bedchamber, Madeline," he said. "There is always the chance that someone else will come along."

Was he teasing? Or was he serious. One could never tell with James. He sounded serious. But he must be teasing her.

"Do you speak from experience?" she asked.

His hand stilled in her hair. She felt his muscles tense. "What do you mean?" he asked.

She kept her eyes closed and her head against his shoulder. But she knew the moment was lost irrevocably. She knew she had somehow said something wrong.

"Only that you must have brought dozens of girls out here in your time," she said lightly, wading further into the quicksand she had taken as her chosen path.

"To whom have you been talking?" he asked. "Who has put such nonsense in your head?"

"It was just that," she said. "Nonsense. I talk a lot of it. Hush, James. Don't be cross."

"It was Beasley, wasn't it?" he said. "What did he tell you about me?"

"Oh, hush," she said, putting one arm about his neck and burrowing her head closer to him. "I was teasing, James. I meant nothing."

He took her by the hips in a very firm grasp and lifted her off him. He turned and laid her down on the grass beside him. His face, she saw with a sinking of the heart, was furiously angry. She fumbled with her shift and pulled it up to cover her breasts.

"I told you to stay away from him," he said. "Now he has poisoned your mind. Well, Madeline, if you believe that you are one of a long string of females to be brought out here to be tumbled, then may you have joy of the thought. If you are interested, you compare quite favorably with all the others. You are well worth the bedding. Indeed, I think I did very well in choosing you as a lifelong bedfellow."

He fumbled for a moment with his own clothing, got to his feet, and strode out of the hollow.

Madeline found when she picked up her blouse that her hands were trembling almost too badly to allow her to do up the buttons. What had she said that was so bad? Why the tirade? Had she hit on a raw nerve?

He had been smitten with Mr. Beasley's sister many years ago, Mr. Beasley had said.

He had fought Mr. Beasley after she had married another man, and he had fought the two brothers of her husband.

Why?

The one child—the oldest—looked quite different from the other three, Miss Trenton had said. He was tall and thin and dark. One would hardly guess that he had the same parents as the other three.

"Henrietta!" Mr. Trenton had hissed, in an agony of embarrassment.

Perhaps even yesterday there had been the tiniest, vaguest uneasiness in her. But so tiny and so vague that it had been forgotten.

What if it was true?

What if *what* was true?

Oh God.

"Did you think I had left you?" James asked from the lip of the hollow, his voice as cold as ice. "I was fetching the horses. Come on, Madeline, let's go home. We just spent too long together this afternoon, that's all. It is tempting fate too strongly to spend more than an hour at a time in each other's company, is is not? And I think it would be wise to keep this sort of activity—" he gestured back to the hollow, "for our marriage bed, where it belongs."

"I could not agree more," she said, pulling on her jacket and willing her hands to steadiness while she buttoned it and pinned her hat to her hair. She glared steadily up at him while she set her foot in his hand so that he might help her mount her horse. "I certainly did not marry you with the expectation of such dealings encroaching on my days. I was told that a wife owed that duty only at night."

"If it is only duty and not pleasure," he said, "it would suit me well to make it much briefer for you, Madeline. I will do so tonight."

"Good," she said, turning her horse's head for home even before he was in the saddle. "It *is* a duty. How could it be anything else?"

And how could she expect such a barefaced lie to be believed? she wondered a few minutes later when her temper had cooled a little. He had only to think back on any of the numerous beddings he had shared with her to know that there had been a great deal more pleasure than duty involved in her response. But of course he was too angry to think rationally.

And now she was probably going to be subjected to nights in which he would take his conjugal rights without ever making love to her again.

The afternoon had started so well. And turned magical when he had talked to her and told her a great deal about himself. And grown delirious when they had made love. But now they were back firmly to the old hostility. And

18

THE SLIM CHANCE THAT THEIR MARRIAGE might have brought them relative contentment seemed to have slipped away during that afternoon when for perhaps an hour they had both known even more than contentment. Had that afternoon not brought them brief happiness, each reflected bitterly, perhaps the unhappiness might have been kept at bay too.

She was sorry she had married him, James convinced himself. She had done so only because he had ruined her on that hillside at Amberley and rushed her afterward into a commitment. She would never have married him if she had had time to reflect.

He thought of the men he had seen her with in London, Colonel Huxtable and others, and of Captain Hands at Amberley. He watched her with Alfred Palmer and Carl Beasley and even young Mark Trenton during the weeks and months that succeeded their disastrous ride on the moors. And he knew that he was not the man for her. He had nothing to offer that would meet and nurture that glow of vitality that was always there in her for other men.

The only way he could please her was sexually. And that enjoyment was despite herself. She did not like him. After that afternoon she rarely spoke to him unbidden.

And because he was hurt by what she had said to him on that occasion, and burdened with the guilt of having forced her into an unwanted marriage, he stopped taking advantage of that one vulnerability in her.

He did not stop their marriage. He was too selfish to do that entirely, he told himself ruefully. And besides, he wanted an heir. Though as for that, he would not mind if she presented him with half a dozen daughters and no sons. He wanted a child—one he could acknowledge and hold and give his name to. One he could love.

If he was capable of love. He was not sure that he was.

And so he continued the marriage. But he no longer made love to his wife. He took her each night in what became a brief and regular routine except for those few days each month after she told him, defiance and triumph in her eyes, that she could not. She had come to enjoy telling him in so many words that he had not succeeded in impregnating her.

Or so it seemed.

Sometimes he tried to be kind to her.

"Mrs. Hurd was telling me at dinner last evening," he said to Madeline one morning when he knew she planned to drive into the village, "that the milliner has some very dashing new bonnets for the winter. Why don't you buy some?"

"Why?" she asked him, looking very directly into his eyes and lifting her chin in an expression he had come to recognize. It was an armor she put on against him. "Am I not fashionable enough for Lord Beckworth's taste?"

"I thought you might like having something new and pretty," he said. "We are very far from London."

"Have I complained?" she asked.

"No," he said, "but it has occurred to me that perhaps

you miss a fashionable center. Would you like me to take you to Harrogate for a week or two?"

"So that we may take the waters and promenade in the assembly rooms?" she said. "I think not, James. We would have to endure each other's company all day long."

"I had not thought of that," he said stiffly. "It would be a terrible infliction, would it not?"

"Yes," she said.

"Well." He rose from the breakfast table and tossed his napkin down beside his empty cup. "If you change your mind about the bonnets, Madeline, you may have the bill sent to me."

"Thank you," she said, "but you have made me a generous enough allowance that I have plenty to last me until the next quarter."

He left the room angry and hurt.

"Your letter this morning was from Dominic?" he asked on another occasion.

"Yes," she said. He thought he was to be punished with only the monosyllable, but she added after a few moments, "And from Ellen. They both wrote."

"They are well?" he asked. "And the children?"

"Yes," she said. "All well." Another pause. "The babies have been cutting teeth. Charles in particular has been very cross. Dom has been walking floors with him at night. It seems that no one else can comfort him."

It was a long speech for her. With him, anyway. She could still chatter brightly when they were in company.

"Olivia is not so bad?" he asked.

"She is sensible enough to fall asleep when she is feverish, according to Ellen," she said.

"Do you miss your family, Madeline?" he asked quietly.

She carefully moved a pile of peas from one side of her

plate to the other. "I am a married lady," she said, "living in my husband's home. I left my family behind when I married. It is the way of the world."

"It is a pity we live so far away from them," he said. "Hampshire and Wiltshire are not so far distant from each other. Your brothers can visit each other with comparative ease."

"Dom and Ellen are going to Amberley for Christmas," she said. "And Jennifer Simpson too."

"Are they?" He sat looking at her downcast eyes as she shifted the peas back to their original position on her plate. "We have been invited to Jean Cameron's wedding to Howard Courtney in Abbotsford just before Christmas. Would you like to go?"

She looked up at him fleetingly. "So that you may have a last look at your old love before she marries someone else?" she said.

He made an impatient gesture to a footman to remove their plates. "I thought you might like to spend Christmas with your mother and brothers," he said. "But of course it would be good to see Jean again. She is invariably friendly."

"Yes," she said, "and pretty."

"Yes."

Silence stretched as it so often did when they sat alone together at meals.

"Do you want to go?" he asked abruptly at last.

"No," she said.

He looked at her, surprised. "Why not?"

He thought she would not answer. She waited until the footman had placed their dessert plates before them and moved back to stand beside the sideboard.

"My brothers both have happy marriages," she said very quietly at last.

She said no more. But she did not need to. Her words cut like a knife. Close as she was to her family, much as she must long to see them again, especially at Christmas, she would stay away from them rather than see her own marriage in contrast to theirs. And she would not have them see what a disastrous marriage she had made.

And did he want Alex to see?

"Well, then," he said, "we will have Christmas alone to-gether here. Did I tell you that my mother has decided to take up permanent residence with my aunt?"

"Yes," she said.

There was no pleasing her. And though sometimes—far too often—he lashed out in anger at her and they quar-reled loudly and bitterly a few times every week, he took the burden of the blame upon himself. It was Madeline's gaiety, her seemingly irrepressible vitality, that had first attracted him to her years before. It was the same quality that had drawn him back to her as a drug early in the sum-mer. And yet now, in the privacy of their own home—though not outside it and in company—the gaiety and vitality were gone. And in their place sullenness or defi-ance.

He had done what he had always known he would do if he married her. He had destroyed her. And in the process his hard-won confidence in himself and faith in life were being fast eroded too.

MADELINE HAD NOT EXPECTED her marriage to be a happy one. She had married because she had to. Not be-cause she had given herself to him on the night after his father's funeral. That had not forced her into marriage. Had that been all, she would have refused him, even knowing the risk she ran of bearing an illegitimate child.

No, it was not that that had forced her into marriage. It had been her knowledge that she had no other choice. For four years she had been obsessed with James Purnell, so much so that she could not find any happiness at all in the prospect of marrying any other eligible man.

She knew she would not be happy married to him. Yet she knew that it was only with him she stood any chance at all at happiness. When the opportunity had presented itself, she could not let him go. She did not have the courage to let him go.

Perhaps, she thought months after her marriage, she could have been marginally happy if the first month had not raised such hopes in her. She had had glimpses of heaven during that month—brief and tantalizing glimpses, but enough to plunge her into the deepest gloom once they disappeared forever.

There was nothing left. No companionship. No affection. No passion.

She had convinced herself during that first month that the physical pleasure without everything else was pointless and even degrading to her as a person. But once it disappeared from their marriage, she knew black despair. She had asked for it, of course. She had told him it was merely a duty to her. But she had not expected to be taken so literally at her word.

It would last for just a few nights, she had thought at first, until his anger cooled. And so she had turned from him on those nights, when he was finished with her, and urged patience on her aching and dissatisfied body.

But those few nights had set a permanent pattern. He

had not kissed her since that afternoon on the moors, or caressed her, or unclothed her. There was only the swift and ruthless penetration of her body, the planting of a seed that never took root.

The moments of blackest despair came each month with painful regularity—even more painful on the one occasion when she was four days late. She was not even to have a child to comfort her, a child of his to love instead of him.

Each time it happened she rode out away from the house and lay on the ground sobbing until she felt that her chest would split in two. And then she would find the stream and bathe her face and sit beside it until the water and the air had repaired the damage done by her tears. Sometime during the rest of the day she would find the opportunity to tell James, but she would never let him see her disappointment. Or know her sense of inadequacy. If she never did have a child, the fault would be in her. James was capable of having children.

She had felt quite sick the first time she saw the John Drummond family at church, all of them remarkably alike, fair, plump, and amiable—except for the tall, dark oldest boy, with his intense dark eyes.

She had never met Dora Drummond face-to-face, or Jonathan Drummond. Somehow they were never at the same entertainments. But that the woman had been pretty—and still was in a matronly sort of way—was perfectly clear.

At some time during their youth James had made love to Dora Drummond, or Dora Beasley as she had been then, and left her with child.

It seemed sometimes to Madeline that there was a knife

permanently fixed in her stomach and twisting and turn-ing at frequent intervals.

She had developed a clandestine friendship with Carl Beasley. Clandestine only in the sense that she did not tell James about it. There was nothing improper in the friend-ship.

He found her beside the stream on one of the occa-sions when she had gone out to cry in private. Fortunately she was past the first stages of grief, but even so it was still perfectly obvious what she had been about.

"Hello," he called across the stream. He was on foot, carrying a gun. "Is it not a little cold to be sitting there?"

It was late in November.

"I had not noticed," she said.

He took a closer look at her and frowned. And he came wading across the water. He was wearing hip boots. The dog that had come panting out of the trees behind him stood looking after him. Carl sat down beside her.

"What's the matter?" he asked quietly.

She was ashamed and embarrassed. "Oh, nothing," she said with a slightly watery smile. "You know us women, sir. Always vaporish."

"But not Lady Beckworth, I think," he said. "You have not hurt yourself? You did not fall from your horse?"

She shook her head and smiled.

"Well, that is a relief anyway," he said. "I would hate to see you with a sprained or broken ankle with all the dances of Christmas coming up."

"That would be a terrible fate, would it not?" she said lightly.

He looked at her in concern again. "I will not pry if you would rather not confide in me," he said. "But sometimes it helps to unburden oneself to a stranger. Is it Beckworth? Has he been unkind?"

She shook her head. "No."

He hesitated and reached across to squeeze her hand briefly. "But you are not happy with him, are you?" he asked.

She stiffened and said nothing.

"We used to be friends as boys," he said. "I don't think he has changed a great deal. He is moody but not cruel. He must be hard to live with, but he is probably fonder of you than he seems. Am I speaking out of turn?"

Despite herself she felt herself relaxing. "Tell me about him as he used to be," she said. "I know so little about his childhood."

"It was not an easy childhood," he said. "His father was a very stern man—did you know him? He was very devoted to his religion and what he considered godly behavior. I'm afraid there were very few people in this neighborhood who were deemed suitable associates for the Beckworths or their children."

"When did you and James become friends?" she asked. "And your sister?"

He smiled. "I imagine your husband is reluctant to talk about either of us, isn't he?" he said. And he proceeded to tell her about the times they had spent together, he and James, and later Dora too, whenever James could get away from his father's watchful eye.

She soon forgot her embarrassment, and the telltale marks of her tears disappeared long before they stopped talking.

"I must be getting home," she said at last. "I have been away longer than I intended."

He got to his feet and helped her to hers. "You may

safely go home," he said with a grin. "No one will know of your tears. It will be a secret between you and me." He winked at her.

Somehow, without their ever making any definite plans, they began to meet at the stream every few days. And they fell into an easy friendship. He was someone to talk to, someone to help her break the terrible silence or the bitter quarrels of home.

She never discussed her relationship with her husband with him, but she knew that he knew. And so she never pretended, either, to a marital happiness that she did not feel. They talked on topics that interested them both. Or he talked about the past. Her hunger to know what James had been like as a boy was insatiable.

He told her, at her request, about the love that had blossomed between James and Dora during that one summer. But he did not make a great deal about it or mention the child.

"You must not feel threatened by it," he said. "It was a very long time ago. And Dora is contentedly married to John Drummond now. Have you been made uneasy by the fact that Beckworth has called on her a few times? You need not, you know. It has been merely one old acquaintance calling on another."

"I did not know he had called there," she said.

"Did you not?" He grimaced. "Then I should not have mentioned it. I am sorry. But really it has been nothing at all. I know. My sister has talked of his visits with the greatest placidity. You must forget that I committed the *faux pas* of telling you something you did not know."

She changed the subject and thought of nothing else for days and even weeks afterward. Why had James been visiting Dora Drummond? And why had he said nothing to her? But then he very rarely talked to her about anything.

She had made several friends in the neighborhood and had been well accepted by everyone. But she particularly enjoyed her friendship with Carl Beasley because it was a private one in which she could relax and talk about anything that came to mind.

"My nephew Jonathan has taken to spending more and more time with me," he told her with a laugh one day. "I'm afraid the lad does not get treated very well by his father. John is always impatient with the boy. I suppose most families have one member who is very different from all the others. Poor Jonathan. He even looks different. The proverbial black sheep. A somewhat moody lad, but he has potential. I enjoy his company."

"Perhaps he does not have enough to do to keep him amused," Madeline said. Her friend did not realize how he was twisting the knife in her wound.

"He will be sent to school when he is old enough," he said. "He will find plenty to occupy him there."

"Mr. Drummond will send him to school?" Madeline asked.

Carl Beasley smiled. "John is not a wealthy man," he said. "But somehow it will be arranged, you may be sure. The money will be found to give Jonathan an education to suit his birth."

They moved on to talk of other matters.

It was Carl too who told her that the Duke and Duchess of Peterleigh were to come sometime after Christmas, though the news was soon generally known in the neighborhood. The duchess, it seemed, was expecting their first child and was to be brought to the country for her confinement.

There was some comfort in the news. The duke and duchess had been married for almost four years.

JAMES SAW DORA for the first time at church. After her husband had recovered from his lengthy illness, they came together with their four children, the youngest a mere baby in arms.

It was a shock to see her. For so many years he had lived through the agony of having lost her beyond trace. He had always imagined their reunion, if ever it was to occur, as a moment of great emotion, when their eyes would meet and all they had meant to each other would be there in their look.

And he had always imagined her pale and haggard, a ruined and an unhappy woman. And seeing her he would know again his guilt in all its rawness. He would still feel as guilty as if he had abandoned her knowingly. He had been enjoying himself at university, enjoying the freedom from his father. And he had not been living a celibate life.

It came as a shock to see her in church, then, and to discover the same Dora ten years later. She had been prettily plump as a girl. Now that plumpness had a matronly quality about it. She had been a placid and trusting girl, always willing to please. He had not had to use many wiles to persuade her to lie with him. And there had been only a few tears afterward.

She looked placid still. There were no outward signs of the dreadful suffering he had imagined. Of course, many years had passed.

She saw him as they were leaving the church, and he inclined his head to her, unsmiling. She colored up and bobbed a curtsy, and turned to say something to one of her children. Not to the eldest, Jonathan.

There was a certain nightmare quality to the moment. He had his wife on his arm, her head turned away as she exchanged some pleasantry with one of their neighbors. And his former mistress was in the church with their child, who looked so much like himself.

How could he have been so mad as to come back? For weeks the whole situation with Dora had lain dormant, almost as if he had thought he could go through the rest of his life without encountering her.

But she was there and could not be ignored. At some time he must talk with her, get some answers finally to questions that had gnawed at him for years. And his son was there. His son. He must do something about the boy. Arrange something for his future. Send him to a good school, perhaps. Arrange for a good career for him.

Yet Madeline was on his arm. And she knew nothing of either Dora or Jonathan. Unless Beasley had told her, of course. She was friendly with Beasley, and years before the man had promised revenge.

She should be told. Sooner or later she was bound to find out. He should tell her. Better that it should come from him than from someone else.

But how could he tell his wife such a thing? Especially when his relations with her were on such shaky ground. How could he convince her that it was a thing of the past, something for which he still felt responsible, but nothing to interfere with his love for her?

What love? she would ask.

And he would be unable to reply. He seemed quite incapable of telling her that he loved her.

And so he led Madeline out of the church and directly

to their waiting carriage, helped her inside, and sat beside her all the way home, looking out through the window in silence. Composing an explanation to her that he never delivered. Composing a speech in which he told her of his true feelings for her. And never speaking the words aloud.

He should not have come home. He should not have married Madeline. He should have returned to Canada and the fur trade, where he could be alone and harm no one but himself.

One afternoon he was riding home from a lengthy visit to one of his tenants, having listened to and finally approved the man's schemes for clearing more arable land, when he saw two small figures walking along the laneway ahead of him. Or rather, the larger child was walking with one arm around the smaller, who hopped on one leg.

Jonathan and Patrick Drummond, he saw as he rode closer. Jonathan glowered up at him as he drew rein beside them. Patrick was sobbing.

"What has happened?" James asked.

"I told him he was not to come," Jonathan said, "but Father said I must let him. And then I told him not to jump down from the top of the stile but to climb down properly. But jump he did and hurt his foot and now it will serve him right if Father thrashes him."

The younger child hiccuped.

"Mother sent me on an errand to Mrs. Potter," Jonathan said by way of explanation.

"Well," James said, resisting the urge to tell his son that he could do with a lesson in compassion and remembering that many children are by nature cruel to each other, "you have a long hop home, Patrick."

The child sniffed and took one hop forward, clinging to his brother's shoulder.

"Unless you would like me to lift you up before me and see if I can coax a gallop out of this stallion," James said.

Two red-rimmed eyes looked up at him.

"Father will be cross," Jonathan said. "He will say that we have inconvenienced you, sir."

"Perhaps I can stay long enough to convince your father that I have not been inconvenienced at all," James said, leaning down from the saddle, taking the smaller child beneath the arms and swinging him up to sit before him. He lifted the child's injured leg with one hand and felt the ankle with gentle fingers. "Can you walk, Jonathan? There must be more than a mile to go."

"Easily, sir!" his son said with some contempt.

"Will Papa be cross?" Patrick asked, looking up at him with wide gray eyes and a running nose.

James took a handkerchief from his pocket and wiped the nose. "I don't know your papa," he said. "But I'll wager that your mama will bathe your foot and make it feel better. And probably cover you with kisses too." He winked at the child, who proceeded to burrow his head beneath his cloak and against the warmth of his coat.

Dora came out of the house behind her servant when the horse stopped at her gate.

"Hello, Dora," he said, swinging down from the saddle and lifting the child down into his arms.

She curtsied. "My lord," she said.

"I am afraid we have one wounded soldier here," he said. "It seems the climb down from a stile was a little much for him, and his ankle turned under him. It is not broken, I think, just badly swollen."

He followed her into the house and parlor, where he set

Patrick down on a sofa. And only then discovered that John Drummond was from home.

He stood watching, his hands clasped behind him, as the servant brought in a basin of water and Dora proceeded to bathe her child's foot. She had first smoothed back his hair and kissed him, as James had expected, and assured him that his papa would not beat him for falling and hurting himself.

"But Jon said he would," the child said accusingly.

"Then you must be thankful that Jonathan is not your papa," she said, kissing him again.

"Won't you take a seat, my lord?" she said finally, flustered, when she realized that James was still standing behind her. "I will have tea brought."

"Don't trouble yourself, Dora," he said. "I merely wanted to see the child safe. How are you?"

Patrick's foot had been bandaged and elevated on a cushion. She turned to her visitor.

"Well," she said. "My last confinement was a difficult one, but I have recovered fully." She flushed.

"Are you happy?" he asked, and wished immediately that he had not tried to make the conversation personal.

"Yes," she said. "I have a good home and a good husband and a growing family. What more could I ask for?"

"It has been a long time," he said.

"Yes." She flushed again. "A long time."

"I have often wondered," he said, "if you were happy."

"Oh," she said. "Yes. It was kind of you."

"My foot still hurts, Mama," Patrick wailed from behind her.

Jonathan came into the room as Dora turned back

to the invalid. "I told him he shouldn't jump, Mother," he said. "He is such a nuisance. He will not do as he is told."

"He fell, Jonathan," she said, whirling on him. "You will say nothing to your father about his jumping. Do you understand me?"

"Yes, Mother," the boy said, that hint of contempt in his voice again.

"This is Lord Beckworth, who was so kind as to bring your brother home," she said. "Did you know? Make your bow to him, Jonathan."

The boy bobbed his head in James's direction. "Yes, I knew," he said.

James took his leave of them. Strange, he thought. It had been so very different from the way he had imagined it would be—he and Dora and their son all in one room together. In the event, he had been able to see her only as the mother of those children. Someone whom he could surely never have desired.

Was it really she he had raged over and almost driven himself mad over?

And for his son he felt nothing but a mild animosity. If he were that child's father in fact as well as in body, he had a conviction the boy would feel the flat of his hand more often than he seemed to do. No son of his would speak to his mother with contempt and escape without a stinging rear end and an earful of home truths.

A strange meeting indeed when he remembered all the passions that had raged more than nine years before. There was an unreality about the whole situation. Almost as if none of it had ever happened. Except that there was Jonathan as living proof that it had.

It was a meeting he did not repeat or want to repeat.

Though he did want to question her. He would never be completely satisfied until he heard the answers to some questions.

It was also a meeting he did not find the right opportunity to tell his wife about. But then he did not tell her a great deal about any of his daily activities. And she told him as little about hers. They were strangers who happened to live in the same house and sleep in the same bed. Strangers who were intimate with each other for a few minutes of each night for a little more than three weeks out of each month.

They meant no more to each other.

Except that he happened to love her. A quite irrelevant fact, it seemed, when one settled down to the reality of a marriage that should never have been contracted.

MADELINE FOUND the winter long and tedious although there were friends and plenty of social activities to attend and to host. But the snow, which she had been warned would be more plentiful in Yorkshire than it had been in the southern part of the country, kept her housebound for days at a time. And being housebound meant having only James for company.

In other words, it meant having no company at all.

Many was the time she almost regretted not accepting his suggestion that they go to Amberley before Christmas. But she would on the whole, she decided, prefer to keep her pride and be lonely than go to Amberley to be with Mama and Dom and Edmund and have them see her misery. And Dom would see it even if the others did not, no matter how good an act she put on. Besides, if she went to Amberley, how would she ever be able to leave again?

Dunstable Hall was her home now, and she must never again see it in contrast to Amberley. And she must never again see her brothers' marriages at first hand and know the inadequacy of her own. She must live out her life in self-imposed exile.

Those brave and gloomy thoughts occurred before the disaster of the duke's spring ball and all that followed it. Everything changed after that, but winter was well and truly over by then.

So was the duchess's confinement. She was delivered of an heir at the end of February. The ball was to be given in honor of the event in the middle of April.

In the meantime the letters kept coming from home. Letters that filled Madeline with nostalgia and discontent. Jean and Howard had married before Christmas, and already she was thought to be increasing, Alexandra wrote, if one were to read any significance into the fact that Mrs. Courtney was driving over to their house every morning to tend a daughter-in-law who could not stand on her feet before noon without vomiting.

Susan Courtney, later Susan Jennings, now Lady Agerton, was also in expectation of an interesting event, Alexandra wrote, adding that the terminology was Susan's own.

It seemed to Madeline that all the world was giving birth except her.

Ellen and Dominic were going to London for at least a part of the Season so that Ellen could be close to her stepdaughter and could visit her father.

The final blow came in a letter from Edmund in March, announcing that Alexandra was with child again.

All the world except her!

The letter came on a particularly bad day. She was from home when it arrived, riding out across a somewhat muddy pasture, unable to see her way because she was crying her eyes out over renewed evidence of her own infertility.

19

JAMES HAD NEVER BEEN FOND OF THE DUKE OF Peterleigh. Seventeen years older than himself, the duke had always appeared as a remote, haughty, and humorless man. He was tall and thin, with a narrow, aristocratic face and piercing dark eyes. He spent most of his time in London on government business, coming into the country for only a few weeks of the year, usually in the early summer.

When he had used to come, he had always visited Dunstable Hall. He was one of the few men of the neighborhood with whom James's father had been on good terms. The two men had shared many ideas on life and morality. Or had seemed to do so. James had been disgusted to discover, when he finally spent some time in London himself, that the duke lived a double life. He kept a mistress with whom he had had several children. And he was rumored to have darker dealings with other ladybirds.

There had been an understanding between Peterleigh and the late Lord Beckworth that the duke would marry Alex when she was old enough. James had always hated the idea. For many years Alex was the only person in his life whom he truly loved. He knew her as a warm and passionate, artistic and imaginative girl. Those aspects of her character would have been squashed by the duke as they were already severely repressed by their father.

But Alex had known so little of life. She had never had friends beyond himself. She had never been sent away to school. By the time she was taken to London at the age of one and twenty, with a view to being officially betrothed to Peterleigh, she was quite resigned to the match. She knew nothing else.

Looking back on that spring now, James could be very thankful to Dominic, Lord Eden, and to Madeline for a stupid incident that should have involved only the two of them but that had dragged Alex in when two of Lord Eden's friends, sent to kidnap Madeline, mistook Alex for her. And so she had been severely compromised when forced to spend a whole night captive in Amberley's town house, unknown either to him or to Eden.

They had both offered for her—Eden and Amberley. James could almost chuckle now at events that had made him beside himself with fury at the time. She had refused them both. Alex was nothing if not courageous—and incredibly naive. Why should she accept either of those two men, she had reasoned, when she was already unofficially betrothed to the Duke of Peterleigh?

Poor Alex. She had learned fast when Peterleigh had cut her in the middle of Lady Sharp's drawing room after every other guest present had already done so, except Madeline. Even then she would have refused Amberley's second offer if he had not almost forced her into accepting him publicly after his arrival at Lady Sharp's.

How fortunately events could sometimes turn out. He had to admit to himself now that Amberley was quite perfect for Alex. He had scarcely been able to believe the outward changes in her when he arrived back from Canada—and all changes for the better.

Most important, she had escaped from the Duke of Peterleigh's clutches, a more fortunate escape than perhaps he had realized at the time. He had heard during the previous spring in London that the Duchess of Peterleigh occasionally dropped out of sight for a few weeks at a time with some undisclosed indisposition. But once or twice rumor had leaked out by way of servants' gossip that on those occasions she was hiding facial bruises.

The duke was not a pleasant character, James concluded. He was quite happy that the man was usually an absentee neighbor. However, when he was in residence, one felt the necessity of being neighborly. He called once, alone, to pay his respects after the duke and duchess's arrival, and once with Madeline after the duchess's confinement. And of course he accepted their invitation to the ball that was being given in celebration of the birth of an heir.

Perhaps the duchess, poor girl, would be treated more kindly now that she had finally performed her main duty, James thought.

Madeline was looking forward to the ball. Not that she said much about it to him. They rarely now exchanged any but the commonest civilities when they were in company together. But she talked with enthusiasm about the event when Mr. and Mrs. Hooper and their daughter called for tea one afternoon. He was talking to Mr. Hooper about crops at the time, but at least half of his attention was on his wife. He could experience that sparkle in her only secondhand these days. She never looked like that for him.

"His grace has hired an orchestra at great expense," Mrs. Hooper was telling Madeline. "They are coming all the way from York, if you would believe it. And candles by the crateful. And extra cooks to help with supper; it will be a very grand occasion, my dear Lady Beckworth. The last time there was a ball at the manor was after the duke's nuptials. And goodness knows when the next will be."

"And there are guests at the manor?" Madeline said with a smile. "Goodness, it will be wonderful to dance again. I shall have to dust off my best ball gown." She laughed gaily.

"Mama is having Miss Fenton make me a gown," Christine Hooper said, "but I'm terrified that it will be dreadfully unfashionable, Lady Beckworth, and that all the guests from London will look at me with contempt or pity."

"But, my dear," her mother said, "you know that Miss Fenton is copying an illustration from a recent copy of the *Belle Assemblée*. How can it not be all the crack?"

"Perhaps Lady Beckworth will give her opinion," Christine said.

"I will be glad to," Madeline assured her. "Shall I ride over tomorrow? Though I am sure that the *Belle Assemblée* is more up-to-date than I am. It is almost a year since I was in London."

Did she sound wistful? James wondered. Did she wish that she were setting out now for this year's Season and all the admiration and flirtations it had always brought her? How could she wish otherwise? She was quite unhappy married to him. He shook off the thought and returned his attention to Mr. Hooper.

MADELINE HAD more than a few rueful smiles at herself in the weeks preceding the ball. She was as excited about it, her mind was as focused on it, as if it were her very first ball in her very first Season. And yet for years during the spring she had attended so many balls and other entertainments that she had come to sigh at yet one more and to feel occasionally oppressed by the tedium of it all. How her life had changed when she could so grasp at a single event.

She had her maid lay out her blue ball gown and the yellow and green. After two days of dithering and constantly changing her mind, she discarded all three and brought out the white and the pink. She even considered once—and laughed at her own madness—dragging James in and asking his opinion. She so very much wanted to wear something he would admire. And she despised herself for the wish.

She decided finally on the pink. She had never considered it her color, but she had fallen in love with this particular shade the previous spring. It was a rich pink that made her feel young and vivid and attractive.

James came into her dressing room on the night of the ball as her maid was putting the finishing touch to her appearance. She was clasping her pearls at her neck. Madeline looked up in breathless surprise when the door that adjoined their dressing rooms opened. She met her husband's eyes in the mirror. He stood just inside the door, his face quite expressionless. But he was looking handsome enough in his black evening clothes to take her breath away.

"Well?" she said, twirling around to face him and feeling herself flush. Just like a girl!

His eyes took their time about inspecting her from head to toe. If only his face were not quite so impassive, his eyes so inscrutable. And if only she did not care quite as much what his opinion would be.

"Wait here" was all he said finally, and he turned and left her dressing room again.

"You may leave," Madeline said to her maid, trying to keep the desperate disappointment from her voice. She sat down on the stool before her dressing table and made a conscious effort not to let her shoulders sag. She was on her way to her first ball in many months and perhaps her last for many more. She was going to enjoy herself. Despite James. Despite her basic unhappiness. Despite everything.

James came back with a large velvet box in his hand. He set it down on the dressing table. She watched him in the mirror as he bent his attention to the back of her neck. He tossed her pearls onto the glass tray in front of her. And then he opened the box.

Madeline swallowed. And gasped from the coldness and weight of the diamond-studded circlet he clasped about her neck.

"Are they not your mother's?" she asked as she lifted her right arm obediently for him to clasp the matching bracelet around her wrist.

"No," he said. "Not these. These belong to the baroness—to the title, not to the person. They are yours for as long as I live."

She did not know what to say. "Thank you" seemed inadequate—and unnecessary since it was not a personal gift. She said nothing, but stared at the jewels in the mirror and at his hands, dark-skinned against the white of her shoulders. And she felt them there, warm and strong.

"They suit you," he said at last. "You are tall and slender and bear yourself proudly."

It was as much of a compliment as she could expect, Madeline supposed. She looked up into his eyes, which were inspecting her in the mirror. Oh, surely there was more in them than usual. Surely it was not just wishful thinking on her part. There was a trace of admiration, surely.

"You look beautiful," he said abruptly. His words sounded almost grudging.

Madeline stood up and turned to face him. She smiled. "And you look very splendid, James," she said. She touched the diamonds at her neck and said something that surprised herself. "I will try to wear them proudly."

She did not know for a moment whether his eyes were on her diamonds or her lips. She thought for the merest fraction of a second that he was moving toward her. She felt her heart begin to pound and the color rise to her cheeks. And then she saw him swallow. And she knew that it was the necklace he looked at.

"The carriage is waiting," he said. "Is this your wrap?"

"Yes," she said, smiling brightly and turning so that he could place it about her shoulders.

She was going to enjoy herself, she told herself later as they sat side by side in the carriage, not touching and not talking. Nothing was going to stop her from enjoying herself.

"Are you going to dance with me?" she asked as they were being driven up the dark driveway to the manor. "Am I to reserve any sets for you?"

"It would be very strange if I did not dance with my own wife, would it not?" he said. "You will dance the opening set with me, Madeline, and the first waltz after supper."

So. He would dance with her because it would look

strange if he did not. And she was being told which dances to reserve for him, not asked. She should not have introduced the subject. She should have kept her mouth shut and forced him to ask if she wished to dance with him.

But it did not matter. Not at all. The main doors to the manor were folded back, and light spilled out onto the cobbled terrace. Footmen in splendid livery were standing in the doorway and beyond. And once the horses stopped and the carriage drew to a halt, they would probably be able to hear voices and music.

She was going to enjoy herself.

JAMES DANCED the opening quadrille with Madeline and the following set with the duchess. He danced with Miss Palmer and Mrs. Trenton and stood and talked with a group of men for a few sets. He doubtless would not have asked Dora to dance if her brothers-in-law had not stood so protectively about her between every set and glowered so menacingly in his direction as if it had all happened only weeks before instead of almost ten years.

Under the circumstances he could not resist sauntering across the room to the little group between two sets, bowing amiably to Carl Beasley and John Drummond, exchanging a few civilities—the first since his return—with the other two Drummond brothers, and smiling at Dora.

"Will you dance the next one with me, Dora?" he asked, deliberately rejecting any more formal way of addressing her.

She smiled at him and curtsied. "Thank you, my lord," she said.

John Drummond began to ask him about his lambs.

It was a waltz. He had not realized that until the music began. It felt strange to hold her again, to be so close to her. The same large gray trusting eyes and amiable expression. The same fair ringlets, though surely not quite as bright as they had been. The same soft feminine body, though plumper, more matronly, than it had been.

They danced in silence for a while.

"When you were good enough to bring Patrick home that day," she said, "I forgot to express my sympathies at your loss of your father, my lord."

"Thank you," he said. "Why do you use my title rather than my name, Dora?"

She smiled. "It does not seem fitting to be familiar with you now that you are Lord Beckworth," she said.

"After what we knew together, Dora?" he said.

She blushed. "Oh, that," she said. "I did not think you would remind me of that. It was very foolish."

Foolish? After the years of agony he had lived through? Well.

"It was very real at the time," he said.

She laughed. A trilling little laugh that he had forgotten. "Just foolishness," she said. "And very indiscreet. I might have got into a great deal of trouble."

Might have?

"I do admire your wife, my lord," she said. "She is very lovely. You must be proud of her."

"Yes," he said, "I am."

"I have never been presented to her," she said with that little laugh again. "I suppose I am not considered quite good enough since I married Mr. Drummond. But I am quite contented, you know."

"Are you, Dora?" he said. "Would you like to meet Madeline?"

"I see she is wearing the Beckworth diamonds," she said. "They look much better on her than they looked on your mother, my lord, if you will forgive me for saying so. And she looks as if she might be the duchess rather than her grace, poor girl. She is dreadfully thin and pale, don't you think?"

"She is only just recovering from a confinement," James said.

"But I was always blooming again just weeks after my confinements," Dora said. "Ask Mr. Drummond. No, the duchess has always looked the same. Of course, it must be dreadful to know that one has been married only because one is of suitable family to bear the ducal heir. She cannot believe that he cares for her, can she?"

And he had loved her? Made love to her? Raged and fought and driven himself to the brink of insanity when she was snatched from him, hidden away from him, and permanently removed from him by marriage to another man? This was Dora as she had become?

James was aghast.

"And yet," he said, "she has borne the heir, a healthy boy from all accounts. And they both look happy this evening."

He took her somewhat reluctantly at the end of the waltz to meet Madeline, and the two women stood and conversed politely until they were claimed by their next partners.

James felt that sense of unreality again. His wife and his former mistress, the mother of his son, had met and talked together. And Dora, that comfortable, placid, rather spiteful matron, was the girl he had agonized over for years. The girl he had taken out of boredom, because she was buxom and pretty and willing. The girl he had later, in his guilt, persuaded himself he had loved.

He joined a group of gentlemen, most of them guests at the manor, and watched his wife dance with the duke and Dora with Adam Drummond.

His curiosity was thoroughly piqued. Had their liaison meant so little to Dora? Had she not been sick with love for him, as he had always thought? Had she not suffered as much as he at the time, snatched away from him and her home as she had been and forced into an arranged marriage with a man of inferior birth? Or had she so schooled her feelings that she could pretend so well? Had the bearing of their child meant so little to her, left so few signs of permanent suffering? Could she look on the father of her eldest son so placidly and tell him that what they had shared had been foolish?

He could not feel satisfied. He had no feelings left for Dora and surprisingly few for his son. He knew that the past was far better left alone than resurrected to the satisfaction of no one. And he knew that his only hope for future happiness lay with Madeline.

But he could not feel satisfied. The urge to know was even stronger in him now that he had danced with Dora and found her so very much the same and yet so very different from the way she had been when he had loved her and lain with her.

He claimed her hand again after supper for a set of country dances. But he had no intention of cavorting about the floor with her, separated for most of the dance by the figures of the set. He needed to talk to her.

"Shall we find somewhere quiet to sit down for a while?" he asked.

"Oh, I don't know, I'm sure, my lord," she said.

"I want to know what has been happening with you in the past ten years, Dora," he said. "We were friends once."

Though perhaps they had never been friends, he thought. Only lovers.

"Well, I am a little footsore," she admitted. "Mr. Drummond bought me a new pair of slippers, and I am afraid to take them off for fear that I have blisters on my heels, and I would not be able to get them back on again."

Sweet and helpless, anxious and talkative Dora Beasley. The qualities had been endearing in a seventeen-year-old.

He took her out of the ballroom and along the hallway past rooms that had all been lit and thrown open for the occasion. Most of them were occupied, either by card players or by gossiping matrons and chaperones. A few were empty. He took Dora into a small salon and left the door ajar.

"Do you remember our last meeting almost ten years ago?" he asked.

She blushed. "I do wish you would not remind me," she said. "It was foolish. But you were very ardent and very insistent and so much in love with me." That trilling laugh.

"And you with me, Dora," he said.

"Yes," she said. "Very foolish. You were so handsome, my lord. As you still are, of course."

"Why did you do it?" he asked. "Why did you marry Drummond, Dora? Did they force you?"

"He was kind," she said, "and said that he wished to marry me. Although he was given a large dowry, of course. My papa did not leave me destitute, and his grace added to what he had left me. Carl was very insistent. He said it was the best thing for me and would save me from ruin."

"Did you write to me?" he asked. "I have always wondered if you tried, and if they withheld your letters."

"Write?" she said. "To you? Oh, no, I never did."

He laughed a little bitterly. "I was a fool," he said. "I thought you loved me. I thought you had been dragged kicking and screaming to the altar."

"Oh, no," she said. "Not really, though I was a little disappointed, I must confess. Carl explained to me that I had been very foolish. Gullible was the word he used. I suppose I was, too. I was only seventeen, you know. He did say at first when he knew I had..." She stopped and blushed. "Well, you know. When I told him about you and me. He said that perhaps we might use that. But I would not hear of it. I might have been foolish, but I was not lost to all conduct. And I was fond of you, I will admit to that. Besides, Carl said after he had had time to think it over that it would not do. His grace would not have allowed it, he said, because he had an understanding with Miss Purnell."

James frowned. "He did not think it would have been right for you to marry me because of Peterleigh and Alex?" he said. "What did that have to do with anything?"

"Well, you know," she said pointedly, blushing again. "Because."

"Because what?" he asked.

"Well, you know," she said. "On account of its being his."

James went very still. Dora had seated herself on a love seat and was pleating the silk skirt of her gown between her fingers.

"Explain to me," he said. "There is something I don't understand here."

"Didn't you know?" she said. "I suppose you might not

have, since we were sent away right after the wedding and Mr. Drummond has been working on one of his grace's estates ever since—well, until last autumn anyway. But I thought everybody would have known, especially when we came back. Have you not wondered why Jonathan looks so different from my other children? It was embarrassing. I hoped he would take after me, but he didn't. He took after his father instead."

"I had noticed." James felt rather as if he were suffocating.

"I suppose it doesn't matter now," Dora said. "It was all years ago, and he has been married for years and now has a son with her. Though I did half wish it would turn out to be a daughter. Carl and I, you know, were just as gently born as she, except that our papa had no title. But we were just his wards, you see, and Carl told me after it had happened that I could not expect him to marry me. I had thought he would. Was not that foolish? And I could not even say that I was forced exactly. He was a handsome man—a little like you, tall and dark, though he was already graying at the temples, and very persuasive. I think that was why I liked you. You reminded me of him. But I should not have let you—*you* know, because I had already been increasing for almost two months at that time. I might have been in real trouble with him if he had found out."

"And he did not find out?" James asked.

"I don't think he could have," Dora said. "He would have come up from London and beaten me for sure, wouldn't he? He had beaten me for less."

"My father had no hand in marrying you to Drummond?" James asked.

"Oh, for sure," she said. "Yes, Carl said he was furious. I

think he thought it was yours at first, but Carl set him right on that. Even so, I suppose it was natural that he would want me married and have everything hushed up on account of Miss Purnell. It was his grace, though, who was good enough to suggest Mr. Drummond and to give us another home to live in for a few years. Mr. Drummond has been kind to me. A better husband than *he* would have been, I daresay."

"Jonathan is the Duke of Peterleigh's son, then?" James said. He felt as if he were in the middle of some bizarre dream.

"He looks like him, doesn't he?" she said. "It is a little embarrassing, and I wonder sometimes if she looks at him and knows the truth. But I don't suppose she minds, does she? When your husband is a duke or someone like that, you have to expect such things. And she has the title and the heir and all that. But I don't think she is as pretty as I, is she? Or as amiable. I could have made him more comfortable, I'll wager. Not that I am complaining. I have a good husband and I have been able to present him with three children of his own. And his grace looks after us, you know. He will send Jonathan to school when he is a little older and find him a suitable situation when he is grown up. I can't complain, can I?"

"I suppose not," James said, seating himself on the edge of the love seat next to her.

Well.

Well.

But before he could get his thoughts in order, the door crashed inward on its hinges and he looked up, startled, to see Benjamin and Adam Drummond filling the doorway.

"Out, Beckworth!" the former said. "Immediately, or it will be out of the house on your ear for all to see."

James stood up and brushed at his sleeves. Dora jumped up beside him.

"Oh, dear," she said, "we were just talking, dear brother. I have blisters and Lord Beckworth was kind enough to bring me somewhere where I could sit down."

"Out!" Adam Drummond said. "And don't come near her again, Beckworth, if you value your life."

"I will acknowledge and be civil to a neighbor whenever I happen to meet her," James said, checking the folds of his neckcloth unhurriedly.

"We know what sort of a neighbor you are, Beckworth," Ben Drummond said. "Sitting close beside her with not a pin space between the two of you. If you plan to cuckold her husband, it will be over my dead body. You can turn your lecherous eyes on all the other women in Yorkshire for all I care. But you will keep them from my sister-in-law."

"Indeed," James said. "Ah, is that a single threat, Drummond, or does it include your brother? It seems to me that the last time I encountered you, it was together. Have you learned since then to fight one at a time?"

"Oh, dear me," Dora said from behind him. "You are not going to fight over me, are you? My lord? Brother?"

"No, we are not going to fight, Dora," James said, turning to look back at her. "None of us is so ill-mannered as to wish to cause a scene at a celebration ball. May I take you back to your husband?"

"You will leave now, Beckworth, and alone!" Ben Drummond said from between his teeth. "My brother and I will convey our sister-in-law back to the ballroom."

James raised his eyebrows. "Ah," he said, "but I brought her here and I will return her, Drummond. Dora?" He bowed and extended his arm for hers. She looked nervously from him to the other two men, and then took his arm. "Gentlemen?" James waited for them to stand aside.

"You are right," Ben Drummond said. "This is not the occasion. But watch yourself, Beckworth. If your wife is not enough for you, there are brothels enough in Harrogate or closer than that, I daresay."

James raised his eyebrows again and led Dora from the room.

"Oh, dear," she said. "Perhaps we should have sat in one of the other rooms, my lord. How foolish of me. I'm afraid I do not always think of what is proper until it is too late."

MADELINE HAD SEEN THEM GO. She had danced the country dance with Sir Hedley Grimes from London, and had smiled at him and conversed with him whenever the pattern of the dance brought them together. And the knife had twisted and twisted in her.

Where had he taken her? Where had they gone? And for what purpose?

He visited her regularly, Mr. Beasley had let slip by accident on that one occasion when she had met him. There was nothing in the visits, he had added, trying to reassure her. Nothing to be concerned about at all.

But James had never mentioned the visits to her. And he had never mentioned Mrs. Dora Drummond to her, or their child.

She was a pretty lady. A little plump, it was true, but plumpness was not always unattractive. Dora Drummond was pretty. And she had a nine-year-old son who was James's.

For how long had they been lovers? How deeply had they loved? Why had they not married? Did James regret now not having married her? And did she regret it too? How often did they meet? And were they alone when they did so?

Were they lovers again?

Madeline had been tormented with the questions for weeks. Even months. And now, almost in public, he had led her from the ballroom, and they were still away when the music ended.

She must train herself not to care. She must smile and converse until the dancing began again. The next dance was to be a waltz—the one she had been told to reserve for her husband. She must wait for him as if she did not have a care in the world. Surely he would not just leave her standing while he remained with his mistress.

The word had come unbidden. *Was* she his mistress?

But Madeline could not wait. Under pretense of going in search of the ladies' withdrawing room, she slipped from the ballroom and looked about her. There was a buzz of conversation coming from the ballroom itself and from other rooms along the hallway. And two of the Drummond brothers were at the door of one room and crashing it back against the inner wall.

Madeline felt sick and drew closer quite against her will.

She could not see inside. But she did not need to do so. Obviously they were in there, and had been alone. And had been discovered sitting very close together. She stood and listened until the two large figures of the brothers stood aside to let the occupants of the room pass.

She did not want to see him. And she did not want him to see her. She did not want to see them together.

She turned and fled in the direction of the ballroom, arriving there hot and distraught. But she was saved from the embarrassment of entering the room thus, where surely several people would have noticed that there was something very wrong with her.

Carl Beasley was standing outside the doorway, facing her as she ran toward him. He took her firmly by one arm.

"Come," he said quietly, turning her in the direction of the stairway. "We will go down and stroll outside for a while. You need a little time."

Madeline allowed him to draw her arm firmly through one of his and hurry her downward.

20

"WOULD YOU LIKE ME TO HAVE YOUR CLOAK fetched?" Carl Beasley asked Madeline when they stood in the doorway leading outside.

She shook her head. "It is not a cold night," she said, and shivered.

There was no one else outside. Anyone who was taking the air was doubtless walking on the terrace outside the ballroom. He led her across the cobbled driveway toward a marble fountain and flower gardens beyond.

"I could not help but hear what was happening," he said, covering one of her hands with his own. "I wish I could have saved you from that pain." They stopped beside the fountain.

"It was nothing," Madeline said. "They were merely talking."

He looked at her rather sadly and said nothing for a while. "Alas," he said, "neither of us believes that, do we?"

Madeline pulled her hand from his arm. "I must go inside," she said. "I will be missed."

"Lady Beckworth," he said, taking her by the shoulders and looking down into her face, a look of concern on his own, "talk about it. If you are angry, let out your anger on me. If you are upset, cry on my shoulder. I admit that I am not as much involved in all this as you are, but I am her brother, and it grieves me to see this happen."

"Perhaps nothing is happening," she said. "Perhaps we are overreacting."

"I hope you are right," he said. "Perhaps you are. It all happened so long ago, you know, that I really thought there would be no danger in their living in the same neighborhood again. But I suppose what they shared does not die so easily."

"I should go inside," she said.

"He told you about it, did he not?" he asked hesitantly. She shook her head.

He grimaced. "I am sorry, then," he said gently. "Perhaps you would prefer that I said no more. Sometimes it is better only to imagine the truth than to know it."

Madeline dropped her head and examined the ground between their feet. "Why did they not marry?" she asked.

"It was rather sad," he said. "Your husband was at university at the time. I suppose he and his father felt that he was too young to take on the responsibilities of marriage and fath—" He paused and took a deep breath. "Did you know about Jonathan?"

"I had guessed," she said, closing her eyes.

"I am not saying that he did not love her," he said. "I believe he did. But I suppose very young men tend to panic in such situations. He was probably sorry after our cousin the duke had found her another husband. He is probably still sorry. And Dora, of course, though she is not desperately unhappy, is married to a man of inferior birth. It must be hard for her to see Jonathan's father come into his title and estate. And one must admit that he is a more personable man than John Drummond."

Madeline took a deep breath but let it out slowly without saying anything.

"But all that does not excuse either of them for what they are doing now," he said. "For better or worse they have both made their choices. And there are other people to be hurt if they rekindle their love. *If,*" he said bitterly. "I think it is already too late for *if.*"

"We don't know," she said, her voice shaking. "Perhaps we are being too hasty."

He removed his hands from her shoulders and clasped hers very tightly. "I am so very sorry," he said. "I would not have breathed a word of any of this if you had not witnessed that rather ugly scene upstairs. I wish you would forget it, though that is easier said than done, of course. But perhaps nothing has yet happened. Perhaps they are just indulging in a little nostalgia. How could any man be married to you and bear to look at any other woman? He would have to be insane."

"I should go inside," Madeline said.

"I will take you," he said. "But you are shivering. Perhaps I really should have said nothing. Perhaps it is worse for you to know than to imagine. I really would not for the world have hurt you. I admire you more than I can say, Lady Beckworth. I would comfort you if I could."

He had drawn her hands against his chest and bowed his forehead against the top of her head.

Madeline closed her eyes, her mind awash with bewilderment and anger and misery.

"This is my dance, I believe, Madeline," a cold and quiet voice said from beside them.

. . .

WHEN JAMES RETURNED DORA to her husband's side, John Drummond smiled amiably at him and continued his conversation with a group of neighbors. He seemed to have been unaware of either his wife's or his brothers' absence from the ballroom.

James strolled away and looked about him for Madeline. The next dance was to be a waltz, the one he had reserved with her.

He felt a little like laughing, though his mind was in such a whirl that he knew he would not be able to sort out his thoughts to his own satisfaction until the next day. But he felt like laughing. At himself.

The great love of his life! He had cut short his university career, established a lifelong enmity with his father, half-killed Carl Beasley, been half-killed himself by the Drummond brothers, made lasting enemies out of all three of them, lived a life of torment for years afterward, held himself back from Madeline because he had felt morally committed to another woman and her child, exiled himself in Canada and beyond for four years, spent those years in deep and often painful self-analysis, and come back home to live a life that he had felt could never be quite unblemished or whole.

All because of the love of his life. Dora.

And she had never loved him. She had turned to him because she was disappointed at being abandoned by Peterleigh, who must have been at home earlier that summer—he could not remember—and had carelessly impregnated her as he had doubtless done over the years with a dozen other women and more. He had reminded her of Peterleigh! She had already known at the time that she was to have Peterleigh's child.

And had he loved her? But he knew the answer. He had

asked the question before in the past few months. If he looked back with perfect honesty, stripping away everything that had happened since, he knew that he had never really loved her. Not even with a very young man's ardor. She had simply been a pretty and attractive girl who took his summer's fancy. And she had been his first—as he had not been hers. He had been so inexperienced that he had not even recognized that fact!

James nodded and smiled in the direction of a group of older ladies who were sitting at the side of the ballroom, fanning themselves and gossiping. Where was Madeline? Couples were already on the floor ready for the waltz to begin.

Surely it was only later, when news reached him that Dora was pregnant and married to John Drummond and removed to some unknown destination, that he had conceived his great passion for her. A passion born of guilt and anger that others had so ordered his life and Dora's and their child's—as he had thought—without consulting him. It had been born of the frustration of knowing that it was too late for him to do anything about it. And of his concern for Dora, who had been so young and helpless.

It was not easy for his mind to assimilate the knowledge that Jonathan Drummond was not after all his own son, but Peterleigh's. For nine years he had thought he had a son.

His mind had not assimilated the facts. But his emotions were beginning to do so. He felt an enormous relief, a huge lifting of a burden. He had no child. And no responsibility for Jonathan's future. And need feel no more guilt over what had happened to Dora.

He was free. Free to love Madeline as he had always wanted to love her. By God, he was free to love Madeline!

His first child with Madeline would be his only child. If only he could have children with her. They had been married for almost eight months already.

Where was she? The music had begun. Couples were twirling past him on the floor. She had been gone for a long time.

By the time he had looked even more carefully around the ballroom and outside on the terrace and in each of the rooms along the hallway, he had noticed that Carl Beasley was also missing. And he was hoping that there was no connection between the two absences.

But there was, of course. When he went downstairs and looked out through the front doors, which were still open, he saw them together beside the fountain. They were facing each other, their hands clasped together.

They were so engrossed in each other that they did not see him approach. By the time he was close enough to speak to them without raising his voice, they had drawn even closer together. They were about to kiss.

"This is my dance, I believe, Madeline," he said.

She jerked her head upward and pulled her hands away from Carl's. Carl on the other hand looked at James with an expression that could only be described as a half-smile.

"Oh," Madeline said, "has the waltz begun? I did not realize."

James bowed to her and extended an arm. She took it. But he turned back to Carl Beasley before leading her away.

"If I were you, Beasley," he said, "I would keep out of my sight for the rest of this evening. And you will keep your hands off my wife for the rest of a lifetime if you know what is good for you."

Carl's smile broadened. He gave James a mock half-bow.

They walked into the house and partway up the stairs in silence. Madeline was holding herself very straight. Her chin was high.

"We will walk into the ballroom together and dance what remains of the set of waltzes," he said, not looking at her. "And you will smile for the rest of the evening. I will deal with you when we are at home in the privacy of our own rooms."

"You will deal with me," she said, her voice as cold as his own. "How do you expect me to dance for the rest of the evening, James, with such a threat hanging over me? My knees are knocking together in terror."

They were at the top of the stairs, opposite the open doors into the ballroom. The music was loud and spirited. He glanced across at her. Her face was flushed with animation, and she was smiling dazzlingly.

She continued to smile beyond his shoulder as he led her into the waltz.

MADELINE WAS FINALLY ABLE to let go of her smile two hours later when she was inside her own carriage again, her husband next to her. But she would not relax the determination that had kept her back straight and her chin high in the Duke of Peterleigh's ballroom. She felt rather as if she would break into little pieces if she tried to relax.

They traveled in silence.

So much for the decision to enjoy herself, she thought wearily as she swept up the stairs and into her dressing room ahead of James. It was rather difficult to enjoy one-self on the very evening when one discovered that one's husband was having an affair with a former lover, the mother of his child.

A little difficult, yes. She sank onto the stool before her dressing table and allowed her maid to remove her diamonds and brush out her curls.

And to have that same husband discover one being comforted by a friend and hear him threaten that friend and promise to deal with her. Doubtless the whole blame for a ruined evening would be placed squarely on her shoulders.

A ruined evening! She would have laughed if her maid had not been standing directly behind her unhooking the back of her gown. A ruined marriage, rather. If there had been anything left to ruin. A ruined life.

She was very tempted when she had washed and donned her nightgown and dismissed her maid for the night to go into her own bedchamber, the one she had never slept in, and climb into the bed there. But James would come after her as surely as the world was turning. And she would not have him misinterpret her actions and think her too cowardly to face him. She went out into the hallway rather than go through his dressing room and into the bedchamber she shared with him.

She had not expected him to be in their bedchamber ahead of her. She was not quite ready for the encounter. But he was standing at the window, his back to her. She closed the door firmly behind her.

"Well," she said, "here I am, James, knocking knees and all, ready to be dealt with."

"You will not make a mockery of this," he said, turning from the window to look at her with eyes that had her suddenly thinking that the detail about her knees was not entirely false. "How long has it been going on, Madeline?"

"You mean my affair with Carl Beasley?" she asked, her chin lifting and her eyes sparking. "Now what exactly are you asking, James? How long I have known him? I believe I confessed to that first meeting. How long I have been stealing away for clandestine meetings with him? I am not quite sure. Since before Christmas, I believe. How long have I been his mistress? I am not quite sure of that either. Since sometime after Christmas, I believe."

She stopped and smiled at him, though in reality she was terrified. His face had blanched so that his eyes looked darker and wilder in contrast. He crossed the room to her in a few strides.

"What are you telling me?" he said—no, he whispered, so that she felt almost paralyzed with fright. "What are you telling me, Madeline?"

"You don't look pleased," she said. "I'm sorry. I thought that that was what you wanted to hear. You would not believe me if I said there was nothing between us, would you? I always aim to please my husband."

He grabbed her arms in a painful grip and jerked her toward him so that her head was forced back at an unnatural and painful angle.

"Don't play games with me," he said. "You are playing dangerously with fire. Have you forgotten that you married the devil? I want to know what is going on between you and Beasley."

"He is my friend," she said. "I talk with him. I confide in him. I have no other man to talk with." Her neck muscles were aching.

"You have a husband." He spoke through his teeth. "Have I not told you to stay away from Carl Beasley?"

"Yes," she said. "But I choose my own friends, James. And if it is my disobedience you complain of, then I will say this. I would obey you, perhaps, if I respected you. Or if I liked you. Or loved you. As it is, I feel I owe you nothing."

He took a half step back, though he did not release his bruising grip on her arms. She was able to lift her head, which felt as if it were about to drop off her neck.

"I want the truth from you," he said. "No more games or defiance or mockery. Are you and Beasley lovers?"

She smiled. "What will you do if I say yes?" she asked. "Spurn me? Beat me? Divorce me? Tell me, James. I must know the consequences of my answer."

And then she was grabbing for the lapels of his dressing gown as he shook her so violently that she completely lost her balance.

"Answer me," he said. "Have you slept with Beasley?"

She clung to him, dizzy and gasping. "No," she said. "We have not made a cuckold of you yet, James. Not yet. But I am thinking of it. I need a lover too. And I do not need to be very particular. I could hardly do worse than what I already have, could I?"

"By God, Madeline," he said, jerking her against him again so that her hands were imprisoned against his chest, "you have a wicked tongue."

She fought against his mouth when it covered her own, twisting her head from side to side. When one hand spread itself behind her head to hold it firm, she went limp in his arms until he lifted his head.

"I want to go to my own bedchamber," she said. "if you take me tonight, it will be rape. I suppose a husband cannot ravish his own wife, can he? I am, after all, your possession to be used as you will. But in your heart you will know that you have ravished me, James. I hate you and despise you for what you have done to me."

"For what I have done to you!" he said, watching her lips. "And what is that, pray? Making you want me against your will? You want me already. Do you think I cannot feel the heat of you? Do you think I cannot look down and see the tips of your breasts hard against your nightgown? Don't talk of rape to me, Madeline. Are you ashamed of wanting your own husband? Is such wantonness appropriate only between lovers?"

She made no resistance when he lowered his mouth to hers again. She would hold herself lifeless in his arms, she decided. Anything he got from her that night would have to be taken.

But it was a ridiculous resolve, as one part of her mind realized almost instantly. He had been right. She was already hot and panting for him. He was her husband and her lover and her passion, and there was no room for thoughts of his infidelity, of his long love for another woman, of the son he shared with that woman. No room for thought at all. Not yet.

There was room only for feeling. And loving. And being loved.

When he stripped away her nightgown, she matched his actions, tearing at his dressing gown and nightshirt, sending a button flying in her haste.

She could not get close enough to him. She had both arms wrapped about his neck, her naked body arched against his, her mouth wide for the invasion of his tongue. And she sobbed to be closer.

And closer yet.

And yet after he had laid her on the bed, his hands and his mouth aroused her further, as rough as her own on him. She twisted against him, moaned against him, begged him with eager body and incoherent pleas.

And if she had never fully known it before, she knew it then with a conviction far too deep for thought.

James. He was her world. The only world. The only place where there was air to breathe and food to eat and water to drink and beauty to delight in. The only place capable of sustaining life in her.

He was her universe.

"James. Please. Oh, please. James."

And then he penetrated her. Deeply. To the heart of the ache that was in her. And moved and moved, thrusting and thrusting against the ache until she became mindless and twisting need. Need to be taken and held and loved. Need to give and to hold and to love.

"James!"

It sounded like someone else's voice, very far away. But it must have been her own, because the sobs that followed it gradually became hers. They were coming from inside her, hurting her chest even as the rest of her seemed to have turned to jelly.

And it was against his chest that she sobbed. He was lying on his side, holding her close against him with one arm while his free hand smoothed through her hair.

"Hush!" he was whispering. "Hush now, Madeline. My God, what have I done to you? Hush now."

If she held her thoughts completely blank, she did not believe she had ever felt so happy. She was in James's arms, the only place where she had ever really wanted to be, and his hand was soothing in her hair and his words were gentle, his breath warm against her ear.

She wanted to stay there forever and ever. And even longer than that.

When she finally stopped sobbing—she could not even begin to explain to herself why she had been doing so—she let herself relax completely and pretended to be asleep. If she were awake, she would feel obliged to pull back from him and announce that she was a perfect goose for crying just because he had made love to her again after so many months of the other dispassionate encounters. Or else she would have to confront him with her own accusations.

And she did not want their relationship to return to normal again. Not yet. Tomorrow there would be all sorts of things to consider, which she absolutely refused even to think of at the moment. But tomorrow would come soon enough. For now she would pretend sleep, and perhaps he would hold her awhile longer.

But not for nearly long enough. She felt obliged to continue to feign sleep when he eventually slid his arm very slowly from beneath her head and rolled away from her. He got out of bed and she knew, though she did not open her eyes, that he stood for a long time looking down at her.

She watched him for a few minutes as he stood at the window again, looking out from a darkened bedchamber onto a darkened world. He was still naked and magnificent in his nakedness.

She closed her eyes as he turned his head toward her once more. And then she heard the door into his dressing room open and close.

He did not return for the rest of the night. Nor was he at breakfast the next morning. He had ridden out, Cockings told her when she asked. But by that time it no longer mattered. She did not want to see him.

Ever again.

• • •

HE HAD RAPED HER. The thought pounded through his brain like the regular beating of a drum for the rest of the night and on into the following morning as he rode, he did not know where, out on the moors. He had raped his wife.

He had raped Madeline. The woman he loved.

Some love! Some way of showing an emotion that was supposed to be all giving. He had taken from her in the worst possible way a man could take from a woman.

He had raped her.

Oh, it was true that she had been willing after he had actually started to do it to her. More willing than he had ever known her. Wild and wanton in her desire. He could still feel the sting on his back from the raking of her fingernails.

But she had not wanted it to happen. She had told him before it started what he would know in his heart afterward. And he knew. It did not matter that she had enjoyed it while it was happening every bit as much as he had. She had cried immediately after.

Her sobs had killed something in him. He had exulted in their lovemaking, in the sound of his name as she begged him to come into her and shouted out as he took her through the climax. He had been finding her ear with his own mouth so that he might whisper her name.

And then had come the sobs, tearing at her, tearing into him. Telling him what he had become.

A man who would force his own wife against her will. A man who found it necessary to do so. "I hate you and despise you," she had said to him.

James spurred his horse into a fresh gallop.

And why had it all happened? Did he really believe that

she had given herself to Beasley? He would not believe it of her, could not do so. Not Madeline. She was not the sort of woman who would be unfaithful to a husband, no matter how she hated and despised him.

And if she ever were and was confronted with her infidelity, then she would react with tears or some sign of inner torment, not with laughter and defiance.

She had not been unfaithful to him. She had met Beasley, she said, because she could talk with him and confide in him. She had no other man to talk with.

And whose fault was that? It certainly was not hers. He could distinctly remember that at the start of their marriage she had made an effort to speak with him, to make a friend of him. And he had found himself unable to respond.

If she did take a lover, the fault would be more his than hers.

He looked about him in some surprise to see that he was riding in daylight and that the sun was not even newly risen. It must be well past breakfast time already. He ran a hand over the rough bristles on his jaw and grimaced.

He should go back to her. Talk to her. But what did one say to the woman one had raped the night before? I'm sorry? It will not happen again? I was distraught with the fear of losing you to another man? It was not really rape because you enjoyed it?

What could he say to her?

But he was free at last. Free to love her. He had not ruined another woman's life. He had no son.

He was free and whole for Madeline. That was what he had wanted to celebrate with her the night before.

If it were possible for him now to love openly.

Perhaps it was too late.

Perhaps the events of last night had proved that. Perhaps he was incapable of giving love. Perhaps he could only take it for himself with violence, destroying what he loved most in the world.

But he must try. If he did not try, he would never know.

Perhaps it was not too late.

"I hate you and despise you for what you have done to me," she had said.

He frowned. For what he had done to her? Shutting her out of his life? Killing the glow that had always been the main source of beauty in her?

"I need a lover too," she had said.

Too? As well as whom? Him? Did she think he had a lover? Had she seen him with Dora? Or more to the point, had she seen him leave the ballroom with Dora? And did she know about Dora? About Jonathan?

She was friendly with Carl Beasley. Once Carl had vowed to get revenge on him for what he had done to Dora. But what had he done to her beyond lying with her when she was already with child? And Carl had known that. Why the threat of revenge, then? Carl had allowed him to believe a lie all those years ago. But he must surely have forgotten that foolish threat. He had smiled the evening before, though. Not a pleasant smile.

What had he been telling Madeline?

There really was only one thing to do. If he had the courage to do it, that was. He must go home to her and somehow persuade her to sit down and have a long talk with him. He must tell her everything—the whole of his past and the whole of his present. Dora and Madeline. Madeline. His present and the whole of his future if she would forgive him. He must make her understand. He must somehow find the words.

He did not know when he reached the house whether he should go up to his room first and change his clothes and shave before finding her, or whether he should find her out immediately. But he would lose his courage if he put off the moment. And he would lose the words, which were now bursting from his lips.

Surely after she had heard him out she would understand the reason for his haggard and untidy appearance.

"Where is her ladyship?" he asked Cockings, handing him his riding whip and hat.

The butler coughed. "Not at home, my lord," he said. "I believe she left a note with your valet."

James went very still and looked closely at the man. "Then send him to me without delay," he said, striding in the direction of the library.

She had not even taken a carriage from their coach-house. She had taken a gig into the village and presumably the stage or the mail coach from there. Her destination was undoubtedly London, though she did not say so. She knew no one in York or Harrogate or any other northern town.

"If you follow me and bring me back," she had written, "you will have to keep me locked up. I shall leave again whenever I am able."

She would be going to her mother. And to her twin. They would both be in London. She would be safe.

"I will not be a thing to you," she had written, "to be used as a toy for your pleasure. If you still love Mrs. Drummond, then I am sorry for you. And if you pine for your son, then I feel for you. But under the circumstances you should not have married me, James. I am a person and I have feelings and needs, and I am not the sort of wife who will turn a blind eye to her husband's philanderings and smile bravely for the benefit of the rest of the world."

God!

"You may go to hell and welcome to it," she had written above her signature.

James closed his eyes and crumpled the letter in one hand.

He did not go after her for almost a month.

MADELINE SAT SILENT and dry-eyed throughout the long journey by mail coach to London.

She would live with her mother. For a time, anyway. And Dom and Ellen were in town for the Season. After a while she would set up her own establishment somewhere. She did not know on what. But Edmund would not see her destitute. And her needs would be modest for what remained of her life.

And if James came after her, she would fight him all the way back to Yorkshire and leave him again as soon as she was able. Time and time again if necessary until he gave up coming for her.

It was true, perhaps, that she did not despise him one half as much as she despised herself. But she hated him for what he had made of her.

A woman who had panted and begged and sobbed for his favors only hours after discovering that his heart—and probably his body too—belonged to someone else.

A woman who had allowed herself to be taken against her will without clawing and fighting every step of the way.

A woman who had enjoyed being ravished.

What kind of a woman was that? What kind of a woman had she become?

"I have done with you, James Purnell, Lord Beckworth," she told him, her eyes on the scenery beyond the coach's window, her lips not moving. "Five years is long enough for any sick obsession. I have done with you now. I have my own life and my own pride to piece together again. And there is no room in either for you."

She withdrew the glove from her left hand slowly without taking her eyes from the passing hedgerows, and coaxed her wedding ring off her finger. She earned a frown of annoyance from a clerical gentleman sitting in the opposite corner when she pulled down the window with the apparent purpose of drawing some deep breaths of fresh air.

Her right hand, resting on the window, dropped the ring to the roadway.

21

IN A SALON IN THE EARL OF HARROWBY'S London house, Lord and Lady Eden had just sunk down onto a sofa, side by side. They were laughing.

"I have only just begun to really appreciate my mother," Lord Eden said, draping his arm along the back of the sofa behind his wife's shoulders. "How is it that she is sane and serene after having brought up Madeline and me? I may well be in Bedlam long before Charles and Olivia reach their majority."

Ellen laughed. "I have heard," she said, "that once children reach their fourth or fifth birthday, they finally learn to walk, not run."

He looked at her with mock gloom. "You mean we have only three or four years to wait?" he asked.

"Of course," she said, "in the meantime, we could abandon them to a nurse's care and merely tiptoe into the nursery when they are sleeping to gaze adoringly at them. It is not obligatory to take one's children walking in Hyde Park every day, you know, Dominic."

"I would be accused of cruelty to my own servants," Lord Eden said with a grin. "Why is it, Ellen, that Charles must always not only run but also make off in quite the opposite direction from that favored by everyone else? Does he take after your side of the family by any chance?"

She turned her head and met his lips briefly. "Let us be thankful that there were enough daisies in the park to keep Olivia busy," she said. "At least she was relatively stationary while she was picking the heads off the flowers. And besides, Dominic, you know that you almost burst with paternal pride every time some dowager pauses to admire the twins."

"Hm," he said, placing his free hand beneath her chin so that he might return the kiss at more satisfactory length. "Are you intent on staying here much longer, love, or shall we go home soon?"

"I miss it," she said, smiling at him. "I always said that I would be happy if I could but live in the country, and I have not changed my mind now that my dream has come true. I just wish Jennifer was settled. She is not happy."

"She is only twenty," he said, "and has enough suitors to make one dizzy remembering all their names. But I know what you mean. Is she still pining for Penworth, do you think?"

"Oh, yes, undoubtedly," she said. "But he was too proud to beg her grandfather for her last year, you see, and she was too proud to beg him to do so. So there was an impasse. Perhaps he will come back this year. But there is no point in our waiting around in the expectation of his arrival, is there? Perhaps we should go home."

"We'll stay another week," he said. "Kiss me again, Ellen. We seem to have so little time to ourselves these days."

"Mm," she said, laying her head back against his arm and offering him her mouth.

But there was a tap on the door before they could settle

too deeply into an embrace. Dominic cursed quietly under his breath before the butler opened the door.

"From Mama," he said with a frown, getting to his feet and glancing at the letter he was handed. "Perhaps she wants us to take her up in our carriage tonight after all."

"What is it?" Ellen asked a couple of minutes later, watching his face as he read the letter.

"Madeline has arrived," he said.

Ellen clasped her hands to her bosom and beamed at him. "Oh, they have come," she said. "I am so glad for you, Dominic. You have been missing her, I know. Oh, how wonderful. When will we see them?"

"Not *them*," he said, still staring down at the letter. "Madeline. Alone. She came on the mail coach today. And apparently collapsed into bed immediately afterward and has been sleeping ever since."

"On the mail coach?" she said. "And without James?"

Dominic swallowed and looked up at her. "She has left him," he said.

"Oh, Dominic." She took a step forward and lifted his free hand to her cheek.

"I REALLY CAN'T get up, Mama." Madeline rolled over onto her stomach and buried her face in the pillow. "I am so tired. I just want to sleep."

"Come down for dinner at least," her mother coaxed. "And then come back to bed early."

"I'm not hungry," Madeline said. "I just want to lie here. I want to die."

Her mother sat on the edge of the bed and sighed. She set a comforting hand on her daughter's head. "I know," she said. "I don't know quite what you are going through,

Madeline. I have never lost a man in that particular way. But I can remember how I felt when Papa died. It was the most wretched feeling imaginable. The bad part is that life continues. The good part is that the pain goes away."

"This never will," Madeline said, her voice muffled by the pillow.

"Come downstairs and talk to me," Lady Amberley said. "I have sent word to Cedric not to come tonight. We will be alone. Come and tell me what happened exactly. It sometimes helps to talk."

"I hate him and I have left him forever," Madeline said.

"Yes, dear." Her mother ruffled her hair gently. "You told me as much when you arrived. But there must be a great deal more. I am not going to force information from you. You may sleep all night, if you wish, and all day tomorrow. But I will be dining alone if you want to talk with me. In less than an hour's time." She got to her feet and left the room.

And paradoxically Madeline felt abandoned. She rolled over onto her back and stared upward. She felt so very, very alone. She was in London and Mama was downstairs and Dom was in town. And there must be any number of her friends within visiting distance.

She could talk again. There were people around her to whom she could talk nonstop if she wanted. People who loved her and would listen to her and participate in her conversations. Her loneliness was over. No more of James's silences and morose moods.

But she was so lonely that her stomach ached and her throat ached, and she felt such a massive inertia that she could scarcely move on the bed. She had not realized until after she had thrown away her wedding ring how she had been in the habit of playing with it on her finger. Her finger was so terribly bare.

And though they had never touched in bed during the nights after he had finished his business with her, the bed she was now lying on felt huge and cold and empty without him. She turned onto her side and spread an arm across the undented pillow beside her.

He was not there. He never had been there and never would be. She was back in the home she had shared with her mother for several years. She was back home. Where she was loved and wanted. And Dom would probably come the next day or she would go to see him. And Ellen and the babies. No longer babies—they were more than a year old.

She was back home. She could forget the nightmare of the past eight months. She could relax and let the healing begin.

But the bed was so very empty. She would do anything, she thought, closing her eyes tightly and clenching her hand into a fist on the empty pillow—anything!—if she could just open her eyes and see him there, morose expression and unfathomable eyes and all. And the lock of dark hair that would inevitably be down over his forehead for her to brush back.

God. Oh, God, she really did want to die. There could be nothing left to live for. It was her left hand that was on the pillow. Her ringless left hand.

James.

"James. James." She whispered his name over and over again.

James and Dora Drummond. And their son Jonathan.

She sat up with a jerk at the side of the bed, throwing back the bedcovers. What in the name of heaven was she doing? Pining away for a faithless husband? Wallowing in self-pity because she had been fool enough to marry him in the first place?

Never! She was Lady Madeline Raine and not some weeping, vaporish female who would crumble under the least adversity.

No. She paused in the action of throwing off her nightgown. She was not Lady Madeline Raine. She was Lady Madeline Purnell, Lady Beckworth. But names notwithstanding, she was not one to give in to her fate. If James was ever interested enough to inquire after her, he would not find a poor cringing creature, destroyed by his infidelity.

Not by any means. She pulled a wrap about her and rang the bell for her maid.

Her mother was forced to sit through dinner with a brightly chattering daughter, who talked almost without ceasing on a wide variety of topics, not one of which was of a remotely personal nature.

The dowager countess was quite relieved to have the flow of monologue stemmed for a while in the evening by the arrival of Lord and Lady Eden.

"Ellen!" Madeline rushed across the room to hug her sister-in-law. "How lovely it is to see you again. You are looking so very well. Have Charles and Olivia grown a great deal since I saw them? And are they walking? But they must be. They are more than a year old."

She turned to her brother without waiting for any response to her questions. "Dom," she said. "Dom." And she was being held against the tall, strong, and comforting body of her twin and feeling all her resolves sag.

"We weren't sure you would be up," he said, kissing the

top of her head. "Did you ride all the way on the mail, Madeline, without once stopping off to sleep?"

She looked up at him a little dazed. "I think I must have done," she said. "I don't remember any inns. I think I came all the way without stopping."

"You don't even know for sure?" he asked.

She pulled away from him and smiled brightly at the other occupants of the room. "There is so much to see on such a long journey," she said. "And one sees so many strange characters. Really one misses a great deal when one travels by private conveyance." She launched into a description of her journey, surprising herself with the amount she remembered. The only detail she had consciously recalled before she started to talk was dropping her wedding ring from the window and fighting the panicked urge to stop the coach and jump out of it for more than an hour after.

"Mama," Ellen said, getting to her feet after an hour had passed and numerous cups of tea been drunk, "you wished to show me your new ball gown. There was no time yesterday, if you will recall."

"Quite right," the dowager said, smiling at her daughter-in-law and rising from her own chair. "How good of you to remind me, dear. I would have been annoyed if I had remembered after you left."

The two ladies went upstairs to examine the fictitious gown.

"I will need some new ball gowns too," Madeline said to her brother. "The ones I have must be dreadfully *passé* this Season. I must go shopping tomorrow. I wonder if Mama will be free to accompany me. Or perhaps Ellen would care to come. If she is not busy, that is. If the two of you do not have other plans. You must have all sorts of engagements. Do you?"

"Hey," he said quietly, forcing her to look directly at him for the first time that evening. "This is your twin, Mad."

"Don't," she said with a little laugh, putting out her hands defensively. "I'm not ready for this, Dom."

"Was it just a quarrel?" he asked. "Did you just act impulsively, as you so often do?"

She stared at him wide-eyed. She shook her head.

"Something more basic?" he asked.

"I never loved him," she said almost in a whisper. "I always hated him. It was just an obsession. It is over now."

He sat back in his chair and looked at her searchingly. "You loved him," he said. "And you love him."

"Don't be too clever, Dom." She got to her feet in some agitation and crossed the room to the window. "I have been married since last August. You have not seen either me or James since then. You don't know. I loathe him, and if I never see him again, it will be far too soon."

She had not heard him come up behind her. She jumped when his hands came down on her shoulders.

"Tell me what happened," he said.

She shrugged and looked sightlessly out into the darkness. "I don't know him at all," she said. "That sounds foolish, does it not, after eight months of marriage and living together. He does not talk to me or smile at me. I can never see beyond his eyes. He is possessive and dictatorial. The only times we talk are when we are quarreling."

"He is possessive?" he said. "He must have some feelings for you, then."

"No, none," she said. "I am a mere possession."

"A buildup of all these things would not lead to a headlong flight on the mail coach," he said. "What happened, Mad?"

She put her head back against his shoulder and closed her eyes. "The world came to an end, that's all," she said.

"Melodrama?" he said. Then he squeezed her shoulders. "No, sorry. You don't have the energy to rip up at me, do you? You mean it. What happened to end the world?"

"Ellen took Mama away deliberately, didn't she?" she asked.

He laughed softly. "You must be off form if you have to ask that," he said. "It was not very subtly done."

"You made a wonderful choice of wife, Dom," she said. "I am so glad for you."

"Thank you," he said. "I'm glad for me too. Why did the world come to an end?"

"He has a mistress," she said. "And he has a nine-year-old son by her. The boy even looks like him. And yet I am to be raged at when I make a friend of another man."

"A particular man?" he asked.

"The Duke of Peterleigh's steward," she said. "An amiable man who has been kind to me. It is his sister who is James's mistress. It hurt him to tell me."

"It hurt whom?" he asked. "James or the steward?"

"Carl," she said. "Carl Beasley."

"He told you?"

"Only when I had seen enough to thoroughly arouse my suspicions," she said.

"And this man is your friend?" Dominic asked. "And your husband objects to the friendship?"

"Yes," she said dully. "I think he thought we were embracing, but Carl was merely holding my hands after he had been forced to tell me."

Dominic muttered an oath that Madeline was too weary to object to. "You are quite sure that what he told you is true?" he asked.

"Yes, quite sure." Her voice was toneless. "They were alone together in a room just before Carl took me outside."

"And yet," he said, "what your husband thought he witnessed was not quite the way it seemed, was it?"

"You are saying that James's being alone with Mrs. Drummond was innocent?" she said, lifting her head away from him and turning to look at him with weary eyes. "I think not, Dom. And there is the child."

"_Mrs._ Drummond?" he said. "And what is Mr. Drummond's role in all this, pray?"

"I think he probably does not know," she said. "Though he must know that the boy is James's. He looks so different from the other Drummond children. But his brothers found James and her together and were furious. They even threatened him."

Dominic sighed and put a hand to his brow. "Did you confront him with all this, Mad?" he asked. "Or did you just take fright and flight, in that order?"

"He was too busy raging at me over Carl," she said. "I left the next morning."

"And what happened during the night between?" he asked and watched her flush deeply and bite her lip. He raised his eyebrows. "One of those fights, was it? I don't know, Mad. I should go up there perhaps, should I? Find out the truth and kill him or draw his cork if what you say is true?"

She looked at him indignantly. "You will do no such thing," she said. "I have left him, Dom. Forever. I told him in the note I left behind that he may go to hell for all I care, and I meant it. I have no more interest in James Purnell, Lord Beckworth. He was an unfortunate, unpleasant episode in my life. Now I have the rest of my life to get on with. You see?" She held up her left hand, palm in. "I have thrown away his wedding ring."

"Mad!" he said gently, taking her by the shoulders and drawing her against him as her face crumpled before his eyes and she began to wail. "Oh, Mad."

"How humiliating!" she said, sniffing and snorting and hiccuping. "How dreadfully mortifying. And it's all your fault. I was not going to tell anyone anything. It's nobody's business but mine. It's certainly not yours, Dominic. You have your own family and are managing it beautifully. Do you think it is not humiliating to come crawling back home like this from a broken marriage and a husband who prefers another woman to me? And always did. The child is nine years old." She pounded the sides of her fists against his chest.

"Hush," he said soothingly against her ear. "Hush now."

And she sagged against him and stopped the tirade abruptly. She could hear someone else's voice, also against her ear, telling her to hush. And she could feel someone else's arms about her as he said it. And she had quietened for him because he had loved her and satisfied her and not turned away from her immediately after.

She pushed away from her brother. "Do you remember in Brussels?" she said. "After you and Ellen had broken up? And you started to fight back to life, determined that you were going to get better and not let yourself be destroyed by anyone, even if you loved her? Do you remember, Dom?"

He nodded. "It's one of the hardest things in this world to do," he said.

"But you succeeded," she said. "And you would have made a meaningful life for yourself, wouldn't you, even if you had not married her after all?"

"Yes," he said, "if there had been no help for it, I think I would have gone on living. Not just surviving, but living."

"Well," she said, "I am not your twin for nothing, Dom. I am more than a survivor too. I love James. I can't hide that from you, can I? And at this very moment I am terrified and quite convinced that life can hold nothing for me if I don't have him. But I don't have him and never will, for I have far too much pride ever to share him with another woman. And so I must learn to live without him. And I will learn. Don't expect me to weep all over you ever again."

"And glad I am to hear it," he said, setting a comradely arm about her shoulders and leading her to a sofa. "My valet sweated blood tying this neckcloth and now it looks like a limp rag. He will sulk for a week."

"Oh, Dom," she said, "I have missed you so."

"We were hoping to see you at Christmas," he said.

"James said we might come," she said. "But I would not because I did not want anyone to see that we were not perfectly happy together. A laughable scruple under present circumstances, was it not? What do you think of Edmund and Alexandra having another child?"

"I am delighted for them," he said, "since they are so very pleased about it themselves."

"I am so envious," she said. "I wish I could have had just one child before all this happened. But how foolish. I could not have left then, could I, and he would not have let me go. Do you think Mama and Ellen are counting sequins on that gown?"

"What gown?" he said, and they both chuckled.

• • •

THE EARL OF AMBERLEY stood in the doorway of the music room and watched his wife. She was playing her own composition on the pianoforte, as she so often did, while Caroline stood beside her, her elbows on the stool, her chin resting on her hands, staring up at her. Christopher was lying on his stomach at the other side of the room, painting. Nanny Rey would scold them all indiscriminately. According to her notions, paints had no business anywhere else but in the nursery.

They all saw him at the same moment. Caroline danced across the room and hugged one of his legs. Christopher picked up his painting and brought it for inspection. Alexandra smiled at him and stopped playing.

"You are back already," she said. "I thought you were to be at the village all morning, Edmund."

"I decided to come back early," he said, swinging his daughter up into his arms, tousling his son's hair, and advancing into the room. "Kisses, princess?" He turned his head to meet the puckered mouth of his daughter.

"Come," Alexandra said, crossing the room and setting her hands on her son's shoulders after looking carefully at his painting, "let's take you back to Nanny Rey. I will play for you again tomorrow, Caroline, shall I? Are you going to wash your own brushes, Christopher, so that Nanny doesn't scold?"

She soon had the children upstairs and settled. She left the nursery and tucked her arm through her husband's.

"What is wrong?" she asked, leading him in the direction of her sitting room.

"How do you know there is something wrong?" he asked, smiling at her.

"Edmund!" she said. "I have been married to you for

almost five years. A poor wife I would be if I did not know instantly when you had something on your mind."

"It used to amaze me," he said, "how Madeline and Dominic used to understand each other so well even without the medium of words. Now I can experience it too with you." He leaned down and kissed her on the nose before standing aside so that she could precede him into the sitting room.

"So," she said, turning to him as he closed the door behind them, "what is it?"

"I intercepted the mail in the village," he said. "There's a letter from Dominic. Madeline is in London."

Her face lit up. "Will they come here?" she asked. "Or can we go there? Can we, Edmund?"

"She is alone," he said.

She looked at him in incomprehension.

"She has left James." He looked at her as she sat down straight-backed on the nearest chair. "Dominic did not give details, but it does not sound like a petty quarrel. She has really left him. Are you all right, Alex?"

She was sitting pale on her chair, staring at him.

"I knew it could not work," she said. "It would have been too good to be true. He gave up so many years to stay with me until I could be happy. And all I have ever wanted for him is his happiness. I thought perhaps he would find it. I thought perhaps Madeline would be right for him. And he for her. But it would have been too good to be true."

"She is pretty distraught, according to Dominic," he said. "Putting a brave face on it, as one might expect with Madeline, and smiling and talking and declaring that she will make a new life for herself. But quite broken up and ready to fly into pieces at the smallest provocation."

She bit her lip. "But why did James let her go?" she asked. "Where is he, Edmund?"

He shook his head. "Not in London when Dominic wrote this letter anyway," he said. "What do you want me to do, Alex? Write to him? Go to him? Will you be hurt if I go to London to see Madeline?"

"Hurt?" She frowned. "Why should I be hurt?"

He sat down opposite her and smiled ruefully. "It has struck me throughout the return ride from the village," he said, "that you and I could easily be caught on opposite sides of the fence on this one, Alex. Whatever has happened between them, it would be natural for you to take James's part and equally natural for me to take Madeline's. Can we talk sensibly now and prevent that from happening?"

She leaped to her feet. "Oh, no," she said. "That is absurd, Edmund. I love Madeline, who is my sister by two separate close ties. I could not turn against her. And as for taking sides, that would be the most stupid thing we could do. They have a problem, and doubtless it has been compounded by foolishness and all the misunderstandings and stubbornness that come so easily when one lives close to someone else. You taught me very early in our marriage how to combat those occasions. You have always made me talk to you, and you have always talked to me. Are we to quarrel over someone else's quarrel when we have learned to avoid our own?"

He sat back in his chair and smiled at her. "You are angry with me," he said.

"I certainly am." Her eyes were flashing. "Don't you trust me to be as committed to your family as I am to my own? My children are your family. They have your name."

He was on his feet too suddenly and taking her by the

arms. "I am sorry, love," he said. "Forgive me? I was terrified that your attachment to your brother would cause you to fly off in a fury with Madeline. I don't know you as well as you know me, I suppose. Forgive me?"

She smoothed the lapels of his coat and lifted her face for his kiss. Then she twined her arms about his neck and laid her head on his shoulder.

"What can have happened?" she said. "I so wanted them both to be happy, Edmund. What could have happened to make her take such a drastic step? She has left him. What did he do to her to make her leave? There is so much love in James. It sustained me for years. But somehow he has driven her away."

"If you can manage without me for a few days," he said, "I will go up to London and see what I can find out. Perhaps it is just a foolish quarrel after all that can be settled with some cool mediation. Though perhaps those few days will have to be extended if I need to go to Yorkshire."

"No, I cannot manage without you," she said. "And I can't stand here wasting time in your arms, Edmund, comforting as they are. There is a great deal of work to do if we two and the children are to be ready to leave for town within the next day or two. Have you sent word to town to have the house opened up?"

"No," he said. "But if you will release my neck, Alex, I can get a messenger on his way before morning is out. Are you sure you are up to the journey?"

"You know I have never been able to sit doing nothing when I am increasing," she said. "And I am certainly not going to remain here without you. The very idea!"

He kissed her on the lips and looked deeply into her eyes before turning to leave the room. "Try not to worry too much," he said. "I have a feeling those two belong together. They are just too stubborn and hotheaded to make an easy transition from the single state into marriage. They will, given time, and be as happy as you and I."

She touched his cheek. "I couldn't wish better for them," she said. "Go now."

22

JAMES WAS STANDING IN THE STABLEYARD OF the Duke of Peterleigh's manor, one booted foot propped on a mounting block, an arm draped over his raised knee. He was looking at Carl Beasley, who was tapping a riding whip against his boot and seemed eager to be on his way. A couple of grooms were busy in the stalls behind them, but they were well out of earshot to all but raised voices.

"I always thought I was the one who had ended our friendship," James said, "by punching out your lights after you had let Dora be sent away. I did not see your actions at the time as hostile, merely misguided. I often felt sorry afterward for taking out my frustration on you. But they were hostile, weren't they? You took me for a fool and were clearly right in your judgment. I was a fool."

Carl shrugged. "It was all a long time ago," he said. "We were both much younger, Beckworth, and a great deal less wise."

"Why did you never tell me that it was Peterleigh's child?" James asked. "Why did you let me believe it was mine?"

"I suppose Dora told you," Carl said. "I might have known she would. It might have been yours, though. You were laying her out there in the heather. You and Peterleigh both. But it was nothing to feel very guilty over, was it? Dora and I were never of great importance. We were only Peterleigh's wards."

"There was never any question of my looking down on either of you," James said. "You and I were friends. And I cared for Dora. You knew that. You knew I would have married her without any hesitation at all."

"It was all very well to rage and tear your hair and break my nose when there was nothing you could do about the situation," Carl said. "I doubt you would have married her if there had been a real chance. Like Peterleigh, you would have looked for a way out. And do you think your dear papa would have permitted you to marry my sister?"

"Did he know?" James frowned. "Did my father know that it was Peterleigh's?"

"Never." Carl laughed. "If Dora were only a little better endowed with brains," he said, "I would say that she laid an excellent trap for you, Beckworth. In reality, of course, it all happened by chance. But it was certainly better to let everyone believe that you were the culprit. You were easy to excuse—young and sowing your wild oats and all that. On the other hand, many people would have condemned Peterleigh. He was almost forty years old and Dora's guardian. And it might well have been you, after all."

"So," James said, "you and Peterleigh between you let my father believe an untruth. You caused a rift between us that never healed and let me live through agonies of guilt and remorse for years."

"You deserved it all," Carl said. "You ruined my sister as effectively as Peterleigh did."

James nodded. "Yes," he said. "I did. I was much to blame. But I fancied myself in love, and I would have taken the consequences. I never did realize that you hated me so much, Carl, and resented my position as son with a living father. I never knew you felt so inferior. But you could not take out your resentment on Peterleigh, could you? You were dependent on him. So I was the scapegoat of your need to avenge yourself on the world. The blame was put on me. But of course Dora could not be allowed to marry me, could she, because I was brother to the duke's prospective bride. The child would have been his son and his nephew both. Besides, it is hardly likely my father would have countenanced that match if he had known the truth. Peterleigh was one of the few men he thought worthy of his regard. Ironic, wouldn't you agree?"

"Forget it," Carl said. "When all is said and done, no great harm has been done. Dora is reasonably contented and the child is well looked after by Peterleigh. And you have done quite well for yourself." He turned and strode from the stableyard in the direction of the house.

But James went after him. He caught him by the shoulder and swung him around so that his back was to the trunk of a giant oak. He took him firmly by the lapels of his coat.

"Has no great harm been done?" he asked. "Is a ten-year anguish no harm? And what about your vow all those years ago to revenge yourself on me for the beating I gave you? Has that been forgotten too?"

"I don't like your hands on me, Beckworth," Carl said icily. "And what nonsense are you talking now?"

"I want to know about your friendship with my wife," James said.

Carl smiled. "I suggest you ask her," he said. "I don't want to tell tales, Beckworth, and get the lady into trouble."

"Oh, no." James's eyes narrowed dangerously. "I was not asking you about the nature of the friendship. I was not asking you to smear my wife's name. And if you don't want your nose broken again, you had better think twice about volunteering any lies on the subject. I am asking what you have told her."

"Many things," Carl said. "We have met many times, Beckworth. To our mutual satisfaction, I might add."

James's hands tightened on his lapels.

"What did you tell her about Dora?" he said. "And about the boy?"

Carl Beasley smiled again. "I did not need to say much," he said. "She saw you alone with Dora, you know, and she heard the interchange between you and Ben and Adam. I merely comforted her."

James dropped his hands and watched as Carl straightened his coat. "You told her that Dora and I were lovers?" he said. "And you let her believe that the boy is mine?"

Carl brushed at his sleeves with careless hands. "I was amazed that you had not already told her yourself, Beckworth," he said. "Anyone would think you still had something to hide."

"Just one more thing," James said, taking a menacing half-step forward. "Did you lead Madeline to believe that there is still something between Dora and me?"

"She saw for herself," Carl said. "I did not have to say a word."

"But you did, didn't you?" James's eyes narrowed again so that for the first time Carl looked wary. "In the way you have always had, of seeming to say only what the other can be supposed to know already. And always in a manner to make the other suppose you to be a concerned friend. It was against me you felt resentment, Beasley. It was me you wanted to hurt. Why must my wife be made to suffer too?"

"Just because she *is* your wife," Carl said, his eyes mocking.

"The last time we had an encounter like this," James said, his voice quiet and level, "I punished you. In a young man's way, with violence. I have learned that unnecessary violence settles nothing. I will only say this, Beasley. You will stay away from my wife in future. You will neither speak to her nor come near her. If you do, I will find a way of dealing with you. Do I make myself clear?"

Carl smiled. "And how is the lady to be kept away from me?" he said. "Are you going to lock her up, Beckworth? You do not seem to have done a great job of making her happy so far in your marriage, do you?"

"Fortunately," James said, "neither my wife's happiness nor mine nor the state of our marriage is any concern whatsoever of yours, Beasley. Good day to you." He turned and strode back into the stableyard to retrieve his horse.

But almost a month passed before he finally went after her. His instinct at first had been to go at once, to find out whether she had gone by stage or by the mail, and to pursue her and bring her back home.

But bring her back for what reason? To force her to continue being his wife? To force her to manage his household and entertain his guests, to sit beside him at meals and with him in the drawing room during the evenings? To force her to share his bed at night and cater to his pleasure? To bear his children—if they ever could have children?

To know himself hated? To know that everything she did in his home was done because he was insisting upon her obedience? To know that at any time when he had been from home he might arrive back to find her gone and have to go after her all over again?

Was that what he wanted? Madeline at all costs?

It had happened as he had always known it would happen. He had loved her and married her and destroyed her. And now there seemed to be nothing he could do to reverse the process.

Perhaps if he had known a long time ago what he knew now, things might have been different. He would not have spent years consumed with guilt and feeling that other people had destroyed any chance he had at pride and self-esteem. He would not have lost all faith in life and other people. And he would have felt free to love and be happy. Free to love Madeline, whom he had fought for years not to love.

Perhaps he could have offered her himself, not just his body on a hillside at Amberley and his hand and his name at an altar a week later.

Perhaps he could have made her happy and himself happy.

Perhaps. But it was pointless to think in terms of what might have been. The fact was that he had made a mess of his marriage and made his wife so unhappy that she had taken the almost unheard of course of leaving him.

He could not go after her and bring her back. If he loved her as much as he professed to do, then he must let her go, he must let her find whatever happiness she could without him.

He showed his love for her for a month by staying at Dunstable Hall, going about his daily business as if nothing had happened. He continued the improvements for both his tenants and his laborers that he had begun months before. He continued to keep a close eye on the activities of his bailiff and on the books. He visited his neighbors and smiled and informed them all that his wife had gone to London to visit her family and that yes, he was missing her greatly.

And at home he noticed with a pang of regret that the servants were beginning to revert to their old ways. The pretty curls and dimples that had begun to appear on the younger maids began to disappear again as Mrs. Cockings once more took charge of the running of the household.

He missed Madeline with an emptiness that was a pain. But unlike most pains, it did not lessen as time went on but grew worse and worse until he had to force himself to get out of bed in the morning and force himself to carry on with the day's activities and then force himself to climb back into the empty bed again at night.

He had heard nothing from her and almost nothing about her. Only one letter, hastily penned, from Alex to say that they were on their way to London, having just heard that Madeline had arrived there. There was some comfort in the letter. At least he knew she was safe.

But safe with her family. Where she belonged and where she would stay for the rest of her life. Away from him, where she was not safe and not happy.

There was never a letter from her, though his days began to revolve around the daily arrival of the post.

He finally went to London himself. He rationalized his decision. He must see her. If they were to live apart, then there were arrangements to be made. He would have to see her properly settled with a comfortable allowance. And he must at least tell her the truth about Dora and Jonathan. Somehow—would it be possible?—he must apologize for what had happened on her last night at home.

He did not know if he had a good reason for going. But by the time he went, he did not need a good reason. He went because he had to go. He had no choice in the matter.

THE DOWAGER Lady Amberley leaned back on the sofa, rested her head against the back of it, and closed her eyes. She sighed.

"I really should not be here," she said. "I should have left with your other guests. I could become the *on-dit* of the week, Cedric. Alone in a gentleman's rooms at eleven o'clock at night."

"Relax for a while," he said. "You have been looking tired lately."

"Mm," she said. "I must admit it is lovely to be quiet here with just you. You are a peaceful companion."

He sat down beside her and took her hand. "I think perhaps you have become too involved in Madeline's problems," he said. "You worry too much, Louisa."

"She is so desperately unhappy," she said. "No one who did not know her would realize it, of course. She is as involved with the entertainments of the Season as she ever was and has just as large a court as ever, too. And she is in good looks, though somewhat thinner than usual. I cannot think what will happen to her, Cedric. A broken marriage! That has always been something that happened to other people. Never within my own family."

"She is seven-and-twenty," he said gently. "Cruel as it might sound, my dear, it is her problem. She must solve it.

With your love and support, of course. But you must not take her burdens on your own shoulders."

"To be fair," she said, turning her head on the cushion and smiling at him, "that is what she has told me more than once. But we are Raines. We stick close together. There is Edmund planning to leave for Yorkshire as soon as he can persuade Alexandra that she would be putting her new child at risk if she goes too. And Dominic planning to take Madeline into Wiltshire and set up the dower house for her. And Madeline fighting us all and enjoying the Season quite furiously. Oh, dear."

He slid an arm beneath her head, leaned over her, and kissed her quite deliberately. "Take some time away from your concerns," he said. "Concentrate on me."

"Mm," she said, touching his cheek with one hand. "Have I been neglecting you, Cedric?"

"Yes," he said.

"I haven't meant to," she said. "You are like a rock for me. I would go all to pieces if you weren't there."

"I need to be more than a rock," he said.

"Kiss me, then," she said. "And hold me. I am beginning to depend upon this too, you know."

He kissed her deeply and slid her gown from one shoulder so that he could kiss her shoulder and her throat too.

"Oh," she said after a while, her head on his shoulder, kissing the underside of his chin, "you feel so good, Cedric."

"Stay here for the night," he said.

"Cedric?" She turned her head to look up at him. "What are you saying?"

"Stay here," he said, "and make love with me. I need

you, Louisa, more and more each day. And I'll take your mind off all that is making you weary."

"Yes," she said, pulling away from him and sitting up, "you certainly would do that. Oh, dear, Cedric, I have progressed a long way since last summer. The prospect is distinctly appealing. I feel tingles all over. But no, of course we must not. Goodness, the very idea! Can you picture me crawling back into my own house at some unheard of hour of the morning with a crumpled gown and disheveled hair?"

"Stay here until morning," he said, "and have breakfast with me."

"And arrive home in broad daylight in an evening gown," she said with a smile. "No, Cedric, you naughty tempter. I have a better idea. I will marry you. Do you still want me to?"

He reached for her hand again. "You know you don't need to ask that," he said. "Let's do this properly, though, shall we?" He stood up, drawing her to her feet with him. He took both her hands in his. "Louisa Raine, will you do me the honor of being my wife?"

"Louisa Harvey," she said with a smile. "Lady Louisa Harvey with no 'dowager' attached. I like it. Yes, I like it very well. And I like you very well, my friend. We will remain friends afterward, will we not?"

"I think it is possible to be friends and lovers at the same time," he said.

"Lovers too?" she said. "Oh, I like the sound of it more and more. I want to be your lover, Cedric, even at my very advanced age. Yes, I will marry you, dear, just as soon as you care to arrange the ceremony. Kiss me to seal the bargain."

He kissed her.

"Mm," she said after a few minutes. "What was that about staying all night?"

"I shall escort you home immediately," he said, putting her away from him. "I will not countenance even the risk of gossip surrounding my betrothed. You ought not to have stayed here after the other guests left, you know."

She smiled at him.

MADELINE WAS SITTING in her mother's drawing room, her cousin Walter on one side of her and Jennifer Simpson on the other. She was laughing with Jennifer at the account Walter had just given of a bizarre bet made at one of his clubs.

"But then," she said, patting her cousin on the hand, "all the wagers at the gentlemen's clubs are bizarre, from what I have heard. Are all of you constantly in your cups when there, Walter?"

He began to protest.

They were surrounded by family members and friends of the dowager countess's and Sir Cedric's. They had all met for an informal afternoon celebration of the betrothal, which had surprised them all.

Not that it should have been surprising, Madeline thought. Mama and Sir Cedric had been very close friends for years, and they did make a handsome couple even if Mama's hair was liberally streaked with gray and Sir Cedric's was completely silver. Perhaps it was the very length of the friendship that had made the betrothal so surprising. Any expectation that the two of them would eventually marry had long been put to rest.

But marry they would, just as soon as the banns had been read. And the newly married couple were to go immediately after the ceremony to the Continent for a winter of travel. And probably the following summer too, Sir Cedric had said, lacing his fingers with Mama's and smiling at her in a way that had tugged at Madeline's heart.

She was happy for them. After the initial shock she was more than delighted. They were friends as well as being very fond of each other. Their marriage would have every chance of success. Friendship was an essential element of any marriage if it was to be successful, she had learned. Edmund and Alexandra were friends as were Dom and Ellen. She and James had never been friends.

She got up restlessly to cross the room to another group of people.

"Your husband will doubtless come down from Yorkshire for the wedding, Lady Beckworth," one of her mother's friends said.

Madeline smiled. "He is very busy," she said. "And it is such a long way to come."

"But a wedding is excuse enough to rejoin such a lovely wife," someone else said with a wink. "And don't tell me that he is not looking for excuses, ma'am."

Madeline smiled brightly and moved on.

"I am to have the honor of leading Mama down the aisle and giving her away," Edmund was saying. "Not many sons have that experience, do they?"

"And will you be overjoyed to hand her over to someone else's keeping at last?" Uncle William asked with a broad wink.

"William!" Aunt Viola said. "The very idea. Take no notice of him, Edmund. He is just teasing. Your own sister too, William."

Edmund laughed. "Well," he said, "I will be quite

confident in placing her hand in Sir Cedric's. I could not wish better for her."

Aunt Viola tucked Madeline's hand beneath her arm and patted it. "And what are you planning to do when your mama goes away, dear?" she asked. "William and I would be delighted if you stayed with us for a while."

"Oh, thank you," Madeline said with a broad smile. "But I will be making some definite arrangements for my future soon. It is quite exciting, you know, to be starting a new life again." She slipped her hand free and moved on.

Her mother's butler tapped her on the arm and handed her a card.

"The gentleman would not have me announce him, ma'am," he said with a bow. "He directed me to ask you if he could be admitted."

Everything around her receded. Sights faded, voices became a distant buzz. All that existed was the card in her hand.

"No," she said after what might have been seconds or minutes. She closed her hand about the card. "Tell Lord Beckworth that I do not wish to see him."

The man bowed and withdrew.

Dominic was miraculously there beside her. He took her elbow and she smiled at him. She did not know if she would have fainted otherwise. She did not know if everyone in the room was aware of what had just happened. She did not look about her to see.

She did not notice Alexandra slip from the room.

"That coat is Weston's creation, is it not?" she said. "I have been meaning to tell you how very splendid it looks, Dom."

"Thank you," he said. "Ellen was all admiration too when I put it on for the first time earlier this afternoon."

"She was more likely all admiration for the man inside it," she said.

"Well, there is that too, I suppose," he said. "Not that I am conceited, of course."

"Of course not," she said, and they grinned at each other.

"You are all right?" he asked quietly.

"Perfectly," she said. "Why would I not be?"

He drew her arm though his and they sat down with a group that included their mother and Sir Cedric.

He was in London. He had been downstairs just a few minutes before. He had come for her. Oh, God, he had come for her. At last.

More than a month had passed. What had he been doing in all that time? Had he been at home? Had he missed her? Had he been as relieved to see her go as she had been to get away?

Had he missed her?

He had not written at all.

Why had he come? Was he going to play the tyrant and drag her back home against her will? And could he do so? Did he have the right to do so? She was very much afraid that he did. But she would not go. He would have to tie her and gag her for the whole distance and then keep her behind locked doors for the rest of her life. She would not go. Besides, Edmund would not allow her to be taken back by force. And Dom would not allow it.

But they were merely her brothers. He was her husband. Would they do the honorable thing and stand aside and refuse to interfere?

"I am afraid not," she said with a smile to the lady sitting beside her. "He is too busy and it is too great a distance to come."

But he was here, she thought. He was in London.

Perhaps he would not force himself on her. Perhaps he would not drag her back home. Perhaps he would go away now that she had refused to receive him. Perhaps he would return home alone.

Panic grabbed at her. Perhaps she would never see him again.

Her mind was effectively brought back to the topic that was never far from it. Could it be true? It would just be too ironic after all those months of anxious waiting and agonizing disappointments. Now that it could not be true without hopelessly tangling her life, it looked as if it might be true. Three weeks overdue already.

It was the emotional turmoil she had lived with for the past month and a half. That was the cause of it. There were no other symptoms. No morning sickness. No unusual tiredness. Nothing. Only the fact that she was three weeks late. And the latest she had been in the months previous was four days.

She did not want it to be true now. He would never let her go if she was carrying a child of his. He would force her to go back. She did not want it to be true. She did not want to go back.

But several times every day she looked anxiously for signs that it was not true and lay on her bed staring upward as if the very stillness of her body would stem a flow of blood.

And he was here. He had come. He had come for her. He had come to her.

James.

"I was very, very nervous about telling my children," her mother was saying, her eyes on Madeline. "I was afraid they would disapprove of my choice or feel betrayed."

"Oh, Mama." Madeline leaped from her chair and crossed the short distance to her mother. She hugged her and sat on the arm of her chair, an arm about her shoulders. "I could not possibly be more happy for you. My only complaint is that you did not make Sir Cedric our steppapa years ago." She wrinkled her nose at Sir Cedric. "Will you expect us to call you Papa?"

The whole group laughed.

Where was he now? Madeline wondered. Would he come back? Or would he go away and never come near her again?

She would die if he did not come back.

And yet over the next ten days she denied him admittance ten times.

"James." The butler had delivered his message, and James had turned away before Alexandra was halfway down the stairs. She hurtled the rest of the way down as he turned back and opened his arms to her. "James." She pulled him toward a small salon.

"Alex," he said, hugging her again when they were inside. "How good it is to see you again. You are losing your figure already."

She pulled back after a while and looked at him. He was quite haggard, his face thin and sallow, his eyes very dark and haunted. His hair was overlong. She lifted a hand to push back the lock that had fallen over his forehead and into his eyes.

"I knew you would come," she said. "Edmund has been planning to leave for Yorkshire, but I knew you would come."

His smile was almost a grimace. "The grim elder brother?" he said. "Coming to dish out punishment?"

She lowered her hand to his shoulder. "You are talking about Edmund," she said. "He is a concerned elder brother, James. He was coming to see if anything might be patched up."

"I doubt it," he said. "She has just refused to see me."

"James," she said, smoothing her hands over the lapels of his coat. "Oh, James, it is not true, is it? Dora is not your mistress?"

He grimaced. "I suppose everyone has been told that," he said, "and believes it. It's not true, Alex."

"I knew it could not be," she said, "though Dominic told Edmund that that was what the trouble was. James, when did you last sleep? You look dreadful."

His eyes held a moment's amusement. "Do I?" he said. "Perhaps it is as well she would not see me today, then. Will she see me, Alex? How is she?"

She shook her head. "Busy and smiling and enjoying the Season," she said.

They looked into each other's eyes. "She is miserable, then," he said.

"Yes."

He turned from her and walked to the window. "I made a mess of it," he said. "I should never have married her."

"I thought you loved her," she said, her voice flat and unhappy.

"I do," he said. "That's the whole trouble."

She put her arms about him from behind and rested a cheek against his back. "I thought you had changed when you came back last summer," she said. "I thought you had put all the old troubles behind you and started to live again. I was very happy when you married Madeline. I love her too."

"I *had* changed," he said. "I had come to terms with myself and life. I had even begun to find some meaning. God, perhaps, though not the God we were brought up to know, Alex."

"He is not the real God," she said quickly. "Edmund taught me that, and my life with him has shown me that he is right."

"But I suppose there was still something in me," he said, "that told me I did not deserve a wife I loved. Or happiness either."

"Dora?" she said. "Is she very unhappy? Has she suffered as much as you have? And does she still suffer?"

He laughed rather bleakly. "She seems perfectly content," he said. "And there is no sign that she suffered greatly even at the time it was all happening, though there was some disappointment, I gather. She expected marriage to her son's father."

"It was not your fault," she said tightly. "You must stop blaming yourself, James. And Papa too. He did only what he thought best at the time, though it was very wrong of him not even to consult you."

"The child is Peterleigh's," he said.

Her arms fell from his waist. "The Duke of Peterleigh?" she said rather foolishly.

"The same," he said. "The very duke for whom you were not good enough, Alex, after being kidnapped and forced to spend a night alone in Edmund's house."

"Dora's child is *his*?" She stared at his back, her eyes wide and disbelieving.

"We were dupes," he said. "Papa and I, I mean. It was better, apparently, to smear our names than to lower

Peterleigh's in everyone's esteem. Not that I was blameless, of course. It might have been my child, and Dora was only seventeen at the time."

"But . . ." she said, and seemed lost for words for a time. "All this burden you have borne, James. It was all unnecessary?"

His fists were clenched at his sides. "And Madeline has been destroyed by it all," he said. "That is the worst of it. I have destroyed her."

"No, James." She hugged him from behind again. "No, that is not so. Nothing is ever so bad that it cannot be put right. She will understand when you have explained to her. There is still time to put everything right. You love her and I am convinced she loves you."

He laughed. "If she had feelings for me at the start," he said, "I don't think they could possibly have survived, Alex. And she will not see me."

"But she will," she said. "If you persist, she will. You won't give up, will you?"

"I will call on her every day for as long as it takes," he said. "But I won't force myself on her. I have no right. There are other things, Alex, that you don't know and that I am not about to tell you of. Unless she has told you, of course. But I doubt it."

"Whatever do you mean?" she said.

He shook his head. "I must leave," he said. "I have no right in her mother's house at present."

"Where will you go?" she asked. "Come and stay with us, James."

He turned and smiled at her. "Absolutely not," he said. "Would you have me put your husband in such an awkward position? I'll stay where I stayed last spring." He reached out to touch her cheek. "How are the children?"

"Well," she said.

"And you? Are you happy to be increasing again?"

She nodded.

"Well," he said, leaning forward and kissing her on the cheek, "go back upstairs, Alex. I don't want to cause any dissension between you and your husband."

"You won't," she said. "We are very close friends, James."

He smiled. "Ah, yes," he said. "Friendship. The essential ingredient." And he opened the door to let her out into the hallway ahead of him.

23

THE EARL OF AMBERLEY ORGANIZED A BALL in honor of his mother's betrothal. It was hastily arranged, coming as it did two weeks after the announcement and two before the wedding. He was not at all sure that many guests would come since it was early in June and the members of the *ton* still had a vast number of entertainments to choose among.

"But enough people will come, Edmund," his wife assured him. "And I shall put off my mourning for the occasion, shall I? Does it matter that not quite a year has passed, do you think?"

"I am longing to see you in colors again," he said, kissing her.

"Perhaps the ball can serve another function too," she said, looking at him a little warily. "Perhaps we can get Madeline and James together at last. May I invite him?"

"Of course," he said. "But you must also tell Madeline, love. She has been quite adamant about not receiving him."

"Yes, I will," she said, and sighed. "Is she not foolish, Edmund? It is perfectly obvious that nothing can be settled between them unless they talk. And it is equally obvious that she is as miserable as he is."

"It is their marriage," he said. "They must work out their problems as best they can. Are you ready to take the children walking?"

"Yes, I am," she said.

MADELINE ARRIVED with her mother and Sir Cedric at the ball. She had seriously considered not going at all, but she could not absent herself from such a family celebration. Besides, she must come face-to-face with him eventually. For two weeks she had lived in terror that he would eventually stop calling at her mother's house and sending up his card. Surely the day would come when he would decide that he had had enough.

And yet she could not send down the message that he might come up. For some reason she could not bring herself to do so. She did not want to see him. She did not want to be persuaded to go back home with him. She wanted to be left to herself so that she could begin a new life. And she longed for him and pined for him.

She was altogether bewildered by her conflicting feelings.

She handed her wrap to her brother's footman and ascended the stairs at her mother's side. She smiled at the people in her direct line of vision and dared not turn her head to either side. She drew confidence from the new gold ball gown she wore and her new coiffure—her hair had grown long enough that her maid had been able to pin it on top of her head, with a liberal shower of curls cascading down the back of her head and along her neck.

"Edmund," she said, hugging him after he had released her mother. "There will be a veritable squeeze here this evening, believe me. Everyone I have spoken to in the past week is coming. Alexandra, what a lovely shade of blue. It seems strange to see you again without your blacks."

"I am not at all sure it is the thing to be hostess of such a very *tonnish* function in my present, ah, shape, though," Alexandra said, flushing.

"What nonsense!" Madeline said.

Alexandra smiled. "Edmund's exact words," she said.

Madeline turned her attention to Dominic and Ellen and Lord Harrowby, who had also arrived early. She had not told anyone of her own almost certain pregnancy. Five weeks late now. And her feelings about it were as ambivalent as her feelings about seeing James. She did not want a child now. A child would complicate her plans to live apart from her husband and begin a new life. And yet beyond the realm of rational thought there was a warmth and a complaisance and a joy that she would not allow to bubble to the surface.

She was going to have a child. She was going to be a mother at last. And it was to be James's child. She was carrying a part of him within her.

She had seen him once. For the first week after his arrival, she had been afraid to go out. She had received her friends at her mother's house and made laughing excuses not to go riding with them or to the theater with them or anywhere else with them. But after that week she had resumed her normal way of life—or what had become normal since her arrival in town. She would not hide from him or anyone else. And she would not care what sort of gossip was going on about her living apart from her husband. She would not cower indoors for fear that he was waiting in ambush beyond the front doors, ready to bear her off back to Yorkshire.

She had been riding in Lord Carrondale's phaeton

when she saw him. He was on foot, walking along a busy thoroughfare. He had seen her too. But he had made no sign and kept on walking. And she had smiled and twirled her parasol and turned to say something to her companion. But every part of her insides had performed a somersault, and she had still felt weak at the knees and short of breath when Lord Carrondale had handed her down outside her mother's door a full half hour later.

Madeline stood in the doorway of the ballroom, lifted her chin, and looked deliberately about her. But of course there was scarcely anyone there yet. And he was not among those few who had come very early.

And how foolish she was to take for granted that he would come. It was very possible that he would stay away. After all, she had been snubbing him for all of two weeks. And he was under no great obligation to come. Mama was not his mother. Perhaps she could after all relax and enjoy the evening.

It was a depressing thought. And yet one that she had to accustom herself to. Two hours later she was dancing with Mr. Rhodes and laughing at his outrageous compliments on her hair and realizing that it was the fourth set of the evening already and that even most of the usual stragglers had finally put in an appearance.

She had been right. Edmund's ball was one of the squeezes of the Season, for all the short notice everyone had been given. It would go down as a great success. Edmund and Alexandra were gracious hosts, and Mama and Sir Cedric were so glowingly happy that they looked ten years younger than they had looked a month before.

It was a great success. Everyone was happy. James had not come, and on the whole it was as well that he had not. Nothing should happen, even in her private world, to spoil the evening. And she must keep on remembering that she really did not want to see him ever again. For however much she loved him and longed for him, and however real her pregnancy had become, he was still an adulterer. He still had his mistress and his son. Her child would not even be his firstborn.

She was glad he had not come.

"Oh, come now," she said to Mr. Rhodes with a giggle. "I think you have gone a little too far, sir. Are you quite sure I rival the sun? Do you find it quite impossible to look at me?"

"Quite, quite impossible," he said, squinting his eyes and frowning as if in pain.

Madeline giggled again. And met the dark eyes of her husband across the room. He was standing in the doorway, his hands clasped behind him. He looked very noticeably different from any other gentleman in the room, dressed as he was in black evening clothes.

"And my hand is too hot to hold?" she said to Mr. Rhodes.

He winced and sucked air though his teeth. He released her hand for a brief moment. "Excruciatingly hot," he said. "Quite like the sun, Lady Beckworth, as I said at starting."

"Flatterer!" she said. "I like it."

EVEN WHEN HE WAS all dressed up for the evening, James was still not quite sure that he would go to the ball. After all, she had consistently refused to see him for two weeks, though he had persisted in presenting his card at her mother's house every day since his arrival.

And on the one occasion when he had seen her, she

had not acknowledged him in any way, or shown any sign of recognition. She had merely passed on by—his wife in another man's carriage, looking as lovely and as animated as she had ever looked. He had thought afterward—after a hard ride of at least ten miles out into the country—that it was probably a good thing he did not know the identity of her companion. He might well have sought out the man and killed him.

But she had clearly meant what she had written. She did not intend ever to come back to him. And she clearly meant her refusal to see him. It was no token refusal of two or three days before she felt she had made her displeasure sufficently obvious that she could now admit him.

James sat for a while in his carriage before directing his coachman to take him to White's. But the words did not come out quite as he had meant them to.

"The Earl of Amberley's house on Grosvenor Square," he said curtly.

After all, she knew he had been invited. He had been very adamant on that point when Alex had asked him. He would go, he had said, only if Madeline clearly understood that he would be there. She knew, but she had not sent any message that he must stay away. And there was little likelihood that she would stay away herself. The ball was in honor of her mother's betrothal.

Did she want him to come, then?

Or did she not care?

Or did she plan to make a very public scene? He shuddered at the thought. But no, Madeline was sociable and vivacious, but never vulgar.

He did not know if he would be able to bear to see her in a party mood. Glittering for other men. How would he be able to keep his hands off any man she smiled at?

He would not stop the carriage now in the middle of a busy street. He would wait until it stopped on Grosvenor Square, and then redirect it to White's. He would call at her mother's again the next day and send up his card.

"Thank you," he said, nodding absently to the footman who opened the door of the carriage at the end of his journey. He stood outside his brother-in-law's house for a few moments, looking up at the lighted windows, and then walked resolutely up the steps and into the hallway.

He was very late. The house seemed filled with the sound of music. There was no receiving line outside the doors to the ballroom. There was a set in progress. He stood watching the dancers, his hands clasped behind him.

But no, he did not stand watching the dancers. For him there was only one dancer in the room, and his eyes found her immediately. She shimmered in her gold ball gown, which caught the lights of the candles with her every movement. But if she had been dressed in drab gray, she would have shimmered just as surely.

For she was Madeline. As she always had been and always would be in his eyes. Except that he could only watch from afar. Whenever he came too close to the light and the flame, he put both out.

And so he stood and watched. And when her eyes met his across the room for the merest moment, there was only a flicker of hesitation. She danced on and talked on and laughed on.

As if he did not exist. As if he were not her husband. As if he never had been. As if he had never been anything at all to her.

And perhaps he had not.

"James!" Two warm hands were taking his, and his gaze shifted to the flushed and happy face of his sister.

"Hello, Alex," he said, smiling. "I am sorry to be so late. But I came, you see."

MADELINE HAD SEEN Jennifer Simpson waltzing very slowly earlier in the evening with a young man. But she had been too preoccupied with her own anxieties about James to look closely at the gentleman. Now, however, she was looking desperately about her for some distraction.

Jennifer was still with the same young man, standing and talking with Walter and his latest flirt. And Madeline realized with a start that Jennifer's companion was Allan Penworth.

"You may take me to my cousin, Mr. Carrington," she said to Mr. Rhodes when the set was at an end. And she smiled dazzlingly at him just in case she was being watched.

"Allan!" She held out both hands to her former fiancé as she drew close. "I did not even recognize you. How splendid you look."

He took her hands and raised one to his lips. "I could say the same of you, Madeline," he said. "How are you?"

She pulled a face. "Perfectly fine," she said.

He squeezed her hands. "I have heard," he said quietly. "I am very sorry, you know."

"But I have just realized why I did not recognize you," she said. "You no longer look like a pirate, Allan. Whose idea was it to wear a flesh-colored eye patch instead of the black one?"

"My mother's, actually," he said with a grin. "Inspired, don't you agree?"

"You look quite dashing," she said. "But Allan—" she paused and gaped quite inelegantly at him for a moment, "you were waltzing. You were dancing with Jennifer."

"So I was," he said. "With my betrothed—though the announcement is not to be officially made until next week when Jennifer's grandfather is hosting a grand dinner in our honor." He smiled down at the girl, who had slid a hand beneath his arm. "You don't mind my telling Madeline, my love?"

"Not really," Jennifer said smiling impishly. "I suppose former fiancées should be the first to know such things. Wish us happy, Madeline?"

"But of course I do," Madeline said. "Were you really dancing, Allan? And where are your crutches?"

"Somewhere in Devonshire," he said with a grin. "I told Jennifer last year that when I was able to walk her down the aisle of a church from the altar, I would come and ask her to walk to that altar on her grandpapa's arm. But not unless or until I was able to do that."

"He is so foolish," Jennifer said, clucking her tongue. "As if I could not love a man on crutches. I spent the whole winter in the sullens and swearing that Allan was the last man on this earth I would ever agree to marry." She giggled and looked fondly up at her betrothed.

"Well—" Madeline said.

"Madeline?" The light touch on her arm burned through to the bone. The quiet voice was like a fist in the stomach, robbing her of breath. "Will you dance?"

She turned away from Jennifer and Allan without a word of farewell. She ignored three gentlemen admirers who were standing close by, walking past them without even seeing them. She had totally forgotten that one of those gentlemen had signed her card for this very set. She stopped when she reached a clear space on the ballroom floor, and turned. And she stood looking at the black embroidery on her husband's waistcoat while the orchestra prepared to play.

They began to play a waltz.

SHE HAD DANCED with him for all of five minutes, one hand rigid on his shoulder, the other cold in his own. Her eyes had been directed at his waistcoat the whole time. Her face was quite without expression.

"Smile," he said. "Do you wish to draw attention to yourself?"

She raised calm green eyes to his. "Quite frankly, James," she said, "I do not care the snap of two fingers what people think. And I have done taking orders from you. I do not feel like smiling, and I will not smile."

He had made a disastrous beginning. That was not what he needed to say or wanted to say at all.

She looked dazzlingly beautiful. Her hair must have been growing all the time she had been living with him. But he had not noticed until tonight, when she was wearing it in a new style.

She returned her gaze to his waistcoat.

"I will be going back to Yorkshire," he said. "Within the week. It is clearly what you wish. I will send a solicitor to your mother's house. He will have authority from me to make any settlement on you that you think acceptable."

"Are you sure you trust me not to take your whole fortune?" she said.

"You may take it and be welcome to it," he said, and watched her eyes lift to meet his for a moment again. "I had to talk to you before returning home, Madeline. Just once. Did you feel I was harassing you? I needed just one meeting."

"You have it," she said. "I am a captive audience. And though I will not smile and pretend to be enjoying myself, you know very well that I will not create a scene. Not at my mother's betrothal ball. It was cleverly done, James."

"I told Alex I would come only on condition that you had been warned I would be here," he said. "You could have sent word that I was to stay away, Madeline. I would not have forced myself on you as I have not done in the past two weeks. I could have done so, you know. You are my lawful wife."

"Yes," she said. And those icy green eyes were on his again. "I know all about that, James. It would not have been the first time you forced yourself on me, would it?"

He closed his eyes briefly and danced on. "I want you to know," he said, "that Dora Drummond is not my mistress and has not been for ten years. I have no mistress and no casual amour, either. I have had no woman but you since our marriage or for a considerable time before that."

Her chin lifted, but her eyes remained on his waistcoat.

"And Jonathan Drummond is not my son," he said, and found himself looking full into her eyes again. "He might have been, Madeline. We were lovers, Dora and I, briefly, when I was twenty and she seventeen. And I thought he *was* my son until just over a month ago. But he is not. He is Peterleigh's son."

He watched her swallow and look down again.

"Dora was forced to marry," he said, "and move away from Yorkshire when she was found to be with child. I was at university at the time and knew nothing about it until it was too late. I did not see her or hear from her again until I took you home as my bride. I have talked to her twice since, once when I took one of her younger children home after finding him on the road with a sprained ankle, and once at Peterleigh's ball. I discovered the truth there."

"How nice for you," she said.

"But it was too late," he said. "For years my life had been blighted by guilt and bitterness because of the lies I had believed. And now it has been destroyed by the same person's lying to you."

"Mr. Beasley?" she said.

"Beasley, yes," he said. "He has been wreaking a little revenge for a thorough beating I gave him after Dora disappeared."

"A sad story," she said. "She had the wrong man's child and married the wrong man. Quite tragic, really."

"I have no feelings left for her, Madeline," he said. "It was a young man's infatuation blown out of all proportion by the events that followed. I have no feelings for her at all. Or she for me."

He waited for her to say something, but she said nothing. Her eyes were lowered again.

"But it was not Beasley who destroyed our marriage," he said. "I did that."

"Yes," she said.

He spoke very softly. "I ravished you, Madeline," he said. "I took what were my rights as your husband, but it was ravishment for all that. And I have no excuse. I cannot even apologize to you, for an apology would be totally inadequate. I can only promise to stay away from you and take care of your needs for the rest of your life. You may have whatever you want that is mine to give. You have only to tell my solicitor."

"You are generous," she said.

"And you are bitter." He looked down at her bowed head with an ache of remorse for what he had done to her life in less than a year. "I cannot blame you, Madeline. I told you you were marrying the devil, that you were caught in the devil's web. I did not even realize myself at the time how close to the truth my words were. I did not mean to destroy you."

"You have not done so," she said, looking him very directly in the eyes. "No one has the power to destroy me, James, unless I choose to be destroyed. You are not important enough to me to have accomplished anything quite so devastating. We shared a physical obsession. We were both agreed on that when we married. Well, nine and a half months have been long enough to satisfy that obsession. Quite long enough. And there really is not anything else between us, is there?"

"No," he said after gazing down at her for a long moment. "There is nothing else. Only that. This is good-bye, then, Madeline. After five years we will finally be free of each other, apart from the small matter of a marriage that binds us legally, of course. But you need not fear that I will ever press any claim on you that relates to that. You can be free of me at last. And you are still young and still beautiful."

He watched her lift her hand from his shoulder and felt her fingers brush back a lock of hair from his forehead. And he watched her frown and bite her lip and lower her eyes again.

He schooled his expression to blankness and watched her. For the last time. A five-year obsession. Finally at an end. For her. For him it would end when he drew his final breath. And perhaps not even then.

He had loved her and married her. But they had not

lived happily ever after. He had lost her. Not through Carl Beasley's fault or his father's or Dora's or Peterleigh's or anyone else's.

Through his own fault.

He led her to Lord Eden's side when the music came to an end, bowed to both of them, said a few words to Alex—he could never afterward remember what—and left the ball, half an hour after he had arrived.

24

"AT LEAST HE CAME, MAD," DOMINIC HAD SAID.
"All the way from Yorkshire, I mean. He has been
trying every day for a fortnight to see you. And it seemed
to me, watching the two of you dance, that he was doing a
great deal of talking."

"Yes, he did," she had said. "He said a lot."

"But nothing to persuade you to reconsider?"

"He is going back home within the next few days," she
had said. "I will not be seeing him again, Dom. I don't
want to see any more of him. I just want to forget and start
again."

He had led her into the next set.

And she had danced for the rest of the evening.

She lay on her bed two days later staring at the canopy
above her. Her mother was out somewhere with Sir
Cedric. Madeline had been invited to take tea with
Edmund and Alexandra but had declined. Aunt Viola and
Anna had invited her to accompany them on a shopping
expedition. She had declined. Lord and Lady Carstairs had
invited her to join them and Lady Carstairs's gentleman
cousin on a drive to Kew. She had declined. The day before she had sent her excuses to avoid an afternoon picnic
and an evening visit to the opera.

She could no longer pretend that she was Lady Madeline Raine again, free to enjoy all the pleasures the Season had to offer. There was no enjoyment and no pleasure. She must plan for her future.

And her future would be independent of Mama and Edmund and Dominic. They had their own lives to lead and it would be unfair to burden any one of them with her presence. Much as they loved her, she would nevertheless be an intruder on their domestic happiness. And besides, she had no wish to be dependent upon them.

She was dependent upon James. That was the way of the world. But at least he was going to allow her some measure of freedom. She would use it. She would decide where and how she wished to live, and she would arrange for the financing of those needs when his solicitor called on her.

It was all very simple really. All she needed to do was do it.

She should have told him about the baby. He would have to know about that. And that fact might change everything. He might insist after all that she go back home with him. She would write to him within the next week or so.

She closed her eyes. She had so wanted him to ask her to come back to him. It was shameful to admit. Did she have no strength of will and no pride? She had wanted him to ask or even insist. It would have been easy if he had insisted. There would have been no decision to make. She could have gone with him because she had no choice, and she could have blamed him for the rest of their lives if they had continued unhappy.

They were shameful thoughts. Was the responsibility of making something of their marriage entirely his? Was she content to be a passive victim? But under the circumstances, she had not even had a chance to be that. He had decided to be noble and give her the freedom he thought she wanted. He had neither asked nor commanded.

And so she was free. Free to live where and how she wanted, though of course she would always be bound to him by the ties of marriage. She was free.

An empty victory.

She could just see James as he had been the first time she saw him. He was standing in the middle of Lady Sharp's drawing room the night the *ton* decided to snub Alexandra. She, Madeline, had been the only person to cross the room to them, though she had never seen either one before. He had been looking as if he could commit murder, his face thunderous, his eyes burning with fury. She had felt unaccountably frightened of him.

And it was a feeling that had persisted all that summer, while their dislike for each other had grown alongside their attraction to each other.

She could remember him kissing her with fury in the valley at Amberley and with passion and tenderness on the night of Edmund's ball. The night he had put her away from him and told her that his feelings were lust only. The night he had ridden away. The last time she had seen him for four years.

She remembered listening to Alexandra read aloud his letter in which he told her he was coming home the following summer. And her feelings afterward: excitement, hope, caution. She had spent a year persuading herself that his coming meant nothing to her.

And then seeing him again last spring. And the rekindling of passion and dislike.

Their good-bye at Edmund's ball again.

It would have been far better if he had not come back, if he had already sailed for Canada before news of his father's heart seizure could reach him. By now she would have put him from her mind again.

Again? Had she ever put him from her mind from that first meeting on? Would she ever be able to do so?

And if she could go back, knowing then what she knew now, would she choose not to marry him? The nine and a half months of their marriage had been hell.

And heaven.

She had lived almost eight months of that marriage with James. Miserable much of the time, but with him nonetheless. And there had been good times. Precious few, it was true, but a few nevertheless.

There had been that afternoon on the moors before their bitter quarrel. The rare feeling of togetherness. The rare openness of his conversation. The magic of their shared lovemaking. They had been so close on that afternoon. So close to bursting through the barrier that always held stubbornly between them.

So very close. One word, perhaps, by one of them might have changed the course of their lives. If he had said her name, if she had called him her love, perhaps they would have gone crashing through that barrier together.

And there was nothing between him and Dora Drummond. He had no son. He had had no woman but her since their marriage. Carl Beasley had lied to him and to her—from what particular motive she could not fully understand. Mr. Beasley had destroyed him, James had said.

And James had destroyed their marriage. She had agreed with him on that. He had forced himself on her at a time when she was hurt and bewildered and had asked to be left alone. He had taken her anyway.

But it had not been rape. She had said that she did not want him, but she had wanted to be ignored. She had wanted him with a powerful need and an overwhelming passion. Just as she had wanted two evenings ago to be overpowered. She had refused for two weeks to see James, but she had wanted desperately for him to break in upon her. She had left him, but she had wanted him to tell her that she was going back with him.

Madeline opened her eyes and stared upward again. How difficult it was, sometimes, to know and understand oneself. She had always thought of herself as a forceful character who knew her own mind and who would never stand for anyone else walking all over her. And yet her relationship with her husband proved her wrong on all counts. She wanted to be mastered and dominated. And when finally James had refused to do either and had left her free, she must take to her bed in order to wallow in misery and self-pity.

Self-knowledge could be the most distressing knowledge of all.

Madeline was off the bed and jerking on the bell pull before another ten seconds had passed.

"My blue walking outfit," she told her maid, her voice almost panicked. "And before you get it, send word that a carriage is to be sent around without delay."

She was sitting in the carriage less than half an hour later, having rejected a number of options. She might have sent a note around to him asking him to call. She might have driven over to Lord Harrowby's to ask Dominic to accompany her or to Edmund's to ask him. Or if she was wary of involving her brothers, Walter would doubtless have come with her. Certainly it was not the thing for an unaccompanied lady to call on a gentleman in the particular club where James had his lodgings, even if that gentleman was her husband.

But she had decided to go herself and to go alone. There was too much inaction involved in sending a note. And it would be wasted time to go in search of a male escort. He was to return home within a few days, he had said. And he had said it two days before. Perhaps he had gone already. Perhaps even now she would be too late.

She was. The doorman at the gentlemen's lodging house bowed stiffly, looked her over from head to toe in the not-quite-insolent manner that some servants could achieve to perfection, and informed her that his lordship had left.

"Left for the afternoon?" she asked. "Or left for good?"

He bowed again and looked at her with the pity and scorn he might accord to an abandoned courtesan. "We are not expecting his lordship," he said.

He was gone. She was too late. She looked haughtily along her nose at the doorman and enjoyed watching him bow obsequiously as she handed him a coin he had done nothing to earn.

He was gone. She placed a gloved hand in that of her mother's footman and climbed wearily back into the carriage.

"Take me to Lord Amberley's," she said on sudden impulse, and sat back against the seat, her eyes closed, willing it not to be true, willing some other explanation of his absence to be waiting for her when she reached Alexandra.

"Where is her ladyship?" she asked Edmund's butler coolly, handing the man her bonnet and gloves.

"In the drawing room, my lady," he said, bowing.

But she could not hold on to her coolness. Instead of waiting for the butler to climb the stairs ahead of her and announce her, she went flying up the stairs and pushed open the double doors of the drawing room without even knocking.

"Alexandra," she cried, oblivious to all but the figure of her sister-in-law, on her knees beside Caroline on the floor, "has he left already?"

And then her eyes traveled past Alexandra and Edmund and Dominic and Ellen and all four children to focus on her husband, dressed for travel and standing before the empty fireplace, his hands clasped behind him.

HE HAD DONE everything he could. Having ruined his own life and ruined Madeline's chance of ever making a happy marriage unless he were to die young, he had done everything possible to make matters as right as they could ever be.

He had engaged a solicitor to handle her affairs and had given the man strict instructions to grant her every wish, regardless of expense. And he had called upon his mother-in-law and both his brothers-in-law.

"I am sorry," he said to the dowager countess. "You must dislike me quite intensely. And you are right to do so. All this has been my fault. But I want you to know that I am making all the reparation I can, ma'am. Your daughter will never be in need. She has only to wish for something and I will grant it."

"You talk of money," she said, surprising him by crossing the room to where he stood and taking both his hands in hers. "She has other needs, James. Can you grant those too?"

He shook his head. "No," he said, "I am afraid not. I have made her very unhappy."

"Then I am afraid that no one will ever be able to make her happy," she said, "if you cannot. I know my daughter very well, James."

He returned the pressure of her hands. "I am sorry," he said. "I truly am. I do love her, you know."

"Yes," she said, smiling rather sadly at him. "Sometimes it just seems that love is not enough, does it not?"

He said much the same to her brothers. Neither heaped blame on his shoulders, though he had fully expected that Dominic at least would do so.

"Do you love my sister?" Dominic asked.

"Yes," James said.

"You have not thought of insisting that she go back home with you?"

"No." James looked his brother-in-law squarely in the eyes.

"You know," Dominic said, "Madeline likes a confrontation. She likes to fight. She hates it when there is nothing to fight against. She tends to give in."

"I will not force her into anything," James said. "Not anymore."

Dominic raised his eyebrows.

"You are her twin," James said. "I know she is closer to you than to anyone else. Will you write to me occasionally and tell me how she is? It is a great deal to ask, I know. Alex will write to me, of course, but with you I will know that what you say is true, and not what Madeline wants people to believe is true. Will you let me know if she is in any need?"

"She is already in need," Dominic said.

James raked a hand through his hair. "I meant a need I can supply," he said.

"That is what I meant too," Dominic said.

At the end of it all he was not sure he had accomplished anything by his journey to London. He wanted to talk to Madeline again, explain himself to her more clearly, make sure that she understood that her life was now her own to do with as she wished. He wanted to see her again, to have one more chance to imprint the image of her on his memory.

And he wanted to go away, to have done with it all. Two days after Edmund's ball he called upon Douglas Cameron. His old friend was planning to return to Montreal at the end of the summer, even though he was tempted to stay yet another winter in order to see Jean safely through her confinement.

"But she doesn't need me any longer, lad," he said with a laugh. "There comes a time when one must kiss a lass good-bye and be on one's way. Especially when there's another man become the apple of her eye."

James was very tempted to go with Douglas. To go back to Montreal, take up his old job again, and set off with the canoe brigades again the following spring for the inland wilderness where he had found a measure of peace once before. And what, after all, was there to stay for?

It was an idea that grew on him for the rest of the morning as he rode aimlessly about London, neither seeing nor hearing what went on about him. If he went back to Dunstable Hall without delay and made all the necessary arrangements to settle his affairs, he could be on the boat with Douglas before the summer was out.

If he did so, he would be released from the temptation to keep finding Madeline to assure himself that she was alive and well. The temptation to see her and perhaps after all try to force her to come back to him.

Luncheon time found him not eating, but pacing his rooms while his man packed his belongings. The afternoon was not the time to begin a journey. He should wait and set out early the following morning. But he could not bear the thought of inaction. By nightfall he could be well on his way.

But there was something he must do. He must say good-bye to Alex. He could not leave without a word to her.

When he arrived at his brother-in-law's house, he asked for a private word with the countess. She joined him in a small downstairs salon, but when she saw his traveling clothes and heard his errand, she insisted that he join the rest of her family in the drawing room.

"Madeline is not here?" he asked. "And is not expected?"

"No," she said. "Dominic and Ellen are here, James, but you should say good-bye to them. I wish, oh, I do wish things had turned out differently. And I cannot for the life of me understand why they have not." She hugged him and shed a few tears before taking him by the hand and leading him upstairs to the drawing room.

There really was not a great deal to say, though they were all cordial. Edmund and Dominic shook his hand and Ellen surprised him by hugging him. Christopher came obediently to be hugged, and Dominic's twins came to stand side by side in front of him, Olivia's thumb in her mouth, until he stooped down and ruffled their hair and hugged them both together. Madeline's nephew and niece.

Alex knelt down on the floor, where her daughter was

sitting. "Are you going to give Uncle James kisses, sweetheart?" she asked Caroline.

His niece gazed up at him with her solemn dark eyes that reminded him so much of Alex as a child.

And that was when the double doors of the drawing room were thrown back without warning and Madeline, pale and wild-eyed, stood there.

"Alexandra," she cried, "has he left already?"

And then her eyes met his and nothing and nobody existed for many seconds or minutes or hours. At the end of it, when the world started to come back, she closed the doors behind her and leaned against them.

"You were not expected back at your lodgings," she said. "I thought you had gone."

"Come along, tiger," Edmund was saying to Christopher.

Alex had Caroline by the hand. Ellen and Dominic were holding a twin each.

"Up on the shoulder it is, then," Dominic said. "Hold on tight, Olivia. We have all discovered pressing business to be carried out in the far corners of the house, Mad. Stand away from the door, love."

She stood obediently to one side without taking her eyes from James's, and four adults and four children disappeared from the room.

HE WAS DRESSED for travel, not for an afternoon's visiting. He was thinner. Surely he had lost weight. His face looked almost gaunt. He looked impossibly handsome.

"I thought you had gone," she said again.

He clasped and unclasped his hands behind his back. She was still pale and looking dazed. And very beautiful.

"I am on my way," he said. "I called to say good-bye to Alex."

She looked about her. They were alone. And he had seen her burst into the room demanding information about him. How humiliating.

"Are you?" she said, walking farther into the room. "Is it not a little late in the day to begin a journey, James?"

He shrugged. "I might as well be a few miles on the road by nightfall," he said. "There is nothing left for me to do here."

"No," she said, smoothing her hands over the upholstery along the back of a sofa, "I suppose not."

"I will say good-bye, then, Madeline," he said. "I am glad to have seen you again. Will you shake my hand? Can we part at least not the bitterest of enemies?"

She held out her hand to him and smiled. "Why not?" she said. "We were never really meant for each other, James. I remember your telling me last summer at Richmond that it could not work between us. You were right. We just forgot that for a while after your father's passing. Now we know it cannot work and we can go our separate ways without regrets."

"Yes," he said, taking her hand, feeling its smooth slimness.

His hand was warm and strong, the hand of a man who had worked for a living.

"Good-bye, James."

"Good-bye, Madeline," he said. "My solicitor will be calling on you."

"Yes," she said, and dropped her hand to her side as he released it. She smiled.

"Well, then," he said after a pause, "I will be on my way."

"Yes."

He turned away and strode to the door. It seemed a million miles away. But she spoke as he set his hand on the knob.

"What did you expect?" she cried, her voice shrill. "What did you want of me? I have never been able to understand that. I tried. I did try, James. I tried to talk to you even when you did not encourage me. I tried to make your house more of a home by pitting my will against that dreadful Mrs. Cockings. I made friends of your neighbors. I always tried to look my best for you. I tried to please you in—in bed. I could never please you. What did you want of me? Why did you marry me?"

He looked down at his hand on the door handle. "I took you for comfort on the night of my father's funeral," he said. "Remember? I had to make you respectable again after that."

There was a pause. "No," she said. "That was not the reason. You took me because you had decided to marry me. That was the way it was, wasn't it? But why? We were never friends. We were never comfortable together. There was only the passion. And if that is why you married me, then you were a fool. For that died too, didn't it? For months before I left you took me as if I were just another of your daily chores. You should not have married me, James. It was not fair to me."

He turned to face her. "And what of you?" he said. "Why did you marry me? Are you an innocent victim in all this? You have a head on your shoulders too. You knew as well as I the chance we took of running into just the disaster we have met. You knew when I took you up into the hills that night what was going to happen. I did not notice your footsteps lagging or find you at all reluctant. I have had whores who gave themselves with less abandon."

"So," she said, straightening her shoulders and lifting her chin, "that is what I was to you, is it? The truth at last? I have been your whore. Better than a whore because more eager. And I came cheaply—at the expense of a special license and a wedding ring. But I will cost you now, James. There will never be a cast-off mistress more expensive than I. And I threw away your wedding ring. I threw it from the mail coach window." She held up her hand, palm in.

He made an impatient gesture. "Theatrics," he said. "You should have been on the stage, did you know that, Madeline? You would make a magnificent Lady Macbeth."

"I would be even more magnificent in the green room," she said.

"Perhaps," he said. "You are determined to make yourself into a victim, I see, and into a proud woman scorned. The fault was not all mine, Madeline. Mostly mine, I will admit, but not all. Why did you make a friend of Beasley against my wishes?"

"Don't you mean against your commands?" she said. "You are good at giving commands, James. I am not good at obeying them. I saw no reason for not being his friend."

"But events have proved you wrong," he said. "Sometimes commands are given for another person's good and not for the mere love of exercising power. Did you ever think of that? Did you ever think that perhaps I had good reason to tell you to stay away from him?"

"Then why did you not give me the reason?" she said. "Have you ever talked to me since we have known each other? Have you ever shared anything of yourself with me? Have you ever given me reason to want to obey you?"

"We are not all easy conversationalists, Madeline," he said. "You could have respected my silence. And you could have kept your mouth shut about our business outside our home."

Her eyes widened. "What is that supposed to mean?" she asked.

"Carl Beasley," he said. "He seemed to know something of the sad state of our marriage, Madeline. I think we behaved with enough decorum in public that he would not have known unless you had told him."

"Well!" she said, nostrils flaring and bosom heaving. "So I am to blame for everything after all. And now enough has been said."

"And almost the first question Alex asked me when I came down here was if it was true that Dora was my mistress. Where did she get that idea from, Madeline?"

"Doubtless from Dominic," she said. "Did you expect me to come here, James, and pretend to my own family that I had come to enjoy the Season?"

"I think we might have kept our own problems at home," he said. "You might have told me that you wished to leave. We might have worked something out in privacy and with some dignity. This has all been performed on a very public stage, has it not?"

She advanced on him. "Nothing had to be played out on any stage," she said. "I left you because I wished never to see you again. I did not ask you to follow me. I did not ask you for anything at all."

"Well," he said, "if you wish never to see me again, Madeline, you are about to have your wish. And I will not follow you anywhere else in this life, you may be assured of that. I think we are both fortunate to be free of this entanglement."

"I could not agree more," she said.

"I will be going back to Canada at the end of the summer," he said. "I won't be in England again, Madeline."

"To Canada," she said, her expression falling blank.

"You will be well rid of me," he said.

"Yes," she said.

"And I of you."

"Yes."

"I must be on my way," he said. "I am wasting precious daylight hours."

"I would hate to be responsible for that," she said.

"Yes, I'm sure you would," he said, turning back to the door. "Good-bye, Madeline."

"Good-bye," she said.

He did not hear the rest of what she mumbled. "What?" he said, looking back over his shoulder with a frown.

"I am going to have a child," she said. "I thought you should know." Her head was tilted proudly back.

There was a buzzing in his head. "*My* child?" he said.

Her eyes blazed. She picked up a cushion from the sofa beside her and hurled it at him. It caught him on the shoulder. "I don't know whose it is," she yelled at him. "It could belong to any of a dozen men. We will just have to wait to see whom it resembles, won't we? Perhaps it will have neither dark hair nor dark eyes."

"Madeline," he said.

"Perhaps you would like to divorce me," she shrieked, "and I could go from one to another of the dozen seeing which one would be willing to marry me after all the scandal. I think that would be a good way of settling the matter, don't you, James? Don't you touch me. *Don't touch me!*"

But he had her arms in a vise and her body against his

own and her face pressed among the folds of his neck-cloth.

"Madeline," he said as she pounded his chest with her fists and sobbed noisily against him.

"It's your baby," she said. "It's yours. But you may think what you like. I don't care. I hate you anyway. I told you only because I thought you should know. And I have not told anyone else, even Dom. There are some things I can keep my mouth shut about, you see."

"Madeline," he said, his arms holding her to him like iron bands. "Madeline."

She threw back her head suddenly to reveal red and swollen and flashing eyes. "I suppose you will want me back now," she said. "Now that I can put a child in your nursery. You will want me back now because I can give you heirs. Because I am not infertile after all."

"*Because I love you,*" he said between his teeth. "Because I love you, and for no other reason in the world. Because I can't live without you, Madeline. Because my soul will die in me if I walk out through that door without you. I want you back because I love you."

She did not even try to stop the angry tears that ran down her reddened cheeks and dripped from her chin to run down her neck. "You don't," she cried. "It is because of the baby. And I am not coming back just because I am a breeder and suddenly valuable property. I am not coming back. You don't love me."

"That's what it is, isn't it?" he said, his hands on her arms holding her close to him still. "That's what it has always been. Not just an obsession. Not just a passion. It's love between us, Madeline. On both sides. We both have too much to give to have been satisfied with what we have had. And the fault has been mine. I have been too caught up for years in my guilt over what I thought I had done to Dora to be free to love you. But I have loved you from the beginning. I have longed to give myself to you. All of me. Everything that is me."

She was shaking her head.

"And you love me too," he said. "You said yourself a few minutes ago that you tried to make our marriage work. You gave and you gave, but I would not receive. I poisoned your love and have put you through all this. Forgive me, Madeline. For your own sake as well as mine, forgive me."

"I dare not," she said. Her voice was flat. "For five years, James, nothing has worked between you and me. I cannot take any more punishment or misery."

"We were lovers," he said. "For the first month or two, Madeline, we were lovers. We were beautiful together. And that last night we were lovers. It was not rape, was it? We loved on that night."

"Yes," she said, "we loved."

"While our minds and our wills have warred," he said, "our bodies have accepted the truth. And our love has created life, Madeline."

"Yes," she said.

"Give me a chance," he said. "Come back to me. Give me a chance to learn how to give you myself now that I am free of my past. Give me a chance to tell you with all of myself, and not just with my body, that I love you. Come home with me."

"Home," she said, resting her forehead against his chest.

"It was becoming a place of happiness," he said. "After you left the maids lost their smiles and their curls. You were making it a happy place, Madeline. Come home with me. It is not the loveliest place on earth, but we will make our own beauty."

"I love the moors," she said.

"You were out on them only once," he said.

She lifted her hands to rest on either side of his waist. "I love the moors."

"Will you come home, Madeline?" He found he was holding his breath.

Madeline had her eyes closed very tightly. If this was a dream, she would not wake up yet. She would not. She would remain asleep by sheer willpower.

"Because I love you," she said. "Not just because of the baby. I could manage very well on my own with the baby. But because I love you and don't think I could live without you. Because I have died a little every day since I left you. Only because I love you, James. Don't lift my face. It is a dreadful mess."

"Have you ever known me to grant your requests?" he asked, lifting her chin with a firm hand. But although the words were light and teasing, his face held its usual seriousness. But his eyes! His eyes were intense on hers and she could see through them into the man himself. She could see for herself that the words he had spoken were true.

"James," she whispered. "Oh, James."

"I'm going to take you home," he said while she gazed and drowned in his eyes. "The day after your mother's wedding. We are going home to Dunstable and our child is going to be born there. Our children. I'm going to take you home, Madeline."

"Yes," she said. "Oh, yes. I wish we could go tomorrow. The day after the wedding? We will not delay longer?"

He shook his head. "In the meantime," he said, "I hold

all the home I really want in my arms. My wife and my child. My lover. And the woman I am going to make my closest friend."

"Yes," she said, smiling slowly at him, the glow back in her eyes despite their redness. "My husband and my lover. And at last the father of my child. And at long last my friend."

They savored the moment, smiling into each other's eyes before the inevitable moment when their mouths would meet.

But the door opened hesitantly before that moment came and Alexandra peered in. If the two occupants of the room had looked, they would have seen Edmund, Dominic, and Ellen in the hallway beyond.

"James?" Alexandra asked. "Madeline? Is everything all right? There was so much yelling. Is everything all right now?"

James did not take his eyes from his wife's. "Alex," he said, "this is your house and I do love you and all that, but would you be good enough to get out of here?"

The door closed quietly as his mouth came down on his wife's.

25

"WELL, MY LOVE." THE EARL OF AMBERLEY had finally got his wife alone in a room swarming with relatives and friends, all merrily celebrating the wedding that had taken place a few hours before. "How does it feel to be the only Lady Amberley?"

"It feels good," she said with a smile, "because it was time for your mother to move on to another name, Edmund. Have you ever seen a couple look more happy?"

"You on our wedding day," he said. "I cannot speak for the couple—I did not look in a mirror a great deal that day. But I know that I felt as happy."

"Edmund," she said, "what a very lovely day it is, even if it is raining and miserable outside. Your mama and Sir Cedric looking so very happy; Jennifer and Mr. Penworth announcing their betrothal just three days ago; Anna and Sir Gordon surely about to announce theirs soon if the looks they keep exchanging are any indication. And Madeline and James! There always was a glow about Madeline, but now she fairly sparkles. And James can smile. You see? I always told you he could. He looks now just as he looked in a portrait I once painted of him. I am so happy for him I could weep for a week."

He chuckled. "Perhaps it is as well, then, that they are going home to Yorkshire tomorrow," he said.

"And they are to have a child," she said with a sigh. "How wonderful they must feel about that. In fact, I know just how they feel. I am not at all sorry about this third one even though we did not plan to have it quite so soon. Tell me you are not sorry either, Edmund. I worry about it sometimes."

He clucked his tongue. "I am only sorry to be putting you through all this discomfort again, Alex," he said. "The pure male in me is thoroughly delighted to see my woman swelling with my child—again. And you know how much I love our children and will love this new one. Weddings are strange things, are they not? I am almost overcome by the strangest urge. I want to kiss you, in view of all these people. Have you ever heard of anything quite so shocking?"

She smiled at him.

"And you are of no earthly help at all," he said, bending forward and kissing her very briefly on the lips. "You are supposed to frown and look repulsed when I say such things."

"Oh," she said, flushing but continuing to smile, "I do love you, Edmund."

He grinned back a moment before they were joined by four of their guests. "I am a mite fond of you too, love," he said.

LORD EDEN CAME UP behind his wife as she was helping herself to a cream cake from a side table. Both of them were free of other company for the moment. He set his hands on either side of her waist.

"I would hate to put my hands here one day," he said, "and find your waist gone altogether."

"Dominic!" she said. "How horrid. You know I am not forever eating cream cakes. It is just such a special occasion."

He reached past her, picked up a cake, and bit into it. "It is, isn't it?" he said. "I can't for the life of me think why they did not do it years ago. Something about being loyal to their first spouses, I suppose."

"Yes," she said, "that would be it. Sir Cedric loved his Anne very dearly. He showed me her miniature just a few weeks ago. And your mama loved your father, of course. They have doubtless felt guilty over loving each other even though so many years have passed."

Lord Eden looked closely at his wife and circled her waist with one arm. "Do you have any regrets, Ellen?" he asked quietly.

She looked up at him, startled. "Regrets?" she said.

"You were rather forced into marrying me, weren't you?" he said. "With the children on the way, I mean. And Charlie so recently gone."

"Oh, Dominic." She put her head to one side and gazed earnestly up at him. "You don't ever doubt that I love you, do you? Or that I married you only because I wanted to do so more than I wanted anything else in this life? How foolish you are. Oh, how very foolish. And I can see by the twinkle in your eye that I have played into your hands, you rogue. You merely wanted to hear me protesting my love. Well, now you must hear the whole of it. I think I am probably the most fortunate and the happiest woman in the world. So there."

"Ah, an extravagant claim," he said. "I think you have some competition in this room, love."

"Your mother?" she said. "You are right. Perhaps I will relinquish my claim for this one day only. For there is nothing quite like the happiness of one's wedding day, is there?"

"Yes," he said, "there is the happiness of the day when one's twins are born."

"And when they first smile and first walk," she said.

"And when they first sleep through the night and leave their mother to their father's care," he said into her ear.

"And when one's husband comes up behind one in the midst of a large gathering," she said, "and stands indecorously close and blows into one's ear."

"Shall we go and talk to Madeline and James?" he said. "They will be leaving tomorrow."

"And there," she said, "I will have to relinquish my claim yet again, won't I, or at least share it? Just look at Madeline, Dominic. She is positively beautiful. And I swear I did not realize just how handsome James is. That smile transforms him."

"Let's go," he said, taking her by the hand.

"And Jennifer and Allan, Dominic. They are going to be happy too, aren't they?" she said.

He grinned down at her. "Sometimes," he said, "when one is happy, it seems that the whole world is happy too. And on this occasion I don't think that is an illusion. Did you see the kiss Edmund just stole from Alexandra? Edmund! That pillar of propriety. Whatever is the world coming to?"

JAMES DID NOT have to find a moment to be with his wife. He had had his fingers laced with hers almost the whole time since they had left her mother's house that morning.

And at the church and while they conversed with other guests at the reception, his thumb and one finger played with her new wedding ring, turning it on her finger.

He had bought it for her on the very day of their reconciliation, taking her from Edmund and Alex's house straight to a jeweler's.

"And you are not to feel bad about throwing the other one away," he had told her later that night when they were alone together in her room and he was sliding it onto her finger. "I am glad you did. We are starting a wholly new marriage, Madeline, and it is fitting that I give you this new ring. It is to stay on your finger for the rest of our lives. And that is a command. It will stay there because I wish it and because you will wish it. I swear you will."

"Yes," she had said, her eyes dreamy, "that is a command I will obey without question, James, because I want to do so. Make love to me. Oh, I have missed you so much. Make love to me."

They had not slept all that night. They had talked and made love alternately all night long. And he had stroked his hand over her flat abdomen and they had both expressed impatience for the time when it would be large with their child.

"I am so happy for Mama," she said to him now, her eyes with that old glow in them and far more besides, but now focused entirely on him, "and for Sir Cedric too. He lost his first wife when he was quite young, you know, and carried her miniature around with him for years. But he and Mama belong together now, don't they?"

He smiled. "They are certainly doing nothing to hide their joy," he said.

"And now I know just how they feel," she said, "just how happy they are. They are close friends, James, and now can mean even more to each other. We did things the other way around, didn't we, but we have arrived in the same place. At last." She squeezed his hand. "My friend. I never thought I would be able to say that to you, but I can, can't I?"

"Yes," he said, and there was a twinkle in his very dark eyes, "my prattler."

"Oh," she said, "unfair. I have not done all the talking in the past two weeks, James. Not by any means."

He smiled. "Are you looking forward to going home?"

She nodded. "Mm," she said. "You know I am."

"You will not miss your family dreadfully?"

"Of course I will miss them," she said. "But we will see them all again with some frequency, I am sure. And even if it meant never seeing them again, James, you know that I would come with you without any hesitation at all. You know that, don't you?"

"And will hold you to it," he said in her ear as Dominic and Ellen approached, "for the small matter of a lifetime."

She lifted her free hand and put back the truant lock of his hair.

THERE WERE A MERE few seconds of grace between the turning away of one group of smiling well-wishers and the arrival of the next. Sir Cedric Harvey set one arm loosely about the shoulders of his bride.

"Soon now, darling," he said very quietly. "Very soon now."

"Edmund and Dominic and Madeline have gone to so much trouble to make this a perfect day for us," she said. "And they have succeeded very well, Cedric. I know I will remember this day for the rest of my life and the way our relatives and friends have come in such numbers to wish us well. But oh, dear, I wonder if the three of them remember how impatient they were on their wedding days to be off on their own afterward."

"Mm," he said. "I want to hold you in my arms, Louisa, and know that this time I do not have to let you go again. For the first time I will not have to let you go."

"I am having the most shameful thoughts," she said, "considering the fact that we are surrounded by so many people and are the focus of attention."

"But they are not shameful any longer," he said. "I am your husband, remember? Think on, darling. And soon now I will be your husband in very deed and doing all the things you are thinking of and far more besides. I promise."

"A toast," Lord Amberley was saying, and there was a sudden hush in the room, "to our mother and our new stepfather."

He was standing in the middle of the room, his arm linked with Alexandra's and hers with James's, his with Madeline's, hers with Lord Eden's, and his with Ellen's.

"To our mother," the earl said, "who taught us from childhood on that love and friendship are the only essential ingredients of a happy life. And whose teaching we learned well and are applying in our own families. And to our stepfather, who has been a valued person in our family for more years than I can remember, and who today has become more than an honorary member."

The bride looked along the line of her children and their spouses. "I am going to cry, Cedric," she murmured. "I swore I would not. It is foolish to shed tears at a wedding."

The bridegroom delighted the wedding guests by hugging his wife to his side and kissing her briefly on the lips.

"Ladies and gentlemen," Lord Amberley said, raising his glass, "I give you Sir Cedric and Lady Harvey."

And he smiled down at Alexandra while Dominic winked at Ellen and Madeline pressed her cheek against James's shoulder.

And they drank the toast.

About the Author

MARY BALOGH is the *New York Times* bestselling author of the acclaimed Slightly novels: *Slightly Married, Slightly Wicked, Slightly Scandalous, Slightly Tempted, Slightly Sinful,* and *Slightly Dangerous,* as well as the romances *No Man's Mistress, More Than a Mistress,* and *One Night for Love.* She is also the author of *Simply Magic, Simply Love,* and *Simply Unforgettable,* the first three books in her dazzling quartet of novels set at Miss Martin's School for Girls. A former teacher herself, she grew up in Wales and now lives in Canada.

Read on for a sneak peek
at the next enchanting novel
in Mary Balogh's series
featuring the teachers at
Miss Martin's School for Girls.

Simply Perfect

CLAUDIA MARTIN'S STORY

Coming in spring 2008
From Delacorte Press

MARY BALOGH

SIMPLY PERFECT

Simply Perfect

on sale spring 2008

CLAUDIA MARTIN HAD ALREADY HAD A HARD day at school.

First Mademoiselle Pierre, one of the nonresident teachers, had sent a messenger just before breakfast with the news that she was indisposed with a migraine headache and would be unable to come to school, and Claudia, as both owner and headmistress, had been obliged to conduct most of the French and music classes in addition to her own subjects. French was no great problem; music was more of a challenge. Worse, the account books, which she had intended to bring up-to-date during her spare classes today, remained undone, with days fast running out in which to get accomplished all the myriad tasks that needed doing.

Then just before the noonday meal, when classes were over for the morning and discipline was at its slackest, Paula Hern had decided that she objected to the way Molly Wiggins *looked* at her and voiced her displeasure publicly and eloquently. And since Paula's father was a successful businessman and as rich as Croesus and she put on airs accordingly while Molly was the youngest—and most timid—of the charity girls and did not even know who her father was, then *of course* Agnes Ryde had felt obliged to jump into the fray in vigorous defense of the downtrodden, her Cockney accent returning with ear-jarring clarity. Claudia had been forced to deal with the matter and extract more-or-less sincere apologies from all sides and mete out suitable punishments to all except the more-or-less innocent Molly.

Then, an hour later, just when Miss Walton had been about to step outdoors with the junior class en route to Bath Abbey, where she had intended to give an informal lesson in art and architecture, the heavens had opened in a downpour to end downpours and there had been all the fuss of finding the girls somewhere else to go within the school and something else to do. Not that that had been Claudia's problem, but she *had* been made annoyingly aware of the girls' loud disappointment beyond her classroom door as she struggled to teach French irregular verbs. She had finally gone out there to inform them that if they had any complaint about the untimely arrival of the rain, then they must take it up privately with God during their evening prayers, but in the meantime they would be *silent* until Miss Walton had closed a classroom door behind them.

Then, just after classes were finished for the afternoon and the girls had gone upstairs to comb their hair and wash their hands for tea, something had gone wrong with the doorknob on one of the dormitories and eight of the girls, trapped inside until Mr. Keeble, the elderly school porter, had creaked his way up there to release them before mending the knob, had screeched and giggled and rattled the door. Miss Thompson had dealt with the crisis by reading them a lecture on patience and decorum, though circumstances had forced her to speak in a voice that could be heard from within—and therefore through much of the rest of the school too, including Claudia's office.

It had *not* been the best of days, as Claudia had just been remarking—without contradiction—to Eleanor Thompson and Lila Walton over tea in her private sitting room a short while after the prisoners had been freed. She could do with far fewer such days.

And yet now!

Now, to cap everything off and make an already trying day more so, there was a marquess awaiting her pleasure in the visitors' parlor downstairs.

A *marquess,* for the love of all that was wonderful!

That was what the silver-edged visiting card she held between two fingers said—the *Marquess of Attingsborough.* The porter had just delivered it into her hands, looking sour and disapproving as he did so—a not unusual expression for him, especially when any male who was not a teacher invaded his domain.

"A *marquess,*" she said, looking up from the card to frown at her fellow teachers. "Whatever can he want? Did he say, Mr. Keeble?"

"He did not say and I did not ask, miss," the porter replied. "But if you was to ask me, he is up to no good. He *smiled* at me."

"Ha! A cardinal sin indeed," Claudia said dryly while Eleanor laughed.

"Perhaps," Lila suggested, "he has a daughter he wishes to place at the school."

"A *marquess?*" Claudia raised her eyebrows and Lila looked suitably quelled.

"Perhaps, Claudia," Eleanor said, a twinkle in her eye, "he has *two* daughters."

Claudia snorted and then sighed, took one more sip of her tea, and got reluctantly to her feet.

"I suppose I had better go and see what he wants," she said. "It will be more productive than sitting here guessing. But of all things to happen today of all days. A *marquess*."

Eleanor laughed again. "Poor man," she said. "I pity him."

Claudia had never had much use for the aristocracy—idle, arrogant, coldhearted, nasty lot—though the marriage of two of her teachers and closest friends to titled gentlemen had forced her to admit during the past few years that perhaps *some* of them might be agreeable and even worthy individuals. But it did not amuse her to have one of their number, a stranger, intrude into her own world without a by-your-leave, especially at the end of a difficult day.

She did not believe for a single moment that this marquess wished to place any daughter of his at her school.

She preceded Mr. Keeble down the stairs since she did not wish to move at his slow pace. She ought, she supposed, to have gone into her bedchamber first to see that she was looking respectable, which she was quite possibly not doing after a hard day at school. She usually made sure that she presented a neat appearance to visitors. But she scorned to make such an effort for a *marquess* and risk appearing obsequious in her own eyes.

By the time she opened the door into the visitors' parlor, she was bristling with a quite unjustified indignation. How dared he come here to disturb her on her own property, whatever his business might be.

She looked down at the visiting card still in her hand.

"The Marquess of Attingsborough?" she said in a voice not unlike the one she had used on Paula Hern earlier in the day—the one that said she was not going to be at all impressed by any pretension of grandeur.

"At your service, ma'am. Miss Martin, I presume?" He was standing across the room, close to the window. He bowed elegantly.

Claudia's indignation soared. One steady glance at him

was not sufficient upon which to make any informed judgment of his character, of course, but *really*, if the man had any imperfection of form or feature or taste in apparel, it was by no means apparent. He was tall and broad of shoulder and chest and slim of waist and hips. His legs were long and well shaped. His hair was dark and thick and shining, his face handsome, his eyes and mouth good-humored. He was dressed with impeccable elegance but without a trace of ostentation. His Hessian boots alone were probably worth a fortune, and Claudia guessed that if she were to stand directly over them and look down, she would see her own face reflected in them—and probably her flat, untidy hair and limp dress collar as well.

She clasped her hands at her waist lest she test her theory by touching the collar points. She held his card pinched between one thumb and forefinger.

"What may I do for you, sir?" she asked, deliberately avoiding calling him *my lord*—a ridiculous affectation, in her opinion.

He smiled at her, and if perfection could be improved upon, it had just happened—he had good teeth. Claudia steeled herself to resist the charm she was sure he possessed in aces.

"I come as a messenger, ma'am," he said, "from Lady Whitleaf."

He reached into an inner pocket of his coat and withdrew a sealed paper.

"From Susanna?" Claudia took one step farther into the room.

Susanna Osbourne had been a teacher at the school until her marriage last year to Viscount Whitleaf. Claudia had always rejoiced at Susanna's good fortune in making both an eligible marriage and a love match and yet she still mourned her own loss of a dear friend and colleague *and* a good teacher. She had lost three such friends—all in the same cause—over the course of four years. Sometimes it was hard not to be selfishly depressed by it all.

"When she knew I was coming to Bath to spend a few days with my mother and my father, who is taking the waters," the marquess said, "she asked me to call here and pay my respects to you. And she gave me this letter, perhaps to convince you that I am no impostor."

His eyes smiled again as he came across the room and placed the letter in her hand. And as if at least his eyes could not have been mud-colored or something equally nondescript, she could see that they were a clear blue, almost like a summer sky.

Susanna had asked him to come and pay his respects? *Why?*

"Whitleaf is the cousin of a cousin of mine," the marquess explained. "Or an *almost* cousin of mine, anyway. It is complicated, as family relationships often are. Lauren Butler, Viscountess Ravensberg, is a cousin by virtue of the fact that her mother married my aunt's brother-in-law. We have been close since childhood. And Whitleaf is Lauren's first cousin. And so in a sense both he and his lady have a strong familial claim on me."

If he was a marquess, Claudia thought with sudden suspicion, and his father was still alive, *what did that make his father?* But he was here at Susanna's behest and it behooved her to be a little better than just icily polite.

"Thank you," she said, "for coming in person to deliver the letter. I am much obliged to you, sir. May I offer you a cup of tea?" She willed him to say no.

"I will not put you to that trouble, ma'am," he said, smiling again. "I understand you are to leave for London in two days' time?"

Ah. Susanna must have told him that. Mr. Hatchard, her

man of business in London, had found employment for two of her senior girls, both charity pupils, but he had been unusually evasive about the identity of the prospective employers, even when she had asked quite specifically in her last letter to him. The paying girls at the school had families to look after their interests, of course. Claudia had appointed herself family to the rest and never released any girl who had no employment to which to go or any about whose expected employment she felt any strong misgiving.

At Eleanor's suggestion, Claudia was going to go to London with Flora Bains and Edna Wood so that she could find out exactly where they were to be placed as governesses and to withdraw her consent if she was not satisfied. There were still a few weeks of the school year left, but Eleanor had assured her that she was perfectly willing and able to take charge of affairs during Claudia's absence, which would surely be no longer than a week or ten days. Claudia had agreed to go, partly because there was another matter too upon which she wished to speak with Mr. Hatchard in person.

"I am," she told the marquess.

"Whitleaf intended to send a carriage for your convenience," the marquess told her, "but I was able to inform him that it would be quite unnecessary to put himself to the trouble."

"Of course it would," Claudia agreed. "I have already hired a carriage."

"I will see about *unhiring* it for you, if I may be permitted, ma'am," he said. "I plan to return to town on the same day and will be pleased to offer you the comfort of my own carriage and my protection for the journey."

Oh, goodness, heaven forbid!

"That will be quite unnecessary, sir," she said firmly. "I have already made the arrangements."

"Hired carriages are notorious for their lack of springs and all other comforts," he said. "I beg you will reconsider."

"Perhaps you do not fully understand, sir," she said. "I am to be accompanied by two schoolgirls on the journey."

"Yes," he said, "so Lady Whitleaf informed me. Do they prattle? Or, worse, do they giggle? Very young ladies have an atrocious tendency to do both."

"My girls are taught how to behave appropriately in company, Lord Attingsborough," she said stiffly. Too late she saw the twinkle in his eyes and understood that he had been joking.

"I do not doubt it, ma'am," he said, "and feel quite confident in trusting your word. Allow me, if you will, to escort all three of you ladies to Lady Whitleaf's door. She will be vastly impressed with my gallantry and will be bound to spread the word among my family and friends."

Now he was talking utter nonsense. But how could she decently refuse? She desperately searched around in her head for some irrefutable argument that would dissuade him. Nothing came to mind, however, that did not seem ungracious, even downright rude. But she would rather travel a thousand miles in a springless carriage than to London in his company.

Why?

Was she overawed by his title and magnificence? She bristled at the very idea.

At his…*maleness*, then? She was uncomfortably aware that he possessed that in abundance.

But how ridiculous that would be. He was simply a gentleman offering a courtesy to an aging spinster, who happened to be a friend of his almost-cousin's cousin's wife—goodness, it *was* a tenuous connection. But she held a letter from Susanna in her hand. Susanna obviously trusted him.

An *aging spinster*? When it came to any consideration of age, she thought, there was probably not much difference between the two of them. Now *there* was a thought. Here was this man, obviously at the very pinnacle of his masculine appeal in his middle thirties, and then there was she.

He was looking at her with raised eyebrows and smiling eyes.

"Oh, very well," she said briskly. "But you may live to regret your offer."

His smile broadened and it seemed to an indignant Claudia that there was no end to this man's appeal. As she had suspected, he had charm oozing from every pore and was therefore *not* to be trusted one inch farther than she could see him. She would keep a *very* careful eye upon her two girls during the journey to London.

"I do hope not, ma'am," he said. "Shall we make an early start?"

"It is what I intended," she told him. She added grudgingly, "Thank you, Lord Attingsborough. You are most kind."

"It will be my pleasure, Miss Martin." He bowed deeply again. "May I ask a small favor in return? May I be given a tour of the school? I must confess that the idea of an institution that actually provides an *education* to girls fascinates me. Lady Whitleaf has spoken with enthusiasm about your establishment. She taught here, I understand."

Claudia drew a slow, deep breath through flared nostrils. Whatever reason could this man have for touring a girls' school except idle curiosity—or worse? Her instinct was to say a very firm no. But she had just accepted a favor from him, and it was admittedly a large one—she did not doubt that his carriage would be far more comfortable than the one she had hired or that they would be treated with greater respect at every toll gate they passed and at every inn where they stopped for a change of horses. And he was a friend of Susanna's.

But really!

She had not thought her day could possibly get any worse. She had been wrong.

"Certainly. I will show you around myself," she said curtly, turning to the door. She would have opened it herself, but he reached around her, engulfing her for a startled moment in the scent of some enticing and doubtless indecently expensive male cologne, opened the door, and indicated with a smile that she should precede him into the hall.

At least, she thought, classes were over for the day and all the girls would be safely in the dining hall, having tea.

She was wrong about that, of course, she remembered as soon as she opened the door into the art room. The final assembly of the school year was not far off and all sorts of preparations and rehearsals were in progress, as they had been every day for the past week or so.

A few of the girls were working with Mr. Upton on the stage backdrop. They all turned to see who had come in and then proceeded to gawk at the grand visitor. Claudia was obliged to introduce the two men. They shook hands, and the marquess strolled closer to inspect the artwork and ask a few intelligent questions. Mr. Upton beamed at him when he left the room with her a few minutes later, and all the girls gazed worshipfully after him.

And then in the music room they came upon the madrigal choir, which was practicing in the absence of Mademoiselle Pierre under the supervision of Miss Wilding. They hit an ear-shattering discord at full volume just as Claudia opened the door, and then they dissolved into self-conscious giggles while Miss Wilding blushed and looked dismayed.

Claudia, raising her eyebrows, introduced the teacher to

the marquess and explained that the regular choirmistress was indisposed today. Though even as she spoke she was annoyed with herself for feeling that any explanation was necessary.

"Madrigal singing," he said, smiling at the girls, "can be the most satisfying but the most frustrating thing, can it not? There is perhaps one other person out of the group singing the same part as oneself and six or eight others all bellowing out something quite different. If one's lone ally falters one is lost without hope of recovery. I never mastered the art when I was at school, I must confess. During my very first practice someone suggested to me that I try out for the cricket team—which just happened to practice at the same time."

The girls laughed, and all of them visibly relaxed.

"I will wager," he said, "that there is something in your repertoire that you can sing to perfection. May I be honored to hear it?" He turned his smile upon Miss Wilding.

"'The Cuckoo,' miss," Sylvia Hetheridge suggested to a murmur of approval from the rest of the group.

And they sang in five parts without once faltering or hitting a sour note, a glorious shower of "cuckoos" echoing about the room every time they reached the chorus of the song.

When they were finished, they all turned as one to the Marquess of Attingsborough, just as if he were visiting royalty, and he applauded and smiled.

"Bravo!" he said. "Your skill overwhelms me, not to mention the loveliness of your voices. I am more than ever convinced that I was wise to stick to cricket."

The girls were all laughing and gazing worshipfully after him when he left with Claudia.

Mr. Huckerby was in the dancing hall, putting a group of girls through their paces in a particularly intricate dance that they would perform during the assembly. The marquess shook his hand and smiled at the girls and admired their performance and charmed them until they were all smiling and—of course—*gazing worshipfully at him.*

He asked intelligent and perceptive questions of Claudia as she showed him some of the empty classrooms and the library. He was in no hurry as he looked about each room and read the titles on the spines of many of the books.

"There was a pianoforte in the music room," he said as they made their way to the sewing room, "and other instruments too. I noticed a violin and a flute in particular. Do you offer individual music lessons here, Miss Martin?"

"Indeed we do," she said. "We offer everything necessary to make accomplished young ladies of our pupils, as well as persons with a sound academic education."

He looked around the sewing room from just inside the door but did not walk farther into it.

"And do you teach other skills here in addition to sewing and embroidery?" he asked. "Knitting, perhaps? Tatting? Crochet?"

"All three," she said as he closed the door and she led the way to the assembly hall. It had been a ballroom once when the building was a private home.

"It is a pleasingly designed room," he said, standing in the middle of the gleaming wood floor and turning all about before looking up at the high, coved ceiling. "Indeed, I like the whole school, Miss Martin. There are windows and light everywhere and a pleasant atmosphere. Thank you for giving me a guided tour."

He turned his most charming smile on her, and Claudia, still holding both his visiting card and Susanna's letter, clasped her free hand about her wrist and looked back with deliberate severity.

"I am delighted you approve," she said.

His smile was arrested for a moment until he chuckled softly.

"I do beg your pardon," he said. "I have taken enough of your time."

He indicated the door with one arm, and Claudia led the way back to the entrance hall, feeling—and resenting the feeling—that she had somehow been unmannerly, for those last words she had spoken had been meant ironically and he had known it.

But before they reached the hall they were forced to pause for a few moments while the junior class filed out of the dining hall in good order, on their way from tea to study hall, where they would catch up on any work not completed during the day or else read or write letters or stitch at some needlework.

They all turned their heads to gaze at the grand visitor, and the Marquess of Attingsborough smiled genially back at them, setting them all to giggling and preening as they hurried along.

All of which went to prove, Claudia thought, that even eleven- and twelve-year-olds could not resist the charms of a handsome man. It boded ill—or *continued* to bode ill—for the future of the female half of the human race.

Mr. Keeble, frowning ferociously, bless his heart, was holding the marquess's hat and cane and was standing close to the front door as if to dare the visitor to try prolonging his visit further.

"I will see you early two mornings from now, then, Miss Martin?" the marquess said, taking his hat and cane and turning to her as Mr. Keeble opened the door and stood to one side, ready to close it behind him at the earliest opportunity.

"We will be ready," she said, inclining her head to him.